Deborah Masson was born and bred in Aberdeen, Scotland. Always restless and fighting against being a responsible adult, she worked in several jobs including secretarial, marketing, reporting for the city's freebie newspaper and a stint as a postie – to name but a few.

Through it all, she always read crime fiction and, when motherhood finally settled her into being an adult (maybe even a responsible one) she turned her hand to writing what she loved. Deborah started with short stories and flash fiction whilst her daughter napped and, when she later welcomed her son into the world, she decided to challenge her writing further through online courses with Professional Writing Academy and Faber Academy. Her debut novel, *Hold Your Tongue*, is the result of those courses.

www.penguin.co.uk

hold your tongue

DEBORAH MASSON

CORGI BOOKS

TRANSWORLD PUBLISHERS
61–63 Uxbridge Road, London W5 5SA
www.penguin.co.uk

Transworld is part of the Penguin Random House group of companies
whose addresses can be found at global.penguinrandomhouse.com

First published in Great Britain in 2020 by Corgi Books
an imprint of Transworld Publishers

Copyright © Deborah Masson 2020

Deborah Masson has asserted her right under the Copyright,
Designs and Patents Act 1988 to be identified as the author of this work.

This book is a work of fiction and, except in the case of historical fact, any
resemblance to actual persons, living or dead, is purely coincidental.

Every effort has been made to obtain the necessary permissions with
reference to copyright material, both illustrative and quoted. We
apologize for any omissions in this respect and will be pleased to make
the appropriate acknowledgements in any future edition.

A CIP catalogue record for this book is available from the British Library.

ISBN
9780552176521

Typeset in 11/14pt ITC Giovanni
by Integra Software Services Pvt. Ltd, Pondicherry.

Printed and bound in Great Britain by Clays Ltd, Elcograf S.p.A.

Penguin Random House is committed to a sustainable
future for our business, our readers and our planet. This book
is made from Forest Stewardship Council® certified paper.

1 3 5 7 9 10 8 6 4 2

To Mum and Dad

Thank you. I love you, and I know you both would've been chuffed to bits.

Twenty years ago

The woody, sweet scent of cinnamon punctures the darkness where he sits at the kitchen table. An oversized pot, half full of mulled wine, still lies on the cooker top. Beads of condensation beneath the pot's glass lid shimmer in the soft orange glow seeping through the window above the sink. He leans forward, reaches over the plate in front of him and picks up the bottle again, his knuckles turning white as he takes a drink and enjoys the silence.

From where he sits he can see thick icicles hanging from the gutter. Lamp posts, their tops heavy with snowfall, throw shadows against the council houses that line the street. A cold wind drives frenzied snowflakes against glass-encased bulbs.

His sigh is loud as he turns towards the panelled door leading to the living room. They had sprayed white foam into the corners of its panes and, through the clear glass above the fake snow, he can see the silhouette of the tree in the corner. Its plastic branches are tired, limp ends bowing beneath the weight of handmade decorations – old, but they can't bear to replace them. The cold wooden chair creaks as he leans back and closes his eyes.

The moan disturbs him.

Shifting his weight to the edge of the seat, he looks beyond the small circular dining table to the floor.

She's moving.

The back of her white nightdress looks rust-coloured in the shadows as she drags herself across the linoleum. If only she'd stayed in bed. He reaches towards the plate on the table, his icy finger poking a hole in the cling film, ripping at it before pulling a biscuit from the top of the pile. It breaks easily, a chunk shoved into his mouth before he picks at the small crumbs that have fallen into the buttons of his pyjama top. They taste soft and sickly sweet, the way he likes them.

As per tradition, they had made them and the wine together that day. Family time, she liked to call it. Pretending everything was all right, as fake as the snow on the door's glass panes. They forced themselves to smile, trying to maintain a sense of normality. He went along with it to keep them both happy, feeling guilt and a rage that he feared would erupt and scorch them all, knowing who deserved to burn. But he kept it hidden, bubbling beneath.

She always allowed them one biscuit each; this year only three were taken instead of four. And then she double wrapped them in cling film and promised they could have whatever Santa didn't eat. Except that now Christmas wouldn't be coming.

His teeth bite into biscuit; he keeps biting until there's nothing left, dark eyes watching her matted hair as she crawls across the cold floor, small movements leaving a black trail in the dark. Glass crunches beneath her.

When he stands up, he's careful not to scrape the chair legs against the linoleum. It's important not to wake him upstairs. He crouches, moves the glass handle away from her side – the only thing that didn't shatter when he smashed the water jug against her head. Her wet hair feels heavy as he tucks it behind her ear, taking no chances as to whether she can hear him.

'It's all your fault.'

Her body resists as he strains to roll her over on to her back, but he does it. She needs to see him, to see that he's his own man. Her breath comes in short rasps, and her eyes are wide, pleading. He jabs his finger towards the ceiling and puts it to his lips, where the flicker of a smile lies, signalling for her to stay silent.

The cheap material of his pyjama bottoms rustles as he straightens and goes to the kitchen drawers. In the top one, he sees the pink plastic spoon next to blue, the only ones they kept: a reminder of the baby years. In the next drawer, he curls his fingers around the worn wooden handle of the bread-knife. It will do. She has to pay, and today is the perfect day. He sees the kitchen tongs and smiles as he lifts them from the drawer and moves towards her, the knife blade glinting in the gloom.

'Please, I love you.' Desperate. Breathless.

He kneels, drops the blade and tongs by his side and clamps his hand over her mouth, stares into her eyes. She's struggling to keep them open, blood pouring from her head wound. He listens, relieved that he still hasn't heard movement from upstairs. Nothing.

He sits astride her, his weight bearing down on her, and prises open her mouth, dirty nails digging into her tongue's strong, slippery flesh. Pulling at it, he lifts the tongs and holds her tongue fast. With his other hand, he lifts the knife. Her eyes fly open as she bucks against him, trying hard to clamp her mouth shut but unable to as his hands and cold metal fill the space between her lips. Her hands claw at his, legs kicking against the floor. Impressing him with what little strength she has left, using it to jerk her groin upwards in a vain attempt to throw his bulk from her.

Her wet eyes never leave his.

He hears the creak of the floorboards overhead, the unmistakeable soft footsteps making their way down the carpeted stairs. It is the cry that makes him look towards the door, deep into terrified eyes.

For that, he is sorry.

Chapter 1

Thursday, 24 October

DI Eve Hunter sat upright in the leather chair, not even trying to look comfortable. They both knew it was the last thing she felt.

'You're welcome to use the sofa.' Dr Shetty, the Police Consultant Psychiatrist, swept an arm over to the corner of the tastefully decorated room, a collection of rainbow-coloured bangles jangling against one another on her wrist as she did. Her voice was soft, traces of the Indian heritage still strong.

Eve shook her head, resenting the soothing tone to the doctor's voice that had lulled her into saying more than she'd meant to over the past twelve months. Even though her leg would have thanked her for the lie-down, she'd rather sit opposite the psychiatrist, both of them in armchairs: more chance of being in control and with her wits about her. That and the fact that if she lay on the sofa, there was no escaping the reality that she was in therapy.

'How have you been?'

Same question every time. Eve lifted her hand, tucked her long fringe behind her ear, the smell of burning incense almost suffocating. She concentrated. Today was important. 'Fine.'

Eve hadn't been other people's definition of fine in a long time, but it was the only way she knew how to answer. She shifted, leather upholstery creaking in the silence. 'It'll be good to get back to work.'

She ignored the flash of doubt that passed across Dr Shetty's face. Eve was used to the doctor displaying a full range of emotions. An open book whereas Eve kept hers firmly shut.

Dr Shetty smiled. It was that smile that never reached her eyes, the one that set Eve's jaw on edge. 'It's a big day for you next week. But I do feel progress has been made.'

Eve almost laughed. *Since the first period of enforced leave or the second?*

'Your resilience was something the first time around, but to then have to go through what you did on your return to work . . . the injury . . .' Dr Shetty stared at her. 'It's been a long road.'

Eve closed her eyes, kept them closed, knowing Dr Shetty was looking for some kind of reaction. Knowing everything she said was designed to prompt an answer that would then be scrutinised and analysed. Eve had learned fast what was expected of her. Shows of emotion, times of reflection, signs of making peace with the past, seeing a way forward. But what Eve really saw was the woman lying there. Lynne. Almost a year ago to the day, slumped on the damp-ridden tenement floor in North Anderson Drive, blood pooling beneath her, the three teeth that had been knocked from her mouth scattered across the shabby vinyl. Brutally battered. Raped. Her long-term partner Johnny MacNeill Jnr the perpetrator, a local hood from a family known for trouble in the city.

The sound of a car starting had propelled Eve and her partner DS Nicola Sanders from the third-floor tenement and down the stairs, both of them leaping two steps at a time. Eve ran to their squad car, jumping into the driver's seat, Sanders letting her take the lead. The woman lying there, broken, was a scene too close to home for Eve. It ignited a rage and a need for justice that fuelled the chase as she drove too fast, too hard. Erratic. She could still hear Sanders' sharp intake of breath, see her hand reaching for the dashboard as the car in front veered off the road, flipping into the air, seeming to pause, Johnny Jnr being thrown around in front like a rag doll before the vehicle crashed to the ground, on to its roof, leaving him with life-changing injuries.

The subsequent investigation and therapy sessions after the car accident had taken their toll on Eve. Her privacy had been shattered by the invasive questioning to determine her state of mind that night, and to assess whether the events would affect her ability to work effectively afterwards. She was left powerless, with the decision over her fitness to work lying in the hands of others.

Eve had also been hounded by the press. Local hack Claire Jenkins, in particular, had become a mouthpiece for Johnny's family, especially his father, who had made it his mission to bang on in the media about the injustice of it all: the police recklessness, their responsibility for his son's injuries. A joke considering what he did for a living. Eve was eternally grateful to the force's press man, Elliott Jones, for his attempts to protect her from the onslaught, but the stress and sleepless nights had her at breaking point.

No one had been as shocked as Eve when she was cleared of any wrongdoing. She returned to work, straight into the wrath of MacNeill Snr, who decided to take matters into his own hands. His actions were to change everything.

Eve opened her eyes, shook the memories from her mind. Dr Shetty studied her, head cocked to the side, fountain pen poised between forefinger and thumb, hovering above the ruled notebook on her lap. The doctor brought her head to centre, her large hooped earrings swaying as she did.

Eve hated that she felt as vulnerable as a kid when she was here. She could only blame herself for that. Over time, she'd convinced herself it had been the stress – the relentless intrusion of the media, the pressure of the upcoming investigation findings and the threat she might lose her job – that had seen Eve, to her horror afterwards, telling Dr Shetty the one thing she'd spent her life hiding.

Dr Shetty. Of all people. The expert at prodding. A stranger. Uncovering the secret that had driven Eve the night of the crash. The resulting rage she had always feared would ruin her one day. So few people knew. She understood the doctor was bound by patient confidentiality but she still hated having to reveal her darkest secret.

'Do you feel ready?'

What mattered was that Dr Shetty felt she was ready. She needed the doctor's validation if she were to stand a chance of getting back to work. But the crushing doubts were never far away.

'Eve?'

Concern was creeping into the psychiatrist's voice. Eve composed herself, sat a little straighter, ignored the grumbling in her leg. She'd taken extra painkillers to make sure she'd get through the meeting. Everything depended on her answer.

She nodded as Dr Shetty laid the pen flat against the lined paper, the bangles on her arm clanging together. The doctor balanced the pen and notebook on her crossed knees, stopping the pen from rolling to the ground. Eve was doing the same with her answers, trying to keep them steady, knowing Dr Shetty's report today would go a long way to stopping Eve's world from toppling off its axis. She cleared her throat, knew she needed to sound confident. Convincing. 'Obviously I have concerns about my return. Mostly about how the team will handle it. Whether I'll still have their respect, their belief that I'm capable.'

That part, at least, was the truth. Her job was her life. She needed to be good at it, craved the validation from her fellow officers, even though she would never admit or show that. She had a reputation for being a law unto herself, but she did what she had to in order to get the job done. Her and her team. Only the bad guys suffered in the long run. At least, that's what she used to believe.

Her team. DS Mark Cooper. He would welcome her back, regardless of the fact he'd been covering her role. Cooper was a solid family man, and he had been a good friend to Eve. He brought out the good in her. The smooth to her rough. They'd always had each other's backs. She'd never doubted that.

She wasn't sure about the new DC who'd been taken on. She didn't even know her name, only that she was a woman. Then there was DC Scott Ferguson, some-one who wouldn't be pleased to see her return, along with the officers throughout the station who hung around with him. He had little respect for Eve, and their relationship had deteriorated between her return to work after the car chase and then what happened to DC Sanders. Guilt on his part, perhaps, when it came to Sanders. Whatever the reason, there was no disput-ing he was a good officer. Possessing an uncanny intuition, he played a vital part in her team, even though it sometimes felt as if she was overseeing an unruly teenager. Regardless, if her boss, DCI Jim Hast-ings, and the management above him sanctioned her return, then Ferguson would have to wind his neck back in.

'How's the sleep?'

Eve paused, trying to keep the irritation from her face. The doc was searching for reasons, any reason, to advise she wasn't ready. How many times would she have to answer the same questions? Hopefully the dark circles beneath her eyes weren't obvious. 'I'm sleeping no problem.'

Dr Shetty looked like she might even believe her. The doctor presumed her difficulty in sleeping after the car accident was the result of misplaced guilt with what had happened to MacNeill Jnr in the crash. A guilt she believed they had tackled in their time together. Eve had let her believe it, had even encouraged it, knowing all the time the real reason was the stress of having to hide the fact that she was to blame for the car ending up on its roof.

She had never voiced that revelation in this room or anywhere else, and never would. A couple of people had their suspicions, didn't believe the official line that it was the actions of Johnny Jr himself that had caused the car accident. But not one of them ever had the balls to say it to her face. It wasn't a confession from her that would either shock or confirm suspicion. It was the fact she had no regrets for taking the vicious sonofabitch out of the picture.

Her only regret – the thing she could never forgive herself for – was that her actions that night had led to MacNeill Snr's need for revenge, and then what happened to Sanders. The woman and colleague who had worked by her side for as long as she could remember.

Eve could take the gruelling rehabilitation and follow-up physiotherapy for her injured leg; her real punishment came from her visits to Sanders. She didn't know what was worse: seeing her colleague's devastating injuries or Sanders' deafening silence, the lack of eye contact, the refusal to forgive. But the difference

11

this time, what made it worse than any car accident or investigation, was that Eve welcomed the guilt and regret. She wanted it to consume her. And that was something no amount of therapy would ever help with.

Chapter 2

Monday, 4 November

THE HOTEL LIFT, WHEN it came, was empty. Eve pressed the button for the second floor and groaned as the door slid shut. She'd looked better. She tutted, wished she could get rid of the deep shadows beneath her hazel eyes. Eyes she hated. She pulled at the fringe of her choppy bob that had frizzed in the wet wind. Eve straightened her blouse collar for the umpteenth time. It didn't help. She pulled at the lapels of her fitted grey suit jacket and looked at her trousers, cursing their bottoms, which had sponged the wet from the pavements, the sand from the snow gritters more than likely going to leave a white line behind once they dried. She tried to get her head ready, even if her clothes weren't up to the job.

She was back.

Hastings had rigidly steered things in her favour, with Dr Shetty supporting her case.

They'd gone for it.

A return to Chief Investigating Officer with the Aberdeen Major Investigation Team, but with an unspoken threat not to balls it up. The real test and a private talk with Hastings were yet to come.

The lift doors squeaked open. The tall, skinny female standing in the corridor straightened, stepping forward to block her exit until Eve showed her ID. The officer nodded but said nothing, her thin mouth set in a tight straight line. She stepped back, hands behind her, repositioning herself against the corridor wall.

Eve turned left, the blue-and-white police tape visible out of the corner of her eye, and walked the short distance to the end of the corridor, conscious of her limp with each step she took away from the woman. Was everyone going to be as friendly? Her feet sank into the plush carpet. It smelled new. The expensive embossed wallpaper was dotted with framed black-and-white images of monstrous steel structures rising from the freezing depths of the North Sea. A nod to Aberdeen's oil industry. The boom town it had become in the 1970s, when its population almost doubled.

She glanced at the photographs: a reminder of the current struggles in the downturn, the city's fight to establish itself as a place of learning and new technologies before the day when the oil ran out. A long shot maybe, but Aberdeen still boasted the highest number of millionaires in the UK outside of London. Like anywhere, though, the wealth was offset by poverty-stricken areas. The sudden money pouring into the city had brought its fair share of problems: drugs and prostitution, amongst many others. All problems that kept Eve in a job. Debatable sometimes whether she'd picked the right job, and she questioned it again now as she looked along the corridor.

A Scenes of Crime Officer (SOCO) stood at the door of the suite, his bulk and more tape blocking the entrance. She'd worked with him before, but he was as talkative as the officer at the lift had been. Eve signed in before getting suited and booted. Her heart raced. It had been six months. Once she ducked beneath the tape and opened the door, there'd be no going back. Her hand wrapped around the brass door handle, squeezed and froze. She counted to three in silence, then forced herself to push the handle, hoping the officer standing beside her hadn't noticed her pause, and opened the door into a scene ripped from a crime drama.

What would be classed as a large suite was now cramped due to the number of people filling the space. The room was dark, walls and bedding matching the hotel reception: red, black and white checked tartan interrupting the black and silver in places. SOCOs moved about the room, their white suits rustling as they photographed, recorded and bagged. They floated around the room like ghosts. Not one of them interrupted their focus or turned in her direction.

The room was freezing. Thankfully, someone had already switched the heating off. There was a door to her left, which she assumed was the bathroom. She took a deep breath. A SOCO came out of the bathroom carrying a bag, the tight elastic of his white hood framing his face like the cover of a home-made jar of jam.

'OK to go in?'

The hood turned to Eve. 'Yeah, we've got what we need.'

'Hey . . . Eve.'

She stopped mid-step, the voice behind her making her turn.

DS Mark Cooper's smile seemed genuine. 'Good to have you back. Hastings said you'd be coming.' His brown eyes didn't meet hers. Not the norm, but one thing hadn't changed. Her old friend and colleague still defied his age, his gangly frame and smooth face making him look like he should be getting up for a paper round in the morning.

'Thanks.' For the first time ever, Eve didn't know what else to say or how to be around him.

Cooper motioned to a woman standing by his side, a woman Eve didn't recognize. 'This is Jo Mearns. She's the new DC.'

Eve's heart lurched, realizing this must be Sanders' replacement. She went to lift her hand to greet Mearns but stopped when she saw the blue eyes blazing beneath knitted eyebrows, the small plump mouth closing over the gap in her two front teeth, lips pursing as she looked at Eve. Spiky.

Eve stayed put, staring at her, a mere inch between them in height, their bodies so close that she could feel Mearns' breath on her face, see the challenge in her eyes. Her attitude stopped Eve from bothering to introduce herself. Not that she had to. After the last year, she'd be hard pushed to find someone on the force who didn't know her face. The woman had a problem with her. Eve had enough of her own.

'Pleasure, I'm sure.'

Mearns had the decency to step aside at Eve's clipped tone, dodging around her outside the bathroom's doorway.

Cooper raised his arm towards the open door. 'In here.'

Eve turned into the room. 'Jesus . . .'

What she could see of the body was propped against the tiled bathroom wall, legs outstretched. The pathologist, Brian MacLean, was kneeling just beside it. Eve could see black trousers sticking out past him, stockings covering the feet. A woman. Her head was bowed forward, long brown hair hanging limp, obscuring her face. As if she'd sat and fallen asleep. Eve could see nothing else, but her instinct told her this was going to be a bad one.

The bathroom was as big as Eve's bedroom, small black tiles covering the walls, larger tiles on the floor, grout that once would have been white. A wet room, but what lay on the floor and was splashed against the wall wasn't water. The blood was everywhere.

She took a deep breath, tried to calm herself, conscious of the new DC assessing her from the doorway. A DC who, for all her attitude, looked a light shade of green. Eve wondered if it was her first dead body. She looked at Cooper. 'What's the story?'

'Cleaner found her this morning.'

'We got a statement?'

Cooper nodded, reached into his inside pocket for his notebook and flipped it open. 'Nadia Koprowski. Came to work expecting to strip beds, clean toilets and stepped into this instead. Puked when she found her. Thankfully made it to a bin.'

'Who called it in?'

'The guy on the desk downstairs. Got a statement off him too.'

'What about the manager?'

'Down south on a course. Antsy on the phone, distraught even. Not about the victim, of course. More worried about the hotel's reputation.'

Eve moved her weight on to her other foot. 'Any ID for the vic?'

'Yeah, Melanie Ross. Eighteen years old, according to the driver's licence in her handbag. Got her address. No one's been notified yet. We were waiting until you got here.'

Today had to be hard for Cooper. Six months of covering her role, of experiencing that step up, and now he was having to hand over the reins. Hopefully it wasn't going to be a problem between them – professionally or personally. She realized she hadn't seen DC Scott Ferguson yet, someone she fully expected to have problems with.

'Where's Ferguson?'

The question threw Cooper for a second, DC Mearns still by his side staring at Eve with a face that looked like it was sucking something sour. 'Hastings has got him working on something at the station.'

Eve nodded once. 'Anything else on the victim?' She kept her voice firm, in control, determined not to let Mearns unnerve her.

'Her purse and ID weren't the only things in the bag. Seems our Melanie knew her way around a

18

sex-toy catalogue – implies she knew who she was coming to meet.'

Eve took a minute to think. 'Did she check in alone?'

'That's the thing.' Cooper waved his notebook. 'She never checked in. Room was booked for single occupancy by a Mr Phillips. Done over the phone with a card registered to the same name.'

'Anything on this Mr Phillips?'

'They're trying to trace him. The mobile given at the time of booking is switched off. DC Ferguson is trying to get access to bank details for contact info.'

'Anyone remember Mr Phillips checking in?'

Cooper shook his head. 'The guy downstairs, Andrew . . .' Cooper checked his notebook again, 'Slessor, Andrew Slessor, said that he was on yesterday and would've checked him in, but he can't remember specifics. We've asked for the CCTV tapes, but there's nothing available for the back entrance. Camera's been faulty for weeks.'

Eve tutted. 'Thanks, Cooper.' And she was thankful to him, for more than having the bases covered today. Namely the professionalism and familiarity he was displaying to counteract the attitude coming from DC Mearns. She nodded over to MacLean, who was kneeling by the body. 'Has he got a time of death?'

'Reckons early this morning. Says he'll know more once he gets her to the lab.'

MacLean looked to be finishing.

'I'll have a word.' Eve signalled for Cooper and Mearns to step away. She had to take charge, draw a line from today.

'OK. But be prepared. Her face is a mess.'

Cooper was making the transition easy for her, looking out for her welfare as he'd always done. Eve walked towards MacLean, who stood, ready to leave, then saw her and stopped.

'I'd say welcome back . . .' MacLean was staring at her but seemed to be fixed on a spot above her head, or at least one eye was. Eve was never sure which eye she was supposed to focus on. His greying moustache twitched. She shook the slim hand that MacLean was offering and looked at the woman. *Her face.* She crouched. It was hard to make out her features. Her cheeks and forehead had been slashed, the blood turning black and crusty on top. The criss-cross of wounds reminded Eve of a lattice-topped pie. It was a bizarre image, but one she couldn't shake.

'Who did this to you, Melanie?' Her voice caught as she leaned in closer to the girl. 'I'm going to find out, I promise you that.' She straightened. She had to hold herself together.

'Poor cow.' MacLean lifted his bag from the floor.

Nothing had changed in MacLean's manner. Abrupt and with a warped sense of humour, he wasn't always appropriate, but it was a mechanism that he adopted to cope. A sense of humour went a long way in this line of work.

'What can you tell me?'

'She's been dead since the early hours of this morning. Wounds to the face were inflicted while she was still alive. Looks like a scalpel was used. No sign of it though.'

'Christ.'

'Aye, he's a real charmer. Only comfort you can take from it is that I'm fairly certain she was drugged. I'm not sure what with yet, but her hands were tied with cord. Looks like some sort of venetian-blind cord, and there's no sign of struggle. No marks on her wrists, no trail of blood. She sat there and let it happen.'

'What?' She must've heard the last bit wrong.

'My guess is that the drug left her unable to move. We can only hope it numbed the pain too. I'll know more once the test results come back.'

'What kind of sick—'

'Nothing queerer than folk, Eve.'

Eve checked the bathroom again. 'What's with all the stuff?' There were mirrors, magazines and make-up strewn across the floor. No, that was wrong. They'd been placed. Staged. The magazines were fanned out like they were on top of a glass table in a waiting room, the mirrors all facing the body.

'It's your job to work that one out. Although, judging by her face and what was left on the body, I think our man's trying to send us a message.'

'Left on the body?'

'They haven't told you yet?'

Eve frowned.

'Newspaper cutting, pinned to her top. It's with forensics.'

'Saying what?'

'A headline – "Aberdeen Model Through to Finals of Competition".'

'That's it?'

21

'Yup.'

'Anything else?' She hoped to God there wasn't. It was obvious the woman had suffered enough, and this thing was getting more twisted by the minute.

'Fully dressed, no obvious signs of sexual activity. I'll know more once I've examined her at the lab. It's a work uniform she's wearing.'

'Any idea where?'

MacLean nodded towards the woman. 'Don't need an idea. Her work badge told us. Boots the Chemist. Guys bagged the badge and took it away.'

Eve made a mental note to have someone contact Melanie's employer.

'One more thing. Probably the most important.'

Eve closed her eyes, not sure she wanted to hear it.

'It seems our killer's into souvenirs. But I think it's safe to say he's probably not into small talk.'

'How come?'

'Her tongue's missing.'

Chapter 3

'MISSING?' DCI JIM HASTINGS echoed. 'What do you mean?'

Eve held the mobile phone away from her ear, her boss's growl still audible.

'Taken, sir.'

'For Christ's sake.'

Eve shook her head. Her boss was making it sound as if it were her fault. She parted the black vertical blinds with her forefinger and thumb and looked out at the grand granite-housed businesses opposite, across the never-ending stream of traffic travelling up from the city centre along Queen's Road. A frozen stream, cars and buses at a standstill in the thick snow that was falling fast, collecting on roofs, blanketing pavements and slowing pedestrians too. Maybe the countless 4×4s would get a shot at what they were built for.

'Eve?'

Her attention was dragged back to the call. 'Yeah, MacLean reckons the tongue was removed with a scalpel. Her face is a mess. Looks like she was drugged. Probably awake but unable to move, although we won't know for sure until the lab results come back.'

'For fu—'

'It gets worse. I think the scene was staged.' A crackle of silence. She wondered if her boss would trust her instincts, bracing herself for the explosion. She turned towards the reception desk, letting the silence stretch down the line. The man sitting there was immaculate, dressed to match the black-and-silver decor. An expensive suit, pristine white shirt, perfect knot on his glossy grey tie. Even his black hair, with its precise parting shining in the glow of the white lights on the countertop Christmas tree. Christmas was arriving earlier every year, but at least the tree complemented the colour scheme. He'd already called for the floor to be mopped where her shoes had left puddles on her arrival. The receptionist ducked his head and shuffled papers as if he hadn't noticed her.

'What was at the scene?'

'Mirrors, magazines, make-up. On the floor around the body. All brand new; none of it belongs to the hotel. And a newspaper headline, pinned to her clothing.' Eve recited the headline from memory, no need for her notebook.

'Can we get anything from the stuff? Do we have the article that went with the headline yet?'

'All run-of-the-mill items, but they've been bagged and tagged. You never know, we might get something in amongst the masses that've probably handled it all before it left the shops. I'll get Elliott on the case about the article.'

'What the hell does it mean? Should we be expecting another one?'

Eve shifted the weight off her aching leg, needing painkillers, still standing by the window. 'Your guess is as good as mine. But it's not the usual, is it? Hard to tell what she looked like, but, one thing's for sure, someone obviously had a problem with her face.' At least Hastings was willing to take her opinion on board.

'Hopefully just hers and no one else's.'

There was a slight pause down the line. Eve lowered her voice. 'Sir?'

'How're you bearing up?'

The question threw Eve. She hadn't realized she was back in bloody therapy. 'I'm fine, sir.'

'Has there been any word on the owner of the card, the guy that booked the room?' Hastings seemed oblivious to her annoyance. She let it go.

'No, but we should have details soon. Cooper said DC Ferguson is looking into that and the CCTV.'

Hastings tutted. 'How the hell can no one have heard or seen anything?'

'The rooms either side of the suite were empty last night. Sign of the times. We've got nothing to go on until we get details for Mr Phillips from the bank.'

'What's happening now?'

'They're moving the body. Van's parked out back. Trying to contain things as long as we can.'

'It's a hotel. Some nosy bugger will have called the press.'

'Maybe not, sir. It's a Monday. Most residents are here for work, those that still have a job, and probably left the hotel before we arrived. There are a few customers in the bar and restaurant, but I think they're mainly visitors, maybe a couple of business lunches. Staff are doing a good job of putting on a front.' Eve half expected to see reporters arrive any minute.

'Still, like you say, it's not the usual, so we better be ready for them. I'll get Elliott on it, that and the article. Are Cooper and Mearns with you?'

'Yeah, they're waiting upstairs until the body's cleared.'

'OK. Have the family been notified?'

'No, but we've got an address. Craigiebuckler area. Must be the parents' place, as I can't see an eighteen-year-old shop assistant being able to afford a shed there. I'm going to head round, see if anyone's home.' Eve's mouth went dry.

'You OK with that? I need you on top of things.'

There it was again. Questioning her ability. 'Course, sir.' She did her best to keep her voice steady, hating that she had to.

'Then you better go before they hear about it on the bloody news.'

'Elliott's good at keeping them at bay.' Eve had a lot of respect for the force's media guy, knew he'd tried to save her when the press had come sniffing around after what happened to Sanders.

'Take Mearns with you; she's good at that sort of thing. I'll make sure Elliott has all the bases covered on the PR front; can't have the media scumbags accusing us of being uncaring and incompetent.'

Eve hadn't forgotten the earlier encounter with Mearns. 'Sir, I—'

'And get Cooper back here. He can start by getting the incident room set up and the team ready.'

Melanie Ross's mother was as small as a child herself, but the short grey hair and deep wrinkles lining her face betrayed her age. She was perched on the edge of an oversized two-seater floral sofa, and it was doubtful whether her feet would've reached the floor otherwise. She sat wringing a damp handkerchief between liver-spotted hands that lay on her pleated skirt. Her neck was covered in red blotches. She raised a trembling hand to her thick glasses and nudged them to dab at her eyes.

The tick of the grandfather clock in the corner dominated the space, the only other sounds a far-off kettle boiling and the occasional clink of china as DC Mearns moved about the kitchen. Eve sat on the armchair opposite, grateful Mearns was somewhere else, giving Mrs Ross time to take in everything that was pointing towards the fact her child was gone. There was a quiet pop as the woman's lips opened, her mouth struggling to move against the dryness.

'Are you sure there's no mistake?'

Eve wanted to relieve Mrs Ross's pain but didn't want to give her false hope. 'Nothing's definite yet. We believe it to be Melanie due to the reasons I explained, but she'll need to be formally identified.'

Mrs Ross tilted back and forth. 'I know it's her. I mean, her work uniform, her bag, her phone . . . the fact she didn't come home. I . . . I can't take it in.'

The words were broken by sobs. She looked fragile, as if the sofa's plump cushions could swallow her whole at any minute. Eve didn't know what to say to her, how to comfort her. Emotions had never been her strong point. Mrs Ross rocked faster, staring at the floor, lost in her own thoughts.

The walls were covered with framed pictures. Family pictures. Mrs Ross and her husband. Mrs Ross and Melanie. The couple and their daughter. Melanie as an adult. She was, had been, stunning. Some of the shots hanging above an old piano looked professionally done. Eve couldn't see a trace of the Rosses in their daughter's features. How had this rather plain-looking couple produced someone so beautiful?

Melanie, as she'd found her, flashed into her mind. She swallowed the lump in her throat and gazed at a rectangular hatch which separated the living room from the kitchen. In a street where the latest model 4x4s dominated the driveways, the decor of the large semi-detached granite house was old fashioned but homely. Mrs Ross reminded her of her grandmother. Softly spoken with a kind face, but Eve's grandmother had possessed a personality big enough for two.

Mearns was visible through the hatch, going about the kitchen, methodical, opening and closing cupboards and drawers as if she knew where things would be. Ordered, like her appearance, trousers looking as if they'd been collected from the dry-cleaners that morning, her long mousey-brown hair fastened tightly in a bun at the nape of her neck, blonde highlights catching the overhead kitchen light.

Eve didn't know what to make of her. She sure as hell wasn't short of self-confidence or attitude. They hadn't a chance to exchange more than a few clipped comments on the drive over, barely more than five minutes from the hotel. But Eve had been surprised to hear Mearns' broad Bolton accent. She'd apparently transferred from the force down south. Mearns must've hit the ground running, Scottish law differing from English. Eve got the sense Mearns thought she had something to prove – and that she definitely had a problem with Eve.

Mrs Ross continued to stare at the floor as Mearns came into the room and slid a saucer and cup across the glass tabletop towards her, a finger of shortbread balanced beside the teaspoon.

'Thank you,' she whispered.

'I thought something hot and sweet might help with the shock.' Mearns sat next to her on the couch and placed a hand on the woman's arm.

She sounded like Peter Kay and Paddy McGuinness. It seemed inappropriate to be thinking about comedians considering the situation they were in, but the Bolton accent was alien to Aberdeen, and Eve's only real experience of it was off the telly. Somehow that connection made Mearns' accent seem familiar, soothing and homely. What was needed to comfort Mrs Ross. Good to see a soft side to her new colleague, but she doubted she would be experiencing it herself any time soon.

Mearns patted Mrs Ross's arm. 'Our family-liaison officer, Sarah, is on her way to sit with you, to help out, and your husband shouldn't be too long.'

Melanie's mother lifted the cup with shaking hands. The tea slopped over the edges, dripping light brown liquid on to the immaculate cream carpet. She didn't seem to notice.

Perhaps that was how Sanders' husband had looked when he was first told what had happened that night, the shock probably worse than the dirty looks that he gave when Eve found the courage to visit. She stood, needing to shake the thoughts from her head.

'Do you mind if I help myself to a glass of water, Mrs Ross?'

The woman shook her head, sniffling.

In the kitchen, Eve filled a glass at the sink and took the bottle from her suit jacket pocket. She shook a couple of pills into the palm of her hand, knocked them back and bent over to rub her thigh now that she was standing and alone. A door opened. Eve jumped as it slammed shut.

'Ellie? Ellie?'

Eve turned round to see Mr Ross arriving home, his voice loud, panic at its edges. He was overweight and breathless, an open camel coat, snow lying on its expensive shoulders, shirt buttons straining at his gut. His wet white hair was thinning; a bulbous nose and puffed cheeks shone red below it. The man visibly froze when he spotted Eve.

'Who the hell are you?'

'I'm DI Hunter, Mr Ross. Why don't you come through and sit?'

'I don't bloody want to sit. I got a message from my PA saying I had to head home urgently. Where's my wife? What the hell is this all about?'

If only family liaison had arrived. Her first day back, and what a day it was turning out to be. 'I called your work, Mr Ross. Please, your wife is in the lounge.' Eve raised her arm towards the door. Mr Ross inched forward, searching Eve's face for answers, looking at the door, wondering if what lay beyond it was about to change his life for ever. When he saw his wife, his face drained to the same colour as his hair.

'James. Oh, James.' Mrs Ross jumped up and flew across the room, collapsing into her husband's arms as if she'd used any energy she had left to get to him. He held her by her upper arms, pushed her from his chest and looked into her eyes, catching his breath as he did.

'No . . . not Melanie. Please no. Not Melanie. Not my baby girl.' He sank to the floor, rocking, his sobs mixing with those of his wife.

The tea tray came out for the second time that afternoon, carried by Sarah, who had finally arrived. Traffic was horrendous, she said. First sign of bad weather in Aberdeen and things came to a standstill. For a city that didn't often enjoy good weather, Eve could never understand why they weren't better prepared. Mr and Mrs Ross sat side by side on the sofa, Mr Ross fitting the furniture better than his wife.

'Why has this happened to our daughter?' The man's voice was weary, devoid of any authority.

Eve answered. 'We still have to be sure it's her. I know this is hard, Mr Ross, but, due to her injuries, it may be best to do it through fingerprints rather than having you or your wife identify her.'

Mr Ross shook his head. 'No. I need to see her.'

31

If Mrs Ross was to see her daughter, it would be the end of her.

'If that's what you want, then I can't stop you. We would only need you to come with us, unless your wife wanted to join you.'

The relief on Mrs Ross's face was evident. Part of her would be wrestling with the guilt of not being there for her daughter one last time, hoping that her husband would in time tell her that she made the right decision, to stop the inevitable doubts from gnawing away at her.

'Mr Ross? Are you sure you want to see her?'

The man nodded, tears dripping off his jawbone. 'Yes. I'm sure.'

Mearns spoke from where she stood at the window. 'Mr Ross, I promise you we are doing everything we can to find who did this.'

Hastings was right: she was good at this stuff. She made Sarah look surplus to requirements with the tea and the comfort. A small voice in Eve's head had her worried Mearns might make her look the same if she didn't stay on top of the game, if it turned out she wasn't ready. But she was glad to see Mearns' professionalism here, even if it hadn't been evident at the hotel. She was taking the back seat, letting Eve take charge, no matter how grudgingly it was being done below the surface.

Eve leaned forward. 'You've no idea what she might've been doing there?'

'I told you, she left early for work and told us she'd be late home.' Mr Ross sighed. 'We realized this morning that she hadn't come home, but we didn't think anything of it.' His hand reached for his wife's. 'Melanie had a habit of staying out once in a while, usually at a friend's. We argued over her not calling or texting to let us know, but she was eighteen – no longer a kid.' His voice trembled, and he took a moment to gather himself. 'Usually she headed straight to work.'

Eve nodded. 'Did work call to check where she was?'

Mrs Ross's eyes flickered to the sideboard where the phone was. 'They might've. I was at my flower-arranging class at the local church this morning. I wasn't long home when you arrived.' There was hope in her eyes, thinking maybe they didn't call, maybe this was all a terrible misunderstanding.

'OK. Can I ask, did Melanie do some modelling on the side?'

Mrs Ross stood and shuffled to the dresser. She opened a drawer and lifted a thin A4 notebook from it. She passed it to Eve. It was a scrapbook. Filled with pictures and small newspaper cuttings throughout, the last filled page containing the headline that had been found on Melanie's body, along with the article. Blank pages still remained that would never be filled.

Eve spoke. 'Could we borrow this, please?'

Melanie's mother looked over at her husband, who nodded a silent agreement.

'Thank you. We'll make sure it's looked after and returned.'

Mrs Ross nodded once. 'How did you know Melanie modelled?'

Eve hesitated, not sure how Melanie's folks would take the next bit of information. 'There was a headline left at the scene.' She flicked the scrapbook open and pointed: 'This one.'

Confusion clouded Mrs Ross's face.

'We don't know the significance yet, but we wondered if you might be able to tell us anything?'

Mrs Ross said nothing, dabbed at her face, her husband not moving.

Eve kept on with the questions. 'Did Melanie have a boyfriend?'

Neither Mr nor Mrs Ross answered straight away, a look passing between them. Mr Ross coughed, fidgeting on the sofa. 'No.'

Eve wasn't sure how Mr and Mrs Ross were going to handle what she was about to say. 'I'm sorry, but it appears that she went to the hotel to meet someone.'

'How the hell do you know that?' Mr Ross boomed. 'She could've been taken against her will. Maybe she thought she was going to meet a girl friend.'

Eve answered. 'I doubt it, Mr Ross. The bag had items in it to suggest she knew about the meet.' She didn't expand on that. Neither parent argued the point, and the look that had passed between them before preyed on Eve's mind. She continued.

'We have a name. We don't know if it's connected yet, but it would help if you could tell us if it means anything to either of you.'

Eve could have sworn she saw a flicker of panic on both their faces. Mrs Ross's hand gripped her husband's tighter. Mr Ross rubbed a hand across his forehead, dragged it over his eyes.

'What's the name?'

'Mr Phillips.'

'The bastard!' The venom in Mr Ross's soft whisper made more sense when the man jumped to his feet and shouted it the second time, as if it had hit home – dragging his wife with him, knocking the tray from the table. His wife made a choking sound, a scream catching in her throat, any hope in her eyes gone.

Eve was by the man's side in a second. 'Easy, Mr Ross. Tell us what you know about him.'

Melanie's father looked at Eve and sank to the sofa, head in hands. 'Mr Phillips,' he spat, 'Ryan, is Melanie's brother.'

Chapter 4

EVE STARED AT THE curtains, standing shoulder to shoulder with Melanie's father. The chemical smell was overpowering even through the sheet of glass behind the divide. James Ross's breathing was laboured. In through the nose, out through the mouth. An attempt to steady himself, waiting for the two thick lengths of material to be drawn, trying to be ready for what they were about to reveal.

Mr Ross had brought his brother, as two people were required to confirm identification. Eve knew the men next to her would never be ready. If only Mr Ross had listened, hadn't felt the need to be here . . . but she wasn't a parent. And she'd never had a father who cared about her.

She put a hand out to offer some kind of comfort but quickly withdrew it, the gesture as unwelcome to her as it probably would be to him. His brother stood rigid on the other side of him. The pulley squeaked. Eve braced herself. The curtains inched back, a chink of light at their centre, the space becoming wider, revealing the white expanse of a sheet pulled taut, a lump beneath. The starched material was bright in contrast to the gun-grey metal sides of the gurney, a colour that dominated Aberdeen Divisional HQ's mortuary, hidden in the basement, away from the living. Mr Ross had stopped breathing, holding tight to the air in his lungs, waiting for the curtain to open far enough.

Her head was the only visible part of her. That was enough. Eve waited, ready, catching Mr Ross as he stumbled, his brother still standing frozen. Eve gripped to stop him falling over, letting him scream, sob and to finally vomit all over her shoes.

Eve shifted forward, ignoring the throbbing in her leg, and poured a glass of water from the jug on the low round table at the centre of the worn armchairs in the family room. She passed the glass to Melanie's father and watched him take it with trembling hands. His brother had gone home.

'I'm sorry.'

'I can't believe it.' Mr Ross shook his head and stared into the glass.

'I know. I apologize for the timing of this, but now that we have a formal identification, I have a few questions that I need to ask.'

Melanie's father raised his head and looked at Eve for the first time since arriving at the mortuary. He nodded.

'You said that Ryan Phillips was Melanie's brother?' Eve didn't question Ryan's different surname or venture towards where her mind had already gone, thinking of the contents of Melanie's bag.

Mr Ross's eyes darted away. Eve let the silence stretch, giving him time to figure out how to tell his story. Mr Ross knocked back the water, probably wishing it would give him the courage of something stronger, and fixed Eve with his stare.

'You've got the room booking and the other stuff. I think you've worked out that Melanie and Ryan were together in another way.'

Eve didn't react. Of course that's where the evidence had taken her. She wasn't shocked. There wasn't a lot she hadn't come across during her years on the job. Compared to other things, this was nothing. But not to the man sitting in front of her. It was as if he'd shrunk in front of her eyes, the words finally spoken out loud taking away a piece of him.

Mr Ross pinched the bridge of his nose. 'There's no point in me concocting a version of the truth, is there? I mean, would it avoid tarnishing my daughter's memory? Would it see justice done?'

Eve swallowed. 'No, it wouldn't and, as difficult as it is, I know justice is what you'll want to see happen.'

Mr Ross's flat palms rubbed at either side of the glass, painstakingly slow, turning it this way and that. His voice cracked when he spoke again.

'Melanie and Ryan were always close. Even when they were little. The real inappropriate behaviour between them started in their early teens. Uncomfortable, the looks between them, their exchanges. Ellie and I didn't want to believe what was happening in front of our eyes.'

He ran his finger around the lip of the glass, staring at it as he did, needing something to distract him from what his mouth was doing.

'Our attempts to stop what was going on only made them more determined. Ryan especially. He was always a confident, cocky kind of kid. Gave us a lot of trouble over the years.

'Melanie was completely different, always eager to please. Or at least she was until all the stuff with Ryan. But even then, I think it was him. He could be frightening.' Mr Ross paused.

'He had a way about him that made others do what he wanted. Melanie didn't stand a chance. She was timid then, awkward, didn't realize how beautiful she already was. He played on that, fed into her insecurities.'

Mr Ross shifted in his seat.

'I threw him out six months ago. We were terrified Melanie would follow him, but he had nothing to offer her, at least not in the financial sense. He was working in a bar, moved in with a pal renting a poky flat, the last we heard. We were estranged from him after that. Ellie was heartbroken.'

Mr Ross fell silent, his face showing memories that haunted him. Eve filled the gap. 'Would you have an address for the flat?'

'Ellie does. She felt better knowing where he was.'

'I understand. We'll need a photo of Ryan too.'

Mr Ross nodded and reached for the overcoat that he'd slung over the arm of the chair. His hand disappeared into the inner pocket, pulling out a leather wallet when it came back into view. He flipped open the wallet and picked at something beneath one of the transparent folds, his shaking fingers struggling before he was able to pull it free. He held out his hand.

Eve took the small photograph from him. 'Thank you.' A dark-haired, good-looking young man with intense brown eyes stared at her from the little square. It wasn't lost on her that Mr Ross still carried it around with him. 'Please, carry on.'

He looked like it was the last thing he wanted to do, but he did. 'At first, we kidded ourselves that they might've finally seen sense, but, although we never spoke about it, we both knew it never stopped between them. We'd only made it easier for them. No more nagging at them under the same roof, no idea whether they were together when Melanie was out.

'We wondered if maybe he'd got his own place, especially the nights Melanie didn't come home. We had a savings fund that was to be released to him at twenty-one. A substantial amount. They both did. We never changed that. I wanted to, but Ellie said no. His was released to him last month. I think it relieved Ellie's guilt a little.'

'Guilt?'

'That we'd somehow failed him. That we could still do right by him by giving him a decent start in life financially, could give them both that. I, on the other hand, never felt responsible for who he was.' He stopped, his face registering that Melanie would never receive her fund.

Eve gave him a moment before speaking. 'Forgive me, but lots of teenage girls feel awkward, it goes with the territory, but they don't go running into the arms of their brother.'

Mr Ross knocked his jittering leg against the table. 'Detective, Melanie and Ryan were adopted.'

Eve fought to keep her expression neutral. Now the difference in surname made sense. 'From the same family?'

'No. Different parents. When he moved out, he returned to his birth name of Phillips. Melanie was three, Ryan six when we adopted them. Ellie always wanted kids. We always wanted kids. Tried for years. When we found out that we couldn't, I was willing to leave it there. But not Ellie.'

It explained why Mrs Ross had reminded Eve a little of her grandmother. 'But surely that changes things with regard to the nature of their relationship?' she said tentatively.

Mr Ross glared at Eve, authority returned. 'It changes absolutely nothing, Detective. We may have been a ready-made family, but we were still a family. To neighbours, friends, our extended family, we were parents, they were our kids – brother and sister. It's all we ever wanted, and what they were doing was taking that away from us.'

Eve saw a broken, bitter man. She felt sorry for Mr Ross, but she couldn't help feeling the same for the teenagers that Melanie and Ryan had been. How Ryan might have felt that he was never as good as Melanie in his adoptive parents' eyes. All the framed family photos she'd seen at the house. Not one of Ryan.

How exciting Ryan must've seemed to Melanie, the good little girl who always did the right thing. What if Melanie had been cooling towards him? How threatened would he have felt if even she was starting to think he wasn't good enough? Maybe Ryan's cockiness was all part of an act, knowing Melanie was the favourite.

Melanie's father put the glass on the table, the expression on his face showing he still had more to say. 'But, you know, as bad as things got with Ryan, I was willing to believe that he at least loved her.'

'That's what we need to find out, Mr Ross. There could be a hundred different reasons, but it only takes one to provide motive.'

Chapter 5

Now

He sits at the small, square Costa table downstairs in the Bon Accord Shopping Centre, the aroma of coffee wrapped tightly around him. One of the crowd.

The overweight woman on the table diagonally opposite him, her backside overhanging the chair, chomps into an iced sponge, taking almost half of it into her blubbery lips. She might as well smear it across her face. A blob of white icing sticks to the corner of her mouth, bobbing there as she chews.

He glances sideways at the elderly man whose skeletal hand shakes, spilling coffee on his brown flannel trousers every time he lifts the cup. Seemingly oblivious as he stares into space, his time left on earth seeping away, much the same as the brown liquid soaking his lap.

Both of them have no idea of what he's done.

He looks at the moving metal staircase of stressed shoppers being spat out on the upper level of Christmas chaos: some scurrying into Next, others preferring Laura Ashley, thinking *the choice defines them. The barista in the purple top and stained black apron behind the counter smiles and pretends to love filling cups for a living.*

Not one of them have any clue.

He relishes this small stolen moment of being normal. So precious to someone who never has been.

But was anyone normal? Or was it all a big lie?

Each and every face a painted version of themselves. A mask.

He of all people knows about that.

He looks around at the bodies swarming here. There. Everywhere. Hears snippets of conversation, Doric slang, foreign tongues, swearing, laughing, babies crying. Mistaken that their lives are important. He likes to pick one at random and try to work out what their story is.

He likes stories. And he has an important one to tell. After today, people will listen.

He will be feared. Him. He knows because he saw the terror in Melanie's eyes.

He lifts the toastie in front of him, bites into it, enjoys the sensation of cheese filling his mouth. Just as the blood had filled Melanie's.

He looks at the unsuspecting bodies surrounding him. Smiles. Wonders what they did last night. Knowing it would be so different from what he'd done.

Today his work was found. He knows his days of being normal are numbered.

The fat woman heaves herself from her chair, looks at him as if he is nothing.

But he isn't nothing. Not any more. Soon he'll be everything. People will know what he did.

He has a story to tell. And it has begun.

Chapter 6

THE FLIMSY DOOR SQUEAKED on its hinges. A pair of blood-shot eyes peered out through the gap.

'Yeah?'

The young man's voice was hoarse, a waft of bad breath hitting Eve and making her want to stop breathing through her nose. She waited a beat before she spoke.

'Michael Forbes?'

'Yeah. Who's asking?'

Eve showed her ID. 'We're looking for Ryan Phillips.'

The young man looked confused for a second. 'That dickhead hasn't been here in weeks.'

'We have a few questions we'd like to ask. Could we come in?'

Michael Forbes tutted but released the chain and moved from the door. Eve stepped over the threshold, the smell of greasy fast food from George Street's kebab shops below strong, mixed with stale sweat. The street was a multicultural collection of shopfronts, looking more tatty with each passing year.

Cooper coughed behind her as the three of them jostled for space in the tiny hallway. She was glad Cooper was with her – she'd instructed Mearns to head back to HQ to help look into CCTV and bank records, effectively getting rid of her, if only for a short while. Eve stared at the hallway walls, which seemed to be closing in on her. Melanie's father hadn't been wrong when he'd described the flat as poky.

'Is there somewhere we could sit?'

Forbes groaned. 'Look, lady, you woke me up.'

Eve stared at him until, with a loud sigh, Forbes pushed open one of the three doors off the small, square hallway. The room was ice-cold and dim, lit only by grey winter light breaking through the closed, unlined curtains.

Eve's eyes adjusted, making out basic furniture: two sofas, blankets spread over them, hiding God only knows what beneath; an old-fashioned glass-topped table littered with overflowing ashtrays – some suspect stubs lying within them – and mouldy dishes.

Tie-dye hangings and posters of half-naked women covered the walls. It looked like bad student digs. Eve would bet it was a long time since Forbes had studied anything, if he ever had. Cooper's nose crinkled. The place was dirty, stinking and sad.

Forbes lifted a fag packet from the table, shook one free and threw the pack down. Turning towards them, he lit the cigarette with a Zippo lighter from the back pocket of his jeans. He inhaled, watching them as he held on to the first hit of nicotine before exhaling with force, eyes squinting through smoke, his yellow-stained

46

forefinger and thumb pinching at the filter. He didn't offer them a seat. Eve was happy to stand.

'What's he done now and how come you're asking me?' Forbes plonked himself on the sofa beneath the window.

'Done now?' The surprise in Cooper's voice matched Eve's.

'I reckon you're not here unless he's been up to something.'

Eve was careful. 'Is it unusual for Ryan to be up to something?'

'Fuck, no. Unusual for him to get caught.' Forbes flicked his fag, ash floating to the carpet.

Eve followed the ash with her eyes. 'How do you know Ryan?'

'Worked with him at Beagles nightclub on Justice Mill.'

Justice Mill Lane. A road parallel to the main drag of Union Street. A strip of bars, the young crowd all over it at the weekend.

'How long did you work with him? Did you know him before?' Cooper took the baton this time. Eve let him go with it. She'd worked with Cooper long enough to know she could. She felt a hankering for the old days, knowing they were long gone without Sanders. She took a deep breath, focused on Michael Forbes' answer.

'I'd never seen the guy until the first night we were put on the same shift. Would've been about a year ago.'

'Did you get on?' Cooper prompted.

'Yeah, we got on. He was up for good times, like.'

Those good times likely involved drugs, if the flat was anything to go by. 'You spent a lot of time together?'

'Yeah, not in some funny kind of way, if that's what you're getting at.'

Eve cocked an eyebrow, waited for Forbes to continue.

'We had a bit of banter at work, drinks after a shift if the ladies were sniffing. Good thing about our line of work is you're there to catch the ten-to-two brigade when they fall.'

'Ten to two?' Cooper asked the question Eve already knew the answer to.

Forbes sneered, licking his lips before answering. 'Club shuts at two a.m. Drunken tarts get a little desperate come ten to.' He dropped his hand casually to the denim at his groin, his gaze never leaving Eve's. 'Always happy to make a girl feel special.'

Cooper sighed.

Bravado oozed out of the pathetic, acne-faced twenty-something male lounging on the sofa. The reality was he probably rode on Ryan's coat-tails, more than happy to snatch up his leftovers. In the photo Mr Ross had given her earlier, Ryan had the looks, and by the sounds of things the personality, for persuasion.

'You and Ryan picked up the ladies together?'

'Most shifts, yeah.'

How drunk and desperate did a girl have to be if she came back here? 'You'd bring them home with you?'

'Once Ryan moved in. He kept the place straight. He always said he had standards.'

Eve stopped herself from saying 'except with women' and let Forbes babble on.

'Thing is, Ryan came from posh and he might've spoke proper, but there was nothing proper about the guy.'

'Where else did you go apart from here?' Maybe it would give them some clue as to where Ryan was.

'Anywhere. Some nights it was good times at the casino. But there were times we didn't have to go further than the side alley of the club. Some girls wanted a little shared fun, if you know what I mean.'

Eve sighed, not trying to hide it. The poor women. Had Forbes enjoyed the closeness to Ryan? Most of the women were probably too drunk to realize what was happening or, at least, how they would feel remembering the next day. Taken advantage of. She wanted to smack the bravado right out of the little shit. Eve had to be impartial, but scum like Forbes picked away at old scars.

Cooper stared at her. She snapped out of it. 'When did Ryan move in?'

He looked like it was the most difficult thing he'd been asked all week. 'About six months ago. His old man was giving him earache, threw him out.'

'Did he say why?' Maybe he'd known about Ryan and Melanie.

'Nah, it's what the folks do sometimes, ain't it? Get rid of us.'

It was something Eve's mother would never have done. She focused on the task at hand. 'Did you ever meet any of his family?'

Forbes wasn't quick to answer, the fag squeezed between his fingers pausing in mid-air before meeting his lips. He took a deep drag and an exaggerated exhale.

Eve looked at Cooper.

'Yeah.'

The cocky tone had disappeared.

'And?' Eve was watching Forbes' every move.

'His sister. Melanie.'

Eve said nothing, letting the silence stretch, waiting for Forbes to continue.

'Ryan was funny about her. Didn't like speaking about her, hated if I tried to.'

A hint of jealousy, but she suspected it was more to do with Ryan than Melanie.

Cooper must've sensed it too. 'What made you want to talk about her?'

Again, the slowed drag, peering at them through the smoke as he blew out.

'She was a looker. Ryan seemed obsessed with her.'

Eve glanced at Cooper, knew by his face he'd picked up on it too. *Was* a looker. They hadn't said anything about Melanie's murder, knew it hadn't made the news yet.

'What happened to have you refer to him as a dickhead?'

Forbes scowled. 'He disappeared about four, five weeks ago without a word. Owed me rent, took off with some of my shit. No surprise there. I was an idiot to think he wouldn't. And he left me to explain his ass to work.'

'You've heard nothing?' Cooper sounded doubtful.

'Nope, and he better hope I don't.' The tone of his voice said different. He was either lying about not having heard from him or was making an empty threat about what would happen if he did.

'Do you know where he might be?' She was looking for that flicker of doubt, sure she could sense it.

'I don't know shit about him, lady. Doubt I ever did.' Forbes stubbed the fag out, threw himself back on the sofa, looking like he wasn't going to be offering anything else.

Eve studied the scrawny, greasy excuse for a guy. Hard to believe he could be capable of what had happened to Melanie, even harder to think he might have somehow overpowered Ryan and was responsible for his disappearance too. More probable that Forbes was covering for Ryan.

Forbes was pretending to be half-asleep on the sofa already, not a care in the world. They weren't going to be getting anything else out of him today. But when they left here, it didn't mean they wouldn't be seeing each other again.

Chapter 7

'VERY PROFESSIONAL.'

DC Jo Mearns smirked as Eve shook a white blouse from its hanger. Eve was in her bra, standing in the incident room as Cooper kept himself turned towards the wall. She stared at Mearns, said nothing.

Eve felt unsettled being back at North East Division HQ. Like returning to an old home that hadn't changed, but yet she had. Queen Street, at the heart of the city. Eve had missed the old grey seven-storey concrete building. It sat a stone's throw away from countless bars and entertainment venues, including the Lemon Tree and the Arts Centre. Adjacent to the council buildings and Sheriff Court.

'Thanks for getting this, Cooper.' Eve pushed her arm through the sleeve, the thin material cold against her already freezing skin. The snow outside wasn't stopping, and the heating in here was useless. More bloody budget cuts. She twisted round to catch the other sleeve and pulled the blouse together at the collar before fastening the buttons.

Cooper turned. 'No problem. Couldn't have you looking like a dog's dinner in front of Hastings.'

They both knew it wasn't only about that. The blouse she'd put on that morning, which seemed like days ago, had been in a bad enough state to start off with, but the visit to the mortuary with Melanie's father hadn't made things any better. Death had a way of clinging to the living. The smell of greasy food and sweat from Michael Forbes' flat hadn't helped.

'Plenty of blouses at home, none of them ironed. I see you went cheap.'

Cooper smiled. 'You know what they say about us Aberdonians – drop a pound coin and it'll be hitting the back of our heads before it reaches the ground. Anyway, I was already heading to the Bon Accord Centre; it was no problem.'

'How'd it go?' Cooper had dropped Eve at the station and gone to Boots the Chemist on the lower floor of the Bon Accord Centre – Melanie's work – to see if he could talk to someone there. Eve made the excuse that she'd get started back at the office, but the real reason was her leg wasn't happy and in need of a break. She tried to ignore the pain, glancing at her jacket slung over the chair where her pills were.

Cooper answered the question that for a moment Eve had forgotten she'd asked. 'Spoke to Melanie's boss.'

'And?'

'Young guy, especially for branch manager. Bit strange. Looked like he's never had to shave yet, personality of a sponge.'

'Upset? What did he say?'

'Shocked. Didn't know her well. A guy like that would be a gibbering wreck around someone like Melanie. There's a reason he's made it to management at his age: probably not got a life outside work, never been laid.'

'That's what? Your expert opinion as a married copper?' Mearns smirked.

Cooper sighed. 'Something like that, except that these days, round my hours and the kids, I'm lucky if I get laid.'

Eve let herself smile, surprised Cooper would be this open in front of Mearns. It was the kind of banter they had always shared between the two of them, but it seemed he and Mearns had formed a close bond while she was gone. She glanced towards Mearns, who was smiling at Cooper and shaking her head. The first real smile she'd seen from her. Eve became conscious of Cooper's stare. She swallowed, the pain in her leg increasing by the minute. 'You said he didn't know her well?'

'Yeah, said he didn't deal with the shop floor, put me on to her supervisor, Lydia Clark. Seems our Melanie was destined for bigger things than working on the make-up counter in Boots.'

'What's that then?'

'As you know, she'd done a fair bit of modelling locally, was starting to do all right. Lydia said she'd got some professional shots done, won that competition mentioned in the headline. It was a UK-wide competition that was getting her some attention. She planned to send her portfolio to agencies in London.'

Eve thought back to the photos she'd seen at Melanie's parents' place, the originals not going anywhere now.

'What else did this Lydia have to say?'

'She was in bits. Mr Jobsworth let me use his office. She and Melanie were good friends, socialized a lot out of work. Sounds like Melanie was a bit of a good-time girl but conscientious in her job. Lydia flagged it straight away when she didn't show and wasn't answering.'

'She have any clue to what might've been happening?'

'You mean with Ryan? No, she didn't mention it, and I made sure that I dropped family into the conversation.'

Eve finished fastening her blouse sleeves, glanced again at her fitted suit jacket hanging over the chair and thought of the pills. She was desperate to take them, to dull the pain, but determined not to do so in front of her colleagues – especially Mearns. 'Our Ryan's managed to stay off the radar.'

Mearns cut in. 'Do you believe his flatmate?'

Eve had updated her on the visit to Forbes' flat while they were waiting for Cooper to return. Mearns' tone was abrupt, as if she was challenging Eve, testing how Eve would dissect the situation.

'No. He's pissed off, but I think it may be more to do with his affections for Ryan.'

Mearns' blue eyes widened. 'You think he's got anything to do with Melanie?'

'Honestly? No.' Eve inhaled sharply, pain piercing at her thigh.

Cooper stepped forward. 'You OK?'

She nodded, offering nothing more.

Mearns stood, looking awkward in the moment. 'I got one of the tech guys to do a check through social media. Unless he uses an alias, you're right, Ryan likes to stay off radar.'

Eve couldn't help but be impressed: she'd not long updated Mearns. 'Good call though. Jesus—'

Eve slammed her backside into the chair beside her, grasping at her leg, unable to hide the pain as her face scrunched. Cooper rushed forward.

Eve lifted her hand, the sharp pain subsiding. 'I'm OK.' She took the bottle from inside her jacket pocket, not caring any more who was watching. She shook out two tablets. Mearns turned on her heel and left the room. Eve turned to Cooper. 'What the hell . . .?'

She was silenced, surprised, as Mearns returned with a plastic cup of water from the machine outside. Eve took it, gulped the pills. 'Thanks.'

Mearns said nothing, her face blank. Maybe she'd shocked herself.

Eve stayed seated, the cup in her hand, keen to move on. 'Did Lydia mention any other boyfriends, Cooper?'

Cooper looked like he wanted to make sure she was OK first but knew better. 'No. She said Melanie got hit on all the time but didn't want to be tied down, reckons she would've known about any guys, especially if there was someone serious. Wasn't aware of anything out of the ordinary at work either. Dead end, I think. Got her details if you want to follow—'

The door burst open. The three of them jumped. Hastings was in full throttle, with Elliott Jones, Police

Scotland's North East Divisional Headquarters' media guru, and DC Scott Ferguson by his side. Eve reddened as she stood, looking to make sure her blouse was definitely buttoned. She tutted and finished tucking it in but didn't miss the slight smirk on Mearns' face, the moment of kindness forgotten. Elliott stepped in front of Eve and cupped her shoulder.

'Good to see you, Eve.'

Ferguson, who was now standing next to Mearns, said nothing. Eve stared at him. Nothing about him had changed. His trendy, straight-out-of-bed haircut was still perfectly gelled to say he'd actually been up a good while, the goatee on his chin still trimmed with precision. She waited for eye contact. He didn't even try.

It stung more than she wanted to admit, but she chose to focus on Elliott. 'Thanks.' His sentiment was genuine. The guy had been a lifeline for her when things got messy before her leave of absence. Immaculate in his tailored suit and polished shoes, the day was young enough that his prematurely salt-and-peppered hair was still neat. Facial stubble nowhere to be seen. 'You'll be battling it from here on in, Elliott. If it helps, you won't need to track that headline article: we got a copy from the mother.'

Elliott put his thumb up.

Eve didn't envy him his job. Elliott oversaw a press team covering a large territory comprising a mixture of urban and rural communities in the north-east of Scotland – Aberdeenshire and Moray, the City of Aberdeen and its suburbs. Eve had enough to deal with in the office.

He'd be working into the night, the tie around his collar loosened by then, shoes kicked off under the desk and hair dishevelled after raking his hands through it in frustration. But he was good at the job.

Elliott shook his head. 'Bloody nightmare. Press has got wind of it already. No surprise. I'm waiting for the Rottweiler to attack.'

Claire Jenkins. Local hack. The woman had haunted Eve's dreams and her waking hours for the last year as she dissected Eve's professional life in the press. After all, there was nothing to tell about her personal one. Jenkins hadn't cared whether anything she unearthed from a 'reliable source' was true or not, conveniently forgetting all the times over the years that Eve had dealt fairly with her where other officers hadn't.

Elliott knew she wouldn't want to hear the actual name, especially on her first day back. They'd always had a mutual professional respect for one another, but during Eve's recovery they'd become friends of a sort.

Hastings dragged a hand across his forehead. 'Right. Press briefing's been organized for first thing tomorrow morning.' He looked at Eve. 'I'd appreciate a word. My office in five.'

DCI Jim Hastings sat behind the cheap office desk and waved at Eve to come in, mobile jammed against his ear, his voice so loud it was debatable whether he needed the phone. The office hadn't changed, neither had her boss. More the pity for Hastings. Still too thin, a faint smell of sweat in the air. The saggy skin on his face looked dead – yellowish, green under certain light. Only his nose seemed to fight against gravity, turned up at the end as if some imaginary hand was pinching it: excessive amount of nostril on show, unnaturally high above the wispy white whiskers of a moustache and what might, on a bad facial hair day, pass as a beard. They called him the Grinch. Not to his face, but he probably knew and, if honest with himself, wouldn't dispute it.

Eve put down one of the vending-machine sludges that she'd brought in with her. Hastings' stare was on her and had been from the door to the table. She was conscious of her walk, glad she'd managed to take the painkillers and hadn't spilled the coffees. She found a space in between the paperwork littering the desk and put the other cup down. Brown-nosing wasn't her style, but today it wouldn't do her any harm.

She took the seat opposite Hastings, the springs beneath the burst upholstery squeaking and tilting to the side when she sat. Nope, nothing had changed. The framed photo on the desk had been knocked out of position by files and sheaves of paper. It half faced Eve where it lay. Hastings' wife was beautiful in a strong kind of way – not small and dainty but assured, her confidence evident in the way she held herself, the fashions she wore. Thankfully, Hastings' teenage daughter had taken after her mother. Rumour was that Hastings had been a catch in his younger years too. Eve had never seen a sign of that and wondered if that's what the job would eventually do to them all.

Her boss threw the phone on to his desk, laced his spindly fingers behind his head and pushed back in the cracked black leather chair. 'Incompetent bastard.'

'Sir?'

'Never mind. Usual shit around here.'

Welcome back.

'OK.' Hastings slouched forward, picked a manila file from beneath the organized chaos and flicked through it. 'Six months you've been off the job. We've got the reports.'

'We covered all this with the board.'

'No, you know we danced with the board, led them around the floor and bowed when the time was right.'

Here came the chat. Payback time for what Hastings had done. It wasn't that Eve wasn't grateful – she didn't know what she would've done if he hadn't let her return to work. But she wasn't sure she had the answers her boss was looking for. It wouldn't help her case to tell him that she didn't sleep well since the attack on her and Sanders, that she still saw the men in her nightmares, the spider's-web tattoo sprawled across one of their temples, or that the specialists weren't sure whether she'd have a permanent limp. Nor would it do anything for her to confirm that she visited DS Sanders regularly, and that, no, it wasn't out of guilt, though that's what she felt every minute of every day. And telling the truth, that what those scum got would never be enough, that she dreamed of getting in a sealed room with them, wouldn't keep her on the job.

'How am I feeling about things? Ready, sir.'

Hastings stared at her over the lip of the folder. 'How did you find the psychiatric assessments?'

Eve lifted the plastic cup to her mouth and sipped, playing for time. 'To be honest, sir, I was a little disappointed.'

Her boss snorted, dragging his nose even further up his face.

'I was expecting to be lying on a red-velvet chaise longue, listening to whale song while we explored the depths of my mind. All I got was a chair and a desk.'

Hastings' mouth hinted at a smile. 'Eve, I'm serious.'

'Look, sir. I'm sure you can imagine what I've gone through. I'm not going to lie to you.' Eve shrugged. 'It affects you. Nobody's going to be the same after something like that. Physically, my leg's still a work in progress. Broken femur, pins, and there's still pain there that they say should go in time with regular physio. Hopefully the limp too. But I've passed everything else they've thrown at me. I'm deemed fit for work, subject to regular reviews and ongoing physio. You said all that yourself. You sent me to the hotel today.'

Hastings laid the file on the table and walked over to the window, snow melting to water and sliding down the glass of the second-storey window. The concrete monstrosity of Marischal Square, which had climbed into view day by day the year before, lay where the old Aberdeen City Council buildings once stood.

'Eve, you're one of my best. That's why I fought the board. But it's about the team.' Hastings clasped his hands behind his back. 'Look, I don't give a shit what they've thrown at you or what you've managed to wing. You need to prove I was right to fight to get you back here.'

The team. Ferguson and Mearns weren't going to be an advert for how to be a team player, but it was her job to manage that, to be a team leader. She couldn't show any hesitation or doubt about whether she should be back.

'Sir, after DC Sanders, there's no way I'd take any risks with the team. I need this. I'm ready. I swear I am.' Eve hated the needy whine that had crept into her voice.

Hastings turned to face her, pity on his face. A look she didn't appreciate. He dropped his hands to his sides.

'What happened to Sanders was not your fault, I believe that. That's why I did what I did on Friday. But you have to make peace with it, move on.'

Eve opened her mouth, shut it again, the grip of shame spreading its icy fingers over her. 'I'll try. But either way, I won't let it affect my work.'

Hastings sighed. 'You were under a lot of stress, as well as the expectations you put on yourself. But I know what you're capable of. It's why I put you on this case.'

'What? To redeem myself or to see if I screw up?'

'Exactly.'

Eve wasn't expecting the honesty.

'But it's on my terms, and as long as I have your word that you'll be upfront with me. No bullshit.'

'I can do that. I—'

'I said no bullshit. No pretending you're coping.' Hastings paused. 'You won't be able to anyway. We've had to agree to weekly meetings between you and the force quack.'

Eve bolted forward in her seat. 'What? Dr Shetty? But I'm fine. Monthly, they said.'

'That was before they agreed to let you return. They want weekly reports from me and a face-to-face between you and Dr Shetty.'

'But, sir, I . . .'

Hastings glared at her. Eve wanted to say more, but she knew when to shut up – when to take what was being offered. She nodded, stood and shook Hastings' hand.

Chapter 8

Tuesday, 5 November

THE SMALL PRESS ROOM was warm and full of chatter as the reporters took their places, the fusty scent of cold, wet coats slowly drying in the heat. Eve spotted the odd spare seat, small pools of muddy water collecting around the chairs' rubber-stoppered legs.

She stood at the front of the room by Hastings' side behind the table, a whiff of BO wafting from her boss's jacket, even at this early hour. Cooper, Ferguson, Mearns and Elliott were seated off to the side. Melanie's father sat beside them, adamant he was attending even though they'd advised otherwise. Her mother had stayed at home with Sarah, the family-liaison officer.

Eve pulled back the plastic chair, careful not to bump into the vertical blue Police Scotland banner that had been erected behind her for the benefit of the cameras. She wondered if she looked as tired as she felt after the restless night she'd had.

The men and women slouched before her had note-pads, pens and phones in hand, faces saying they'd nothing better doing. There was a lone cameraman, not even one of the big guns, the large furry microphone looking like a stuffed cat sitting on his shoulder.

Eve sweated beneath her jacket, and not with the heat. Somehow they'd landed lucky, keeping the story contained and, by some small miracle, off social media. If they hadn't, the press bodies would've been spilling into the corridors. Still, it was busy, considering. There must've been a lack of news overnight. That was about to change. Hopefully she and Hastings had made the right decision. Let the games commence.

She cleared her throat, stopped mid-croak as she was blinded by the flash of a camera, blinked and tried again. 'Yesterday, we found the body of a young woman in a suite of the Malmaison Hotel in Queen's Road. She has been identified as Melanie Ross, aged eighteen and local to the area. We are awaiting post-mortem results, but the incident is being treated as suspicious. We would urge potential witnesses or those with any information to come forward as soon as possible. An incident room has been set up, contact details are as follows . . .'

Eve barely finished her statement before being drowned out. They were on their feet, had something better to be doing now, questions coming like bullets from a shotgun, reporters reloading with professional speed.

'How was she murdered?'

'Was she sexually assaulted?'

'Have you made an arrest?'

Eve looked across at James Ross, the loss of his daughter evident in his red-rimmed eyes and gaunt expression.

Had he expected this when he'd expressed a wish to talk to the press? Eve wanted to usher him to one side, tell him he didn't have to do it. But instead she leaned towards the microphone.

'Please. Melanie's father, James Ross, would like to say a few words. I ask that you respect his feelings during this difficult time.'

Mr Ross stood and moved towards the front of the room, cameras clicking and flashing as he walked. His eyes blinked rapidly, white light striking his face over and over, making his movements look like one of those flip-book animations. Eve could see he was trying to hold himself upright, to stand strong and proud. The room hushed as Mr Ross pulled back the empty chair by Eve's side. He sat, the chair squeaking as he pulled himself closer to the table. He unfolded a crisp white sheet of paper and leaned towards the microphone, looking unsure as to how close his mouth should be, never raising his eyes to the reporters in front of him.

'The last time I saw my daughter she left the house for work just like any other day – leaving a pile of wet towels and dirty breakfast dishes in her wake.' The tremor in his voice could be heard throughout the room. He coughed. 'Melanie is . . .' Now he did lift his gaze, the pause as he did, deafening. 'Melanie *was* so young. Independent, beautiful, her whole life in front of her.'

The television camera whirred as it zoomed in.

'But someone took all that from her, and in the most terrible of ways.'

Eve watched the paper shake in his large hands, wondering if he was thinking of Ryan, knowing that he wouldn't be mentioned here, not by her or Mr Ross. She waited, along with everybody else in the room, as Melanie's father gathered himself. When he did, he lifted his gaze again, stared hard down the lens of the camera. The cameraman looked like he'd struck TV gold.

'If you, if anybody watching this right now knows something, anything, I urge you to come forward. Did you see something? Hear something? Has someone you know been acting differently? Disappeared? Help me to stop this torture, for both me and my wife. Because if you don't come forward, you are letting Melanie's killer go free.'

Eve wondered what the press would make of it when they found out Melanie had a brother – no mention of his torment. She didn't, couldn't, stop looking at Mr Ross. Her and every other person in the room.

He raised his voice, still fixed on the camera. 'It's up to you. Please.' He sat back.

The crowd was up on its feet, baying for blood. And then, from further back, 'Mr Ross. You say it's up to the public. What I want to know is whether you think DI Hunter is up to running this investigation?'

The voice cut through the throng: a confident, unmistakeable drawl that had provided a soundtrack to Eve's lowest moments. Her heart plummeted. She felt Mr Ross's stare on her skin, confusion in his eyes when she glanced his way before looking towards the disembodied voice. Claire Jenkins from the local rag, the *Aberdeen Enquirer*.

The reporter's hair was more severe, dyed bright red and dragged back off her face, but the dark-rimmed glasses and sharply cut suit were still the same. Eve's pulse throbbed in her neck, a trickle of sweat running between her shoulder blades. She forced herself to stay seated and tried not to glower at Jenkins, conscious of the camera.

Elliott rose from his seat. Mearns was staring; Eve could almost feel the cold glare on her skin. Cooper looked angry, whereas Ferguson looked like he was enjoying the show. Elliott was on high alert, making a visible effort to smooth the scowl from his face, the result not much better. 'Ladies and gents. Please. The capabilities and dedication of all our officers is never under question. Let's stick to why we're here, please.'

Hastings stiffened next to her. Jenkins licked her lips, the blue stone of her tongue piercing flashing in the lights of the cameras, reminding Eve of Melanie all over again. When Jenkins spoke, it was with an icy tone. 'But don't you think with DI Hunter's recent history that—'

Elliott looked at Melanie's father. 'Thank you, Mr Ross. The gent in the red tie, please, what was your question again?' Elliott pointed beyond Jenkins, dragging the attention away from her.

Eve relaxed, grateful for the intervention. Jenkins seethed, mouth pursed, eyes dangerous, as proceedings continued around her. Eve answered the next question, but her mind was on the vicious article that Jenkins had written after MacNeill Jnr's car accident. Every word dripping with accusation. Pointing the finger at her:

Local police officer being investigated after suspect run off the road . . . witness says officer was breaking the speed limit and driving recklessly . . . total disregard for fellow officer's life . . . life-changing injuries to Johnny MacNeill Jnr . . . father wants justice . . .

Eve would pay for her unanswered questions later.

The next half an hour was a sea of questions. Hastings missed plenty of openings to wrap things up. Eventually, Eve took it upon herself. She coughed, making sure her voice would be steady and seem confident through the mic. 'That's all we have for now. Further information will be given as soon as we have it. Thank you.'

The reporters were on their feet again. Still an onslaught of questions. None of them satisfied with what was essentially a holding statement. Such a statement was usually made without the press in attendance, but in light of the severity of the case they had hoped the face-to-face briefing to be the right PR move. A move that said they weren't hiding from the media, even though they were in every sense of the word: no details on the tongue, the headline attached to the clothing, or the nature of the crime scene, and no hint towards Ryan Phillips at this point in time.

Eve stood and followed Hastings out, her lopsided gait more pronounced than ever. Elliott took hold of her arm, steadying her through the crowds, making sure she got outside and across the uneven corridor to the lift. She never wanted to be seen as a victim, but this was one time she appreciated the help. Melanie's father was being escorted home to his wife. The din was still clear as the lift doors closed and they made their escape.

Only Elliott spoke. 'I'm not sure the plan worked.'

Chapter 9

Then

The playground's crowded, filled with deafening squeals and screams of children set free from school, if only for a short while. He stands with his back to the red-brick wall, pressing hard against its uneven rough surface, the fat rolls spreading, enjoying the feeling of it through his thin school shirt.

It's shaded here. Sheltered by a cracked asphalt flat roof that the older boys come to climb on after school hours. This is where he always stands. At the junior end of the play-ground even though he's a senior. Away from the crowd. From them. Invisible. Alone. Except he doesn't feel alone, not as long as he can see her.

Her long brown hair flies out behind her as she runs here and there with her friends, sunlight catching its strands, glowing like a halo, like the angel she is. She waves over to him, grins, and he doesn't feel invisible any more.

'Hey, Fatty.'

His cheeks clench as he hears Mason, sees him and his four-strong gang rounding the corner of the school. He starts stumbling in the other direction, the only place he's able to go – the school car park. Figuring he'd rather take the wrath of the head teacher any day over what he knows Mason is looking to hand out. He hears them starting to run, feels his own feet picking up speed. Hopes she isn't watching. Watching him run. Scared.

The punch to the centre of his back propels him forward, bending his upper half over his lower. He reaches out for the metal barrier between the playground and the car park, touching the flaking red paint with his fingertips, trying to stop himself from falling, grappling to grab hold of the bar too late, hitting it with his chin instead as he crashes to the ground.

He hears laughter. Right before the kicks start raining down on him, jabbing into his ribs, stamping on to his back. His cheek's pressed hard against concrete, gravel in his mouth, sticking fast against the tears on his face, mixing with the snot running from his nose.

'Down this end to see that sister of yours again?' Mason's out of breath with the effort of the blows he's dishing out. 'Watching her run around in that little skirt of hers. Hoping for a flash of her knickers?'

He lifts his head, shakes it violently against the lies, seeing the blur of faces gathered around him. All of them standing by, watching his humiliation, enjoying it.

'Maybe we should check out her knickers. She's obviously got something you can't find anywhere else.'

He clenches his teeth, fists curling beneath him, scraping against the stone, oblivious to the pain, anger spreading across his chest, making him get to his knees. No longer seeing the crowd, only Mason. Only Mason. He lunges for him, wonders why his lower legs are circling air, going nowhere, until he realizes he's being held from behind. By someone bigger than him. The headmaster, Mr Bellingfield.

And then he's being dragged backwards, carried along as if he doesn't weigh what he does, towards the office. Aware he's shouting, swearing, kicking, unable to stop. Seeing everyone then. Each and every face. Finding his sister's amongst the many.

He focuses on it. Sees tears on her cheeks glinting in the sunlight. Stares at her, calming himself. Needing to be there for her. Wanting her to be proud of him, not ashamed.

But then it's her screaming. Pleading with them all to leave him alone. Her brother. To stop all the lies. Making everyone turn to stare. Making him want to start kicking again.

Chapter 10

THE COLD AIR WAS thick with the smell of coffee, officers hugging plastic cups between freezing hands, the muster room lacking decent decor and heat. Eve scanned the faces in front of her. Some had the 'been there, done that' air about them, hardened to most things these days. Others were still wet behind the ears, eager to please, hungry to climb. Everything she'd told them, they'd probably already gleaned from the usual HQ canteen gossip.

She cleared her throat and ploughed on. 'DC Ferguson is looking into the CCTV footage between Melanie's work and the hotel.' Eve heard grumbling, no doubt from DC Ferguson.

'There's no record of Melanie entering the hotel – either on CCTV or checking in. We believe she may have used the back entrance to the Malmaison, where the CCTV has been faulty for some time. It's fair to say she knew who she was meeting and, judging by how she entered the building, that she'd been there before.

However, on checking, Melanie has never officially been booked in. At least not under her own name.'

'Why do we think she knew who she was meeting, ma'am?'

The wiry-haired officer was new, sitting posture perfect, craning his neck over those in front of him. One of the keen ones. Clearly he hadn't been there long enough to have his opinion of her warped by all the gossip, unlike some of the more familiar faces looking back at her now.

'Good question.'

The officer tried and failed to hide the pride on his face. She felt like a dog trainer throwing a titbit for good behaviour.

'Melanie told her parents she was going to be home late, but not why. The bag she packed in advance, found at the scene, answers that. The contents were of a sexual nature. I don't think there's any need for me to spell that out.'

'Might add some excitement to the morning.'

Once more, Eve blanked DC Ferguson, but her hackles were starting to rise. The press briefing earlier had been enough for one day. Her fingers flexed.

'Could the contents of the bag have been placed at the scene? Had she been raped, ma'am?' The question came from the same enthusiastic, Brillo-padded head bobbing above the others.

'According to MacLean, there were no signs of sexual activity, but we are awaiting post-mortem details to confirm that.'

'Waste of a good bag.' There was a spattering of laughter, the usual suspects, with DC Ferguson at the heart of it. Eve glared at him, not willing to ignore him this time, irritated by the DC's artfully ruffled hair, arms draped over the plastic chair, toned muscles visible through his shirt. 'Knock it off, Ferguson.' She held the stare, pulse throbbing in her head, until the laughter was cut short.

Now was not the time to deal with him, but it would have to happen at some point. And definitely before she lost it with him. She broke eye contact and looked towards Hastings, an unspoken agreement between them that Ferguson's attitude had been noted.

Eve raised her voice. 'As I said earlier, it was a brutal attack. Severe disfiguration to her face, believed to have been caused by a sharp instrument, perhaps a scalpel. MacLean thinks it may have been the same thing used to remove her tongue.'

The silence that followed the collective intake of breath was heavy. No longer any doubt who was in control, any reservations and distractions forgotten. Then a buzz of chatter charged through the room.

'Do we know if she was alive when it was cut out?' It was Ferguson again. Hopefully this time his sensible question wasn't leading somewhere stupid.

'Again, we are awaiting results, but it looks like she was.'

The groans hit her from all sides. Ferguson kept quiet.

Eve carried on. 'MacLean thinks she was drugged. Unable to move but awake.'

She let that sink in before signalling to Elliott, who leaned forward, staying seated, more used to being behind the scenes in the press room.

'Thanks, Eve. We've managed to keep the finer details out of the media after the briefing this morning. I know if they were to get out how difficult your job would become with the press baying for blood. The panic from the general public. We'll try to hold them off for as long as we can.'

Eve looked around the room, making sure everyone was getting Elliott's message. No leaks. She saw Ferguson's scowl as he looked at Elliott and then glanced over to Mearns. She could take two guesses as to what his problem was – Mearns staring back at Elliott. But it was the least of hers.

'Thanks, Elliott. As I'm sure you'll all appreciate, this is not your standard murder inquiry. On top of that, the scene looked staged. Mirrors, magazines and make-up were all placed around Melanie's body. A headline from the local newspaper about a modelling competition that Melanie had made the finals in was pinned to her body.' Eve passed crime-scene photos around the room, watching each officer grimace in turn. 'I think our guy is trying to send us a message. I hope I'm wrong, folks, but we need to be all over this.'

The atmosphere in the room was electric. Even the hardened were animated. Eve felt buoyed. Back in the game. She sensed movement from the side of the room. Hastings. White hair flapping, upturned nose twitching. Her boss placed a clammy hand on her shoulder and faced their audience.

'Ladies, gents.' His voice was gruff, authority rumbling across the space without the need for volume. 'I have to go, but I want to take this opportunity to welcome DI Hunter back to the team. Some of you have worked with her previously; some of you are new to her. Whatever preconceptions or misconceptions you might have, you get on board and give her the best of you. Eve, I'll catch you later.'

The door closed. Eve turned to the crowd, the blur of faces waiting for her reaction. Her eyes were drawn to DC Ferguson, the smug look all over his face. Eve took a moment, her clenched hand unfurling and reaching to fuss at her blouse collar. Mearns seemed to be enjoying her discomfort alongside Ferguson.

Was she supposed to show gratitude for Hastings' backing? In truth she was pissed off, feeling like she'd had to pass some kind of test; to earn the right to be standing where she was. Maybe a swift, hard punch to Ferguson's face would help the throbbing in her temples. If only. She gulped, plugging her rising anger in order to refocus.

'We should expect preliminary post-mortem results later today, tomorrow at the latest.' Her voice quivered, with anger not nerves. 'The crime scene is a forensics nightmare; news on that front could be a long time coming.'

A shout-out from the back: 'Do we have any leads?'

Eve rocked on her heels. 'We have a firm lead, but again the following information is to be kept confidential and within the murder-inquiry team.'

The room fell silent.

'A Mr Ryan Phillips booked the room. After speaking with Melanie's parents, it has been verified that he's Melanie's adoptive brother.'

Eve let the flurry of comments fly. Christ knows what would've happened if she'd announced, as she'd first assumed, that Ryan had been Melanie's biological brother. She raised her hand.

'Obviously this is highly sensitive for the family. They're estranged from Ryan and have been for some time. Efforts to track him yesterday were unsuccessful.'

'Any word on the phone?' Mearns said it like a petulant teenager.

'Another dead end. Looking like it's been destroyed.'

Eve spun round to the whiteboard behind her and pinned up an A4 photo of Melanie and the most recent photo of Ryan that Mr Ross had been able to provide.

'I'll assign some of you to help with the CCTV; others will be working through the statements taken from the hotel staff.'

Eve turned to the wall, hoping she looked confident. 'Let's get down to business.'

Chapter 11

DC MEARNS RAISED HER head above the computer monitor and saw DS Cooper sitting opposite her staring intently at his own.

'Square eyes?'

He smiled. 'Getting there.'

He'd been good to her since she'd joined the team six months ago, had made it easier coming in under the circumstances she did. Sanders had been a force to be reckoned with. The team was fiercely protective of that reputation; of making sure it wasn't forgotten. If Mearns had arrived without the easy nature and strong work ethic she possessed, things could've been different. This was the first time that easy nature had been threatened, coming face to face with Eve. But she didn't want Cooper to think less of her for the opinions she held; she knew he admired his boss.

'Fancy a brew?'

He shook his head. 'I was thinking it was about time we headed off.'

'You did a good job getting Hunter out of here.' Mearns couldn't bring herself to call her Eve.

'It's been a hell of a couple of days to return to. She won't have switched off though. She'll be waiting for an update.'

'You've got a lot of time for her.'

'Best boss I've had. Fair. And as long as you do your job, you know, show respect, she's not too anal about rank.'

Show respect. That wasn't something Mearns was willing to do. Not with what had happened to Sanders. 'And do people do that? Respect her, I mean?'

'Yeah, Eve's not up her own arse. Treats folk equal; people want to please her. Doesn't mess about if folk take the piss though; you don't want to see that side of her.'

Like Sanders had? And she hadn't even been taking the piss. But from what she'd been told, Eve definitely had. Mearns tried not to show how she felt, didn't want the woman's return to affect her relationship with Cooper.

'Must've been tough for her.' She meant all the press intrusion and gossip after the attack – something Mearns thought Eve deserved.

'Tough for anyone, worse when you hold yourself responsible no matter what folk say. One thing you can be sure of though, Eve will always have your back.'

She doubted that and was glad when the incident-room door opened, stopping the conversation.

'What's the scoop?' DC Scott Ferguson swanned into the room.

'Nothing. Chewing the fat. Talking about Eve.' Cooper sighed and turned towards his screen.

Mearns was aware of how little time he had for Ferguson.

Ferguson tutted. 'Plenty to talk about there. And none of it good.'

Cooper turned, glaring at him. 'Fergu—'

'OK, OK. Suit yourself. Still can't believe they let her back though.' Ferguson shrugged, that lazy smile spreading across his face, blue eyes twinkling as he looked at Mearns. 'You needing a lift tonight?'

Mearns nodded. 'Yeah, that'd be good.' She looked at his hair, strangely fascinated by how it always looked the same even at the end of the day, no matter the weather, no matter the job. She admired his dedication to personal grooming.

She had fallen into a kind of car-share agreement – in that she shared Ferguson's car now the weather was turning, as she didn't have her own. Not that she wouldn't have walked the fifteen minutes it took her, but he'd refused to take no for an answer.

'Good.' He turned, facing both of them. 'I came in to let you know about the CCTV from the hotel, in that there's nothing to know. Guy that checked in looks down the whole time, aware of the camera. He had a black baseball cap on, plain, no logos, and a black jacket, same. Nothing to even try and get a better look at.'

She leaned back in her chair. 'And you'll have run the image past the Malmaison guy that booked him in?'

Ferguson winked – something Mearns had noticed he only did to her. A lot. And she knew why. 'Of course. You know you can count on me.'

Mearns looked across at Cooper, saw the pursed lips imitating a kiss. 'Piss off, Cooper.' She hoped the embarrassment wasn't visible on her face. Cooper smiled as Ferguson stood there wondering what was going on.

Unbeknown to Ferguson, Cooper had told her a couple of months ago that he'd been asking whether she was single. She'd surprised herself by feeling flattered, not that she'd told Cooper that. She was glad of the distraction when someone else appeared at the door.

'Eve still here?' It was Elliott, looking like he'd had a worse day than them.

'Not long left.' Mearns noted the hint of stubble on Elliott's chin, the jawline leading upwards to greying temples. Dishevelled. It suited him. Ferguson was staring at her, obviously not happy at the thought of competition.

Elliott sighed and leaned on the door frame, a muscular arm above his head, smooth fingers rubbing at his forehead. 'Phones have been non-stop; think we've managed to ward them off. Still, the papers are going to be full of it again tomorrow. It's only going to get worse from here.'

'Nowt new there.' Mearns sighed in return.

'OK, I'll catch Eve in the morning.' Elliott pushed off from the door and disappeared down the corridor.

Ferguson stepped in front of Mearns, eager to get her attention. 'Got Phillips' bank records too.' He paused for effect. 'The guy has one seriously healthy bank balance. A lump sum paid direct to his account from a savings-fund company a few weeks ago. Mainly cash withdrawals, but the bank says the Malmaison payment is there.'

She frowned. 'Doesn't seem to fit that he'd leave a trace through the bank. I mean, this guy isn't stupid, is he? Ready for the CCTV, phone out of service, flatmate the only lead and leading nowhere.'

'But maybe killing Melanie was never the plan.' Cooper shrugged. 'He could've been cagey checking in because of what they were doing.'

'Yeah, maybe. Nothing's ever simple, is it?' Mearns groaned.

Cooper blew out slowly and scratched his head. 'Course not. When is this job ever easy?'

Eve switched off the power sander and laid it down, her ringing ears adjusting to the silence. She pulled the face mask out from her nose, lowered it beneath her chin, leaving it there, nestled against her neck. She lifted her goggles to sit on top of her head. Sawdust and the familiar smell of burnt wood shifted against the winter wind that was blowing its way in through the open windows of the outhouse. The room was freezing, the night black and pressing against the panes, but Eve didn't feel the cold when hard at work. And she needed to be working hard tonight. As far as feelings went, she was chasing away more than the cold.

Going back yesterday had been a lot tougher than she'd imagined. And not because of the case she'd walked into. After an initial awkwardness, Cooper had come through for her – Elliott too, and Hastings. Ferguson and Mearns were another story and she wasn't at all sure how it was going to go. What she had worked out was that Mearns seemed to hold the same opinion of her as Ferguson, and she had a rough idea how influential he'd probably been in that.

But as long as they did the job they were paid to do, she would get on with it, regardless of their issues with her.

Eve ran a hand along the top of the dresser, one of her better finds at the weekly Thainstone car-boot sale. It was held every Sunday, a mere thirty-minute drive north-west of Aberdeen, the Thainstone grounds and respected hotel on one side of the dual carriageway, the small town and royal burgh of Inverurie on the other. There was nothing she loved more than browsing the bric-a-brac out there, the rush of finding a bargain that she could take home, restore and make her mark on, breathing new life into something that someone else had abandoned.

She jumped as her mobile phone rang in her denim pocket. She fished it out, stopping dead when she saw Jenkins' name lighting the screen. Eve's finger shook as she cut the call dead. Jesus, the reporter had a brass neck. Was she honestly expecting her to answer? Eve threw the phone on to the workbench. She needed to lose herself out here tonight.

She crouched, at eye level with the top of the dresser. It was shaping up, would be looking even better once she got in amongst the more awkward bits by hand with good old-fashioned sandpaper. She liked the manual labour, physically tired by the end of it. The work calmed her – gave her a way to deal with the frustration and anger that was all too often in her.

Eve walked over to the workbench, hoisted herself on to the stool and gulped from the water bottle sitting there, half of it gone by the time her thirst was quenched. She turned to the window, the cold wind welcome on her sweating forehead. She loved it out here. A concrete outhouse her grandfather built so many years ago as a workshop in the garden of the two-bedroom detached cottage that was Eve's home. Her grandparents and her mother all gone. Not a day that she didn't wish it could be how it used to be.

The cottage was her haven, tucked down the quiet tree-lined street of Loanhead Terrace, off Rosemount, a bustling residential and retail area of the city. Where Eve's cottage was, she could as easily have been in the countryside. She had the best of both worlds – the Queen Vic pub at the Rosemount Place end of the street, along with convenience stores, eateries and small boutiques – and at the other end, Westburn Road, with access to two of the city parks, Victoria and Westburn, both of them lush, green and floral oases in amongst the city chaos. She liked to think of them as her gardens. Both the parks and the house held happy memories of her childhood.

Eve checked her wristwatch: 10 p.m. She'd been at it for over an hour. And only after she'd done the exercises for her leg that the physiotherapist said she had to do every morning and night if she was to have a fighting chance of the leg returning to normal, the limp going away. Her life seemed to be full of one therapist or another at the moment.

She looked at the dresser. She could continue on into the night if she wanted to, and often did. The neighbour next door was half deaf and happy that someone was there, especially knowing what Eve did for a living.

She took another sip of water, her mind being dragged back to the day job. How alone must Melanie have felt in that hotel room? How scared and betrayed? By a man she thought she knew. Beautiful, young, had her whole life ahead of her. Maybe that was why she wanted to go to London: to get away from whatever hold he had over her, to finally do what her parents wanted.

Was that what the facial disfiguration was all about? Maybe he had been threatened by London, her potential success as a model, her wanting to be somewhere else, with someone else. If he couldn't have her. . . What about the tongue? A nod towards the taboo of what they were doing? It was a fair stretch, but Eve had seen all kinds of weird during her time on the force.

She stretched to the workbench drawer, the thin brown file placed there less than two hours ago. She pulled it out and opened it for the umpteenth time that day. Melanie stared at her, her smile wide and flawless on the photocopy of the 6″ × 8″ glossy photograph that her father had given them earlier. Eve walked over to the cork board on the wall, took out a green-headed pin and pinned the photo to the board, creating her own personal murder incident room.

She stared at the photograph. *Who took that smile from you, Melanie?*

Her fingers played with the edge of the photocopied headline lying in the folder. The article that went with the headline had yielded nothing: a celebratory story about a local girl done good getting to the finals of a modelling competition. A competition that still hadn't seen its conclusion, one that Melanie would never have the chance to reach now. Eve had no idea what the connection was. She pinned the headline next to Melanie's photograph, wondering what it was trying to tell them.

The mobile phone sitting on the bench rang and Eve jumped, the folder slipping from her hand to the floor. 'Shit.' She scooped it up and straightened, wiping sawdust from it.

'Hello?'

'Hey, boss, how's things?'

Cooper. She couldn't help but smile, a little with relief that it wasn't Jenkins again but more thankful for the word 'boss'.

'Same as. Anything happening?' Eve sat on the stool.

'Ferguson found the CCTV footage of the guy who checked in as Mr Phillips. Can't see his face, no obvious markers on the clothing. He ran it past reception but nothing. Bank records came through.'

'Let me guess. Nothing to go on. Huge pot of ready cash paid in about four weeks ago, around about the time he disappeared from his last known address?'

'I see Mr Ross already told you. Where do you want this headed next?'

Eve looked towards the cork board where Melanie stared back at her, the headline taunting her again.

'Has the image been run past Mr and Mrs Ross?'

'Not yet.'

'It would be a good idea to have them take a look at it. They'll know if it's him. I'll get on it tomorrow.'

'OK.'

'We need to find him. He can't hide for ever. Someone must know where he's at. We'll hopefully get some more leads from the parents, maybe pay the flatmate, Michael Forbes, another visit, see if we can't find out the company he's been keeping, other than Ryan. We've got to decide how we're going to use the press if we can't uncover him.'

'Maybe something will come through from forensics.'

'Here's hoping. We should hear from MacLean tomorrow too. I asked him to put a priority on Melanie after Mr Ross ID'd her.'

She pushed the image of Melanie lying stiff on the steel gurney from her mind.

'OK. See you tomorrow then.' Cooper went silent. 'Good to have you back,' he said in a rush. 'Hope you get some shut-eye.'

Eve hung up, stood and pulled the mask up over her mouth and nose, the goggles down over her eyes. She lifted the power sander. Sleep would be hard to come by tonight.

Chapter 12

Wednesday, 6 November

EVE GOT OUT OF the car and joined Cooper at the kerbside. The sloping garden with thick undisturbed snow reminded her of the ready-to-roll icing her mother used to favour. The houses here were huge, money seemingly oozing from the brickwork. Eve clocked Claire Jenkins skulking further down the street. Elliott had been right. It was only a matter of time before the Rottweiler came running.

'Wait here a sec.'

Cooper looked in the direction Eve was headed. 'Eve, leave it . . .'

'A minute, no more.' Eve moved towards the car. Jenkins was opening the window before she got there, her red hair even more brash in the daylight.

'DI Hunter, nice to see—'

'Shut it, Jenkins. Listen, I know empathy isn't a strong point for you, but I'd appreciate it if you'd scarper.'

Jenkins' front page that morning had been screaming about Melanie's murder. Thankfully minus the details that mattered. Still, she'd made her mark with her story, questioning Melanie's life, those closest to her, only adding to the Rosses' pain. Eve knew that feeling.

Jenkins shook her head. 'And I'd appreciate getting the real story here.'

'You know you'll get nothing more than what was said.'

'Hence why I'm here – to get what you're not telling me.'

'Jenkins, for Christ's sake, a girl has been murdered. Her family are grieving. Can you not knock it off for once?'

Jenkins tutted. ''Fraid not. Everything you've said is why I'm here. It makes for essential reading – especially the why.'

Eve pushed off from the side of the car. 'The only why is why you're such a heartless bitch.' She turned and walked back to Cooper.

Jenkins shouted from the car. 'For the story, Eve, and you of all people know I always get it.'

Eve didn't turn around but raised her middle finger behind her as she walked.

'Feel better?' Cooper smiled.

'Nope. I never will when she's around.' Eve walked in silence up the short gravel drive to the Rosses' front door, resisting the temptation to wave at a nosey neighbour.

The Rosses' curtains were closed, upstairs and down. She was willing to bet that was unusual for Mrs Ross at this time of day, and that they would remain that way for a long time to come. Eve rang the doorbell and moved off the front step, Cooper by her side, both watching as a large blur of grey and white approached the door from the other side of the bevelled glass.

James Ross threw back the door. 'I told you lot to piss—' He stopped dead, his shoulders slumping as he realized the fight he was spoiling for wasn't going to happen.

'I'm sorry,' said Eve. 'We should have called ahead. Can we come in?'

Mr Ross stepped aside to let them enter before leaning out of the door and looking both ways, perhaps for nosey neighbours but most likely for press. Probably best for his temper, and hers, that he wasn't aware Jenkins was lurking out there. They waited in the hall as Mr Ross closed and locked the door again, Jenkins left outside where she belonged.

Mr Ross had changed somewhat. His high-coloured cheeks were a sunken grey, a match for the cotton tracksuit he wore, a white T-shirt beneath. His thinning hair hadn't seen a brush. She doubted there had been many days when Melanie's father had dressed casually. Mr Ross motioned for them to go through to the sitting room and followed them in.

'What can I do for you, Detective?' His voice was quiet. 'Ellie's asleep upstairs. I had to get the doc out last night to give her something to help calm her. Damned doorbell never stopped yesterday. Disconnected the thing and still they knocked.'

'I'm sorry to hear that. Sarah should be with you again soon.'

'We don't need any family liaison. We need . . .' Mr Ross swallowed whatever he was about to say and made his way over to the sofa. It seemed an age since the Rosses had sat there side by side.

'I appreciate how difficult this is. We won't keep you.' Eve signalled to Cooper, who moved over to sit next to Melanie's father.

'DS Cooper has a photo of the man caught on CCTV checking in to the Malmaison on Sunday night. We'd be grateful if you could take a look.'

Cooper relaxed his shoulders and passed the A4 sheet to Mr Ross before clasping his hands on his lap. Respectful, giving the man space. Eve noted the professionalism, something she'd always been able to count on with Cooper.

The paper was shaking in Mr Ross's large smooth hands, the emotion of losing his daughter raw and there for all to see. The man stared at the photo long and hard. When he spoke, it was with obvious disappointment, but perhaps with a little unrealized relief. 'It's blurry. It could be anyone.'

Cooper rubbed his thumbs together, hands still clasped. 'Perhaps you recognize the clothing? Maybe his stance rings a bell?'

The paper shook harder, perhaps due to the force of sheer determination radiating from Mr Ross, willing Ryan Phillips' features to reveal themselves beneath the baseball cap. For all this to be over, starting a different kind of torment all together.

Mr Ross passed the paper to Cooper. 'I'm sorry. I want to say it's him, but there's nothing there to tell me that. It's not what he used to wear, but, as you know, it's been a long time since I saw my so— since I saw him.'

Cooper took his time folding the sheet of paper before standing, taking care not to appear abrupt. 'Thank you for taking a look.'

'What now?' Mr Ross's stare bored into Eve.

Eve updated him on the case, offering what felt next to nothing. Mr Ross sat in silence, waiting to hear something that would provide hope of a breakthrough.

'I'm sorry it's not more. If you or your wife can think of any other contacts of Ryan's, we'd appreciate a list.'

Mr Ross stood, looking smaller than yesterday, resigned. 'I'll speak with Ellie and anyone else I think may be able to help.'

Eve nodded. 'We'd appreciate that.' She joined Cooper, already by the door, and made her way out into the hall. There was nothing else to say other than that they'd be in touch. It sounded like nothing because to Mr Ross it probably was.

Eve stood over Melanie's body, alert after MacLean's call, aware it was the first day she had neglected her leg physio exercises.

The white body in front of her seemed luminous. She looked anywhere but at Melanie's face. The smell of dead flesh was thinly veiled beneath the chemical stench in the air. Eve tasted the decay. What she wouldn't give to be behind the glass divide.

'See here?' MacLean pointed to a dot on Melanie's milky-smooth upper arm, the pale flesh reminding Eve of a wax dummy. Eve followed his finger. MacLean, hunched over the steel table, turned his head to look at her, his face alive with excitement, grey moustache twitching, those eyes still with a mind of their own. It made her think of her own hazel eyes. She looked to the floor as MacLean spoke. 'Puncture wound caused by a needle.'

'Which means?'

'Can't be sure until toxicology results come back, but I'm willing to bet that was how our Melanie was drugged.'

'Any idea what with?' Eve took a step back from the table, imagining the thick Y-shaped stitching across Melanie's torso, hidden beneath the sheet, where MacLean would have opened her up and sewn her back together.

MacLean snapped off his gloves, busying himself moving apparatus as he spoke. 'The amount of blood loss and the force of it tells us that the tongue was removed while her heart was still pumping.'

Eve swallowed, conscious of her own tongue.

'As I said at the hotel, everything was pointing towards the fact that she must've sat there and let it happen. No one does that unless there's bugger all they can do about it.'

'Paralysed?' Eve whispered the word.

'Yup. But there aren't many things out there that can do that. I don't know jack-shit about your guy, but I'm thinking he would've steered cleared of any anaesthetics, wanting her to be alive for the grand finale, not taking any chances on respiratory failure.'

MacLean prepared Melanie for going back into the mortuary drawer, moving about the space as if he was at home in the kitchen getting ready to freeze leftovers. He carried on speaking as he worked.

'The needle was inserted into the deltoid upper-arm muscle. You're looking for something that causes paralysis, perhaps unconsciousness in high doses. What springs to mind is ketamine.'

'The ravers' drug?'

'Bravo, Detective. Never had you down as being into that scene.'

'Funny.' Eve wasn't smiling. 'Arrested some folk in my day.'

'I preferred imagining you in a fisherman's hat.' MacLean didn't crack a smile. 'Anyway, in high doses it can cause coma. Would be a slow return to consciousness, probably hallucinations, blurred vision, slurred speech. With the right amount – or wrong, however you want to look at it – paralysis. The only good thing is she probably didn't feel any pain.'

'He knew what he was doing?'

'Not necessarily in the sense that he's any kind of professional in the field. It wouldn't take a genius. Google ketamine and you'll find hundreds of folk willing to advise how to get the best hit on countless forums. Of course, there's always the chance he could be supplying it professionally.'

'Doing what?'

'Ketamine's commonly known as the "cat drug". That's the street name for it because it's used in veterinary practices for operating on cats. Once upon a time it was regularly used in human operations too.'

'You're a mine of information.'

'Mostly useless, I'll give you that, but I surprise myself sometimes. Injected where it was, it would work within seconds and last half an hour to an hour. The side effects can last a few hours after that.'

Eve thought back to where they'd found Melanie. Slumped against a bathroom wall. She would've been alive, unable to move. Terrified. Confused, seeing things, wondering if what was happening to her wasn't all some kind of vivid nightmare. Eve wished more than anything that it had been.

It wouldn't be a surprise if they found that Ryan and his old flatmate Michael Forbes had dabbled in drugs. But was Ryan only out to get Melanie? Or was Forbes? Eve wanted to believe that, but she couldn't shake the feeling Melanie wasn't going to be the last victim. The way the scene had been staged. The newspaper headline pinned to her clothing. The drugs. Melanie's murder had been planned. Her murderer wanted to say something. That fact nagged at Eve. She hadn't been murdered in the throes of a rage or on the spur of the moment. So what was he trying to tell them? But most of all, was he finished?

She stopped staring into space and looked at MacLean. 'Anything else?'

'Cause of death was massive blood loss and the fact she choked on it. No defence wounds or tissue beneath her nails, which isn't surprising as she wouldn't have been able to fight back. And no sexual contact.'

'Wish I could take some comfort from that.'

'One of the worst I've seen, Eve. Murders, I mean. I see worse injuries every week coming in from traffic.'

'I don't know how you do it.'

'No rest for the wicked. You do what you do and catch the bastard.'

Eve nodded, wondering where the hell to go next.

MacLean walked with Eve to the mortuary door, an out-of-place smile on the pathologist's ruddy face. 'Hey, look on the bright side. It's rather apt, don't you think?'

'What?'

'That he should use ketamine.'

Eve turned to him, frowning. 'What're you on about?'

'It's fair to say that the cat got her tongue.' MacLean winked.

Eve shook her head. 'Even for you, that's low.'

MacLean placed a hand on Eve's shoulder as she stepped out into the corridor. 'That's how I manage to do the job.'

And he closed the door.

It was late. Hard to believe Melanie had been found only two days ago. DC Jo Mearns stood and stepped out from behind her desk. She'd stayed even though Eve had told them to knock off earlier, keen to make a tiny show of defiance, nothing to do with showing dedication for the job to a woman she'd decided from the off she wasn't going to like. Anyway, she didn't need anyone to tell her she was dedicated *and* conscientious. Two attributes her boss didn't possess.

Mearns had been on the force here two months when everything blew up after the attack on Eve and Sanders. She'd completed the three-week residential Transferee Conversion course at the Police Scotland college in

Tulliallan. She'd initially wondered whether the course would be open to her if she made the move from Bolton, England, to Aberdeen, Scotland, even with her five years' continuous service. She needn't have worried. Her exemplary record saw to that.

During those first eight weeks at Queen Street, she hadn't directly crossed paths with Eve or any of her team. But then came the incident, after which she was asked to replace Sanders. Asked to step into the shoes of someone who had not left through choice. A DC who was plastered all over the papers at that time, alongside Eve, a DI who was injured and off the job, the fodder for HQ gossip. It had been nerve-wracking, fretting over whether she was ready for such a move, scared of the pressure and expectation as she took someone else's place, questioning whether she'd only landed lucky because of Sanders' misfortune.

What Eve had let happen to Sanders was an outrage. Ferguson had told her the DI was unreliable, impetuous. But she had a reputation for getting results and, regardless of some people's opinion of her, she was still liked and supported by Hastings and others. Definitely before the incident and bizarrely afterwards. Why, she didn't know. Mearns had to be careful of that.

Whatever the reason, Eve Hunter was not going to ruin things for her. For the last six months, since working with the team under Cooper's interim leadership, she'd given the role her all. It had been hard: a new city, a new job. Miles away from home. Away from what she'd known all her life. Alone.

But it was the only way she'd wanted it, the only way she could thrive. By getting out from beneath the stifling blanket of her over-protective parents. Her father especially. To the other end of the country, no less. Getting used to a new way of life, to different ways of living. Feeling like a foreigner.

She'd had to step outside her comfort zone, pressing herself on to others in order to get to know her surroundings. Thankfully only professionally, as a social life didn't bother her. She'd made her mark, been accepted by the rest of the team in Sanders' absence. It had boosted her confidence and self-belief. She might not have shown it to Eve, but she was kind, kick-ass when she needed to be, fair. She put in the hours when others rushed home, took the job home with her and never missed a shift. She'd slowly come to accept that maybe she did deserve the role. And she hated the possibility that it could be threatened in any way. That Eve might think she wasn't up to the job.

But what she detested even more since Eve's return was how she was acting around her new boss. Like a snotty-nosed kid, attitude rolling off her in waves. No matter how shitty she was, Eve had tolerated it so far.

The problem was that Eve was so different from the monster Mearns had built in her head. She was surprised to find that Eve came across as a conscientious detective, and one who clearly valued her team and took the job seriously. She felt a begrudging respect for how Eve had handled her return. But no one took Mearns for a mug. She knew it could all be an act on Eve's part, a ploy to get back on the job and to stay on it.

To be on her best behaviour while she was being observed and reported on. She felt sure her new boss would show her true self before long.

She sighed as she stretched and pulled her hair free of the bun that was starting to make her hairline throb. Tiredness and thirst were getting to her. She shook out her limbs and made her way over to the water machine, rubbing at dry eyes as she walked – too many hours spent staring at the computer. Too many obsessing over her issues with her boss.

She stared at the blank wall in the darkness, the only light the blue of her computer screen and the emerald-green emergency-exit sign above the door. The water glugged inside the plastic canister as it trickled into the cup.

She forced herself to concentrate on the task at hand. Going over all the statements from the hotel staff and anyone else who had thrown in their tuppence worth, doubtful any of it was going to help catch the man who had taken Melanie Ross's tongue. In this job there was no hiding from how many crazy folk there were in this world. Crazy and dangerous.

She jumped as her mobile phone rang in her pocket, the sound amplified in the empty office. She dug it out, saw 'Dad' lighting the screen. She sighed and put the phone to her ear as she answered.

'Hello?'

'Your mother asked me to call . . . see you're not involved in that murder from today.'

Typical of her father. Straight to the point, no attempt to conceal that he had been put up to calling, her mother always choosing to hide behind him the moment anything remotely difficult came her way. Regardless of her issues with her parents, or rather their issues full-stop, it was strangely nice to hear from home, the Boltonian accent that seemed to surprise people when she first met anyone here and made her different.

'What if I am, Dad? It's my job.' She tried to soften at least a little of the defiance in her tone. She told herself it was concern, not control, that was driving the phone call, thinking all the time of Melanie's parents, who no longer had a daughter to worry about. Silence stretched at the other end of the line.

'So how are you and Mum doing anyway?' Safe. Dutiful daughter.

'Your mother would be doing a lot better if you were home.'

Mearns bit the inside of her cheek. The guilt trip no longer surprised her, but her father's habit of using her mother's health as a way to berate her for her decisions in life hit a raw nerve every time. The fact her mother was forever willing to play the weak little wife irked her even more.

'I'm sure Mother is just fine. I'm a big girl.' She stopped herself from saying that her mother was too.

'That may be so, but—'

'Dad, I'm kind of busy right now. I have to go.' She wasn't in the mood for the usual lecture about being married to the job or the fact it was no job for a woman. She'd heard it a million times.

'But—' The indignation was clear in her father's voice. 'I'll call you, OK?'

She didn't wait for an answer before she ended the call. Her father didn't believe any job was for a woman. She pictured him standing there in the striped-wallpapered hallway that hadn't been decorated since her teens, the phone probably still clasped in his hand as her mother looked on, twisting her hands round and round one another, her face creased with worry. She felt a stab of guilt but quickly buried it. She didn't want to be her mother. Who would? A woman at some man's beck and call, with two point four kids, numbed to who she once was, to who she might've become. Hiding behind a man who had, over the years, made her feel she needed him to survive. Well, that wouldn't be her. That wasn't survival; it was a slow painful death. No, what Mearns was doing was worthwhile.

Sure, she'd sacrificed what her friends had settled for, losing them in the process before moving here from Bolton. But it had given her freedom, a way out from beneath her parents' shadow, the chance to climb to where she needed to reach. Another reason she was determined she wasn't going to let Eve ruin it for her. Eve had made it to where Mearns wanted to be, and Mearns wasn't going to be stopped from getting there too. She wasn't going to let some maverick threaten her job or her life, like Eve had done to Sanders.

Mearns looked over at her desk. It seemed such a thankless task sifting through everything, but if it gave them one lead, however small, one that might help to give the Rosses answers, then it would be worth it. She sipped the cold liquid from the plastic cup, forced her mind back to Melanie. Thinking about all the chances she'd missed. Modelling, travelling, perhaps a man who would love her, maybe a family in time. Maybe not. The man Melanie had been thinking about *was* her family. Adoptive brother. But too close for comfort all the same. And it was looking like he was responsible for taking all those years and chances away from her.

She walked to her desk. The silence of the office made her feel alone. The only thing waiting for her at home, a microwave meal for one.

Chapter 13

THE HISSING INHALATION AND exhalation of Sanders' ventilator made Eve feel guilty with every breath she took. When she left the morgue earlier, leaving Melanie's lifeless body behind on that sterile metal table, she knew that this was where she would be headed. A room that seemed as sterile, a body that seemed as lifeless, except that this one, the one sitting in front of her, still drew breath.

The wheelchair seat lifted Sanders high off the ground. An air pipe was in front of her face, which she used to adjust the chair by blowing on it. Eve was small in the low, deep armchair, Sanders peering from a commanding height. It was where Eve chose to sit every time she visited.

'Thank you, darling.'

Eve averted her eyes and tucked her hair behind her ear as Sanders spoke, focusing instead on the oak sideboard while Sanders' husband crouched by her right foot. The dust-free wooden surface was crowded with framed pictures. All of them taken before.

Eve coughed, masking the sound of trickling urine as Archie drained the tube hidden beneath Sanders' trouser leg into a bottle. She didn't look until Archie had stood and the bottle had been hidden away out of sight.

Sanders smiled at her husband, a gesture that reached her blue eyes, reminding Eve of a thousand other smiles in a body that once worked.

'Thirsty, Nic?' Archie's voice was tender as he held a straw to her lips.

Eve baulked at the use of Sanders' first name. Nicola? She was Sanders. Always would be. But Eve knew she would never again be the officer she once was. She looked at Sanders' head, her neck hard against the padded support. Her husband caught a dribble of water from her mouth with a tissue.

'Right. I'll leave you to it.' He turned from Sanders, face darkening as he glowered through horn-rimmed glasses towards Eve before leaving the room.

Eve breathed deep, inhaling furniture polish mingled with disinfectant. She felt slapped again, having not long recovered from the same look when Archie answered the front door. The venom in his voice as he'd said 'You again' causing Eve to step back from the door. 'Do you even stop to think how having you here makes her feel? Flaunting the life and job she used to have?' Eve wanted to leave and would've if Sanders hadn't called on Archie from the front room.

Eve jumped when Sanders spoke. 'You know, you don't have to keep coming here out of some kind of sense of duty.' Spoken in a deliberate, fully formed sentence, only occasionally gasping on a word as she breathed through the ventilator.

Eve let go of her own breath, the sharpness in Sanders' tone slicing into raw wounds, knowing that, under their stilted exchanges whenever she did visit, it was these moments she came for. It had taken weeks for Sanders to even acknowledge her when she'd first started visiting, the tortured silence doing little to mask the rage pulsing from the wheelchair.

Sanders stared at her, waiting for a response. Those deep-set blue eyes, familiar laughter lines at their edges, the only part of her Eve truly recognized. Her hair was short and there was a clammy look to the paper-thin skin covering limbs that never moved. As lifeless from the neck down as Melanie, except Sanders was still in there somewhere.

Blood thundered in Eve's ears. She answered the only way she knew how: 'I'm here because I want to be.'

Sanders scowled. 'If that's true, then at least have the guts to be the woman I knew.'

Eve sat, stung, but she was happy to take it. Needed to take it. Better than the visits when they sat in silence or made clipped polite chit-chat. She swallowed. 'What do you want from me?'

'You need to ask?' Sanders' pupils widened, top lip curling as she spat the words at her.

'I didn't come here for this.' Eve's voice getting louder, forcing herself to stay seated, nails digging into her palms. Both of them knowing this is exactly what she came for.

'That's more like it, Eve. Some fire in your belly.' Venom in her voice.

Eve's heart hammered, her fists clenched, at odds with the lump in her throat. 'I came to see you. To be here for you.' Her voice was a hiss, back teeth clamped like they'd been glued together.

'See me for what? A reminder of who I was? You don't need to be here for that. Or for me. Especially when you can't even see it's still me in here.'

Eve's head snapped round towards the closed door.

'What? You scared Archie'll hear?'

Eve's eyes narrowed, temple pulsing, pushing down the rising feeling of shame. This was more than Sanders had ever said. Moving further than she knew how to deal with. She needed to leave. She wasn't ready.

The room was silent but for the sound of breathing: hers as laboured as Sanders'.

'I've never been any different with you.' Eve whispered the words, not believing them herself.

'Bullshit.'

Eve moved her heavy head from side to side, not able to deny it twice with words. She lowered her eyes to the floor, the carpet blurring. 'What do you want from me?' Feeling pathetic as her voice cracked.

'To stop feeling sorry for me. To come here and speak to me. Not sit there, every single time, staring at me like some rare exhibit. And to stop feeling sorry for yourself.' She paused, gasping. 'Be the woman I knew.'

Eve tried to swallow; it was almost painful when she gulped. Fighting tears. Vulnerable. A place she didn't go. 'I don't know how. You're not the woman I knew.'

How close they'd been. A team within a team. Two women determined to be as good as and respected as their male counterparts. They hadn't failed.

Sanders huffed into the tube, the chair buzzing closer to Eve. 'Maybe I'm not the woman you knew, but you need to stop all the woe-is-me shit; it doesn't do anything for you.' Her voice softer this time. 'I should kno—' She stopped as Archie came into the room.

'Everything OK?' Archie looked between the two women, seemingly sensing the tension in the air. 'What's going on?' He went straight to Sanders, standing in front of her chair as if he needed to guard her.

Eve didn't know what to say. Glad of Sanders' voice when it came, soft and quiet, from behind her husband.

'Darling, please. Everything's fine. We're talking. About things that need to be said. That should've been said.'

Archie didn't move, his glare pinning Eve to the spot.

'Archie, please.'

He stepped to the side, his frame relaxing a little. Eve looked at Sanders. Taking in all of her. Seeing Sanders for the first time in a long time. Surprised to see tears, scared to hear what she had to say next.

Sanders tutted. 'I want to hate you.'

Eve reached for a tissue from her pocket and stood to dry her old colleague's face. Archie blocked her before she could, snatching the tissue from her hand. He turned and bent over to dab at his wife's cheeks. Eve sat, chastised.

'I want you to hate me.'

Sanders sighed, licking at dry lips. 'All this time I've told myself you put me in this chair. I needed to do that. Archie wanted me to. I know that.' Sanders glanced at Archie, whose whole body had tensed once again. 'He kept telling me that although you weren't the one who dealt the blow to my back, what you did that night was what failed to stop it.'

'And he's right.' Eve didn't want forgiveness. She didn't think she could handle it.

'I knew, Eve. I knew where you'd been that night, and I still picked you up.'

'I shouldn't have allowed you to.'

'But you did.' Her voice softer. Sanders glanced at Eve's leg. 'You didn't exactly get off lightly yourself. I'm glad of that.'

Eve looked to her lap. 'You're right to feel like that. To blame me. Archie too, and anyone else.'

'I'm angry, Eve, fucking angry, but, if I'm being completely honest, it's with myself more than you. Me and this useless body. It was easy to blame you – everyone else was doing it – but I didn't want it to be as bad as it got.'

Eve could only guess what Archie was thinking right then.

'That bitch Jenkins didn't help. Reporter scum. Half-truths and ruined lives. Stupid cow managed to get into the ward and classed five minutes with me, off my face, as an exclusive.'

That front page was one of the few that Eve's name hadn't solely dominated at the time. The headline screaming about a long road ahead to recovery for Sanders.

Sanders stopped speaking, panting with all the effort, the silence in the room deafening. Archie reached for the glass of water he'd fed to her earlier.

'I'll go get you some fresh water.'

'No, Archie. I'm not finished.'

Archie let his arm fall by his side, glass in hand. Struggling not to say something.

'The thing is, I'm sick of this anger. I need to let it go, and to do that I need to forgive.'

Archie's face reddened, his fingers curling around the glass, tighter. 'Nic—'

Sanders sighed. 'Archie, please. I need to. And I need you to.'

Eve half expected the glass in Archie's hand to come flying towards her. 'Sanders, you don't have—'

Sanders shushed her, stared at her husband, her eyes glistening. Archie stood, staring at the floor, shaking his head. After a moment, he looked to his wife and held her gaze before nodding once.

'Fine.' He walked to the door, glass in hand – not once looking at Eve – and left the room.

Sanders waited until the door had closed. 'That's as good as you're going to get. He's always had a problem with you.'

'I don't know what to say. I don't deserve your forgiveness.'

Sanders said nothing. The problem was it gave Eve no relief. It would make coming here easier, maybe, but there was no way forward for her when she couldn't forgive herself.

Eve wanted to know more about Archie. 'Did he have a problem with me even before what happened?'

Sanders tilted her chin: her way of nodding. 'In that the nature of the job meant I spent all my time with you, it was all he heard about. Archie always had a problem with anyone taking my attention away from him.'

'How's he handling it all?' She was at a loss for what else to say.

Sanders swallowed. 'With a smile.' She closed her eyes, quiet for a minute. 'I sometimes hear him crying at night.'

Eve softened her voice. 'Don't you ever speak to him about it?'

'I've tried. I even told him to leave. That he deserved a life away from all this.'

'But what would you do?'

'There are places. Ways and means.' Sanders nibbled her bottom lip. 'We have a nurse that comes in every day to help out as it is. She stays on a Thursday night and he gets out for a game of cards and a drink with the boys.'

'At least it gives him some freedom.' Eve regretted the words as soon as she'd said them, aware she was making Sanders' life sound like a prison sentence, drawing attention to the fact she had no freedom herself. Because of Eve.

'To be honest, in some weird way, I think he likes things as they are.'

'What?' It came out higher pitched than Eve intended.

'I know. Go figure.' It was Sanders' turn to look towards the door. She lowered her voice. 'Archie always treated me like some precious doll. I think my job sometimes made him feel less of a man, didn't give him the chance to provide or look after me the way he wanted.'

'But surely he'd never wish for what happened?'

'God, no. But in a strange way, it's given him back his masculinity. Made him feel needed. It lets him treat me like china and to feel, in his eyes anyway, he's finally a better man.'

Sanders' sad smile tugged at Eve as she spoke. 'It's why I need you to do what I asked. Be you and let me be me. For those moments you're here. See if I can let go of this hate. Truly stop blaming you. Because the rest of the time, here with him, I'm that rare exhibit.'

'Sanders, you can't live like—'

The door opened, Archie holding the glass of water, a straw sticking out of it.

'Thanks, Archie.'

He fed Sanders again. Eve was sure she could hear in Sanders' voice that she was thanking him for more than the water. He stayed silent, left the room again.

Sanders sighed. 'Anyway, where were we . . . Yeah, live like what? He's happy. I can give him that. I'm not in some hospital or assisted housing. He cares for me. Am I in despair about it? No. Despair's a bleak word.'

'Do others come to visit? I know Cooper does.'

'At first everyone did, even Hastings. But it fell off after a while. Life's busy, it moves on.' Sanders' eyes watered. 'Hastings, Cooper and you still visit regularly.'

113

'What about Ferguson?'

Sanders sighed. 'I said everyone, but I've never seen Ferguson.'

'What?' Eve couldn't believe it.

'Don't be too hard on him. You know he was one of the first responders that night. I can only imagine he's been living with "what ifs" ever since. What if he'd got there earlier? What if he'd been the one to accompany me that night? I think it's too hard for him to be here.'

It was true, and something Eve had already known. But there's no way he could've changed Eve accompanying Sanders that night. And no matter how many times he'd been told, he wasn't to have known what was happening in that flat. But it didn't change the fact that he hadn't raised concerns about how long they'd been at the call; that he had waited for a neighbour to phone in. It was part of the reason she put up with Ferguson as much as she did. She knew about guilt. But too hard? With what Sanders had to endure? She realized she'd never asked what a day was like for Sanders. Too wrapped in her guilt, seeing Sanders exactly as she'd described, with no real thought for the before and after once she was done visiting. She asked her now, ashamed at the appreciation on Sanders' face.

'What can I tell you?' Grateful to be on safe ground. 'Up at seven a.m., and it's straight into the morning routine. Archie gives me a bucketful of vitamins, then the nurse arrives and together they flex my legs and arms for at least an hour.' Sanders took a deep breath.

'Electrodes are then taped to my limbs, which stimulate my muscles for another hour while I try to eat breakfast. Then they wash, dress and lift me into my chair. My arms get strapped to the armrests, the ventilator pipe gets connected to my throat and hooked up, then the nurse leaves and I have the afternoon left to party.'

Bleak. 'Jesus, Sanders. You deserve more.'

Sanders wrinkled her nose. 'Do I wish this hadn't happened? Absolutely. In my dreams, I'm never paralysed. It takes real effort, there in the silence when I wake, to drag myself into the reality that I can't move my body below the neck, or even feel it. But it's my reality, and one I'm living every day. Positive thinking and all that.' She snorted. 'Anyway, enough of all this self-pity crap. When were you thinking of telling me you're back on the job?'

Eve was taken aback by the sudden change of subject, grateful Sanders had made it easy for her – albeit after a good battering.

'I'm back on the job. Your replacement hates me too, you'll be glad to know. Oh, and it's looking like our latest murderer is trying to send us a message.'

Sanders whistled low. 'You always were a bit of a bitch.' She laughed – the first Eve had heard from her in too long. 'First problem, she'll get over it. Second problem, not easy. What do you say we use this head of mine and you lay the facts on the table? Do a bit of brainstorming, like the old days?'

Eve nodded, her hazel eyes meeting blue. That she could do.

Chapter 14

Now

Tea-tree soap nips his nostrils as he lathers it in his hands. The room's in shadow, light flickering from the television up on the corner bracket: an old portable, the kitchen units even older. The place is cramped, not his style, but it's true what they say: beggars can't be choosers. Beads of sweat glisten on his top lip, the room too warm with the storage heating and cooker on.

He feels for the hand towel, something on the evening news catching his attention, and dries his fingers one by one while he watches. A picture of Melanie. A run-down of the same old details.

He expects more. More from the news reports he's watched. They should be covering his story with a bit more flair, matching the scandal that the Aberdeen Enquirer and nationals have it down as. But he supposes they have to stick to the facts. Report on the lies he's putting to bed, one by one. What was really going on with Melanie. The ugliness beneath the beauty.

The reporter's face up on the screen is deadpan. Is she scared beneath that face, wondering if there'll be another? Wondering who'll be next?

He begins slicing red onions, keeps slicing until they're all done. He mutes the telly, lights the gas ring on the cooker and lowers the frying pan to the flames, the full-fat butter sizzling within seconds. He has no need for volume. The reporter can tell him nothing. Only he knows who is next.

He picks up the green chopping board and scrapes the onions into the pan with his hand, then puts the board into the washbasin. The red chopping board will be used for meat. Like always, he does things properly, has standards.

He picks up a garlic clove, inserts it into the hand press and squeezes it over the frying onions, scraping the pulp off the metal with a knife, all without looking. His mind stays fixed on the task ahead. He glances over to the door, where his rucksack lies. It holds all the tools he will need. He'll be seeing her soon.

He smiles, thinking of what is ahead. The next chapter. When he's ready. For now, he'll eat. After all, he has to keep up his strength.

Chapter 15

Tuesday, 12 November

BRUCE SPENCER STOOD IN the doorway of the dance studio clutching an oversized bunch of keys in one gloved hand, a mobile phone clamped against his ear in the other. He tutted, steam rising from his mouth in the early-morning chill. 'For fuck's sake.' He glowered at the phone screen, watching his call to Duncan being ignored for the third time before jabbing his thumb against the cancel button.

The doorway stank of stale urine, commonplace with the studio being on the homeward stretch for drunks from the night before. Except that normally he didn't have to smell it. Opening was Duncan's job, and this was the second time in a fortnight he'd gone missing. Hadn't come home. And Bruce Spencer didn't like waking alone.

He pocketed his mobile phone and started fumbling with the keys, trying to find the one for the main door. 'Shit.' His hands grappled for the keys as they slipped from his grasp, landing with a clatter and splash as they hit slush on the concrete step. He was going to kill Duncan. He crouched, the smell of piss stronger than ever, grimacing as his fingers brushed against the wet ground and lifted the keys.

Where the hell was Duncan? It was a question that Bruce already knew the answer to. The first time his young lover hadn't come home until the next morning after a night out, he'd made it easy for him – said he believed it was a party that had got out of hand. He hadn't said anything about the bite mark clearly visible on the inside of Duncan's rock-solid, bronzed thigh later that same day. Dancer's limbs. Reminding Bruce of what he'd once been. Before old age had crept up and sucked the youth from him.

He sighed, found the key he was after and pushed it into the lock, frowning when he didn't hear the familiar click. The door was open. His heart lifted a little, already making excuses for his boyfriend. Bruce stepped into the pitch-black reception of the studio, no warmer than outside. He felt for the switch, wondering why Duncan would have the place in darkness. As the harsh orange bulbs overhead flickered into life, Bruce squinted and saw that everything was the same as he'd left it last night. Before Lexie had arrived – a dancer who regularly hired one of the smaller studios after hours, who knew to lock up and post the keys through the door.

Maybe she'd forgotten to lock up and just shoved the keys through the letter box without thinking. Bruce turned in the doorway. No keys on the floor.

'Duncan?' Bruce called into the darkness of the hall-way beyond reception, surprised by the slight tremor in his voice as he did. 'Lexie?'

He closed the main door against the draught and forced his feet to move along the hallway to the studio, stopping when he spotted the thin strip of light spilling out from beneath the studio door. Bruce craned his ear towards the door. Nothing. He lifted his hand to push open the swing door, tried to tell himself the shake in his arm was the cold temperature or old age. Bruce swallowed as he shoved at the wood and froze as the door swung inwards, revealing what waited for him in the studio.

She looked like a pink flamingo in a lagoon of red. Bruce stood, seeing his reflection – the look of horror on his face – in the wall-to-wall mirrors, framed in the background of death. Lexie's slender body, dressed in a leotard and tights, was draped over the barre, one leg stretched out along the dark, knotted wood. Both hands, their flesh bloated and purple, gripped the ankle, dainty fingertips resting on soft leather pumps. What looked like some kind of cord bound the wrists to the ankle, all three tied tightly to the barre. A perverse take on holding the stretch. Bruce covered his mouth, stepping backwards out of the room, reaching for his phone, wishing the call he had to make was as simple as trying to contact a missing lover.

Eve couldn't see the woman's face. The forehead and chest rested on thigh and shin, brown hair on her head pulled into a thick neat bun. Her other leg, long and lean, hung, straight, towards the floor. A featherless elegant bird, standing on one leg. A leg that had a folded piece of paper sticking to it. Eve didn't need to be told what it was.

Blood pooled around the narrow mottled foot on the polished floorboards. And again, further along, where it had flowed from her mouth. The room smelled of copper, with an undertone of sweat-soaked wood. Obvious that the tongue was gone. She wanted to turn away but couldn't, her mind trying to grasp if this could be happening, waiting for someone to tell her it wasn't real, that she'd stepped on to some horror-movie set.

SOCOs were crawling about the corpse like giant white maggots. MacLean was standing over in the corner, mumbling into a Dictaphone.

'Jesus.'

At the sound of DS Cooper's voice Eve turned towards the main door and was met by her colleague's slim, green-tinged face.

'Where's Mearns?' Cooper looked away from the body.

'Interviewing the studio owner. Ferguson's in with her.' She didn't say that apart from telling Ferguson to go with Mearns, they still hadn't said two words to one another. 'Different start to the owner's work shift.'

'You can say that again.'

MacLean pocketed his Dictaphone. Eve made her way over, momentarily shocked to realize that the reflection of a limping woman in the mirror was her.

'You know what I'm going to ask.'

MacLean bent to lift his case, screwing up his face as he felt its weight. 'Yeah,' the word sounded strained, 'and you already know the answer. Same puncture wound to the arm, mouth missing an essential muscle.'

The pathologist shook his head, disgust twisting his lined features, and started towards the door. He shouted over his shoulder, 'I'll be in touch once I've seen her down the lab.'

Eve motioned to Cooper to come over, their own white suits rustling alongside the others already moving about the scene, one of the SOCOs working on carefully removing the piece of paper pinned to the woman's pink tights. An eerie silence fell over the room, the only sound the rustle of newspaper in the examiner's gloves. Eve craned her neck to read what was on it.

'US Dancer Hopes to Inspire Others.'

This thing was getting more complicated by the minute. She herded Cooper off to the side, Eve wanting to talk in private. 'OK, MacLean's confirmed the puncture mark in the arm. What've we got?'

Cooper straightened and puffed out his chest, knowing how Eve liked to work – to give opportunity to those on her team, valuing their input. She was comforted to see him fall into the familiarity with ease.

'Same MO. Injection to upper arm, tongue missing, newspaper headline.' Cooper's eyes scanned the scene as he spoke. 'Body position's been manipulated, staged like the first but different.' He walked over and bent beneath the barre the body was shackled to. He forced air from his nostrils before looking upward. 'No injury to the face.'

Eve frowned. 'No injury?'

'No.'

Eve dipped her chin, signalling to Cooper to carry on.

Cooper straightened, careful not to touch the body or to step in blood. 'Both bodies found in public places . . .' He paused, his mouth moving, no sound coming out. 'A week apart. That's all I've got.' Cooper turned his palms to the ceiling.

Eve took the baton. 'How's he targeting them?' She stopped herself from saying 'Ryan', although it was his face she saw as she spoke. 'What's their connection? What's the significance of these headlines?'

Cooper scratched at his chin. 'Both Caucasian, brown hair, slim. Could be what he gets off on? Could be nothing.'

'Possible. Both feminine, one a promising model, one a dancer, at least as a hobby. Headlines point towards what they do, or want to do, for a living. Did he know her?'

'Did Melanie?'

Ryan's flatmate, Forbes, came into her mind. 'Are the tongues a sexual thing?'

Cooper shrugged. 'Maybe it's about secrets? Tongue's obviously key, and whatever he's trying to achieve with the bodies being placed the way they are.'

'The real question is, where the hell is he hiding? Is Forbes helping him?'

A swing door swished open at the other side of the studio, Mearns blocking the view to the reception area behind it. Her face fell when she looked at Eve but

123

recovered as she walked over to where they stood, silent, their old camaraderie dissolving around her. Ferguson, trailing behind her, didn't bother to hide his disdain.

Eve couldn't have missed Sanders any more than she did right then. Her visit to her former colleague the previous week only magnified how unfair life could be. They'd brainstormed the case together, like the old days. Not coming up with anything concrete, but the process giving them so much more.

'Ma'am.' Mearns hissed the word, as if her mouth was fighting against the respect for rank. Eve wondered how hard she'd had to fight to be accepted as part of the team in Sanders' absence. How well she and Ferguson knew each other and whether Ferguson was responsible for stoking the issues Mearns obviously had with her.

'How'd it go?' Eve looked over Mearns' shoulder, saw the owner hunched over the reception desk, howling into a mobile phone, jewellery jangling on his bony wrist, the other hand dabbing a tissue at streaks of smudged eyeliner seeping into the deep creases of his face.

Mearns cocked her head towards the owner. 'He barely knew her.'

'What's the story?'

'Victim's name is Lexie Jackson. She was renting the studio for dance practice in the evenings. He sometimes saw her if he was working late. He'd left by the time she arrived last night.' Eve watched as Mearns ran her tongue over the gap in her front teeth.

'Do we know for sure?'

Mearns didn't try to disguise the deep sigh. 'I wouldn't have said. He left with two others – the boyfriend and an employee. I've confirmed it with both. I let him finish the phone call to the boyfriend, as you can see.'

Eve's teeth were clenched, temple throbbing at the attitude. Mearns was reminding her of a kid. A kid who had got themselves into some kind of gang and didn't know how to get out of it. But her defiance didn't seem as aggressive as it had the first time they'd laid eyes on one another. It was as if Mearns felt she had to keep up the charade for Ferguson. Nevertheless, she glared at Mearns, as it couldn't be allowed to continue.

Cooper's discomfort was obvious as he looked between them. The smug look on Ferguson's face confirmed her suspicions. She wouldn't bite. She couldn't. Not here. She loosened her jaw. 'She local?'

Ferguson answered. 'No. Moved over from New York with her husband three months ago. Oil contract. She wasn't working here but toured professionally with a dance troupe back home.'

'We got a surname?'

Mearns this time. 'Mr Spencer's boyfriend arranged the rental agreement with the vic, says he'll know where the paperwork is.'

'I take it he knows not to divulge any details from the scene?' Eve glanced to the office again, the owner cradling his head in his hand, still crying into the phone.

Mearns ground her jaw, but it was Ferguson who answered. 'You can take it that she knows how to do her job.'

Eve wanted to slap him. Mearns glanced to the floor; even she looked surprised at his brass neck. Eve flexed her fingers by her sides, staring at them both, like kids called to the headmaster's office. She fought to keep her cool, wanting to get in their faces, to tear a shred off Ferguson. But she knew here wasn't the place.

Cooper cleared his throat, louder and longer than necessary, breaking the tension. But it didn't break Eve's eye contact. Mearns had the decency to keep her own stare to the floor.

Eve and Cooper stepped out of the studio on to the concrete hill of Hutcheon Street. The wet grey pavement was pock-marked with chewing gum and lay in the shadow of a decaying red-brick building, once a slaughterhouse. Across the gridlocked road was a mix of new-build tenements and the granite of old.

Gawking faces looked out from the car and bus windows, while other onlookers gathered on the street; the crime tape and officers a magnet for gossip. Traffic still crawled long after the lights at the junction of George Street changed to green. Eve was well aware that Michael Forbes, Ryan's flatmate, lived on that stretch.

'DI Hunter?'

Her chest constricted. Jenkins. She turned, saw the reporter standing to the side of the barriers closing off the studio. Her nose was as red as her scraped-back hair, black-rimmed glasses severe against her pale skin. Eve was sure Jenkins would see the beats drumming against her chest. 'Jenkins, you don't give up, do you?'

Cooper stepped forward. 'You've got some bloody nerve.' Anger rasped his tone.

The reporter smiled. 'Just doing my job.'

'It's OK.' Eve laid a hand on Cooper's forearm. She wanted to smack the smile from Jenkins' face. The headlines Jenkins would be generating over the next few days would be a hell of a lot more sensational than the two headlines that had been found at the murder scenes. 'Didn't take you long.'

DC Mearns and Ferguson came out of the building. They stopped, looking unsure as to what was about to go down. Jenkins looked them over before answering Eve. 'Anonymous tip.'

White air rose from Jenkins' mouth as she spoke. Dragon breath. 'And what did this anonymous tip tell you?'

'Another female. Something tells me it isn't a coincidence.'

Eve took a deep breath. 'You know the drill. You get nothing.'

'But you know I'll get it. I always do.'

Eve bristled. 'Yeah, and as I've said, you don't care what you have to do or who you have to hurt to get it.'

Jenkins raised a hand and clutched it against her chest in mock horror, her mouth open, a blue flash catching Eve's eye, the glare of car headlights bouncing off the piercing in her tongue. Eve didn't need to be made any more conscious of that particular piece of flesh. She wished Jenkins had been the one silenced instead of Melanie and Lexie.

'Jesus, Jenkins, how do you sleep at night?'

Instead of the reporter, it was Ferguson that mumbled a reply. 'I could ask you the same question.'

Eve whirled around to face him, rage propelling her, forgetting about Jenkins for a second until she spoke again.

'Well, well, it seems not everyone is glad to see you back, are they, Eve?'

Cooper stepped forward but not before glowering at Ferguson. 'Wrap it up, Jenkins.'

Eve tugged at his upper arm and shook her head. 'Leave it.'

Cooper took a breath, trying to calm himself.

Eve's anger bounced between the scum in front of her and Ferguson stood behind her. Her temper caught between them.

She focused on Jenkins, knew she'd have to deal with Ferguson later. Eve didn't doubt the sly reporter would manage to get what she wanted. But for now, at least, she had nothing. Nothing about how the bodies were being found. No knowledge of the tongues or the headlines. No hint that they were looking for Melanie's adoptive brother. If she did, she'd be using it as leverage. Until then, Eve needed to think of a way to keep Jenkins where she wanted her, and it wasn't going to be by losing her temper. She inhaled through her nose, slow as she could.

'Wait here.'

Jenkins' eyes flickered, thrown by her reply, not trusting it.

Eve herded Cooper and Mearns to the side, making a point of leaving Ferguson standing there. She kept her voice low as she spoke, never moving her eyes off Jenkins. After a couple of minutes, she walked over to her, knowing that what she was about to do would test her friendship with Elliott.

'Ryan Phillips. Go see what you can get from that.' She turned on her heel. 'Ferguson, get your ass over here.'

Eve led Ferguson around the corner of the dance studio into the side alley, out of earshot of Cooper and Mearns.

'What the hell are you playing at?' The hushed words came fast through Eve's clenched teeth.

Ferguson stood rigid, his face flushed. It was rage, matching her own, rather than embarrassment. The clenched fists, arms by his sides told the story.

'Answer me.'

'It's a bloody disgrace that they let you back.'

His words didn't surprise her; she'd been waiting for them.

'Well, they did, and if you want to stay on this team, you better get used to it.'

Ferguson said nothing.

She had an overwhelming, immature urge to mess up his perfectly groomed hair. 'You know something, Ferguson? You've always had an attitude, but somehow it made you the officer that you are. Determined, fearless, strong, dedicated. Intuitive.'

Ferguson looked surprised.

'But none of that means jack-shit if you let the attitude control you. You and I once worked great together.' She was so close to saying what she thought the real issue was – his guilt that he hadn't got to her and Sanders in time. That he'd let them down. That he found it easier to blame Eve when there was something to pin on her.

But she knew if she did that, right here and now, there might be no way back for them. Instead, she opted for safe ground. 'You want to make this all about me and my failings, but it's bullshit.' The fear in Ferguson's eyes was clear. 'This goes way back. When I put Cooper forward for promotion to DS over you.'

Ferguson let go of his breath, relief flooding his features. He half-heartedly shook his head, went to argue.

Eve raised her hand, silencing him. 'No, I've let this slide for too long. Once you start letting the attitude into the team instead of directing it out there where it can be used positively, we have a problem. And that problem only got worse with what happened with Johnny Junior and then Sanders.' She stopped short again of saying what she knew was his real problem. 'It gave you even more reason to target me. And it looks like you're intent on taking Mearns down that road with you.'

Ferguson swallowed, not making eye contact with Eve. 'Sanders is in a wheelchair because of you. You and your rage. Your failure to radio or call in what was happening. I was there that night. I saw what had gone down by the time I got there.'

Eve's heart raced, pulse pounding in her throat. He'd actually touched upon it. *By the time he got there.*

Ferguson seemed to take her silence as some kind of admission. 'Same as it doesn't add up that you acted

130

professionally and had nothing to do with MacNeill's car ending up on its roof. You always did what you had to do to get the job done, and I'll admit I used to respect that. At least when you kept it professional on the surface. Who doesn't want to see the scum put away? But you took it too far that night, and Sanders paid for it later. One of our own. And you get off scot-free? Makes me sick.'

Eve swallowed her rage at being challenged by him, emotion threatening to bubble to the surface. She wouldn't tell him that she'd been paying every day since. That she couldn't imagine a day when she wouldn't be. Her anger dropped to a whisper, the edge to it still audible. 'That scum, MacNeill, deserved to go off that road for what he did. I didn't touch him. He was running from me.' She knew that wasn't the full truth, but it was all she was willing to give him.

Ferguson shook his head. 'And what's Sanders' take on all that?'

'Why don't you ask her?'

Ferguson looked to his feet.

'Oh wait, you can't. Because, unlike me, you've never had the balls to sit in that room with her.'

'I don't need to go and feed some kind of guilt.'

But Eve knew that's exactly what he needed to do. Still, she wasn't ready to let him off the hook when he'd never done the same for her. 'No, you don't. You're right. Because you can feel guilty enough from a distance for never visiting.'

Ferguson hissed when he answered. 'Don't you dare lay that on—'

'No, Scott.'

Shock was in Ferguson's eyes as she used his first name. This had gone beyond the job. This was personal. 'Don't *you* dare. I am your boss. Whether you like it or not. And I will not, do you hear me, I will *not* take your bullshit. If you can't find a way to work with me and be on this team, and I mean without your pathetic digs, jokes and general insubordination, then go see Hastings.'

Ferguson jerked his head towards her, his breath warm on her freezing face. 'Fine. I might do that.' But the doubt in his voice didn't match the conviction of his body language.

Eve jutted her chin forward, stepped even closer, challenging, in his face. 'Please do. But remember Hastings got me here. You may be taking on something you don't want to start. You have a choice. You either go get Mearns and track Lexie's husband to break the news, or you go visit the boss.'

Eve didn't wait for an answer before she turned and walked away.

Chapter 16

DR SHETTY PLACED THE mug of coffee in front of Eve and made her way round to the other side of the desk with her own.

An effort from the doc to show how far they'd come – from a stranger in therapy, to friends over a cuppa. Eve wasn't fooled.

'So, how's things?'

Eve worked hard not to show her innards shrivelling at the same old start to these sessions. What could she say when she'd arrived here fresh from finding Lexie bleeding out in a dance studio? The story she peddled to everyone else – that she was fine – didn't wash with Dr Shetty. She had to give something during these sessions – the doc's professional input was still going a long way to keeping Eve in a job. But that didn't mean she had to give anything easily.

'Fine.' Same answer as always.

Dr Shetty sat silent, her owl-like chocolate-brown eyes perched above razor-sharp cheekbones boring into

Eve's. Eve didn't flinch. She could wait out the best of them. Dr Shetty sighed as she broke eye contact and lifted a sheet of paper from her desk.

Eve looked around the office while the doctor's eyes skimmed the paper. Large ornate lampshades glowed around the room, the space otherwise dark without them in the basement of the mid-terraced office. It almost felt like a cloak-and-dagger operation as she skulked down the black wrought-iron stairs from the street level of Albyn Terrace, yet another affluent area of Aberdeen, as if her secrets were only to be shared below ground, away from prying eyes. She jumped now as the doctor spoke.

'DCI Hastings filed his report with me yesterday. Quite a first week you've returned to.'

Eve said nothing.

'How are you coping with it all?'

Same question, rephrased.

'Glad to be back.'

The doctor smiled. That smile. The one that, in a single second, was telling Eve she could play all day long too. Eve forced herself to smile back. 'It's been a tough week, but it would be for anyone. I feel on top of things.'

There. Feelings. That's what the doc wanted. Eve watched her scribble on her notepad, wondered if she was seeing right through everything Eve was saying. Sanders. There was something she could give the doc. She'd leave Ferguson and Mearns out of the picture. Make a real show of doing better.

'I went to tell Sanders I was back.'

Dr Shetty sat forward, all ears. Eve was on level ground, happy to talk. She gave the details of their meeting, at least the ones she was willing to share, and finished with the flourish of her colleague's forgiveness. She sat back, hoping that little revelation would keep the doctor happy for today.

Dr Shetty's wide smile was genuine this time. 'You stayed when things got tough, hearing Sanders out. That must've been painful for you. To have forgiveness, that's a real step in moving forward for you. Perhaps that alone is helping you at least in some small way to deal with the stress of what you're facing at work.'

Eve nodded, playing the star pupil, letting Dr Shetty believe she was doing her job in reading her. What she could've said was that it didn't matter, none of it did, if she couldn't forgive herself.

Instead, Eve smiled and thanked the doctor as they made an appointment for the following week.

Chapter 17

'Evieeeeee.'

Mearns ducked back and narrowly missed being knocked over by the skinny, pigtailed girl who launched herself into Eve's arms before hugging her tight.

'Hannah, let her breathe.' Cooper's wife laughed as she came out of the kitchen into the hallway, wiping both hands on her floral apron. She waited for Eve to put her daughter down before taking hold of her just as hard, smile wide, eyes squeezed shut.

Mearns stood inside the Coopers' front door feeling like an intruder.

'And you must be Jo.'

She accepted Louise Cooper's hug but stood wooden in the exuberant embrace that smelled of garlic and olive oil.

'Come through, guys.'

Cooper stood in the middle of the rustic kitchen, a wriggling toddler in his arms, crayon drawings of Santa and Christmas trees stuck to the fridge beside him.

The house was larger than it looked from outside. It nestled in a quiet street in Cornhill, an overcrowded ex-council estate off Anderson Drive, the long grey strip of dual carriageway that snaked from one edge of the city to the other. The original developers had built upwards: sixteen-floor blocks scraping the winter sky, dwarfing the individual houses below.

Hannah danced around her father's bare feet, making faces at her little brother. Mearns felt strange looking on, seeing her colleagues out of work. It was weird enough them all being out of uniform, never mind the cosy domestic scene. She was surprised to find herself yearning for a childhood she felt she never had. At least not with her father. She couldn't recall a time she ever danced or fooled around with him. She smiled alongside Eve, hiding what she was thinking, letting the smile slip away when her boss looked at her.

Cooper laid a hand on top of his daughter's head. 'OK, Hannah Banana, don't go winding your brother up. It's time for his bed.'

Louise removed her apron, re-clipped her long dark hair at the back of her head and took her small son in her arms. 'Food's out, help yourselves.'

The table in the corner was weighed down by food. Quiche, pasta, bread, chilli, soup . . . Hot. Cold. Every accompaniment imaginable. Too many smells to count, all blending together to make Mearns' mouth water.

Hannah pulled at her mother's cotton top as they left the kitchen, the youngster's high-pitched voice carrying as they went up the stairs, begging her to do the bed-time song.

Eve took a seat at the table. She looked as if she'd sat there a thousand times. Mearns followed her lead but sat on the seat furthest away from her. When she and Ferguson had gone to notify Lexie's husband, Ferguson had told her what happened between him and the boss round the side of the dance studio. Cooper had extended the invite to Ferguson for tonight, but he had made his excuses.

Mearns had sat in the car on the way to Lexie's husband's work nodding her agreement at Ferguson's anger, feeling it alongside him, thinking about everything he'd told her about Eve. Impulsive to the point of dangerous. The maverick approach finally catching up with her with horrific consequences the night of the attack on her and Sanders.

Cooper clattered plates against each other as he walked over to the table, bringing Mearns' attention back into the room. He handed them both a plate and sat. 'Tuck in.'

Mearns wanted to try everything but hid her excitement at the chance to eat home-cooked food instead of listening for the ping of a microwave oven. For a moment, they sat saying nothing, the odd clink of serving spoons the only sound as they heaped their plates high.

'What's the bedtime song these days?' Eve asked while piling a slab of quiche on to her plate.

Cooper laughed, brown eyes twinkling. '"Wind The Bobbin". Thank God "Twinkle, Twinkle" finally burned itself out.'

Mearns wiped oil from her chin and swallowed the bite of warm bruschetta in her mouth. 'My mother used

138

to sing "Rock-A-Bye-Baby" to me.' She felt Eve's eyes on her, aware it was the first time she'd given anything away about herself, annoyed that she had.

Cooper smiled. 'They do say the old ones are the best.'

They sat a while, safe in the small chat. It was Eve who eventually pushed some dishes to the side and laid down the manila file. All three of them knew it was coming, but Eve looked sorry for being the one to bring death to the table.

She opened the file and spread out the photos. Mearns pushed away her own plate. No longer hungry, chit-chat over. Eve's finger touched one of the pictures taken that morning. A macabre moment caught in time. A moment Lexie's husband, found via the rental paper-work for the studio, had been spared.

Mearns and Ferguson had ushered him into an empty office in his workplace a married man and left him there a widower. Just in time for Christmas.

'What the *hell's* going on?' Mearns' voice sounded loud against the tiled walls. She remembered the kids upstairs as she looked across at Eve and Cooper, lowered her voice. 'Sorry. This is Aberdeen we're talking about.' She lifted the photo, sure she could still smell the blood that covered Lexie and the floor beneath her. 'Stuff like this doesn't happen here.'

Cooper leaned back against the kitchen wall. 'It does now.'

'It's going to get worse tomorrow.' Eve pinched the bridge of her nose, her elbow leaning on the table, anticipating the media onslaught from her tip-off to Jenkins about Ryan Phillips.

'Do you think you did the right thing?' Mearns emphasised the 'you', trying to hide the brittleness in her tone, aware that she was in Cooper's home. She didn't care whether her attitude would eventually see Eve's patience waning. But she did care if it would cause a shift in her relationship with Cooper. His friendship and support had been vital to her since she'd joined the team.

Eve didn't look at Mearns when she answered. 'I went to see Mr Ross while you were with Lexie's husband. Obviously he's in shock that there's been another murder.

'He's worried about what it's going to do to his wife once the press start on Ryan, once they realize who he was to Melanie. Elliott isn't happy about what I did. He left a message on my mobile earlier. Thinks I've undermined all his team's work.' That was the one thing Eve regretted. She'd need to smooth things over with him. She sighed. 'It was inevitable though; we were lucky to have gone this far without them sussing out what was going on.' Eve slumped alongside Cooper. 'So, yes, we did the right thing. Jenkins is scum, but she's like a bloodhound. Let her take the rap for whatever scandals she uncovers about Ryan, and we'll make the best use of that if we can.'

That was true. Ryan's face would be all over the news-stands tomorrow. Mearns had read all Jenkins' articles after what happened with Eve and Sanders. It was those front pages of the *Aberdeen Enquirer*, and the reactions from some of her colleagues, especially Ferguson, that had shaped her opinion of her boss.

Cooper leaned forward, picked up photos of both Melanie and Lexie and forced himself to study them. 'What's he trying to tell us? Both tied with venetian-blind cord, both injected in their arm, tongues cut out, headlines from articles they featured in pinned to their clothing. Melanie's face hacked to bits, Lexie's left untouched. Melanie sitting, surrounded by all this stuff. Lexie tied, standing, in a dance pose, nothing else around her.'

Mearns took a sip of Merlot as she looked at the red that dominated the pictures in front of her. 'I don't know how the hell we can even begin to read the mind of someone like this. One thing's for sure though, he's calm, staying at the scene as long as he does to set all this stuff up.'

Eve shifted in her seat before she spoke. 'How's he targeting them? Is it a connection with their mention in the papers? Obviously he knew Melanie; it was easy to get her where he wanted her. Did he know Lexie too? If not, how long had he been watching her to know she'd be there alone?'

Cooper laid down the photos. 'And what about Michael Forbes? I have my suspicions about him, but maybe just because he's a slippery sod.'

Eve slid the photos towards herself. Mearns watched as Eve looked at the images, the overhead light catching the unusual brown tone to her eyes. Greenish brown. Intense.

Eve shook her head. 'I don't think it's Forbes. He's not clever enough. Or bloody clean enough on the forensics front.'

Mearns' forefinger and thumb squeezed at the stem of her wine glass. 'These aren't random rage killings. They're calculated – from the drugs to the tongues to the setting of the scene.'

'I think you're right.' Eve nodded at her.

Mearns was surprised to feel a flicker of pride. She cleared her throat, feeling awkward. 'I know we're still waiting on forensics for Melanie, but I don't expect anything. All part of his planning.'

Cooper sighed. 'How many women are there going to be if we don't figure out what all this shit is supposed to mean? If we don't get to him first?'

'We have to work with what we do have,' Eve said. 'The drugs. The cord used to tie both women.'

Eve took a sip of water. 'I've got the team looking into any links between Ryan and Lexie, or if the women knew each other. We've got to hope something comes of it. Or that Jenkins' front page throws up something tomorrow. Anyway, that's the idea of tonight. A little break away from the office. See if there's anything we haven't explored.'

Two hours later, they were no closer to making sense of anything. Conversation had strayed to small chat, and Cooper's wife had joined them at the table with a glass of wine.

'It's great to see you, Eve. The kids have missed you loads. My husband too.' Louise smiled across the table at Cooper and Eve.

Mearns liked the woman, regardless of her obvious affection for Eve. It was hard not to. She was warm, genuine. Mearns felt at home here. Welcome, in stark contrast to her minimalistic flat. Able to ignore the fact that Cooper's wife was a homebody, just like her own mother, because Louise had somehow retained her own personality and independence.

Eve smiled. 'It was time. The endless hours of nothingness were driving me mad.'

Louise lifted her glass. 'Wine, Eve?'

Cooper snorted. 'Come on, Louise, we know how easily Eve gets bladdered.'

Even Mearns' inhalation was audible. She glanced at Eve, who looked like she'd been slapped. She couldn't help but enjoy the moment.

'Jesus, Eve, sorry. I didn't mean . . .' Cooper looked like he was struggling to find the words.

Louise glared at her husband as she rested a hand on Eve's arm. 'He wasn't thinking, Eve.'

Cooper shook his head. 'No, I wasn't. It was a joke. We all know you're not a drinker, have never been able to handle your drink, even before . . . I didn't think . . .'

Eve was visibly struggling to recover, blindsided by her colleague, her friend's comment. Mearns flicked her gaze between the two of them, wondered if there were things unsaid about that night with Sanders, even if it was subconsciously in Cooper's case. She watched as Eve tried to gather herself, as she fought to speak, relishing her boss's discomfort.

'I went to see Sanders last week.'

Cooper took a glug of his wine, placed his glass on the table.

'You go to see her regularly.'

'This time was different. This time I had to tell her I was back. She tore a strip off of me before I got the chance to.'

Mearns stiffened, Sanders' reaction to Eve's visit only confirming the truth. She couldn't begin to imagine how Sanders must have felt.

Louise placed a hand over Eve's. Comforting. 'What happened?'

Mearns shifted in her seat, uncomfortable with someone being so nice to Eve. She wasn't sure she liked the woman after all. But then Eve began to talk.

Chapter 18

MEARNS SAT IN EVE'S car, the creak of a stiff clutch as Eve changed gears breaking the silence. She could see Eve's face out of the corner of her eye, her features bathed in orange light, then black. Orange, black, orange, black as the car passed beneath streetlights on the deserted road.

They'd barely said two words to each other since leaving Cooper's. She hadn't wanted to accept the lift home, knew it was an offer Eve had felt obliged to make. But Mearns' silence wasn't attitude this time – more a stunned reaction to what she'd just heard.

She'd been wrong.

Mearns had sat frozen as Eve told her story, hiding the heat of emotion. Her anger softened when Eve's voice broke, told how Sanders challenged her. About her guilt.

But not guilt in the sense that Mearns expected. Yes, guilt about what happened, but also guilt for how she'd acted since the accident. How she'd lost sight of the fact that Sanders was still Sanders. She *wanted* Eve to be there for her. She'd forgiven her.

The woman Mearns believed put Sanders in that chair. She'd been so ready to judge, had ignored her gut instinct. Eve wasn't the problem. Fear was. Fear she wasn't good enough. That her father had been right. No job for a woman. For her.

She'd grabbed the opportunity Sanders left behind. Then began to feel bad that she'd profited from someone else's misfortune. Feeling terrible for Sanders' situation but secretly grateful for the opportunity, regardless of how it had come to her. But then there was the fear, the worry she would fail.

It had been easy to listen to Ferguson reel off and then repeat all Eve's faults. To convince herself that she was fighting Sanders' corner by taking the job. That Eve was to blame for the situation she found herself in, for the job even being made available. Eve *had* to be the bitch. Someone for her to undermine to make herself feel worthy.

But now, after listening to Eve relay her conversation with Sanders, she'd come to realize that Ferguson was dealing with his own guilt. Just like her. That he hadn't gotten to Eve and Sanders in time. That Sanders could've been spared the life she now knew in that wheelchair. And they'd both chosen to target their guilt, anger and fear towards Eve.

Eve changed gear, said something about nothing. Mearns jumped as if she'd been burned.

'Touchy.'

Mearns looked round in the muted darkness. 'I was away in a world of my own.'

There it was. Her opportunity to say sorry. Her heart hammered against her chest. She didn't know how to do apologies. She needed to learn fast. They were minutes from her flat.

She took a deep breath, held on to it when Eve spoke.

'Didn't realize you lived close to everything that's been going on. It's a nice area. Must be some pad you have.'

Shit. She needed to get this out. Eve glanced at her every few seconds, waiting for an answer.

She exhaled. 'Bank of mummy and daddy. Wanted to put their princess in a tower when she moved here. And right at the top of it. The penthouse.'

Eve stared at her as the car came to a stop outside the Bastille. Another red-brick building, rare in a city of granite. The supposed silver city. The building was a converted factory. Luxury flats in the middle of less luxurious surroundings. The grand building looked on to a disused crumbling factory on one side and downtown on the other. It sat one street along from where they'd found Lexie, a street up from where Ryan had lived with Forbes.

Mearns felt awkward under Eve's gaze. Unsure what she was thinking. Probably shocked she lived in the penthouse.

Eve shrugged. 'I've no doubt you can handle yourself. No need to be saved.'

Mearns frowned.

'From the tower. Even slay a dragon or two.'

147

Mearns allowed a small smile. 'It's not all that. The place was fancy when it first went on the market. But the whole building is dated, in need of a major refurb. Lift's not even working.' It was the most she'd said to her boss without attitude.

Eve leaned her cheek against the car window, looked towards the top of the building in the dark. 'Still impressive. Anyway, I'll see you tomorrow.'

Formal. Safe.

Maybe one admission of guilt from Eve was enough for tonight. Mearns told herself the moment for apology was over.

She undid her seatbelt, opened the door, the biting cold rushing into the car. 'Thanks for the lift.'

Eve stared ahead. 'Don't let the dragons bite.'

Mearns got out, made her way over to the glass security doors, each step exaggerated across the icy car park.

She swiped her key chain against the door panel and pulled the heavy steel handle of the door. She didn't trust herself to look back.

She listened as Eve drove off.

Mearns waited a beat, and pulled out her phone.

Tonight, she didn't want to be alone.

Eve locked the car door, having managed to get into a space that she might need a shoehorn to get out of in the morning, and walked the short distance to her door, keys jangling as she did.

'What the hell are you playing at?'

Eve jumped at the voice, almost dropping the keys, a dark figure stepping out from her doorway. Elliott.

'Jesus. Near enough gave me a heart attack.' Eve had known Elliott would want to have it out with her but thought maybe she'd get away with an angry phone call this late.

Elliott stepped aside to let her unlock the door, looking about as happy as Eve felt as they went in. Eve busied herself taking off her jacket in the doorway, getting the heating and lights on, knowing what was coming. Elliott was already slouched on the sofa, rubbing his forehead the way he did at work when stressed.

'Nothing like making yourself at home. No gifts? Not even a takeaway?' Feeble, but an attempt at least.

Elliott scowled.

'Fair play. I've already eaten.'

Elliott didn't smile. 'Giving Ryan's name to the Rottweiler? What were you thinking going direct instead of through me?'

'It wasn't like that. She was getting in my face after we found Lexie. I didn't want her sniffing around. Wasn't going to take her long to find out about Ryan; call it throwing her a free titbit to keep her distracted.'

Elliott was glaring at Eve. 'How about you run these bloody titbits past me first in future?'

Eve felt that same stab of guilt as when she'd given the name to Jenkins, and again when they'd spoken about it at Cooper's. 'You're right.'

Elliott shifted in his seat, softening a little. 'Too right. After everything I've done to make crap easier for you this past year, you go and make my job harder than it has to be.'

'I know. I'm sorry.' Eve meant it. Elliott had been there for her both professionally and as a friend during the press chaos after the night she'd found the rape victim a year ago, the same night Johnny Jnr had crashed his car while she was in pursuit. He'd been there for her again when her life imploded with what happened to Sanders. Her face reddened as she remembered sitting outside the pub with him on that summer night. Out the front of the Queen Vic at the end of her street.

They'd crossed paths as they finished shift, decided to go for a drink, same thing they'd done as a team before, Eve usually having one or two at most. In control. At the pub, Elliott had managed to winkle it out of her that it was her birthday. A date she usually tried to forget. They'd ordered steak, agreeing to share a bottle of red. A break from reality.

She hadn't known then what was ahead that night, or the effect just half a bottle of wine would have. But she hadn't taken into account the stress of the last few months and the fact that, apart from the steak, she hadn't eaten that day. Even when she took the call from Sanders, she didn't think she was anything but relaxed. A house call. Routine domestic disturbance. The other officers on duty were involved in a stabbing on Union Street, and Sanders was asking for some back-up on the off-chance Eve could make it, even though she'd finished for the day. Easy. She would accompany Sanders as the secondary officer and then get home. Eve closed her eyes, wishing that was how it had panned out.

She looked at Elliott, the anger about her betrayal today still clear on his face. 'Coffee?' It was the best she could do.

Elliott waited a beat, as if weighing whether to make it that easy for Eve. 'Fine. As long as it comes with a bacon roll.'

Eve tutted but went to make it anyway.

'How's it going?' Elliott's voice echoed through from the living room.

'Let me get the bloody grill on first.'

'You know that's not what I meant.'

Eve looked up from the cooker, Elliott standing in the doorway of the kitchen. She shrugged. 'OK.'

'Bullshit.'

'I'm doing OK.' Eve didn't make eye contact. 'Have you had any luck with the article about Lexie and her dancing?'

'Yeah, a small piece that appeared in the entertainment section of the local rag. Moved over from the States, was really something in the theatre over there. Retired and came here because of her husband's work. She was hoping to start teaching kids dance, give her something to do.' Elliott paused. 'Anyway.'

Eve said nothing, carried on pretending to fuss over the bacon.

'You don't have to lie to me like Hastings and all the rest of them.'

And there lay the problem: Elliott knew. About the drink the night Sanders was injured. About what had happened all those years ago to Eve's mother.

Eve closed her eyes. Elliott had come to see her at the hospital two days after she and Sanders were attacked by MacNeill and his men. She'd been off her face on meds, but she needed to talk. *Wanted* to talk.

Photos had emerged of her and Elliott drinking outside the Queen Vic before she was called to the scene with Sanders – Christ knew who had sold them, but by then they were splashed all over the papers. Everything being dredged up from the past about MacNeill's son's injuries from the car crash and her part in that too.

Eve had talked. Told Elliott things she feared the press would uncover if it turned into a witch hunt for what she'd let happen to a fellow officer. Her mother. Her father. How she came into the world. Why what MacNeill's son had done to his victim had hit her so hard. Her fear of letting anyone in. The terror that her father's blood ran through her veins. After she'd finished, Elliott had left and had never breathed a word of it to anyone. They'd never spoken about it again.

She opened her eyes and felt Elliott staring at her. She looked down at the grill, busied herself with the bacon, ignoring him. He sighed, taking the hint and going back through to the living room.

Eve stood in the silence, trying to ground herself in the present but thinking of the past. Hard to believe her mother had been dead over two years.

Eve was ten when her mother told her the truth. Younger than her mother had planned, but the answers she had given Eve about who her father was, where he was, hadn't stopped Eve's questions. She remembered everything about that day: sitting on the sofa by her mother's side, her small hands cupped in hers, her mother speaking in soothing tones. Soft. Gentle, as always. Her grandparents fluttering by the sitting-room door, anxious. Those three adults and their love her world. Her mother's thumbs had rubbed constantly against hers. Her voice quivering as she spoke, but her eyes never shedding a tear.

'I was on my way home from work when a man appeared in front of me. He smelled bad, looked drunk. It was dark and there was no one else around. I was five minutes from home, living with Grandma and Granda like we do now, but it might as well've been five miles away. I was in trouble. He pulled out a knife, dragged me down an alley that I used to play in often as a child, and he attacked me. Did things I didn't want to do.'

In the years that followed, that day became the one that separated 'before' from 'after'. Until then she'd always felt the good in her, even when her temper flared. And it did, quickly and often. Different from her mother and grandparents, who were soft, gentle. She couldn't remember a time she'd ever heard them shout.

Her mother had explained it away, told her she was a kid finding her way in the world and that could be hard sometimes. But after, after realizing the violence that ran through her blood, her world had turned on its head. She'd known then why everyone commented on her hazel eyes. Unusual, nothing like her grandparents' and mother's. Eyes she'd once loved but had hated every day since. Everything out of order, not normal. She wasn't normal. Questioning more than she ever had. Was her father's evil imbedded in her genes? Could people tell she was created from violence? Was her temper his? The fear sent her off the rails.

She was fifteen when her grandfather died. It hit her hard. Her grandmother died a year later. Eve was headed towards no qualifications, known at school and in the neighbourhood only for causing trouble – feeling none of that was her fault. She was her father's daughter. Terrified to get close to anyone. Scared of men and what they could do. She remained wary of men, preferred to be alone. As her mother had been all her life after giving birth to Eve.

It was standing by her grandmother's grave, her mother weeping beside her, when the sacrifices that her mother and grandparents had made for her smacked her in the face. How brave her mother had been, how she had never given up, never made her feel unwanted, had begged her parents to accept her. And they had, unconditionally. Eve had reached across and clasped her mother's hand, and remembered now the look of surprise on her face, the void that had existed between them for the past five years closing in that single moment.

Eve had made her mother proud when she joined the police. Determined to do good, to put people like her father behind bars where they belonged. Her mother never told Eve her father's name. Eve didn't know if her mother had ever known it. Eve didn't need to know. She wanted to believe that her genes were her mother's. But there was no escaping her eyes. His eyes. Feeling like every time her family looked at her, they were seeing him. Like she did when she looked in the mirror. And there was no escaping the rage inside her that she battled every day.

'Are you OK?'

Eve jumped as Elliott appeared at the door again. She nodded. 'I'm keeping on top of it.'

Elliott looked unconvinced. 'The minute you feel you're not, you let me know. I still feel responsible for that night, Eve. You already had enough on your plate, and then that. Now this. Let me be there. We both know it's a thin line between being on top and falling.'

Eve pulled out the grill to check the bacon. She knew. She'd been there before.

Chapter 19

Then

He waits in the darkness. Heart thundering, unsure what he heard. Wanting something to tell him. And then he hears it. The voice of his father. Talking in hushed tones, the irritation not dampened any. His father's anger a regular visitor to their home these days.

The blue wall's cold against his ear as he leans to listen, pulling the rockets, moons and stars around him, snow swirling in the wind outside, whipping against the window.

He hears his mother. Crying again. He can't hear what they're saying to one another, only the rise and fall of the notes in their voices, like a song playing, stuck on repeat – one that he's not allowed to listen to.

The bang makes him jump. Not loud, not like the guns he hears on TV. More a dull thud. Like a fist slamming against wood. He unfurls himself from the duvet. Sticks a toe out into the cold, then a foot and a leg, shunting himself across the mattress until he can feel the floor with the sole of his foot.

They're still arguing. He wants to hear what about but is always too scared to leave his room and creep along the hallway to stand listening outside their door. Or maybe he's too scared to hear. He takes a deep breath, puts two feet on to the carpeted floor, stands, pulling the duvet around him, his protection blanket.

He pulls the door open wider, enough to step out into the hall. His breathing is loud in his ears, but he's not worried they'll hear, as their voices are getting louder. He steps along the hallway. Big over-the-top steps. Trying to creep, like the burglars in cartoons. Finding it hard to be light on his feet with the weight that he carries.

Their door is closed, a thin line of light escaping from beneath, shining on his toes that stand closest. He clutches the duvet at his throat, wearing it like an invisibility cloak, feeling his pulse against his fist. Thinking that since what happened, they don't see him anyway – no need for the cloak.

'You can't think like that. What you said was wrong.' His father, interrupting whatever his mother said.

'Don't you think there's a chance? Am I terrible to think it?' His mother, desperation in her voice.

'For Christ's sake, woman, stop it. Before you drive us all mad.'

'Why are you angry? Because of what I said or because, somewhere, you think it too?'

'You will go and say sorry. Tomorrow. Like you should've done the day you said it.'

His mother sobbing. 'Why has this happened? To me? To us?'

He hears the springs in their bed. His father moving to comfort his mother. His voice softer. 'It's happening to all of us. We need to stay together. Not let it rip apart what we have left.'

'What if what I said was true?'

His father, his voice stern again. 'It's the loss. Of what could've been. You're not thinking straight. None of us are. It's not his fault. I can't allow it to be. He's our son.'

Chapter 20

Monday, 18 November

NEWSPAPERS FROM THE LAST three days were spread out across the table that dominated the incident room.

They all carried stories about the murders, but it was Jenkins who got the exclusive, a day before the nationals even heard a whisper about the suspect's identity. Eve didn't doubt she'd be basking in the glory.

She leaned forward in the plastic chair, black sludge trying to pass for coffee in her hand, the first of many in what promised to be yet another long day. The office was dead at such an early hour.

Eve's eyes skimmed the papers. Words she'd read a hundred times. Quotes from folk who had worked with Ryan, others who claimed to have socialized with him. The usual shocked neighbours, adamant he'd seemed such a nice guy.

There was little from Melanie's parents or Lexie's husband, other than desperate pleas for anyone with information to come forward. And then there was Michael Forbes, who had capitalized on the harrowing tale of life living with a killer.

None of it had led to Ryan. They'd failed to establish a link between Ryan and Lexie, or Melanie and Lexie. The cord used to tie both girls proved to be bog standard, available in most DIY stores. The only hope came from forensics. A partial fingerprint, hidden amongst many more in the hotel suite, placed Ryan at the scene. Nothing else. But something about this niggled at Eve.

It didn't sit that Ryan would've been careless when nothing else was found. But facts were facts, and it had allowed Eve to pacify her bosses, both of the victim's families and the media, that Ryan had been there and they were hunting the right man.

Eve drummed the edge of the desk with her free hand. Ryan's face stared at her again and again from the same photo splashed across all the papers; different from the one pinned to the incident-room wall. She hadn't asked Jenkins where she got it.

The only other break they'd been given was the car Ryan had been driving. A titbit gleaned from Forbes's newspaper interview. A fact he'd failed to mention when they'd paid a visit to his home. The car was a beat-up Corsa, registered to another unsavoury acquaintance of Ryan's. All forces were on the lookout for the vehicle.

Eve sat back, the cheap seat creaking as she did. She leaned her head over the back of the chair, the thick lip of its back digging into her neck, and stared at the stained ceiling tiles.

What they had was nothing.

The room went from empty to cramped without Eve realizing when it had happened. She looked around, took a mental count of the officers milling about, Mearns and Ferguson coming through the door together as she did – to wolf whistles from most of the other officers, even Cooper joining in.

Mearns tutted as she found a spare seat, pink spreading across her cheeks. 'Yeah, yeah, guys, it's a car share. Get over it.'

Eve didn't miss the smile on Ferguson's face or the sly winks he gave in the direction of some of the other officers when Mearns wasn't looking.

Mearns had seemed different over the past couple of days. Maybe it was to do with her chat about Sanders at Cooper's house, the first time Eve had broached the past in front of her new colleague. Perhaps hearing it from her had put some of Mearns' doubts about her to bed, even though she was probably right to have them. But given the amount of time Mearns had been spending on her phone since that night, Eve was betting something, or rather someone, else was responsible for the change in her mood.

Eve stood and rapped on the desk. Chairs scraped against the floor, the majority of bodies seated within seconds and only a couple of stragglers standing. She launched into the familiar daily run-down, doing her best to show enthusiasm, something she most definitely wasn't feeling. It was getting harder by the day to fire up the team with so little to go on.

She was aware she sounded as unconvinced as the faces in front of her looked. No wonder. How the hell did someone drop off the radar like Ryan had? No sightings, no contact, no bank trace. Nada.

She was kidding herself. People chose to disappear every day. Except Ryan didn't want to disappear. What he was leaving in his wake was a cry to be seen. To be heard. But it had to be on his terms.

Eve was nearing the end of her spiel when she heard feet pounding along the corridor outside. The door to the incident room burst open. An older guy she recognized from the force control room. Out of breath and bright red.

'They've . . . found . . . the . . . car.'

All heads turned. Mearns jumped up, Cooper alongside her. Ferguson not far behind them. Adrenaline coursed through Eve's veins. Was this it? The break she'd been waiting for? She was already moving towards the door.

'Where? Tell me where we can find the bastard.'

The barrel-shaped call handler was shaking his head, trying to catch his breath. 'You won't have to.'

Eve stopped moving. 'What do you mea—'

'He was in the car. There's no chance of him trying to make a run for it.'

The journey was slow, parts of the snow-packed, narrow, winding country road threatening to send Eve's car skidding over the side, the sheer drop in places meaning she'd probably meet her end. Strangely tempting with Ferguson sat in the passenger seat.

The news that Ryan had been found dead at the crash site had forced her to re-evaluate everything. She could only hope that Ryan was responsible for Melanie and Lexie, and that this was a freak accident. One that would put a stop to the murders. But she had to be ready if that wasn't the case.

She'd put Cooper and Mearns on to scouring the Scottish Intelligence Database for any cases similar to what they were dealing with, at a loss as to what to do until she found out more about Ryan. And she'd taken the opportunity of taking Ferguson along for the ride: eighty miles and no escape for either of them when there were things that needed to be said. But so far there had been nothing but stilted small talk. She took a deep breath.

'You decided to stay.'

Ferguson's left arm was upright, his hand holding on to the handle above the door. Eve glanced over, saw his grasp tightening as he shrugged.

She sighed. 'That it?'

'The team's what I know.'

'And me being at the head of it? I take it that's not a problem for us?'

'You're the boss. As long as I'm kept involved. I'd like to do more.'

His reply didn't answer the question, or address the fact that it was most probably himself he had a problem with. That guilt kept at bay as long as he was able to blame her.

'Good.'

Ferguson said nothing, the relief evident in his features as he pointed at the windscreen.

They were there. The recovery vehicle's strip lights flashing by the side of the road and marking the spot. The guys were out of the truck, shouting, arguing over whatever it was they were about to do.

Intermittent flashes of yellow and orange light bounced off the snow that was piled high at either side of the road as she and Ferguson parked and got out of the car. The landscape was white, a nothingness as far as the eye could see to the mountains beyond. Eve peered over the embankment to where the car wheels, which had long since stopped turning, were sticking up and out, the recovery lights reaching and bouncing off them too. It reminded her of the scene from the film adaptation of Stephen King's *Misery*. Except in this case the one in the car had been the psychopath.

She looked along and up the winding road that stretched towards and beyond the mountains. Not a car in sight. The road had been shut off. Again. The Lecht. A remote road through the Scottish Highlands, known for closure in adverse conditions.

Ryan had been found frozen at the wheel. He'd already been cut free of the wreckage, his body taken away. A passing motorist heading for the ski slopes after the thaw allowed the reopening of the road had spotted the tyres – black poking through white – and had wasted no time in phoning it in.

Eve signalled to the recovery guys, asking permission to have a little time, let them go and take a look. One of the guys, his gut too big for his hi-vis vest, nodded and hopped in the truck, looking only too happy, his workmates joining him as quick, all of them lighting fags and taking turns to pour from a flask something that looked hot.

She motioned to Ferguson and started to make her way down the hard-packed path that had already been trodden in the snow by the emergency workers who had gone before her. He followed her lead. She wished she'd worn better footwear. Instead, she took over-exaggerated steps, her thigh grumbling, making sure her feet cleared the mounds of snow and got her over to the car. Ferguson didn't offer to help.

Eve placed one of her freezing hands on an upturned tyre, leaning back into her legs as she crouched to take a look at what was left of the car. Going by the amount of dried blood splattered over the interior, there hadn't been much of Ryan left either. Ferguson peered in from the other side, his face paling at the sight.

Dried blackened blood dominated the crushed dashboard, was congealed on the buckled steering wheel and stained into the footwell. A fitting reflection of Melanie and Lexie's murder scenes.

Eve had already done the rounds of phone calls on her way here. Neither Ryan's adoptive parents nor his former flatmate, Michael Forbes, had any idea what he would've been doing this far from home. There seemed to be no previous connection with Ryan to the area that they were aware of.

Maybe he was running from what he'd done. And ran straight off the road instead. Black ice, perhaps. The deluge of snowfall before and since had obliterated any tyre marks that might've told the story. Gone. Out of the picture. Like Ryan.

Eve pulled her head out from the wreckage, listening. Her phone was ringing from the car above, abandoned on the road verge, door still open from when she'd parked. She watched as Ferguson stumbled up the embankment as fast as he could, surprised when he caught the call. He said little to whoever was on the other end of the line, made his way back down the embankment and passed the phone to her.

'Hunter.'

'Wasn't sure you'd be getting a signal.' It was Cooper.

'What you got?'

'Nothing you're going to be happy about.'

Eve's heart sank, Cooper confirming what she'd already been afraid of. Ferguson stared at her. 'Tell me.'

'MacLean's been on the phone. Preliminary report from the guy who examined Ryan confirms he can't be our man.'

'How come?'

'He's been dead longer than Melanie and Lexie.'

Hastings paced the office, squeezing at the centre of his sweating forehead with a forefinger and thumb. If her boss let his blood pressure get any higher, he'd be in danger of looking healthy.

'This is a balls-up of the highest order.'

Eve stayed seated, the scolded schoolchild. 'With respect, sir, we followed what we had.'

It sounded a poor excuse, even to Eve's ears. She didn't say anything about how she'd been torturing herself, questioning whether someone else would've seen whatever she hadn't.

She hadn't got it all wrong though. She'd been right to feel uneasy about the fingerprint found at the hotel. The room had indeed been booked under Ryan's name. They'd even confirmed he'd stayed there before. But it wasn't Ryan who had checked in the day Melanie was killed. No way it could've been after they'd found his body. It made sense. There was no way of telling the age of a print. Sack the cleaning staff.

The text inviting Melanie to the hotel had been sent from Ryan's mobile, but no phone was found in the car with his body. They could only assume it had been stolen by someone who knew what was going on between them. That theory had proved to be as cold a trail as where Ryan had been found. But Eve had a feeling that Ryan's death wasn't the accident it seemed.

Hastings stopped pacing and placed his clammy palms on the desk. He leaned towards Eve. 'Look, I know you followed the obvious, but tell that to Ryan's father, who's lodging an official complaint. He'll probably sue us. Both his kids dead and a city full of folk who know what was going on between them when it turns out they didn't need to.'

Eve chose her words carefully. 'Mr Ross wasn't exactly against the notion of it being Ryan who killed Melanie. He joined the dots, same as us.'

'Maybe, but he's convinced it's that reprobate Ryan was hanging around with.'

'Forbes?' The doubt was clear in her voice.

'Yeah, you said yourself he might have been jealous. What if something was going on between him and Ryan? Even if it was in Forbes' head? What's to say he didn't kill Ryan in a rage over Melanie? Then killed her?'

Forbes. Acne-ridden, skinny. She doubted he was clever or strong enough to do either.

'Eve, I'm under pressure for results. That doesn't mean making this fit, but I want you to consider him. We have to, especially with the stuff Jenkins is peddling in the press . . . The Rottweiler is whipping the city into a frenzy with her front pages, knowing we have nothing. He's still out there. Women are scared to walk the streets alone.'

'Maybe not a bad thing.'

Hastings glared at her, teeth gritted. 'Eve, don't push me.'

'I'm not. But we're back where we started, with nothing to say that there won't be another. We have leads to follow that, admittedly, we didn't look into because we were hell-bent on pursuing Ryan. But we're on them as of now.'

Hastings threw himself in his chair. 'As of now isn't good enough. You needed to be on them two weeks ago.' Her boss swivelled the chair, hard, towards the window.

Eve stood. It seemed the conversation was finished.

Chapter 21

'I THINK I'VE FOUND something.'

Eve was by Mearns' side before she'd finished speaking. 'Show me.'

She pointed to the Scottish Intelligence Database on her computer screen. 'Here. A year ago. Down in St Andrews.'

'St Andrews? Nothing else?'

Mearns looked at Eve. 'I searched for any murders with similar MOs and I got two hits. This and another going back to the 1990s.'

'Same drugs in the nineties?'

'No drugs. A murder. Partial removal of the tongue. I've ruled that out though, as the perp served his time, been a model citizen ever since. Plus he's an old man and terminally ill. This one though, the St Andrews one, is too close to ignore.'

Cooper stood, pushed his chair out from the desk opposite, where he'd also been searching the database, and came round to join them.

Eve's heart pounded as she scanned the details. Mearns was right. It was closer than close.

'Jesus.' The word whistled through Cooper's lips.

Eve barked at Mearns as she made her way back to her desk. 'Get me the number of the officer who worked the case. Text it to me when you have it.' She grabbed her jacket from the chair. 'Cooper, you're with me.'

Beagles Bar and Nightclub on Justice Mill was grim. Even in daylight, the windowless space was dark, dingy and stank. Not unlike Michael Forbes' flat. They found him behind the bar, only three staff members in, stocking the shelves ahead of the night-time trade. They'd managed to convince the club owner that using his office to talk to Forbes was best for everyone. Forbes sat on the other side of the desk from Cooper and Eve, as slouched as he had been at his flat last time they'd met.

'Nae impressed with you coming to my workplace, like.'

Eve smiled. 'We're not out to impress you, Michael.'

Forbes tutted, fingers rubbing fast against each other. Probably desperate for a fag but not willing to face the wrath of his boss if he lit up in here. 'Fit you wanting this time?'

Eve didn't have him down for any kind of clever. A blunt statement would tell her if he knew anything. She looked straight at him. 'Ryan's dead.'

The colour drained from Forbes' face quicker than Eve had ever seen. His mouth was opening and shutting as if it was on a loose hinge.

'Dead?'

Eve nodded. Forbes clutched at his stomach with both hands, gasping for breath before crying. Crying. Eve and Cooper watched him fumble in his pockets for his fags, his hands shaking, unable to get one from the packet. Cooper stood to help, lit it for him. Eve would placate the boss.

It was clear in that moment that Forbes knew nothing about Ryan. She now had to make sure he hadn't been instrumental in Melanie's death, even though she already knew he hadn't. The lack of forensics jarring against Forbes' poor hygiene, the set-up, the murders since.

But the answer was on the wall of the office they sat in and she would double-check with his boss as they left. She stood, moved over to the rota, saw within minutes that Forbes had been working in the run-up to and during the estimated time of Melanie's murder.

She motioned to Cooper. They left Forbes sitting there in a cloud of smoke, snivelling.

Helen Black died a violent death down a cold, dark back alley in the historic seaside town of St Andrews. A place famous for world-class golf, sandy beaches and a university attended by royalty. It showed that no matter how pure the surface seemed, there was always a layer of rot hiding beneath.

Eve listened as the officer Mearns had found wheezed on the other end of the phone, doing his best to recover after a lengthy coughing fit. Detective Sergeant Jack Allen. Six months retired. Happy to talk to Eve as long as she called him Jack.

'Sorry. Damn near coughed my lungs up there.'

Eve heard the click of a lighter, the slow deep breath in and then the sigh of addiction on the way out. She waited.

'Yeah, I remember it. It was my last case and a big one for here.'

'Can you tell me what you remember?'

'Everything. Bloody thing's stayed with me since I left.'

'The officer I spoke to said you never gave up.'

'Damn right. I knew Helen. She was a good kid. One of the few locals at the uni.'

'I read the reports. Says she was drinking at a local pub with friends that night.'

'Uni friends. It was a regular meeting place for them. Helen left before closing time. Home was a ten-minute walk, but she never made it.'

Melanie and Lexie never made it either. She couldn't help but think of her mother. Only minutes from home when she'd been brutally raped by Eve's father. She may not have been murdered, but she never made it that day either. Eve struggled with the thought that if her mother had, then she wouldn't be standing here.

She remembered the phone in her hand. 'I take it you've heard about the murders here in Aberdeen?'

'Sure have. And I'm assuming you're thinking something connects them to Helen.'

Eve picked at the skin on the inside of her forefinger, the office phone cradled between head and shoulder, thinking how to play this one. 'Both our women had the same puncture wound to the upper arm as Helen, ketamine in their system.'

The other end of the line was silent for a moment. Not even the slightest hint of a wheeze.

'Battered?' The elderly ex-detective's voice was a whisper.

'That's where it differs.'

'How?'

'Same drugs, but the first had her face mutilated, the second had no injuries to her face.'

'The drug's the only thing connecting your victims?'

'That and both their tongues were missing.'

The wheezing returned. Eve held the phone away from her ear as Jack launched into another barking episode.

'I can see why you kept that from the press.'

'Yeah, and there's something else we kept from them. Something I wanted to ask you if it was the same with Helen.'

'Shoot.'

'Was her body manipulated into a position?'

'How do you mean?'

'Did the scene look staged?'

'I'm not sure you can class being beaten black and blue as requiring any kind of precision.'

'I read that in the report. No trace of the guy found. I had to be sure there was nothing else.'

'Understood. But she had her tongue intact.'

'I know, but the drugs and the injection site were a huge coincidence. We only got two hits on the system. Your case and another going back to the 1990s. Guy from that case is now an old man and terminal, so not on our radar.'

'Glad you added the terminal; I was about to say there's life in us old dogs yet.' Jack broke into another cough.

Eve doubted there was much life left ahead for Jack if he kept lighting up. She sighed. The long shot at a breakthrough in the case looked to be falling short.

Jack clicked his tongue, the sound loud in Eve's ear. 'There's no harm in taking another look. Why don't you see if you can get down here, visit the scene, look at the photos, even re-interview the guy that found her?'

'I'm not sure it'd be worth it. Helen died a year ago. We're on the block up here. But it's the first lead we've had since the screw-up that I'm sure you know about.'

'A screw-up's only that if you let it be. Everything was pointing towards Ryan at the time. OK, that was wrong. But look at him as one suspect eliminated. This would be something else off the list.'

Eve wasn't surprised to hear Jack had been following the case closely enough to know Ryan's name. She imagined it'd be hard to step away from the job – retirement or not. She was tempted by Jack's proposal. 'I'm not sure the boss'll go for it.'

'Sell it. Let me help you. If anything comes of it, think of it as you helping me.'

'Eh?'

'We find something that helps put Helen to bed, then I'll sure as hell rest a little easier in these supposedly golden years of mine.'

The photos on the wall of Melanie and Lexie stared out at her. Had Helen been the first?

There was only one way to find out.

'You around tomorrow, Jack?'

Chapter 22

Now

Seven o'clock in the evening. He watches the hand of the oversized clock tick a stiff minute past the golden roman numerals at its top. If it makes any sound, he doesn't hear it.

The open fire crackles. He turns his gaze to the flames, his forearm resting on the soft velvet arm of the hotel lounge's sofa, a whisky glass clutched in his hand. Amber swirls in the tumbler as he circles his wrist, the liquid coating its glass sides. He takes a sip, enjoying the heat in his throat and the warmth of the fire on his skin. It would be easy to let both soothe him, to carry him off into daydreams. He blinks. Lack of focus is dangerous.

He leans forward, past the sofa's padded side headrest, and looks over to where Claire Jenkins sits. A woman who makes a living from exposing lies. The reporter is shovelling food into her mouth faster than she can chew. Silver cutlery waving about in front of her face as she talks to her overweight male companion, a spider's-web tattoo spun across his left temple, *which causes other diners to stare. Jenkins' mouth is full, arms animated, the hair framing her face looking as red hot as the flickering fireplace.*

She greeted the bald man on arrival with a brisk handshake and painted smile. It seemed tonight's meal was business not pleasure. Which was what he'd feared. They were too far away for him to hear what they were saying, the clink of other diners' cutlery and their incessant chat mingling in his ears as murmured mayhem. As he leans back, he knows they can't see him.

How long would he have to sit here? He hopes she'll be leaving alone. She's played the game exactly the way he wants her to: dishing the dirt purposely fed to her, devouring the details he is willing to part with.

He'd been nervous when she started reporting on Ryan but quickly realized he could turn it to his advantage. It was a shame Ryan had been found. The place had been an ingenious idea. He'd gone to a lot of trouble getting that low-life piece of shit up there, Ryan willing to travel the distance for the promise of a cheap score. Liked a good smoke, did Ryan, but liked to save money more, even though it was a deal with some guy that had struck up a conversation with him in a nightclub. They'd been in the middle of nowhere when Ryan realized there was no deal to be had. Had thought getting in his car and driving off would be the end of it.

Chasing Ryan had got his adrenaline going. His more powerful car teasing at the bumper ahead on the narrow, icy Highland road, Ryan's eyes bulging with fear in the rear-view mirror. Running him off the road had been easy. The car being upturned was a bonus, making sure it looked like an accident when the time came for him to be found. Which had *promised to be long enough, what with the forecasted snow. Enough expected to block the road. Far enough away for him to achieve what he needed to. And he would've, had the weather reports been right.*

Panic set in when he heard the local radio station reporting a thaw. He ripped the newspaper to pieces when he saw the picture of the car on its roof two days later. His advantage had been lost. He was in danger of losing control.

But Jenkins came through again, unsettling the city with her words, giving him the glory he deserved, instilling the fear that he, someone, was still out there and would strike again. He owed a lot to Claire Jenkins and this was the perfect way to repay her.

He watches her stand from the table and put on her thick furry-hooded coat. No assistance from her dinner date. She shakes her companion's hand again and leaves him squatting there like a fat frog as she walks past him to the door. She digs in her jacket pocket, takes out her phone. He could reach out and touch her. She's typing furiously, stopping only to open the door, probably already filing her story with her editor.

It's dark outside, but he can make out her denim-clad legs, bathed in the glow from the streetlights above, as they edge up the icy steps outside the basement window. He waits until her limbs disappear before standing and shrugging on his own coat.

One last look over to the man who still sits at the table, a newly delivered dessert in front of him that he most definitely doesn't need. He doesn't doubt what they'd been talking about. It irritates him that she knows, that her attention to detail has rewarded her yet again. What irks him even more is that the guy is selling out. But it doesn't matter. Claire Jenkins' attention will be firmly on him by the end of tonight, and the guy will be silenced.

Chapter 23

Tuesday, 19 November

EVE'S EYES STUNG AS she sat in the back of the beat-up Mondeo. DS Jack Allen sat at the wheel, barely visible through the narrow gap in the gaudily upholstered front seats and the haze of cigarette smoke that filled the car.

Jack was exactly as Eve had expected: skin as grooved as a prune, patchwork teeth and a head of white hair – the thinning quiff at the front tinged a fusty yellow after years of being bathed in smoke. The short, neat, black-haired man sitting in the passenger seat looked the epitome of good health in comparison. As they drove towards where Helen Black had been found murdered, Eve hoped the man, Bob Freeman, would prove to be good luck too.

Eve looked out the window at the passing town. She toyed with her phone, wondering whether she should call Jenkins back. The reporter had left a message on her mobile phone last night. She'd sounded wired, breathless, her footsteps clacking along the pavement in the background as she spoke. 'Eve, it's Jenkins. I need to talk to you. Please call me. I have something you need to hear.' But she hadn't said what. Hung up. Probably nothing more than a ploy to get her attention.

Jenkins would no doubt call again if she didn't hear from Eve soon. She put the call out of her mind, taking in the sights of St Andrews but thinking of home.

Both places had sandy beaches, golf courses, museums, cobbled streets, churches and beautiful architecture. A blend of past and present. But St Andrews just seemed to do it better. Maybe because it was a town compared to a sprawling city, or because of the warmth of the local quarried sandstone compared to the grey of Aberdeen's granite. Or more likely because, unlike her hometown, it was one of the driest parts of Scotland.

'The lane's up ahead,' Jack said, interrupting Eve's thoughts with a grating rasp and the threat of a coughing fit.

Eve glanced over at Cooper, who sat beside her, neither used to being the ones in the back seat. Cooper was staring out the window as she had been, silent in his thoughts.

Eve's belly rumbled. She wished she'd grabbed something from one of the service stations on the monotonous early-morning drive down the A90 from Aberdeen. The only thing sloshing about in her stomach was the cup of tea that Jack had given her when they'd arrived at his home.

She could still taste the dishwater-coloured hotness, gulped while sitting on the burst springs of a two-seater sofa, a swirling mass of steam rising to the brown-stained

Artex ceiling. The tea had tasted like liquid nicotine in her mouth. She'd forced herself to swallow it, Cooper sitting by her side cradling his own chipped mug, not once raising it to his lips. They'd still be stinking of smoke once they arrived back in Aberdeen, whenever that might be.

Jack turned right into a dead-end narrow cobbled lane. He'd have to reverse out. The reason they'd come in one car. Eve got out and gulped at the air, grateful to be free of the fug. Ahead, she spotted the large stainless-steel industrial bin, its heavy, wide plastic lid partially hidden under a blanket of snow. Exactly the same place as it had been in the crime-file photos, the only difference being that Helen Black wasn't lying inside it.

Eve moved towards the bin, conscious of the slippery cobbles beneath her feet, willing her limping leg to do its job. Cooper followed, Jack and Mr Freeman giving them a moment to take in the surroundings that they'd stood in too many times to count.

Eve closed her eyes, saw Helen. Naked. Beaten beyond recognition, with a rage not shown by their killer. Found outside, thrown out with the rubbish, her tongue intact. The only thing connecting her to Melanie and Lexie was the drug in her system and where it had been injected.

'I found her right there.'

Eve opened her eyes and turned, the pain in Bob Freeman's voice echoed on his dark features.

'I've read your statement, but could you go over what happened again for me? Leave nothing out, however insignificant it may seem.'

Bob nodded and glanced over to Jack as he walked to where Eve stood. He might be feeling disloyal to the retired officer, that this case was theirs to be guarded, but he was nevertheless torn by a desperation that a year later they'd failed Helen by not finding her killer.

Jack gave Bob a reassuring look Eve didn't miss. The two men hadn't known each other before the night Helen Black's life was snuffed out, but her death had brought them together. Hours spent both before and after Jack's retirement; two men obsessed with solving a crime that had rocked a small community and still haunted their dreams.

Bob cleared his throat. 'It was a Tuesday morning. Bloody freezing. Christmas time. Streets were a mess – streamers, chip wrappers, spew. The usual stuff for clean-up, a hell of a lot more of it due to the time of year. I was on duty in the one-man street cleaner; you know, brushing the kerbside. It was about six a.m.

'The lane was part of my route. Some of the lads would miss it out – you know, out of sight out of mind, eager to be out of the cold, doing something else. I never missed that lane once.'

The note of pride in Bob's voice was evident. Cooper and Jack stood as engrossed in his words as she was.

'Anyway, I turned into the lane as usual. I was watching the brush; you can get lost in thought watching that bloody thing spinning. Best time of day for thinking too. I looked to see how far I had to go and saw it. A foot – small toes sticking out of the bin.'

Bob stared at the spot where he'd found Helen. Eve guessed he was seeing that foot again as clear as the day he'd seen it the first time.

'It was raining, battering against the window of my door. It made things blurry, but I knew before I got out. I lifted the bin lid. It was the smell. Not of rubbish like you'd expect. Bleach.'

'Bleach?' Eve couldn't hide the surprise in her voice.

Jack spoke. 'The pathologist reckoned she'd been scrubbed.'

Eve stored that for later. She nodded for Bob to continue.

'She was blue. From the cold. But from the bruises too.' His voice cracked. 'She looked like some kind of broken doll. All painted nails and red lipstick, but maybe that was the blood, because her face was . . .'

Eve gave Bob a minute before speaking. 'It's OK. Stick to what happened.'

He looked grateful. 'I leaned over, didn't try to find a pulse or anything; it was obvious she was gone. Her hands were behind her back. I didn't want to touch her, but the way she was lying I couldn't see if they were tied. Didn't know until after. When they moved her out of the bin. I shouldn't have been there by then, but I refused to leave.'

Eve's heart quickened. She knew Helen's hands had been tied after speaking to Jack, but from the limited paperwork she'd managed to get access to between their call last night and the journey here this morning, she hadn't found out what with.

183

'Did you see what they were tied with? Can you remember?'

'I remember everything about that day. It wasn't rope. It was thin stuff. Cord of some sort.'

'Venetian-blind cord.' It was Jack who spoke, confirming what Eve had hoped.

Cooper's face barely contained what she was already feeling.

'What happened then?'

'That's when I phoned the police, and my boss. I stayed with her until the police came. I didn't want her to be alone.'

Eve lay a hand on the man's shoulder. 'Thank you. And thanks for agreeing to come today.'

Bob shrugged. 'No problem. But it's nothing that Jack and I haven't gone over a thousand times.'

'I know, and I appreciate that. But if it in any way has a connection to what's going on at our end, then telling it one more time may help more than you know.'

They sat in a café, condensation on the windows blurring the street outside, Eve and Cooper silently relieved they'd managed to convince Jack to go there for lunch instead of home to the corned-beef sandwich and more dirty cups of tea he'd offered them.

'You think it could be the same guy?' Jack pushed the white rind hanging out of his bacon roll back in before taking a bite.

It was Cooper who answered. 'Seems a hell of a co-incidence with the drug and the cord. Both were used on Melanie and Lexie.'

Jack's eyes widened, bacon roll suspended mid-air, the grease on his chin left to dribble. 'Why didn't you say about the cord when I told you?'

Eve stretched for the tomato sauce. 'By everything you've said, Bob is a man to be trusted, but we're trying to contain things. I'm sure you can appreciate that.'

Jack put down his roll and looked like he was about to argue but said nothing, probably realizing why Eve hadn't extended the lunch invite to Bob.

'I know it's hard for you to keep him out of the loop, but I must ask that you do. Do things by the book.'

Jack would. Retired but still a cop.

'What about the state she was found in?'

Eve scraped some sauce to the side of her plate. 'That's what's not adding up. Both our women were fully clothed, found indoors; any injury to them was intended, calculated. Staged.'

Cooper prodded a sausage with his fork. 'Including the tongues. Or lack of.' He lay down his fork, pushed the plate away.

Eve waited a beat. 'What was the cause of Helen's death?'

Jack stared at her as if she'd asked a stupid question.

'I mean, did they determine whether it was the drugs, the battering? Both? Any sexual assault?'

'Pathologist said it was an overdose of ketamine. No sexual assault. The injuries were inflicted after death. According to the report, the bastard carried on laying into her long after she was dead.'

'Was there ever any kind of lead?'

'Nothing. Not from CCTV, canvassing, forensics. You name it, we did it. Nada. Not even from the footprint.'

'Footprint?' Cooper straightened. 'As in, left at the scene?'

Jack coughed. 'It was left at the scene all right but not on the ground. We found it on Helen's face.'

They fell silent around the table, minutes ticking by.

'He got it wrong.' Eve said it in a whisper.

Cooper sat forward. 'Wrong how?'

'She died before he was ready.'

'What are you saying?' Jack screwed up his features.

'She was supposed to stay alive. She was supposed to watch him take her tongue. But he gave her too high a dosage of ketamine. Instead of paralysing her, he killed her.'

Cooper saw where Eve was going. 'She humiliated him, took his control. He stripped her. Beat her and humiliated her. Stamped her out. Hid his mistake.'

Jack paled, his yellow quiff more pronounced than ever.

Eve sat back, covered her leftover food with a napkin. 'I'm willing to bet Helen Black was his practice run.'

Chapter 24

Wednesday, 20 November

Hastings whacked the rolled-up morning newspaper against the side of the desk and threw it down. 'You get her sorted out. This sensationalism bollocks – digging for every bit of scandal she can on these dead women – is shit enough, but bad-mouthing our efforts at every turn isn't helping anyone or anything.'

Eve, who had already had better starts to her day, having come from Dr Shetty's office after her weekly therapy session, unfolded the paper, revealing Jenkins' latest front page in all its glory. 'Fuck.'

'You got that right.'

The headline *'Dancing on Drugs'* was emblazoned above a picture of Lexie on stage. Eve scanned the article. Jenkins' unnamed source had given lurid details about the buckets of coke he'd been supplying Lexie with since she arrived in the UK. Her out-of-control habit, her desperation and loneliness, her hours dancing at the rented studio, and a husband who didn't care. How the dealer had been the one to give her what she needed – a regular drug lord in shining armour. No comment from Lexie's husband. An altogether different kind of headline from the one that had been left pinned to her body.

A week had passed since Lexie's death, two since Melanie's. They'd approached each day with a sense of dread, sure that Lexie wasn't going to be the last, feeling like they were sitting on a ticking time bomb, waiting for the next city-wide panic to explode in their faces. Today was the day they were suspecting things would go off. Wednesday.

But nothing.

Eve didn't take comfort from that, didn't believe for one minute it was over. Still the unrelenting pressure, the worry of another murder pushing down on her, the grip of desperation that was coming off her boss in waves.

'Give me something positive.' Hastings barked the words.

Eve clutched at what they did have, giving a rundown of their visit to St Andrews the day before.

'It's good to know that your day off gallivanting threw up something, but where does that leave us?'

'It lets us know he's probably been planning this for some time. We need to look into how he might be getting his hands on the ketamine, whether we can make any link to anyone who was in St Andrews a year ago and is in Aberdeen now. Who knows, maybe he was down there for the weekend. I've requested details on the footprint.'

'And what then? Find the shoe that matches, drive around the city looking for a warped version of Cinderella – to whomever the shoe fits?'

Eve didn't answer. There was no point.

'Do what you need to and keep me posted.' Hastings strode across the incident room towards the door. 'And make sure you talk to Jenkins.'

'Hastings is not a happy camper.' Ferguson didn't look up from his desk as he stated the obvious, his hands playing with his mobile phone.

'You don't say.' Eve let the sarcasm drip in her tone.

Mearns was standing over by Cooper, tapping on her mobile, the hint of a smile on her face.

'Something funny, Mearns?' Eve's voice was sharp as she lifted the receiver of her desk phone to call Elliott.

Mearns pocketed her mobile. 'No, ma'am.'

Eve tried to hide her surprise at Mearns calling her ma'am, and without attitude.

Elliott answered on the third ring. 'Could you come to the incident room?' She hung up.

Cooper grinned and cocked his head towards Mearns. 'Someone has an admirer.'

Eve caught the glance between Mearns and Ferguson as he came over to join them. Mearns jutted her hip against Cooper's shoulder. 'Shut it, Cooper.' She looked flustered. 'Where do you want us to start?'

They stared at Eve.

'The ketamine. We start there.'

Mearns looked unsure. 'Short of questioning every junkie out there, where exactly do we start?'

Eve rolled up the newspaper again and hit it against her hand. 'The precision with which this guy plans and carries out what he's doing, I think it's safe to say he's no junkie. The only person from that circle I want to talk to is the guy that was supplying Lexie, and not because I think he has anything to do with this but to rule out that he's not dealing in ketamine. That he can't shed any light on things. The guy we're after is switched on. Maybe we should start with professionals who have access to the drug?'

'You rang?' They all turned as Elliott appeared at the door, two coffee cups in his hands. Eve motioned to him to come in. 'Take a seat, I'll be with you in five.'

Cooper rocked in his seat. 'Professionals who have access to the drug. Vets?'

Eve nodded.

Ferguson tutted. 'What, we interview every vet in the area?'

Eve let the tut go. 'Maybe, but let's start by looking for vets who might not be as white as their coats.'

Cooper's expression showed that, for once, he was in agreement with Ferguson, thinking it was a waste of time. Mearns stood looking towards Elliott. Eve was surprised she hadn't joined in.

Her team still didn't look convinced. Eve shrugged. 'Any better ideas?' She stared at the three of them and was met with silence. 'Go to it then.' She watched them walk off.

'Sorry I haven't checked in.' Elliott slid a cup across the desk towards her.

'No worries. I don't need to be babysat. Anyhow, this makes up for it.' Eve lifted the cup and blew on the hot coffee. 'Our favourite journalist is pissing off Hastings.'

'Today's paper.'

There was resignation in Elliott's voice. She wasn't sure what the hell she was expecting him to be able to do about Jenkins. 'Don't know what she's up to,' Eve continued, 'but she's gone off radar. Surprised I haven't heard from her after she left me a voicemail.'

'Trying to get the scoop?'

'Said she had something I needed to know.'

Elliott shook his head, smiled. 'Ah, good old Jenkins. Anything to get you to bite. Let me guess, she didn't give any clue as to what that might've been?' He stood to leave.

Eve nodded. 'You know her . . . Anyway, let me know if you get hold of her. I'll keep trying too, see if talking to her means we can find Lexie's dealer friend.'

Elliott threw his coffee cup in the bucket by Eve's desk. 'Let me see what I can do.' He walked to the door, then stopped to turn around. 'Not a lot, I expect. I don't think I'll be her favourite person after shooting her down at the press briefing. My favours will be done.' He waved once and disappeared down the hall.

Eve stared at the crime-file photo on her computer screen as she hung up the phone yet again. She'd been trying Jenkins all morning, both at the office and on her mobile, but all her colleagues would tell Eve was that she was out on a job.

Eve shuffled her seat closer to the desk, read the notes accompanying the photo for the hundredth time. The shot showed the bruised and battered flesh below Helen Black's cheekbone, a partial shoe print magnified upon the damaged skin. The young woman was barely recognizable compared to the other picture of her on file – one of her in life: vibrant, beautiful. Just as Melanie and Lexie had been. Was it a coincidence that they all had the same colouring? The same long brown hair, same almond-shaped eyes?

Eve could make out the letter 'C' imprinted on Helen's soft face. Through the miracles of modern science, Jack's people had been able to match the print to 'Carolina' work boots manufactured in America, not a common brand in the UK. It had given them hope but had come to nothing.

Eve made a note to have Ferguson check out work-wear companies that operated or supplied to companies throughout the UK, see if any of them stocked the boots. Something she knew had been done a year ago, but it wouldn't hurt to check again. She smiled, imagining Ferguson's reaction when she gave him the arduous task. They might be finding a way to work together, but she could still take pleasure in the small things. Her moment of enjoyment was interrupted as her team came rushing into the office.

'Something you'll want to see.' The excitement was obvious in Ferguson's voice, and definitely a surprise, as he tossed the press clipping in front of Eve. 'The bell that was ringing for me when you mentioned vets.' Ferguson tapped his finger against the paper. 'Adrian

Hardy. Veterinary assistant for a practice in the West End. *Was*. Sacked over a year ago and done for theft.'

'Ketamine?' Eve felt the familiar stirrings of excitement at a possible lead. She ignored the fact that Ferguson had shown no sign of any bell ringing when he'd tutted and questioned her instruction earlier. But, then again, reading Ferguson and his ways was next to impossible sometimes.

Mearns butted in. 'Yup. And anything and everything else by the sounds of things.'

Maybe it was Mearns who had made the connection. The two of them were in cahoots. Ferguson would be happy to take the glory, and perhaps if there was something going on Mearns would be happy to give him it.

Ferguson nodded. 'Sanders was the arresting officer.'

A memory fought to rise to the forefront of Eve's mind. Countless drug-related arrests over the years. This one obviously hadn't stood out against any other at the time. Nothing more than a coincidence that it had been Sanders who arrested him.

Ferguson paused. 'And he's been in trouble before.'

Eve saw the glint in Ferguson's eye. She was glad to see the fire back in him, regardless of his problem with her. 'Go on.'

'Our Mr Hardy had been cautioned for stalking six months before the theft. Seems he had a bit of a thing for a young lass that lived in his neighbourhood. Never went beyond the warning though. But maybe he had some unresolved issues, if you get what I mean.'

193

Eve did a quick count in her head. 'Issues that he might've still been dealing with around about the same time Helen Black was murdered.'

'Bingo.'

'Anything linking him to her or St Andrews?'

'Not that we've found.'

'We know where he is?'

Cooper hadn't said a word, probably as confused as Eve as to how Ferguson and Mearns had found the connection. Still, it didn't matter. They had a lead.

Ferguson carried on. 'Got off lightly with the theft. Two-year suspended sentence. Did his eighty hours of community service. Last known working at a pet shop. Seems his love of animals might be genuine.'

Eve frowned. She looked at the clock on the wall, realized she'd missed the last dose of her painkillers and that it was a first. Too busy for pain. She opened her drawer and felt for the bottle.

Eve lifted the glass of lukewarm water on her desk, saw Mearns walking to the door. She was making small chat with the guy standing there, signing for something. Eve craned her neck. She swallowed the pills as Mearns turned from the courier.

Mearns was carrying a small brown-paper-wrapped package in her hand, its edges wet from the rain falling outside. Cooper and Ferguson were watching her as she approached.

'For you.' Mearns placed the package on the desk.

Eve picked it up, turning it this way and that. 'What is it?' She felt stupid when she saw Mearns' face. 'Yeah. OK. Open it. I hear you.' She grabbed a pencil

194

and poked a hole in the damp paper before ripping it open.

'What the . . .'

It was a ceramic box. A trinket box of some sort, its lid the face of a crying Harlequin. Taped shut with masking tape. Eve's flesh went clammy.

'Never thought of you as being a girly girl.' Mearns' attempt at humour sounded forced. Cooper and Ferguson stood watching.

Eve laid down the box, opened her drawer again, this time reaching for latex gloves. She wasn't taking any chances.

Not one of them said a word as she prised at the tape with the point of the penknife on her keyring. She ran the blade around the edges of the box, sat back once the seal had been broken.

She looked up at her colleagues, willing them to count to three for her. With trembling hands, Eve lifted the lid.

Newspaper. She breathed out.

The paper was scrunched like the poxy tissue wrap that was all the rage in gifts these days. Eve picked at the wrinkled paper, peeling it back bit by bit, careful not to rip it. She paused. The smell mingling with damp newspaper made Eve want to lift her hand to her nose. But she didn't, keeping the gloves as clean as possible.

One more layer . . . Eve holding her breath, sure she recognized the newspaper article that was being revealed bit by bit.

It was Cooper who broke the silence. 'Jesus Christ.' His voice sounded strangled.

Mearns gasped, grabbing the edge of the desk to steady herself, Ferguson putting a protective hand to the base of her back as she did.

No doubt about the newspaper article. Eve swallowed, stared at the severed tongue in front of her. Gift-wrapped. The blue piercing at its plump centre answering all of her unanswered calls to Jenkins.

Chapter 25

EVE PLACED THE SHEET of paper on the polished oak table in front of Sanders and her husband. Archie took hold of his wife's hand.

'What does it mean?' Archie's trembling voice belied the masculine grip.

Their hands lay together on the padded arm of Sanders' wheelchair. Archie's black-haired, fleshy fingers covering the spindly digits beneath.

She shrugged. 'Whatever it means, it's just got personal.'

A colour photocopy of the original article, the scrunched-up paper in which Jenkins' tongue had been sent lay spread out: red and black ink upon greying paper, Sanders' and Eve's faces looking warped amongst the many creases.

But the thick black letters of the headline were still as bold and loud as they had been back then – shouting at the injustice of Sanders' injuries, the words below whispering at Eve's guilt. Making sure the reader was clear this was the same woman who had run a suspect off the road. The same fellow officer with her at the time whose life had been put in the balance, with the scale finally tipping.

It was Jenkins' front page. The page marking the event that changed their lives for ever.

Sanders' eyes searched Eve's. 'How did they get hold of that article – an original?'

'I've asked Elliott to look into that. But it seems our killer has easy access to these things.'

She didn't say the most obvious answer was that someone had cut them out at the time of publication, intending to use them later.

Eve picked at the side of her finger. 'I was lying in a hospital bed the first time I saw that story. Cooper was there and I was demanding to see you, to know how you were. Feeling like shit, knowing I'd let you down.' She picked harder at her finger, didn't say out loud that Cooper had been telling her over and over that it wasn't her fault.

'Cooper tried to block my view of the trolley as it made the rounds of the ward, to hide the newspaper and the truth of what people were saying – what they were thinking.' She looked to the floor, sat in silence.

Archie set his mouth in a tight line. Sanders said nothing.

'I wanted to silence Jenkins. I hated her – but not for what she was saying about me. It wasn't that. It was how she was able to write what was inside of me. All the guilt, the shame, the anger.' Eve didn't care if Archie might be enjoying her confession.

'I couldn't deal with that, but I kept reading. Every day. Letting her beat me with her words, knowing I deserved them but wanting, praying for her to stop.' Eve paused, letting the silence stretch. 'Jenkins won't be saying anything ever again. Won't be able to do to people what she seemed to always take pleasure in doing. In some strange way I should be glad, but I'm not. I deserved what she did, but no one deserves what she got. Just like you don't deserve that.' She nodded towards the wheelchair, waiting for Archie to lay into her, but he didn't.

'What if all this is because of what I did? I mean, isn't that what this is?' Eve jabbed at the evidence bag, shifting it across the table and on to the floor. She wanted Archie to lay into her. To say what he'd always wanted to say, not buying into the bullshit forgiveness he'd been forced to give. But he sat there, clasping his wife's hand, controlled, contained.

Sanders didn't argue with Eve. 'But why? Who? They're all still inside.'

'I know. But what else can it be?' Eve was pissed at herself, feeling like a whining puppy, wanting instead to be top dog, to be in control of what was going on.

'There must be a reason that front page has been dredged up. It has to be something to do with what happened. Maybe I should go and see MacNeill. Find out whether they're influencing anyone on the outside.'

'Can you trust yourself to be in the same room as him?' Sanders' voice was low, dangerous. 'If I wasn't in this thing, I know I wouldn't be able to control myself.'

Eve carried on. 'In there I can. Outside would be a different story.'

Sanders shook her head. 'They're bad bastards, but they don't fit this. They're not that clever and – as stupid as it sounds, considering – I don't think even they're bad enough for this.'

'Maybe not, but we can write it off, eliminate them from inquiries. Anyway, I think it's time that me and MacNeill had a little chat. I want to see him face to face.'

Sanders was silent for a moment. When she spoke, her voice was resigned, changing the subject. 'Have you got anything at all to go on otherwise?'

Eve filled Sanders in on their trip to St Andrews. 'There has to be a reason why he's waiting a week between. There's a message he's trying to send us. How he's killing them. A reason for everything, even the harlequin on the box he sent. We can't see it yet, but we bloody need to, and fast.'

'Any word on what happened to Jenkins?'

'They found her body at her flat, hands still bound in venetian-blind cord, no sign of forced entry. MacLean reckons she'd only been dead a matter of hours when the tongue was delivered. But she'd been missing since Monday night. It appears the bastard kept her tied up during that time.'

'Have you found the dealer she met with about Lexie?'

'We found out that she met a guy at the Highland Hotel for a meal the night she was killed. Her boss says she phoned in on her way home, around nine p.m. He says she was all excited about the Lexie story. That she typed it up before phoning him. Filed it there and then. But she also said that the story was so much bigger than that. That there was more to come.'

Eve let that sink in before her next revelation. 'And then she phoned me. But I didn't answer. She left the same message as what she'd told her boss.'

'What? Eve . . .' Sanders' expression said what Eve hadn't stopped thinking herself. *If only she'd answered the phone.*

Eve swallowed. 'No one heard from her after that. We managed to get a description of the dealer from the waiter that served them. No CCTV on the premises, but I've got the team trawling cameras in the surrounding streets and the route to Jenkins' home. Maybe we'll get a hit. A search of her flat found nothing related to what she was working on. She was obviously storing it in her head overnight.'

'And do you think—'

'I don't think for a minute he's our guy.' Eve stood. 'But, whoever he is, I believe he's somehow connected to all this. Anyway, I better get going.'

Eve stood, had an overwhelming urge to say sorry again. But she stepped away instead, crouched to get the paper still lying on the floor and looked at the front page again. 'Don't worry. I think this is about me, not you.'

Eve looked at Archie. 'You take care of her.' Archie's lips twitched. She turned once more to Sanders. 'I'll be back to see you soon.'

Eve saw herself to the door, not wanting them to see the doubt on her face. She hoped this was about her.

But she had no idea why it would be. She wasn't linked to the first two women who had been killed. She had no idea who they were or who was targeting them. But that person knew her. Her life. It wasn't some game. Nor were the lives of the women who had lost theirs.

Her life, and someone had got too involved in it. Eve lifted her coat collar against the wind as she walked to the car, shivering as she did, nothing to do with the cold air. What was going on? She was supposed to chase the bad guys and they were supposed to run. But this time it looked like someone was coming for her and, although she'd never say it out loud, it scared the shit out of her.

Chapter 26

Thursday, 21 November

JOHNNY MACNEILL SNR'S FAT bald head gleamed like a polished bowling ball beneath the glare of the strip lights as the massive bulk of him rocked on a chair which remained upright, somehow defying gravity. His solid thick arms were stretched out in front, handcuffed wrists and clasped hands resting on the edge of the table separating him from his visitor.

Eve worked her tongue behind closed lips, trying to draw water into a desert-dry mouth. She hadn't expected fear. Rage, yes, but not fear. Anger had always been her go-to whenever she thought of the man in front of her, but that had abandoned her as soon as she walked into the Peterhead Prison room.

Eve's eyes were fixed on MacNeill's as her guts churned. She would not show weakness, never had, but it was proving harder sitting opposite the person responsible for ripping her life apart and leaving Sanders for dead. She felt shame for being scared – like she was failing Sanders again: a loyal partner trapped within a body that might as well be made of stone.

Beyond MacNeill's mountainous frame, a warder stood by the door in the corner. The room was bright and modern, the new-build a far cry from the old Peterhead Prison, which now served as a popular tourist attraction. Eve could think of better places to go on her time off.

She was still assessing whether the pale, skinny runt of a warder would be of any use to her if things were to turn nasty. When she looked at MacNeill, the sight of the smirk on his flabby cracked lips turned her stomach.

Eve spoke for the first time. 'Looks like your appetite hasn't suffered in here.' In all the imagined conversations she'd had with MacNeill, that was never her opening. Still, she was relieved there was no tremor when she spoke.

'Takes a lot to put me off my grub.'

Eve clenched her fists beneath the table. From what she knew of MacNeill, nothing had ever troubled the man. Nothing apart from what had happened to his son, that is.

'How's Johnny Junior these days?' Eve took perverse pleasure in seeing MacNeill's oversized, tattooed hands flex within the metal shackles, dimpled knuckles whitening beneath faded ink.

'You don't ask about my son.'

'I think I just did.' Eve was warming to her theme, an image of Sanders kept in the forefront of her mind, awakening the rage.

MacNeill's jaw was grinding, several chins wobbling beneath black stubble. 'Doing about as good as that lady friend of yours.'

Barely contained fury, the words hissing through gritted teeth. She leaned back in her chair, keeping eye contact, relaxing her posture. 'And that about sums it up, doesn't it? Tit for tat. Payback.'

MacNeill smiled, chilling Eve to the core. 'Dead would've been good, but the way things turned out? Couldn't have asked for better – the bitch gets to suffer every day, a constant reminder of what she did. You too.' MacNeill motioned towards Eve's legs, hidden beneath the table.

'Your son was a vicious bastard, a drug dealer who terrorized the streets and a rapist to boot. Did you ever see the photographs of what he did to Lynne?'

They were clear in her mind. It tortured her, wondering whether it was how her mother had looked after what Eve's father had done to her.

MacNeill shrugged. 'The cow deserved everything she got. Word is she was putting it about.'

'Come on, MacNeill, your son had her under lock and key. She was terrified, been getting battered and raped by him for years.'

'She needed kept under control.'

Eve's nostrils flared, but she said nothing. There was no point with a monster like MacNeill. The man had reared his son true to his own form. That fact haunted Eve. She'd always feared which traits of her father were in her, what lay beneath the surface of the person she was determined to be. She shook the thought from her mind, focused on MacNeill. Eve struggled to believe that his long-suffering wife, Johnny Jnr's mother, still visited like clockwork.

'Anyway, I'm forgetting. You probably would've enjoyed the photographs, and the last thing I want to give you is any pleasure in life.' Eve lifted the plastic cup of water in front of her, sipped and took her time lowering it to the table before continuing.

'I hear she's thriving. The only good to come out of what happened is that Lynne, after years of trying to leave, finally got away. All thanks to their neighbour finally growing some balls and picking up the phone.'

MacNeill's struggle with that first bit of information was visible. 'I couldn't give a shit how she's doing. What I do give a shit about is the way you pigs went straight round there, no questions asked, and chased my son out of his own home.'

Eve laughed. 'Your son was shimmying the drainpipe before we got to the top of the stairs. He chose to run. The state Lynne was in, he had no choice.'

Lynne lying unconscious in the bathroom: the image she could never shake. Bright-red blood spattered against the white porcelain of the toilet, sprayed across the flaking wall tiles, three jagged teeth lying by the grubby sink's pedestal.

Then the car chase.

Six weeks in a coma. When Johnny Jnr finally woke, he didn't remember a thing, including how to walk, talk or take a shit by himself. Last Eve heard, things hadn't changed.

'You were drunk that night.' MacNeill said the words softly, taking Eve by surprise, not only with his tone.

The warder stared straight ahead, pretending not to hear.

MacNeill leaned forward. 'I'm not speaking about the night you went after Johnny. I'm talking about the night we dealt with you.'

Eve's blood gushed in her ears so loudly she wondered if MacNeill could hear it. She wanted to deny it to his face, even after Jenkins' articles hinting at it time and time again through statements from MacNeill, accusations that were never taken seriously by her superiors, or anyone else. Why would they be from pond life like him – a drug dealer and someone with a grudge to bear?

Only Sanders, her husband Archie, Cooper, and of course, Elliott knew the truth. But there were those, DC Ferguson one of them, Mearns another, who clearly had questioned MacNeill's accusations.

MacNeill's sausage-like fingers were gripped together tight. They looked fit to burst. 'I smelled it on you. Above the mint on your breath and your false steady walk. A walk that I took from you. I smelled it. As you lay there. You know I did. And you know that's why you couldn't save her.'

Eve dipped her eyes to the floor, tried to swallow the ball stuck in her throat, seeing that night playing out like a horror movie in her mind, frame by frame, in slow motion, like always.

Sitting outside the Queen Vic with Elliott. Her birthday. A reminder that she was here only because she'd been conceived through rape. A day she chose not to celebrate. Sanders collecting her from out front of the Queen Vic, and on the way to the call Eve sitting with her head tilted, eyes closed, realizing she was more drunk than she'd thought. Blaming the stress and lack of sleep for how quickly the wine had gone to her head, waving Sanders' concerns away. The call-out wasn't an address they'd ever been to and didn't arouse any suspicion as they got out of the car and approached.

Eve was barely over the threshold when a burly skin-headed guy stepped out from a side room and slammed a baseball bat into her guts, bringing her to her knees – winded, ready to puke, the acid taste of partially digested red wine forced up to her throat.

Her first thought was Sanders. Right behind her. In danger. She tried to stand, but her legs failed her – dizzy with the shock, surprisingly unsteady with the drink.

Then a fist flew towards her, making contact with her cheek and eye, keeping her floored. She squinted, blood blurring her vision of Sanders being propelled along the hallway towards an open door.

She could make out an empty armchair, two more guys standing beside it, knew she'd seen them before. A carpet, 1970s swirls dominating it as well as the armchair, and she wondered why the hell that was registering in her foggy brain. Her eyes went to Sanders, watching the first heavy's hand clutch the bun at the back of her neck, still pushing her forward, Sanders jogging to stop herself from tripping.

She was shoved into the room. And then silence. Eve couldn't see her either. The next sound was MacNeill speaking. They were in trouble, even though the voice was too low to make out what he was saying.

That's where she knew the guys from. MacNeill's heavies, always in the background whenever he appeared on the news or in the press, bumping his gums about his son's downfall.

Eve struggled to her feet, half-expecting the men she could see, one with a spider's-web tattoo on his temple, to come at her. She needed to radio in for help, realized in that moment that she'd left the radio at the station when she knew she was off shift and headed to the pub.

Her mobile.

She patted her jacket pocket. Nothing.

Her trouser pockets.

It was there.

Relief flooded her. She pulled it from her pocket, held it up to her face, the numbered keys swimming in front of her eyes.

How the hell had she got so drunk?

She put out a hand to steady herself against the wall. She felt sick, unsure if it was the blow to her stomach or the drink.

How could she have been that stupid? To drink and then agree to accompany Sanders?

She managed to unlock the phone, heart beating as she scrolled through for the number to dial. Found it. She looked ahead to make sure no one was coming for her . . . and dropped the phone. She moaned as she leaned forward, the hallway spinning as she bent to pick it up. The push to her backside stunned her, toppling her forward, face planting on the floor. She cried out as her nose hit carpet. She looked behind her – the same guy who hit her had shoved her on the backside. He was smiling.

She tried to get up, pushing her palms against the floor, forearms shaking as she did. All it achieved was exposing the mobile phone she had landed on. She watched helpless and in horror as the guy crouched beside her, snatched the phone from beneath her and stood. Her arms collapsed.

So close, just one more button to press and she would've made the call.

She saw the phone being placed on the floor by her head. In slow motion, she went to reach for it as she saw the big black boot come down on it, crushing and cracking the phone in front of her eyes.

And then she was being lifted. Roughly. Being shoved into the room that Sanders had disappeared into.

She steeled herself against the dizziness and the ringing in her ears, doubting the fight she had left in her. Her heart felt in danger of exploding. Eve stumbled, half-held up by MacNeill's man. And froze.

'Nice of you to drop by.'

Even in the rage that clouded Eve's vision, she saw MacNeill weighing down on Sanders' legs. Sanders' radio was lying on the floor beside her, intact.

She flew across the room at MacNeill, all dizziness and unsteadiness forgotten in the adrenaline of fury. And then the baseball bat that had floored her was on her once again. This time targeted at her lower legs, sending her crashing to the floor, face first, her delayed reflexes stopping her arms protecting her from the fall, her stomach slamming against the threadbare carpet, vomit threatening again.

She'd known the heavy would act, but she hadn't cared. She started caring around the fourth whack to the back of her legs and the side of her thighs when the searing pain registered through the red veil that had descended on seeing Sanders lying there.

As she howled in pain, she never stopped looking at Sanders, even when she saw MacNeill lift his foot and stamp on the radio, the crack audible above the chaos. Eve glanced to the smashed radio before looking at Sanders, sure she could see blame in her eyes.

If she hadn't let her temper control her.

If she hadn't rushed at MacNeill but tried something else that could've got her to the radio.

As the hate for herself crept in, Eve's eyes were begging Sanders to fight, to get up. Realizing her colleague's silence hadn't been bravery but thick masking tape stuck fast against her mouth, binding her arms beneath her back, unable to reach the radio, to call for help. Sanders stared at her, pleading, probably desperately hoping Eve had used her mobile phone, tears trickling down the side of her face to the floor, both of them willing their eye contact to block out what was happening, to transport them out of there.

But the blows kept raining on Eve. Which one wrecked her leg, she'd never know. She'd forced herself to open her eyes when the blows stopped, saw MacNeill standing, stepping over Sanders and walking to one of his heavies. Smiling as he took the bat from his hands.

Everything slowed around Eve, every movement magnified, her lungs feeling like the air had been sucked from the room.

Fighting to stop what was about to happen, she dug her nails into the carpet, gathering everything she had left, trying to pull herself over to Sanders – even though she knew she'd never get there in time and could do nothing to stop what had been set in motion once she did.

She felt something weighing her down, turned her head to see what it was. MacNeill's foot. He was stroking Eve's cheek with the baseball bat, enjoying every minute. He lifted his foot and kneeled by her side, leaning in close.

'Had one too many, Detective?'

Eve tried to grab MacNeill, catching fresh air instead.

'Shit aim. It's going to cost you, but your partner over there will pay more.'

MacNeill walked backwards to Sanders, each step painfully slow, never taking his gaze off Eve.

Eve had nothing left, was forced to look on, her brain struggling to process what she was seeing as MacNeill turned Sanders over on to her front, the shock of the attack leaving her as pliable as putty.

The last thing Eve saw was the baseball bat being lifted high above MacNeill's head like a trophy, the fat on his upper arms wobbling as he stretched, and the slow-motion drop of the bat slicing through the air before it smashed into the base of Sanders' spine. Hearing the crack of wood from somewhere far off, feet thudding against the floor, voices shouting, panic setting in around her.

Darkness.

To this day, they had no idea how MacNeill and his men had known they'd be on duty. All she did know was that they'd got what they wanted. Payback.

She and Sanders weren't supposed to survive that night, wouldn't have if Ferguson and another officer hadn't been dispatched after a concerned call from a neighbour. The same way Lynne had been saved. Community spirit wasn't dead after all. And neither were they. But they would never be the same again, Sanders especially. And she knew Ferguson still lived with the guilt that he should have got to them sooner. That no one had followed up on the call-out, even when it had been so long since Sanders or Eve had touched base. No suspicion or checks when perhaps there should have been. The realization his fellow officers were in trouble coming only once the neighbour called it in.

Payback. Nothing more, nothing less. And Sanders had been paying for it every day since.

Eve forced the thoughts away, her backbone now rock hard, fighting an urge to lunge across the prison table, to squeeze MacNeill's fat neck until he took his last breath. Revenge. Prison wasn't – never would be – enough.

'Are you done?' Eve stared at MacNeill.

'Bitch. I'm never done. There's always someone willing to run things out there for me.'

'I'm not talking about running drugs. I meant with us. Me and Sanders.'

'I'll never be done until you tell everyone.'

'Tell everyone what?'

'That you were drunk that night. And the way you chased my son off that road was your fault and yours alone. That if it hadn't been for you, my son might not be a fucking vegetable.'

Eve didn't move.

MacNeill edged closer. 'You think you're safe out there, but I can get to you any time I want.'

Eve leaned in closer still, whispered. 'Yeah, I was pissed that night. I'm not proud of that fact. But I'll never give you your moment. And as for your son? As far as I'm concerned, he deserves everything he got.'

Eve leaned back fast, avoiding MacNeill's attempt to thump her with his bound wrists, dodging the spilled water as MacNeill bumped against the table. She smiled as she sat back in her chair and watched the warder grapple MacNeill into the chair and on to his massive backside again. Not bad for a lightweight.

MacNeill was out of breath. Furious. Wanting to lash out but knowing that if he tried it again, he'd be removed.

Eve sat.

MacNeill was desperate for a bite. 'I'll finish what I started with you if I ever get out of this shithole. Meantime, I know plenty of people on the outside who are more than willing to have a little fun with you.'

Eve couldn't be sure if he was playing her or not. But she did know he was pathetic – hard to believe she'd ever feared him. She reached inside her jacket, saw the warder shifting, getting ready to move again, but stopping when he saw what was in Eve's hand.

Eve put the plastic-covered front page, the one of her and Sanders, on the table, turning it so MacNeill could read the headline.

'You got anything to do with this?'

'Yeah, you stupid cow, I was the one that made sure she wouldn't walk again.'

Eve waited, searching MacNeill's face for any sign he was keeping something from her. 'This was sent to me recently. I wondered if you or one of your heavies were trying to tell me something.'

She didn't divulge what it had been wrapped around, knew that MacNeill would know what had been going on from the papers and prison gossip but not about the newspaper cutting or how it would be connected to that. Nothing about the other headlines.

MacNeill nudged the article with his fist. 'What if I am?'

Her neck pulsed. MacNeill was riling her.

'It's in your interests to tell me, to stop all this, if you are.'

MacNeill shook his head. 'And spoil the fun?'

He was playing her; he had to be. Eve stood, pushed back her chair, not wanting to give him any more time, knowing he wouldn't tell her anything even if he was behind what was going on.

'You enjoy your time in here and the safety it brings you.' She stared MacNeill down, powerful standing above the seated, shackled excuse for a man.

MacNeill wanted to keep her there, to have her under his control. When he spoke, Eve tried to look as if his voice and his words had no effect on her.

'This is all going to come out. It's going to expose you for the lies you told. They're going to bring you down for Johnny Junior.'

Eve walked to the door.

'Do you hear me, Hunter?'

MacNeill shouted over and over again. She stopped when she reached the door and turned, halting MacNeill's tirade.

'You failed to bring me down, MacNeill. And your son? He brought himself down. You think you won something getting me and Sanders that night? You think you're going to win if you do have anything to do with this? You're the one stuck in here.'

Eve walked from the room, wanting to believe that MacNeill was helpless in here – that he couldn't possibly be responsible for what was happening on the outside.

Chapter 27

MEARNS HID IN THE toilet cubicle and sat on the closed lid of the seat, reading the words on her mobile-phone screen again, looking at the smiley emoji at the end of them. *Thinking of you. Want to do it again?*

Mearns had never been short of male attention, and that hadn't changed since her move to Aberdeen. But she'd always said no. No time for anything else but the job – wanting to make sure she held respect as an officer.

Why had she given in this time?

That night when Eve had given her a lift home from Cooper's, the night she'd finally taken a good long, hard look at herself. She'd yearned to make her guilt and her feelings of failure disappear, to simply feel wanted and that she was a good person. She'd waited until Eve had driven away and then texted him to meet up, feeling more and more pathetic as she waited for him to reply. Thinking he was never going to. And then the relief when he had, and she'd gone to see him.

She'd awoken the next morning feeling regret, desperate to make excuses to leave, but he'd been standing there, a full tray of breakfast held in his hands, that side to him he kept hidden. She'd surprised herself by pulling him back into bed.

The last couple of weeks had been out of character. Letting someone in. She wasn't sure it was what she wanted. Maybe she was using him to feel better about herself, to cope with the worst job she'd ever been on. She'd seen things on this case that she knew would never leave her and was more committed than ever to finding the bastard who was doing them.

But for the first time ever she'd been able to step away from the job, if only for a short while. Not to forget about the job exactly – she couldn't ever forget about the women who had lost their lives – but able to find something for herself in amongst the horrors of what she did for a living, to find a little sanity in a world that sometimes seemed mad.

She read the text again. Was she using him? Was that why she hadn't mentioned anything to Cooper and Eve? She sensed it upset him that she wanted to be secretive. It was complicated. Private. Not important compared to what they were working on. At least that's what she'd told him but she knew it was bullshit.

The truth was, she wanted Eve to respect her. And that revelation when it hit her was like a truck – as far removed from how she'd felt when Eve returned to work as she could've ever imagined. And she knew he wouldn't understand, not after everything that had been said about Eve.

It wouldn't hurt to keep things quiet, to make sure it wasn't some whim, that she did care for the guy. Then and only then would she tell anyone.

'Mearns, you in there?'

Mearns jumped up from the toilet lid, opened the door to answer Cooper. The wide swing door into the department's toilets was slightly ajar, Cooper standing outside, only his fingers curled around the door visible.

'One second.'

'No probs. Sorry to interrupt. We found the vet.'

Mearns picked up the plastic cup she'd left behind when she'd gone to the toilet and perched on the edge of Cooper's desk, waiting for him and Ferguson to update her.

Cooper started. 'He's been staying at an aunt's locally. Got in touch with her, seems she can see no wrong in our Adrian Hardy – done for stealing drugs from his work or not.'

'She let him know we want to talk to him?'

'Yeah. Eve's on her way, says she'll meet me there.'

Mearns tried to hide the look on her face. Pissed off, desperate to get more involved. She looked at Ferguson as he spoke up.

'And us? It was me who made the connection.'

He sounded like a petulant kid, but Mearns could understand why he was annoyed.

Cooper shrugged. 'Eve wants you guys to go see Lexie's dealer, the guy Jenkins met with the night she was killed.'

219

'We found him?' Ferguson was sounding a little less pissed off.

'Yeah, turns out the bar staff at the hotel got yapping about what had happened, spoke about the guy, and the barman who'd come on shift recognized the description. He phoned in, says he knows where the guy hangs out.' Cooper ripped off the top sheet of his notebook and passed it to Mearns. 'This is the pub you'll find him at.'

Mearns took the paper, glanced at the address and then Ferguson before pocketing it. 'Classy joint.' She felt appeased – at least a little. 'How did she get on anyway?'

Mearns knew it must've been hard coming face to face with MacNeill.

'She can't be sure. Thinks MacNeill might be toying with her.' Cooper looked at Mearns.

'What's she thinking about Hardy?'

'Says she can't ignore the facts.' Cooper made a point of focusing his attention on Ferguson. 'Facts you brought to her, such as the ketamine, the stalking.'

Mearns didn't miss the straightening of Ferguson's posture, his ego being stroked expertly by Cooper.

Cooper smiled. 'At first, as good as it looked, it was at best a long shot. But on having a nice friendly chat with his lovely aunt, it seems it might not be such a long shot after all.'

Mearns frowned, waiting for Cooper to say more.

'Guess where his aunt moved from last year?'

'You're shitting me.'

'Nope. St Andrews.'

Mearns' heartbeat quickened. It was too much of a coincidence, surely.

Eve drove fast, wanting to leave MacNeill behind in more ways than one. Glad to be heading to Aberdeen, leaving the busy fishing port of Peterhead and her past behind. Peterhead was known locally as the Bloo Toon, supposedly because of the blue stockings that the fishermen originally wore, but Eve chose to believe it was more to do with how cold the bloody place was.

She squinted against the low winter sun bouncing off the wet road ahead but resisted flipping the visor, wanting instead to soak up the brightness of the day: clear blue skies stretching out in front of her, muddy green fields re-emerging from beneath thawing snowfall and speeding ever faster past her.

She turned up the volume on the car stereo, Original FM playing a song that reminded her of her youth. Before everything. The synthetic 1980s beats of OMD vibrated from the speakers, immersing her for a moment in the comfort of childhood memories.

Someone had sent that front page. Wrapped around Jenkins' tongue. And that person wanted to make it clear it was personal. If not MacNeill, then who?

Eve discarded the thought as quickly as it came. She wanted, no, she *needed*, this moment, this break from everything that was going on – no matter how short-lived. Even if it was only going to last the distance left before reaching Aberdeen. She glanced at the dusty dashboard clock. She was making good time for meeting Cooper.

Her mind wandered to Adrian Hardy. That damned front page creeping into her mind again, refusing to go away. The only connection Hardy had to Eve, and a tenuous one at that, was the fact Sanders, a member of her team, had arrested him. But could Hardy be MacNeill's puppet? The ketamine? Had they known each other on the drugs scene? Had MacNeill kept up his supply? Did it have to be connected to her and Sanders? Could it be someone playing with her, trying to shake her? It was whether Hardy would be capable of it, and why. She had no idea.

The vet link had been a stab in the dark. More desperate than she'd let on to her team, though their faces had said they thought it anyway. Now that it had turned up Hardy, with his history of ketamine theft and stalking, it seemed too neat, almost as if Hardy was being delivered to them. But earlier, when Cooper had called her, breathless with excitement at the St Andrews link, it had dampened the voice of doubt whispering in Eve's ear. Package-wrapped or not, the facts couldn't be ignored.

She was distracted by her thoughts when the sign for Balmedie showed ahead. Twenty minutes until she reached the city. She had to think about how she was going to handle Hardy. The possibility they might be on the verge of a breakthrough buoyed Eve, more than she thought possible today. To have hope that this could be the week that they stopped another woman losing her life made Eve press that little bit harder on the accelerator.

Chapter 28

Then

They're downstairs. In the kitchen. Together. Mum and Dad.

The cross-stitched fabric hanging above the bed pulses in the flickering light from the streetlight outside. Dirty yellow creeping in through the flaking painted panes of the window, spreading out across the pale-blue wall, clinging to the multi-coloured threads that never used to mean anything. The fabric hanging that had once hung above her bed now moved to above his.

The letters are embroidered on tiny white squares, material that's always reminded him of waffles. He knows the words off by heart, even the few that manage to shrink away from the light. Taking his time over each one, whispering every line, lines that mean everything. That help to make sense of it all. The lies. All of them.

Satisfied, he burrows beneath the single duvet, brightly coloured rockets, moons and stars covering him – imagining being swallowed by space. Lost in darkness. Glad of the teddy he holds in his hand. He's not alone. Between two chubby fingers he squeezes at fur. Slides his fingers to the top of the teddy's ear before letting go and starting again. A movement he finds comforting.

From downstairs he hears the scrape of a dining-room chair against linoleum. Dishes clattering as they're collected from the table. Water gushing from the tap into the sink. Nothing else. At least he knows they're still here.

When they come to check on him, if they do, he'll close his eyes, breathe deep. Tell a lie like Mum does. Make it easier for Dad. But he'll make sure Teddy's tucked away out of sight. Safe beneath him, because he knows Mum won't like him having it. Not her teddy.

He wonders if they ever liked having him. He knows she's their favourite. He doesn't mind though. Because she's his favourite too.

He thinks about her long brown hair, sees her cute little nose, the way her eyes twinkled when she smiled at him. Eyes that had reminded him of chocolate. Like the buttons in the purple packets they used to get as a treat if they'd been good. The picture of her in his head is clear. Right there. He could almost reach out and touch her. She'd been pretty, but he'd never told her that.

The muffled sounds of soapy water sloshing in the plastic basin drift up the stairs, wet dishes being stacked against each other on the draining board, wooden drawers being pulled open, cupboards being slammed shut. Nothing else. He remembers a time when he would hear them talking, laughing.

But he knows they'll still be standing side by side. At the sink, by the window. Like before. Except nothing like before.

Moving about the kitchen, stepping around each other as if they're doing some silly little dance. Reminding him of a musical they once took them to see at the theatre, but without the sound. Acting. Pretending. Silent. Lying.

Chapter 29

THE WORN TEAK TABLE and scored orange plastic mats reminded Eve of Sunday meals with her grandmother as a kid. It was the rest of the room that let down the memory. Muriel Hardy's kitchen was sparse, lacked warmth and matched her demeanour. The terraced council house in Seaton Drive was badly in need of refurbishment.

Eve jumped as the kettle on the gas cooker top whistled causing Muriel, a floral tabard covering her blouse and skirt, to stand to attention and start clattering cups about on the worktop.

Adrian Hardy sat opposite Eve and had the good fortune of being able to move his chair – unlike Cooper and her, who had been sandwiched in against the wall, their legs crammed beneath, grappling for space amongst the wooden joists holding the side panels of the table that were probably usually folded away to allow for some space in the small room. Eve's leg was starting to throb, but she hid her discomfort, not wanting to show any sign of weakness.

Hardy was sitting poker straight, legs crossed, his hands overlapping on his thigh, jeans riding up pale, skinny legs. He looked a world away from someone who would steal drugs from their workplace, but it had been proved that he had. And what did that kind of person look like anyway?

Criminals didn't come packaged and advertising what was within. Although MacNeill's appearance did give a pretty good indication of what you were getting. Was it possible Hardy knew MacNeill? Would MacNeill trust this guy to do business on his behalf? Maybe that would be the key to everything, but she'd keep it out of the interview for now.

Eve broke the silence. 'Thanks for agreeing to our visit, Mr Hardy, especially at such short notice.'

'I wasn't doing anything better. And it's Adrian. Call me Adrian.'

His voice was nasal, annoying. No wonder he wasn't doing anything better. Stuck in some poky bedroom here, a police record for a theft that cost him his job.

'You'll be wondering why we're here.'

Not a flicker. 'Yes.'

'You'll understand that this is an informal chat and voluntary, but I need to read you your rights and make it clear that you do have a right to legal counsel, should you want it.'

'No need for all that, I'm sure.'

She rattled through the legalities regardless, interrupted only by Muriel banging four cups, two of them chipped, on the table. Hardy nodded when she was done.

Cooper stared at Eve, probably wondering where she was headed. She wasn't sure herself, but she needed to get in the right frame of mind for this, to close herself off from her time with MacNeill. Eve made a show of checking her notebook. Casual.

She focused on Helen Black, the photos from the file. Being at the scene in St Andrews with ex-DS Jack Allen. The poise of Adrian Hardy, the rigid way he sat. His aunt resuming her position by his side, her presence having no effect on the way he eyed Eve across the table.

Eve sensed Hardy was not a man used to female attention – more than likely mocked or rejected by those he longed to be interested in him. Like his neighbour, Sonia Paterson, the woman he'd stalked and been officially warned to stay away from eighteen months ago, six months before Helen's murder. A young woman battered to death. The photos of Helen's face, or what had been left of it, were still clear in her mind. Had this man been responsible for that?

Cooper coughed, helping her to refocus on the task at hand.

Eve closed her notebook. 'Mr Hardy, sorry, Adrian, can you tell me about Sonia Paterson?'

Hardy flinched, thrown for a second. Obviously not a question he'd been expecting. Hardy patted at his denim thigh, smoothing the tough material as if trying to restore order.

'Sonia?' A catch in his voice.

Eve said nothing, but Muriel did, her face stern. 'What's this all about? I thought you were here about the theft?' Her voice made Eve believe that Hardy's nasal voice was genetic.

Hardy placed a hand on his aunt's. 'Why don't you go watch your programmes? I'm fine here.' Talking to her like she was a child.

Muriel looked like she'd rather poke herself in the eye, but she stood obediently and left the room, not before glowering at Eve.

Hardy waited for her to close the door, licked his lips. 'Sonia was my neighbour. Lived in the same block of flats.'

'A friend?' Eve spoke to Hardy like she was someone to be confided in.

Hardy shifted in his seat, uncrossed his legs before crossing them again in the opposite direction. 'I thought she was.'

'You thought?' It was Cooper who spoke this time, his tone sharper. Good cop, bad cop.

Hardy glared at him. 'That's right.'

Eve stepped in again. 'When did you realize she wasn't?'

'When the police came to the house.' Hardy's jaw tightened.

'She phoned the police without talking to you first? Without telling you that, in her eyes, you'd done something wrong?' Eve finished the sentence on a high note, seemingly incredulous at Sonia's betrayal. Hoping it would strike a chord with Hardy.

Eve waited. Not expecting the smile when it came – a twitch of Hardy's top lip. It threw her. She could see then that Hardy was no clown, nowhere near as nervous as she'd first thought or, indeed, as Hardy had put across.

Hardy leaned forward and lifted an unchipped mug to his lips. He blew gently, ice-blue eyes staring coolly across the table. Taking his time. Taking control of the situation, if only for a moment. He took a sip, gave a loud sigh of contentment and put the mug down.

Eve wasn't feeling friendly. 'Why did Sonia phone the police?'

Hardy, still leaning forward, draped one forearm over his folded thighs. 'I think you'll have read that in the file.'

The cocky shit. Eve's pulse quickened. *This nerd thought he knew how to play her*. She leaned against the stiff wooden backing of her chair, her own frame relaxed. 'Trying to keep things friendly, but if that's the way you want to play it, Mr Hardy, *Adrian*, then, yeah, we've seen the file. It seems you wouldn't leave Sonia alone.' Eve was satisfied with the steel edge slicing through her tone.

It was Hardy's turn to lean back, nonchalant – *nothing to worry about here*. 'If you're here for the reason you gave, then there's no call not to be friendly.'

Eve wanted to punch him but waited for him to speak again, knowing it wouldn't be long.

'Don't you think it's a shame how things have changed these days, Detective?'

'I don't follow.'

'Women. Like you. Wanting to be our equals on the one hand but banging on about chivalry being dead on the other. I was trying to be the gentleman that I knew she needed. That I sensed she wanted.'

Cooper didn't bother to hide the sarcasm when he spoke. 'You sensed she wanted?'

'Yes. I'm a man who can read these things. When we first got chatting. You know, the odd occasion that I'd see her on the bus. I'd sometimes help with her bags, see her to her door.'

Eve's mind flashed to her mother. Had her father's logic been that skewed right before he attacked her?

'What changed?' Cooper asked now.

'Nothing as far as I knew. She was always nice to me.'

Hardy changed when he spoke to Cooper. Maybe it was an approach he kept for all men.

Cooper tutted. 'That's not what her statement says.'

Hardy responded to the challenge. 'She's a liar.'

'You weren't standing, every night for weeks, whatever the weather, at the bus stop she came off at?'

That smile flashing on his lips again. 'You make it sound like I was lying in wait. I was *meeting* her off the bus, helping her, making sure she got home safely in the dark.'

'Isn't it true that she asked you on several occasions to stop "meeting" her? That when you ignored her pleas, she started to ignore you? That one night, with someone by her side, she had the courage to challenge you. To make it clear that it was *you* that was making her feel unsafe?'

Eve liked how Cooper was handling it, was reminded of the good old days.

'Rubbish. She was playing with me. Pretending she didn't want me, but I knew by how she looked at me, how she walked, that she did. I looked out for her. That wasn't "someone" with her that night, it was a male work colleague. I hadn't seen him with her before. He acted like he owned her. He wasn't good for her. I could see he was confusing her, controlling her, turning her against me. I was concerned.'

'You started turning up at her work and the places she socialized.' Cooper was prodding, warming him for Eve.

'I wanted to check she was OK. She was looking different. Pale. Skinny. He was always there, stopping her from talking to me. Silencing her. I knew he wasn't good for her.'

Cooper bristled by her side. Those two words, *silencing her*, had hit him in the same way that they'd punched Eve in the gut.

Sonia's 'male work colleague' had in fact been her boyfriend of two years, Michael. He had logged countless calls to the police with concerns over Hardy's behaviour.

An official warning had finally been issued to Hardy after officers responded to a late-night call from Michael. They'd found Hardy kneeling outside Sonia's door, shouting obscenities through her letter box. Still, they'd been surprised when Hardy had appeared to heed the warning and stopped.

Eve had spoken on the phone with Sonia. She'd confirmed everything had stopped that night, but she and Michael had moved anyway. They were happy. Hardy had no idea where they were. She'd pleaded to Eve that she made sure it stayed that way.

What had made Hardy stop? Eve was damned sure it wasn't a warning from the officers. Maybe he had targeted someone else. Helen? Perhaps he decided it was time that he was the one doing the silencing.

Eve took over from Cooper. 'Tell me, if you were concerned about Sonia, sure that Michael was bad for her, why did you then leave her alone?'

'Again, I think you've seen the file.'

'And you listened to the warning? The model citizen?'

'Detective, like anyone, I can only do my best. And I did the best I could for Sonia. Some people can't take the help they're being offered. Don't deserve what they're being offered. He'd brainwashed her. More than I ever realized. But something clicked and I saw her for what she was. Weak. Disloyal. I wasn't willing to waste any more time on her.'

Hardy certainly had an overblown sense of self-worth. His black-and-white warped approach was chilling.

'You found someone else to help?'

'You could say that.'

'Tell me.'

'My, my, Detective, if I were to get into the details of all that, you'd be in danger of wheeling in the psychiatrist's couch.'

Eve gritted her teeth every time Hardy said 'Detective'. The way he used it as an insult. Eve hid her irritation. 'Hey, I'm here to listen. Think of me as your regular shrink.'

'I jest. Regular shrink? Believe me, it's something I've never needed. I know who I am. It's those around me who struggle.'

Eve shifted in her seat, aware Cooper knew she was still visiting the psychiatrist, hating that Hardy's words were making her feel even worse about it.

'Tell me about that then.'

'I'm different. I see the world differently. People don't always see that as a good thing. It's why I prefer animals: they accept you as you are. They let you help them, care for them.'

The career choice of veterinary assistant and, when that career choice was no longer his, the pet shop, made sense to Eve. It seemed Hardy had the intelligence; it was something else that was amiss.

'You turned to animals?'

'No, Detective. I may have my fantasies, but fornicating with our four-legged friends isn't on the list.'

Cooper made his disgust clear.

Eve nearly smiled. 'What is on the list?'

'Basic human needs: sex, affection. Dare I say love?'

'And you found someone who could give you that?'

'The sex, yes, even the affection. And sometimes I choose to kid myself it's not a lie.'

'A lie?'

'As I said, I'm different. I know what you think you see. Some bookish, unattractive guy, socially awkward, too intelligent for his own good.'

Eve didn't say that, apart from the last trait, it was exactly what she saw.

234

'I'm not stupid. I know the reasons women don't want me.'

Nothing to do with being an obsessive psycho. 'They say there's someone out there for everyone.'

'Indeed they do, but some of us need to get out there more often.'

Eve allowed a smile. 'You're making do?'

Hardy nodded.

'Prostitutes?' Cooper sounded surprised.

'Singular. So lock me up for the admission.'

Cooper snorted.

Eve flashed a warning glance at Cooper before continuing the questioning. 'The same prostitute and the only one since Sonia?'

'Yes. And please keep your voice down. My aunt doesn't and has no need to know.'

Eve wanted to speak even louder but refrained. 'How did you meet?'

'The way you do. Online. I perused the goods on offer and chose what I wanted to buy.'

'Is that when you got involved in drugs?'

'Ah yes, from what my aunt said of the call earlier, I could tell you'd done your homework, Detective.'

Eve clamped her back teeth. 'It's my job.' Or rather it had been Ferguson's – he had come through on the connection and then got his hands on all the press reports for the drugs.

Hardy smiled. 'Is that all you're here for? Has there been another theft or something? Are the insipid individuals I worked for at the surgery trying to pin something else on me?'

'Pinning it on you? Are you saying that you didn't steal ketamine from your workplace?'

'I'm not saying that at all. What I will say is that I didn't steal the quantity that they said I did. People see what they want to see. No one wants to believe their own flesh and blood would be capable of stealing from them, let alone why they'd be stealing what they were.'

Cooper had said it was a family-owned business. But she wasn't here to dispute whether the owners' son or daughter was a closet junkie.

'Anyway, my question. Did you get involved with drugs around the same time you started paying this prostitute?'

'Rosie. She's called Rosie.' Hardy's voice was hard, blue eyes sub-zero.

Eve jumped on the show of raw emotion from Hardy. 'It sounds like you have a lot of time for Rosie.'

'She's a good person. She lost her way like many do, but I helped her.'

A common thread. It seemed Hardy wanted to look after a woman like he did an animal. Have them dependent on him for their care.

'How did you do that, Adrian?' Eve hated using his name, her mouth feeling dirty.

'I took her away from the flat her pimp had her operating from, paid her a monthly fee to be mine and mine only. Got her a bedsit. I could afford it then, when I was still working at the surgery.'

Cooper mumbled, 'Eat your heart out, Richard Gere.' Hardy missed it, too busy basking in his own glory.

Eve carried on, liking this side of Cooper. 'And she agreed?'

'Yes. Of course. She was able to keep a roof over her head, to be fed and watered and to have someone looking after her.'

Same requirements as a dog. What did Hardy do if the dog ever defied its master? She thought about the women slain, paralysed but awake, at the mercy of their killer.

'Where did the ketamine come in?'

Hardy was choosing his words carefully. 'When she found out where I worked. I'm a clever man, Detective. I know why these women do what they do. Rosie was no different. She wanted me to add a little spice to our time together.'

Eve was willing to bet that spice wasn't why Rosie wanted it. She'd read the side effects countless times since finding out ketamine was being used on the victims. A feeling of being out of themselves, a disassociation between their mind and body, no concept of pain, paralysis in high doses. Removed from reality. *Removed from Hardy.*

She looked at the pathetic person in front of her. 'Spice. Is that what you call it?'

'You should try it.'

It was Cooper's turn to grunt.

Eve didn't falter. 'I like having my full faculties about me.'

'Believe me, our sex life was even better after that. And I didn't think it could be.'

Yeah, because she was out of it and you could do what you wanted to her.

She thought of Helen Black. Had Hardy been visiting his aunt in St Andrews and needing what Rosie normally gave him at home? Maybe Helen fought him, wouldn't do what he wanted. He went too far. Did something he didn't know he was capable of. The catalyst for his lust for murder. A means to silence the women who had spurned him. Maybe he'd tried it on with Melanie or Lexie in the past. Eve was starting to build a case in her head.

Had he met Jenkins during his time in the press for his theft? Did he flirt with her only to be mocked by her? All 'what ifs'. *Concentrate.* Helen first. 'Did you visit your aunt often when she was in St Andrews?'

Hardy's head snapped up. 'What's my aunt got to do with anything?'

Loyal, protective. A puppy dog himself when it came to his aunt – probably the only woman who had been there for him and accepted him as he was. She didn't want to think what their relationship might be.

Eve continued. 'Nothing. My colleague who spoke to her on the phone said she sounded like she was proud of you. That, like you and Sonia for example, she wants to look out for you.'

'Do not compare my aunt to that tart.'

Cooper shifted in his chair, ready to pounce. Sonia was a tart now. Another Hardy layer unravelling.

Eve played it carefully. 'Sorry, nothing intended other than you seem to have a good relationship. Did you not travel to see her on occasion?'

Hardy sat back, clasped his long bony fingers together and placed them on his jeans. It was a full minute before he spoke. 'Detective, I'll ask again. Why are you here?'

Eve gave the rehearsed answer, the one they'd given his aunt on the phone.

'We've had a spate of crimes linked to ketamine. Initial investigation threw up your name on the system. We are interviewing anyone who has a record with the drug. Process of elimination, nothing more.'

'Detective, like I said, I'm not a stupid man. Sonia. Rosie. St Andrews.'

Was he playing with her?

Eve's eyes bored into Hardy's, looking for that flicker, that sign that he was their man. But instead Hardy smiled. Not the one of earlier. A full-blown smile. A grin. Small sharp teeth on show.

In that grin, Eve saw Melanie – bound, leaning against the cold bathroom wall. Lexie – bound, shackled to the hard wooden barre of the dance studio. Jenkins – her plump pink tongue wrapped in newspaper. And that smile on the smarmy bastard's face in front of her.

Cooper stiffened beside her. The charge in her own body language crackling throughout the room, firing up her colleague, putting him on red alert.

Eve tried to calm herself. Hardy was enjoying the effect he was having on her. *Control.* She watched his grin widen further.

'Careful, careful, DI Hunter. This is my home.'

Eve shifted forward, challenging him. 'You were given your rights when we arrived. They still stand. If you wish legal counsel, it can be arranged. You can come to the station.'

239

A twitch. The smile faltering. Silence.

'What, Hardy? Cat got your tongue?' Eve was trying everything she could think of to get a reaction. The surname, using the animals Hardy loved, hinting at the murders. She wanted to push more, to accuse him of more, to push him to the edge, to force a confession from him.

But Hardy wouldn't be pushed. He just sat there waiting for Eve to compose herself – enraging Eve even further. When Hardy spoke, it was with calm control. *Control.*

'You think I have something to do with those murders. The women. Don't you, Detective? Like most people, I follow the news. Seems you're quite the celebrity. It's certainly true to say you've had your fair share of scandal.'

Was he goading her?

They'd never released information about the ketamine to the press. Had never linked Helen's murder in St Andrews a year ago to what was happening. And he knew about her past. MacNeill. *Did* he know him? Eve grasped the gouged edge of the table in front of her, squeezing.

Cooper startled her when he spoke. 'Could I have a moment, ma'am?'

Eve was pissed off at his nerve. He was showing her up, interrupting her flow at the crucial moment. She sat a moment before giving in.

Chapter 30

Eve struggled to free herself and her damned leg from the table before stalking from the room.

Cooper joined her in the hallway, shutting the door gently behind her, both of them watching Muriel scurrying to the living room, neither of them surprised at her eavesdropping. They waited until she closed the door.

Eve stood there, finding it tough not to have a go at Cooper for having the balls to do what he was doing. She knew he was right.

His voice was a hushed whisper. 'Eve, I'm not sure what was happening in there. I know he's a dickhead, every pore on my body is shrivelling beneath his crap, but we can't blow it. Can't assume anything.'

'Three women, Cooper. How many more? Jesus.' Eve dragged a hand over her hair. 'He's playing us. It's him.' Eve thought again about MacNeill. About what he'd said about knowing people on the outside who would be more than willing to play with her. But how the hell could he have known about Hardy? 'I think he might know MacNeill, or at least one of MacNeill's men might've been supplying Hardy with the drugs, is using him now in all this.'

Cooper looked confused. 'What? Where did that come from?'

Eve didn't want to get into it. 'I'll tell you later, once I've figured it out in my head.'

Cooper looked hurt, maybe thinking that she'd kept him out of the loop on something. 'Fair enough. But maybe he's just a saddo who has to pay for sex. He's clever, clearly unhinged, and he likes to be in control. Maybe that's all this is. But the fact is that everyone knows about the murders, that we're working round the clock on the case. That we're desperate.'

Eve pulled at her blouse collar and let Cooper continue.

'Come on, it's not such a jump for Hardy to think that's what this is all about. It would make sense of the questions we're asking. I mean, yeah, I was going at him too, but not letting the piece of shit lead me. We need to calm down.'

Eve saw Cooper for the officer, the friend, he was.

Cooper looked worried that he'd overstepped the mark.

Eve spoke in a whisper, scared what her voice might do if she didn't. 'Sorry. You're right. I . . . thanks.'

Eve turned and went back into the kitchen, desperate to return to the interview, to work, Cooper following her lead.

She was ready to think straight.

Instead, it was Hardy who spoke first.

'I want you to leave, Detective. Unless you have a reason to take me to the station, that is. But I think you'll find that I have an alibi for any dates you have in mind, because I've done nothing wrong.'

Eve stood glaring at Hardy. There was little she could do.

Hardy smiled. 'There is something you should know though.'

'And what's that?'

'I want to look after people, not hurt them. Go see Rosie. She'll tell you that.'

Eve stared at the mass of ink lines on the incident-room whiteboard. The thick black brushstrokes of inquiries and leads branched off in all directions. And in her head, they were all pointing towards MacNeill.

Cooper lifted the lid of the pizza box between them, steam rising as he took a slice and turned to the board, a piece of pepperoni falling on to his chest. 'Shit.' He picked at the greasy piece of meat and stuck it in his mouth, the fat stain mixed with tomato sauce spreading on his shirt. Eve put her own half-eaten triangle on the napkin in front of her. She wasn't hungry, even though she'd been convinced she was starving.

'Feels like the longest day ever. We're staring at this board as if it's going to give us answers. Why don't you finish your pizza and get home to Louise and the kids?'

Cooper shook his head. 'No need. Louise's folks are round as she's away to the cinema with pals. The kids'll be down already.'

243

Eve glanced at the wall clock, surprised to see it was gone 8 p.m. The windows either side of the clock were black. Beneath the harsh overhead lighting, she could see herself and Cooper reflected in the dark glass. 'I thought Mearns and Ferguson would've been here. We'll see what they have to say and then you should head off.'

'You know, I feel like there's something we're missing. A link that'll join all the dots.' Cooper said exactly what Eve was thinking, something he had an uncanny knack for.

Eve had already updated him on what MacNeill had said – about how he knew people on the outside willing to play with her – and then she'd met with Hardy.

'What have we got?' Eve launched into the tried-and-tested format that she and Cooper had always used – sounding things out together.

Cooper wiped his hands on a napkin. 'OK, Hardy was known for stealing drugs from his workplace and being involved with them, with Rosie at least.'

Eve nodded. 'Drugs being something that MacNeill made a living from. And then there's Sanders.'

Cooper leaned back, lifting his right ankle and resting it on his left knee. 'Sanders was Hardy's arresting officer when he stole the ketamine from his work. And Sanders was the officer who was with you the night Johnny Junior went off the road.'

'Indeed.' Eve picked a piece of chopped green pepper off the solidifying piece of pizza in front of her. 'And it was Sanders that Johnny Senior lured to that address, along with me, when his son still lay in a hospital bed six months later.'

Cooper turned in his seat towards her. 'Coincidence?'

Eve cocked an eyebrow. 'You know, Hardy's a creep with his own sordid past. He likes to control women.' Eve took a sip of water. 'But could MacNeill be using him on the outside? To murder, I mean?'

Cooper stared at her. 'Let's say he is. But why? What does it all mean? How is Melanie connected?'

Eve picked at her finger, the skin open and raw there. 'I don't know, but we do know Ryan dabbled in drugs, with Forbes. But small potatoes compared to the world MacNeill operates in. Although we know Lexie was being supplied drugs too.'

Cooper cocked his head. 'Then there's Jenkins. She knew Lexie's dealer, met with him the night she was killed. And Jenkins links right to you, Sanders and MacNeill.'

Eve couldn't argue with that. 'Yeah, and the newspaper article wrapped around Jenkins' tongue made sure of that. But why the tongues? Why the week apart?'

Cooper lay his head against the seat. 'Jesus, we sound like we did that night at mine. Right back where we started.' He spun his chair around, helped himself to another slice of pizza.

Eve stared past him to the board. *One link. Something that would bring it all together.* She turned as she heard noise in the corridor. Mearns and Ferguson. 'Hey, guys, pizz—' Eve stopped when she saw their faces, Ferguson's especially. All colour gone from it.

'What?'

'We found the guy. We'd missed him for his morning whisky snifter. Barmaid told us he'd be in for lunch, but he didn't show. Finally arrived at seven p.m.'

'And?' Eve wished he would get on with it.

'The one thing the hotel barman hadn't mentioned in his description was the thing I noticed first.'

Mearns stood beside Ferguson, staring at Eve. It was Cooper who spoke. 'Jesus, Ferguson, spit it out.'

'Spider's-web tattoo on his left temple. One of MacNeill's men, Eve. He was there that night.'

Eve felt like she'd been whacked in the stomach all over again. Instantly pulled back to that night. Seeing him standing in that room with Sanders. The only reason he wasn't in prison along with MacNeill was because he hadn't been instrumental in inflicting injury, had just stood there, silent. What a joke. She was glad she was sitting. 'It looks like we've found our missing link.'

It took a while for them to gather themselves, to digest the sheer scale of what they might be looking at. Eve was first to recover.

'He didn't see you?'

'No.' Ferguson looked buoyed, involved. 'And we didn't approach him, as we thought you'd want him left – keep an eye on him, see where he leads us next. The barmaid says he's in there most nights to closing time. I don't think he's going anywhere soon.'

Eve glimpsed the man she used to work with in front of her. 'Good thinking. Look, I appreciate it's getting late, but would you guys be OK to go keep watch until closing time, see where he goes after?'

Mearns and Ferguson nodded without hesitation. 'Thanks.'

Eve updated them on their visit to Hardy, both of them as convinced as she was that he was involved. Cooper too, even though he'd asked her to step back a bit at Hardy's house.

She was feeling as buoyed as Ferguson looked. 'First thing tomorrow, Mearns, I want you to interview the boss at the veterinary practice, the former employer that Hardy stole the ketamine from. See if we can get anything that might link him to MacNeill's guy. I'll speak to Sonia again, see if she ever saw Hardy with anyone.

'Ferguson, I want you to find out if Hardy has any social life to speak of – anyone who resembles a friend. See if we can't pin him to the dates of the murders.'

Ferguson stood to attention, nodded.

'OK, let me know where our dealer man goes tonight. Cooper, since you don't need to be home, you're with me.'

Chapter 31

ROSIE LOOKED ANYTHING BUT ROSY. Eve watched her suck the life out of what was left of her roll-up, the orange tip illuminating her face in the fading light, before flicking it out on to the pavement from the tenement doorway that she stood in. Union Grove, grey blocks of flats running either side, rusting satellite dishes as far as the eye could see, the street tucked off the bustle of Holburn Junction, which led on to Union Street, the heart of the city.

It was an ideal location for punters. Rosie didn't bother to lift her scuffed stiletto heel to stub out the cigarette, the driving sleety rain taking care of that for her. Even from across the road where they sat in the unmarked car, Eve could see that any life left in her had been sucked out a long time ago.

Rosie pulled together the edges of the flimsy unbuttoned black raincoat that she wore; it barely concealed the bony chest in a low-cut top and laddered fishnets beneath a skirt that could pass as easily for a belt.

In the few minutes that they'd been sitting there, she'd smoked two cigarettes. Seemed unlikely she had a punter waiting for her. Eve wondered how many girls were inside. Whether the pimp would be visiting any time soon. She still couldn't believe the changes in the city's prostitution trade over the last decade. The red-light district, a tolerance zone down the harbour area, had been abolished, at first forcing the women on to the city streets but eventually seeing them trading from private flats and homes, brothels on the rise, with Aberdeen being named the brothel capital of the UK in 2016.

What an accolade. But it was the women that Eve felt for. They were invisible, vulnerable and in more danger from the pimps that ran them.

Rosie was staring at them, glazed eyes thin slits, challenging them. She wasn't stupid, she knew not to approach them – had a sixth sense, like any of the girls who worked the trade, about who was a potential client and who was a copper. She'd be off and running as soon as they opened a door. Eve turned to Cooper, who sat in the driver's seat. 'You ready?' Cooper nodded and Eve pulled at the door handle, knowing she wouldn't have to worry about her leg.

Eve took her time crossing the street, making sure her own jacket was fastened while listening to the click-clack-click of Rosie's shoes echoing off the granite tenements as she tottered up the street and attempted to run across towards Albyn Lane. Cooper didn't even have to break into a jog before Rosie was slipping on the wet cobbles of the lane, crashing to the ground and then fighting against Cooper like an alley cat as he attempted to help her.

'Bastards.' She sounded as common as she looked. 'You can fucking pay for my tights.' Cooper shook his head, amused, as she flailed around on the end of his arm.

Eve joined them as Rosie was giving up the battle. 'How about we take you for a cup of something warm instead?' She saw the surprise and then the hope in Rosie's features as she glanced along the stretch of Union Grove to the Foundry pub in the distance. Eve followed her gaze and smiled. 'I was thinking more non-alcoholic.'

Rosie huffed and made a half-hearted attempt at shrugging free of Cooper's grasp on her elbow before letting herself be escorted to the car.

The Asda café at the Bridge of Dee, a five-minute drive from Union Grove, was deserted this time of night. Perfect for parking and a place that, in this quiet hour and with the flash of a badge, wouldn't refuse entry to Rosie's attire. Tea-time trade was over, the rectangular, cheap-looking veneered tables cleared but still in need of a good wipe.

They sat in silence as Rosie bulldozed her way through an all-day breakfast, her cracked, sore-covered lips never closed for long as she chewed. Eve and Cooper sipped at their coffees and waited for her to finish, the fork and knife clattering as she threw them on the plate and grabbed at her own coffee.

'Not like you coppers to wine and dine a girl. What're you after?'

Eve watched coffee collecting at the corners of her mouth, mixing with the drying egg yolk there. 'We wanted to have a wee chat about a friend of yours.'

'Aye?'

'Adrian Hardy.'

Rosie put down her cup, started picking at one of the scabs on her face as she stared at the table. 'What about him?'

'We went to see him earlier today. Wanted to talk to him about some things. He told us to come and see you. Here we are.'

'What do you want with me?'

'I think he reckons you'll be able to give us an idea of what he's about.'

'Eh? Can you not suss that out from talking to him yourselves?'

Eve pursed her lips. 'Let's say it'd be better for him if I didn't go by that opinion.'

Rose looked first at Eve, then Cooper, and drooped her shoulders. 'Is this off the record?'

Cooper winked. 'We were never here.'

Rosie looked at the empty plate in front of her. 'In that case, it won't show on the department budget if I ask for a second helping.'

Eve waved over the elderly woman sat peering at a crossword through the milk-bottle thick glasses perched on her hooked nose. She shuffled towards them with the manner of someone who has been inconvenienced, white thinning curls clapped to her forehead under the regulation hairnet she wore that did nothing for her.

The second breakfast was out within minutes and it was only once it was set down, a fresh coffee alongside it, that Rosie spoke.

'Met him a year ago. Started off once or twice a week he'd come to the flat. Always the same time and always wanting the same thing.'

'Which was?'

'To talk.'

'To talk?' Eve couldn't hide the disbelief in her voice.

'Yeah. I get all sorts. As long as they're paying, I couldn't give a shit if someone wants to yap crap or pretend I'm their mother-in-law.'

Eve hid the smile. 'And was he yapping crap?'

'At first I didn't listen, let him babble on, but he started coming more, and I kinda got to like listening.'

'How come?'

'He was harmless. Lonely. Been given a rough deal from folk. Said they didn't understand him. The usual patter. Course I've heard it all before, but for some reason I believed him and sometimes I talked about my own shit.'

'Why?'

'Cos he was paying and willing to listen. Made a change from being a means to an end and knowing to keep your gob shut – unless they liked a bit of chat, if you know what I mean.'

'What did you talk about?'

'Anything and everything. Not smutty shit, nothing to do with sex. Chat.'

'And he never wanted anything else?'

Rosie hugged the mug of coffee to her goosebumped chest. 'Not at first. I don't think he was experienced. Wondered if he was gay. But then one night he said he wanted to make love to me. No one ever said that to me before. I'm not the kind of lass the word love gets used around.'

'What did you say?'

'I started unbuttoning his jeans.'

Cooper laughed, stopped himself. 'And?'

'He stopped me. Got a bit weird about it all. Started banging on about how he was a gentleman and wanted to look after me.'

Eve's eyes widened. 'And what did you think?'

'That he was a bit weird after all. All mouth and no action. Thought he was scared to do it. But I soon found out he definitely liked the action.'

Eve pictured Hardy and the way he'd been in his aunt's kitchen, felt sick even thinking about him in action. 'What do you mean?'

'He told me that night that he could arrange a place I could go. That if I agreed to be his, he'd keep me safe.'

'You agreed?'

'I ain't stupid. It's not like I love what I do. He wasn't exactly my dream guy, but I stopped believing in fairy tales a long time ago. Better I stick with the weird that I know rather than laying myself open to the dickheads I don't.'

'You think he's weird?'

Rosie bit her bottom lip. 'He's different.'

'Different how?'

Rosie was now pulling at her lip. 'Look, the guy's been good to me. I don't want to drop him in any shit.'

'I respect that, Rosie, but we need to know more about Hardy. Let's say you might be helping other women with their shit.'

Rosie's jaw set, a hardness creeping into her eyes. 'What women?'

'What is it with you and Hardy?'

'Like I said, he looked after me.'

'No funny business?'

'Depends what you mean by funny business. He gave me a place to stay, a cheap Airbnb he paid month to month, made sure I had food and all the rest of it.'

'In return for what?'

Rosie looked at the table, scratching at another sore. 'For being his.'

'And what did being his involve?'

'Not seeing any other punters.'

'That's it?'

Rosie kept her gaze downwards. 'He liked me to stay indoors, always, to be there whenever he needed me. He'd tell me what to wear, how to be.'

'And what did he like you to wear?'

'Simple stuff. Nothing fancy. Nothing slutty.'

'And you did this?'

Rosie coughed, a deep chesty wheeze that shook her small frame. As she covered her mouth, the sores on her hands were as bad as those on her face.

'Yeah. Like I said, he was paying.'

'What else did he tell you to do?'

'He liked to bathe me, to feed me. He'd decide what I was to eat and that. Said he wanted to take care of me.'

'When did the drugs come into it?'

Rosie dropped her hand beneath the table. 'He knew I wasn't the Virgin Mary, even though I think he wanted to pretend I was. And I think we both knew I didn't go into that bedsit without a wee stash. I ran out quick, sitting around all the time.' Rosie shrugged. 'I dunno, maybe he sensed it. Next I knew, he was offering the goods.'

'Did you take ketamine together?'

'Fuck, no. It was something else he liked to provide me with, to give me.'

'How did he give it to you?'

Rosie patted at the top of her arm. 'Needle.'

Eve glanced at Cooper.

'Ever give you enough that you were completely out of it?'

Rosie's eyes flickered. 'Eh?'

She'd struck a nerve. 'As in not able to move.'

It was a beat too long before Rosie answered. 'Wouldn't be a lot of use to him then, would I?'

Cooper shifted in his chair. 'Are you sure about that?'

'Listen, I don't know what you want from me, but I've nothing bad to say about the guy, OK?' Rosie was pulling her coat around herself again.

Eve was at a loss as to why this woman who had been kept like some kind of animal would want to protect Hardy. 'Do you still see him?'

'Yeah, what of it?'

Eve could sense she was losing her. 'Often?'

'Not like before.'

'Why not?'

Rosie's thumb and forefinger were fiddling at one of the buttons on her coat. 'When the shit hit the fan with the theft and his job, he couldn't keep me in the bedsit any more. I had no choice but to go back on the game. Different flat. Different pimp. That bitch that took him in sure as hell wouldn't have had me moving in.'

Eve was taken aback by the spite in her tone. 'What's the story with you and Hardy now?'

'He comes to see me sometimes, to chat again. He still gets me the drugs sometimes.'

Eve's eyes widened. 'How? How did he manage that once he'd lost his job?'

Rosie let go of the button and patted at her lip before wiping blood on her tights. 'Some guy.'

Eve's heart thumped. 'Some guy? Rosie, do you remember the guy's name?'

'No.'

Eve was desperate; she wanted to reach across and shake it out of Rosie. 'You can tell us. We would protect you; no one would know it came from you.'

'I don't need your protection. Hardy's not a guy that likes to share, but he doesn't want to give up on me. He'll protect me.'

She sounded proud of that fact. Eve was reminded of what Hardy had said about Sonia. *'Some people can't take the help they're being offered. Don't deserve what they're being offered . . . Disloyal. I wasn't willing to waste any more time on her.'* But it seemed Rosie was more than willing to take it and remain loyal to him.

Eve wanted to groan. 'Doesn't want to give up on you?'

Eve wanted to shake some sense into the emaciated woman sitting in front of her. What the hell was wrong with her? It reminded her of that cellar girl in Austria, her name escaping Eve – how the girl had been inconsolable to hear of her captor's death. That she still carried a photo of him in her wallet. There was a name for it. Whatever it was, it was the only reason she could think of for Rosie's bizarre attachment to Hardy.

Or maybe it was as simple as the guarantee of having a roof over her head, of feeling wanted in the world – no matter how warped the way in which that person wanted her. She felt sick that someone could be that desperate.

Rosie sniffed. 'That's right. Says he's going to get set up again, that he'll make things the way they were. Until then he doesn't want anything physical, not while I'm seeing other punters.'

Eve looked at Rosie's hands, the raw skin exposed by bitten fingernails. She glanced at the empty plate in front of her, thinking about the speed at which Rosie had eaten both helpings, and Eve pictured the doorway they'd found her in. And she understood. As Rosie said herself, better to stick with the weird she knew.

Rosie coughed again, her fragile body wracked by it, eyes squeezed shut, bones visible through the paper-thin flesh above her low-cut top, black-tinged tears rolling down hollow cheeks. As she fought to recover, Eve saw then how desperate she probably was, and she was willing to bet Rosie would be a ready-made alibi for Hardy.

'Then if he's adamant he won't give up on you, it won't matter if you give us the guy's name who's getting Hardy the drugs.'

Rosie sat, weighing whether she had anything to lose. She shrugged. 'I don't know it, but I can tell you what he looks like.'

Eve felt the chill crawl up her neck and over her head.

'Short guy but solid. Bald. Gappy teeth. A spider's-web tattoo here.' Rosie pointed to her left temple.

Cooper looked as shocked as she felt.

Chapter 32

Thursday, 28 November

'I WANT SURVEILLANCE ON HIM. Tonight. I'll do it.'

Hastings didn't reply but remained standing with his back to Eve, as rigid as the the new city-centre shopping complex that now blocked the horizon.

'Sir?'

Her boss turned, leaned spindly hands on the cracked leather chair behind his desk. 'You need to go home. Get some rest. You look like shit. The three of you do.'

He was right about the hours they'd been putting in. 'But it's important, sir. Another week has passed. Going by his track record, it'll be tonight, if it hasn't already happened. But maybe this time we can stop it.' Eve was aware she sounded desperate. 'If not me, then put Ferguson on it. He said he wanted to be more involved.'

Hastings straightened. 'He been giving you trouble?'

He'd been difficult, but he'd also been so keen. Last week, him and Mearns had followed the dealer, spider's-web tattoo and all, from the pub to a flat in

Portland Street. According to them, he'd looked shifty but more through fear. Kept checking over his shoulder every five seconds. She wasn't sure what to make of that.

Anyway, as tempting as it was, she didn't want to get Ferguson in shit. 'Not trouble, no. Just being his usual pain-in-the-backside self.'

'You do know it's not about what happened with Sanders?' Hastings let go of the chair, walked round to the front of his desk and perched on the edge of it. 'I don't think he even blames you. On another note, Dr Shetty seems happy with you according to her weekly reports.'

Eve had no wish to talk about Dr Shetty or the bullshit Eve had been feeding her. 'Can we look at putting him on to Hardy? I know when I mentioned it last week you felt it didn't merit the manpower but, with the MacNeill link and Sanders being his arresting officer, the fact another week has passed and this now fits the pattern of murders to date, I'd say we have to.'

'Anything else?'

Eve grappled for evidence to support her argument. 'As you know, Cooper and Mearns interviewed the ex-employer he stole the ketamine from. I spoke to Sonia again. Ferguson and the team looked into anyone with links to the guy. Not much came out of any of it. It's a hunch, sir, on what we do have.'

Hastings nodded slowly, not looking convinced. 'And what about the prostitute?'

'Rosie, sir?'

'Yes. Her experience of Hardy sounded twisted, but is it enough? Has there been anything else from her?'

'No, but I think she'll back him all the way. We know she's got some obsession with the guy. Jealousy. And I doubt it's because he's good in bed.'

Hastings looked disgusted.

'I know. I've been thinking about her a lot. She reminds me of that girl.'

'What girl?'

'The one in Austria. Locked in the cellar.'

Hastings stared at Eve as if she was the one who should be locked up.

'I know, but there's something about how Rosie defended Hardy, protected him, like she couldn't see what he's been doing to her. The day the Austrian girl escaped, her captor was found beheaded on a train track. She was devastated. She still carries a photo of him in her purse.'

'Stockholm Syndrome.'

'That's it. Knew there was a term for it.'

Hastings looked to the ceiling, crossed his arms. 'Sounds a bit far-fetched, don't you think?'

'It's better than the other option.'

'What?'

'That she loves the screwed-up sonofabitch.'

Hastings smiled.

'Anyway, it depends if we can put a little pressure on her to rethink. I've got some of the beat guys keeping an eye out for her down Union Grove tonight. Ferguson's got the aunt covered if you put him on surveillance at the house for both of them tonight.'

Hastings sighed. 'Fine. Go home.' He stood. 'Let me break the news to Ferguson.'

Eve was heading out to her shed when her mobile rang. Cooper. Shit. Had they found a body?

'Please tell me this isn't what I'm thinking, Cooper.'

'It isn't what you're thinking. Promise. Not yet, anyway.'

Eve's heartbeat slowed. 'Make it quick then. You're coming between a woman and her escape.'

'I won't pry. Been asked by the better half to invite you to dinner Christmas Day.'

As Eve walked across the snow-covered grass towards the shed, she was trying to think what date they were on, how far away Christmas was. The thought of it all the last thing on her mind.

Cooper spoke again. 'She says if you say no, I'm to put her on the phone.'

Eve smiled, unlocked the shed. 'Doesn't sound like I have a choice.'

Cooper spoke a little quieter. 'Louise wants to invite Sanders and Archie too.'

Eve pushed open the door. 'I can't see Archie and me being a recipe for festive cheer.'

'I said that, but she's adamant it's the way to go.'

Eve tutted but then thought of Sanders. 'I could handle passing the salt. If he goes for it, then OK, but I doubt he will.'

'Great. Louise was asking about Mearns. Doesn't want her to feel left out. Thought she might be alone what with her folks being in Bolton and her life revolving around work.'

'Jesus, Cooper. Are you guys having a Christmas dinner or a work do?'

Cooper laughed. 'You know what's she's like.'

Eve knew exactly what Louise was like. A homebody with a good heart who wanted the world to be a better place, for everyone to get on. A tall order for the world but maybe even more so for Eve and Mearns. Although it seemed there had been a slight warming in the attitude from Mearns recently, spending Christmas together might be pushing it. 'I'm sure Mearns'll be spending it with the new boyfriend. What's the deal with that anyway? All this secrecy?'

'You tell me. Her mobile's been going a lot. I've almost asked a few times if there's something she wants to tell me, but she doesn't strike me as one for sharing at the best of times. Might get a swift kick to my groin.'

Eve smiled.

'Anyway, I can only ask – about Christmas, I mean.' Cooper went silent. 'Boss, I hope to hell it is Hardy otherwise it feels like we're all sitting about letting someone else die tonight.'

'I know. It's shit. Don't know what to do with myself. Not going to stop it from happening by sitting in the office. Or working here either. But what do we have? How the hell do we know where we need to be?'

'We don't.'

Eve switched on the lights in the shed. 'Nothing we can do other than keep an eye on Hardy tonight and hope.'

Cooper clicked his tongue. 'You're not Ferguson's favourite person.'

'When am I ever?'

'True. Last time I saw him today he was dressed like the Michelin Man, getting ready for a long cold night in the car.'

Eve couldn't help but smile. 'Maybe not such a long night if Hardy is our man. And I don't see what Ferguson's problem is when it was him that brought Hardy to the table. I thought he'd be up for proving he's right.'

'Mmm, I'd say it's more to do with being made to do a task he feels is beneath him. Let someone else freeze their bollocks off and he'll take the glory once they have.'

Eve kicked the door closed behind her, reaching for her mask that hung from a hook on the wall. 'We work on Rosie and his aunt. See if we can play them off against one another – get them to admit they weren't always with Hardy on the dates of the murders. See what tonight brings.'

'They both look like they'd take a bullet for Hardy. He's sharp – he'll have them buying into anything that he needs them to.'

Cooper was probably right, but Eve couldn't see what else they had to go on. 'Fair play, but we need to try. Anyway, in the meantime I need to get lost in something, anything.'

'I'm hearing that. I'll go do my husband duty and phone Archie about Christmas.'

'Good luck. You'll need it.'

Eve jumped at the sound of her phone ringing, the TV remote on her stomach clunking on to the floor as she did. She dragged herself up the sofa, where she'd sat to eat the takeaway she'd eventually ordered in, realizing she'd fallen asleep sometime after. She peered over to the telly still flickering in the corner of the room and twisted towards the side table, reaching for her mobile. Cooper. Almost midnight.

She cleared her throat. 'Eve.'

Silence. Eve checked the screen, thinking the line had gone dead, and then heard Cooper. 'It's Sanders.'

It took her a second to process what was being said. She rubbed at bleary eyes. 'Don't tell me you're ringing at this time to say they're not up for Christmas.'

No answer. Something about Cooper's voice before all wrong. Eve's skin prickled. She sat up, rigid. 'What? What about her?' Her voice cracked, heart thumping against her ribcage, mouth gone bone dry, instinct telling her what Cooper hadn't yet.

'You better come.'

Chapter 33

Friday, 29 November

THE FAMILIAR SCENT OF oak furniture polish was there as soon as Eve stepped into Sanders' home but tinged with the sharp smell of copper. She swallowed, willing herself not to puke again, the partly digested takeaway of earlier left at the side of the road on the drive here.

Bodies seemed to swarm the hallway. Eve negotiated them as best she could while avoiding eye contact with faces partly hidden by masks, trying not to see the looks of sympathy she knew would be directed her way.

She walked towards the sitting room, but her body felt like it was being pulled backwards instead, legs heavy, not wanting to lead her towards what lay beyond.

She glanced sideways as she passed the kitchen. Two liaison officers standing inside, one of them moving towards the kettle, revealing Archie hunched over the table, face pressed against the wooden top, body heaving. Tears sprang to Eve's eyes. She wiped at them as she caught sight of Mearns.

Mearns was standing in the sitting-room doorway with Hastings. Her skin grey, eyes hollow. She made eye contact as Eve approached but didn't speak, just gripped the top of Eve's arm and looked to the floor before stepping to the side. Hastings' mouth was moving. Eve watched his rubbery lips, trying to concentrate on what he was saying, searching his face for God only knows what.

'You don't have to do this.'

The words drifted to her in slow motion, from the end of a tunnel. She moved forward, forcing her boss to step back. She stopped inside the room, steeling herself to look at what was a crimson blur in the corner of her eye. In her head she counted to three, turned. Her throat made a noise she never knew it could.

Sanders was looking right at her – wide, terrified blue eyes above a sea of red, as dead as the rest of her body had been in life. She was sat in her wheelchair. The cotton pyjamas she wore lay slick against her slender body, their intricate snowflake pattern no longer white. Her head and wrists still held fast in the cushioned supports, the ventilation tube ripped out and hanging loose, her mouth gaping, tongue gone.

Eve swayed on her heels, the room spinning around her, blood red filling the space. She turned, searching for the door she'd come through, shrugging off hands that reached for her as she moved towards it. She burst out into the hallway, her hand clutching at her chest, struggling to breathe. Eve banged off the patterned wall before slumping her shoulder against it, gasping. Her leg was throbbing in time to the words running through her head. *This is your fault.*

'Eve?'

She raised her eyes at the familiar voice, watched Cooper rushing towards her, concern etched in his features, arms outstretched, Eve unsure whether it was to embrace her or stop her from falling. She let Cooper's arms reach her, allowed them to hold her, clinging to him like a lost child, grateful for Cooper's support once again.

MacLean looked out of place. He was sitting in plain clothes on the brown leather armchair, Eve used to seeing him bent over dead people and dressed in white overalls. But they all knew it was more – that they were watching a professional struggling to report on the murder of a colleague, a friend.

'The tongue . . .' MacLean coughed, shifted in his chair, his eyes brimming. 'The tongue was removed while she was alive. Same as the others, but the scene doesn't appear to be staged in any way this time. They're taking her to the lab. But my initial examination showed no signs of a puncture wound.'

Those last words hit Eve square in the gut. Confirmation that for Sanders there'd been no hallucinations or escape. Her mind had been alert and in that room with the killer, no need for any drug to cause paralysis. Eve's leg jittered, brushing against Cooper's, who sat on the sofa beside her, his hand covering hers, Mearns by her other side.

They all looked out of place sitting there – uncomfortable in the front room of Hastings' home in Hazlehead, where money was evident and the streets clean. Barely two hours since they'd found her. Their boss trying to make this easier, somehow thinking being here would feel better while the rest of the city still slept. Better than being at Queen Street HQ. Eve wanted to laugh; brittle, broken bitterness wanting to burst from within her. Nothing would ever make this better.

She watched her shoe knocking against the polished wooden flooring, as she refused to cry. She wanted out of here, to break free of this crap, but she didn't trust herself to stand.

'Wait a minute . . .' Her brain kick-starting into gear. 'Hardy. Have—'

'Yeah, we checked in with Ferguson.' Mearns had read her mind. Eve wondered if she'd spoken to him, questioning again whether there was more between her and Ferguson than Mearns was letting on. 'Hardy didn't move an inch last night.'

Eve felt like she'd been punched. 'Is he sure? What about the back door, a window?'

'He's sure.' Mearns spoke softly but with enough of an edge to try to convince Eve.

Was she defending Ferguson? Eve didn't know what was going on but let MacLean continue.

'I estimate that she died within a half-hour window before Archie arrived home . . .'

'This is bullshit. It's Hardy,' Eve hissed through clenched teeth. 'Ferguson must've missed something.' Eve leaned forward, ready to fight her point – until Hastings lifted an arm from the armchair he sat in, silencing her. 'It's not him, Eve. Let it go.'

Eve moved to stand, to challenge her boss, but Cooper's arm was on her with a strength Eve was unaware he had, and one that made her rethink.

When Hastings spoke again, it was without anger. 'I can have someone take you home, Eve. Everyone will understand.'

Eve stayed seated, forced herself to set Hardy aside for the moment. 'I'm staying. Why was she on her own?'

'Archie's cards night.' Cooper didn't sound like Cooper. 'They got a nurse to come in on a Thursday to let him meet friends.'

A recollection of Sanders telling her about the nurse teetered on the edge of Eve's memory as she listened.

'The nurse would keep Sanders company, get her ready for bed. Sometimes she waited with her until Archie got home. A couple of times she left because Sanders wanted a little time on her own before he got home.'

'*Left* her?' Eve's pulse pounded in the side of her neck.

'The nurse is in bits. Blames herself.' Cooper's voice was a monotone.

'She should.' Eve spat the words, instantly regretting them, not wishing on anyone what she'd gone through with her own guilt about Sanders. She shook her head. 'Why the hell would you leave her on her own?'

Hastings stood, walked over to the fireplace. 'We all know it was pointless arguing with Sanders. If she was ready for bed, and Archie was due home at a certain time, the nurse saw no reason not to let her have a little independence.'

Eve tutted, looked over to her boss standing by the stone surround dominating the wall. He was leaning on the cluttered mantlepiece, his elbow jostling for space amongst framed family photographs. It looked as if it was his habit to stand there – or perhaps it was because otherwise he'd be in danger of falling over. The night had taken its toll on all of them.

'Even though, sir, surely someone had to be with her at all times?'

Hastings looked uncomfortable. 'Sanders had access to an alarm. The nurse wasn't concerned, said she'd asked to watch some drama she'd recorded, wanted to catch an episode before Archie got home.'

'An alarm? Did she—'

'No.' Mearns cut in, expecting the question. 'Could be that she didn't get time to.'

Eve felt something stirring in her stomach. The words she was trying to squeeze out threatening to stick in her throat. 'Or it could be that she knew her attacker but trusted him. She arrested Hardy, remember?'

No one spoke, trying to digest what that would mean, before the deep, hollow ring of the doorbell broke into their thoughts. Her boss left the room and then Eve spoke, not loud enough for her voice to carry through to him. 'Surely you guys aren't buying into this shit about it not being Hardy?'

'What are we supposed to do if Ferguson says he didn't move?' Cooper shrugged but didn't make eye contact with Eve.

'We don't take it. We go in there – question him, the aunt, Rosie. Put the pressure on.' Eve shut up as Hastings

271

walked back into the room, someone following behind from the hallway. It took a moment for Eve to register who. 'What are you doing here?'

Ferguson's eyes widened. 'I was told to come.'

Eve glared at her boss. 'You ordered this? Told him to leave Hardy's?'

Hastings clenched his fists, a steely glint creeping into his eyes. 'Eve. I said to drop it. We don't have anything on Hardy.'

'How can we be sure? What if he did manage to get past Ferguson? What if he's gift-wrapping Sanders' tongue right now?' Eve was giving in to the rage, the grief. Letting it engulf her, feeling like she was in danger of drowning but couldn't stop it. She was aware of herself, from a distance, shouting in her boss's face. 'Jesus Christ, what if he's already out there, stalking the next one?'

'Enough.' Hastings had turned red, was almost nose to nose with Eve. 'We don't have anything on him and that's the end of it.'

Eve glared at Ferguson, who stood there looking at Mearns, perhaps feeling sure she'd be on his side. She felt the familiar rage building inside her. She had to calm down, get away.

'The hell it is.' Eve grabbed her keys from her crumpled coat pocket and headed for the door. 'I'll see myself home.'

The house was in darkness. A black-and-white cat slunk between yellow pools of light from the overhead street-lights – the only life in the small cul-de-sac that the terraced home lay on. Eve twisted her clenched fists on the steering wheel, watching. Five a.m. Five hours since Cooper had called and everything had changed.

Her view of the front door was clear; she could see how nothing would've got past Ferguson. *If* Hardy had come out that way. But what if he'd sneaked out the back? Where high fencing bordered the gardens of the row of five houses and, behind that, more gardens led nowhere except to the owners' homes? There was scope. Opportunity not visible from the road.

She lay her forehead against the cold leather of the steering wheel, fighting every instinct to get out of the car, march to the door and kick the shit out of Hardy. If he was even there. She shouldn't be here. She scanned the upper floor again, looking for something, anything to give a sign that Hardy was in. When the passenger door flew open, she cried out and spun her head around. 'What the fu—'

'Fancy seeing you here.'

Ferguson. Eve stared at him and dropped her hands to her lap. No use in trying to make excuses, so she waited for Ferguson to say what he was going to say.

'I would've done the same. Problem is, seems Hastings would've too; it's him that told me to come.'

'Great. What now?'

'Quit while you're ahead.'

Eve lay her head back on the headrest. 'Do you think that?'

Ferguson shrugged, didn't look so sure. 'Look, I know I brought him to you with the drugs and the stalking, but what's the motive?'

Eve couldn't answer that, so avoided the question. 'Are you sure he couldn't have got past you earlier?' She watched Ferguson's face for a reaction, saw something she didn't like. 'What? Tell me. What is it?'

Ferguson looked away, out of the window. 'Look, I was pissed off about being put on duty here.'

'So, what – you found the link to Hardy and you said you wanted to be more involved, but you meant only if it's tasks you like?' Eve wanted Ferguson to look her in the eye and leaned forward, trying to see his face again. 'Is that it?'

Ferguson stayed as he was.

'I said, is that it?' Eve's voice was rising.

Ferguson turned round, Eve shocked to see tears glinting in her colleague's eyes. She grabbed hold of Ferguson's upper arm, shook it. 'Talk to me. Are you sure he didn't leave the house?'

Ferguson sat still, his mouth moving but no sound coming out.

'For Christ's sake, Ferguson. Talk to me. Tell me what happened.' Eve was shouting, not caring what time of night it was.

And then it was Ferguson shouting. 'I fell asleep. OK? I fell asleep.'

Eve's heart fell, bile rising. She shoved Ferguson's arm, banging his other shoulder against the window. 'You fell *asleep*?'

'Yeah. OK? Nothing you say or do can make me feel any fucking worse about it.' A single tear dripped down Ferguson's cheek, surprising Eve, even in her anger. But she didn't trust herself to speak, let alone move.

Ferguson stared at her. 'By midnight I was bloody freezing and knackered with the hours we've been putting in. I didn't mean to drop off, couldn't've been out more than a couple of hours, but it was the call from Jo checking in that woke me.'

Mearns. Eve flexed her fingers, thinking about them together, wondering how Mearns could be that stupid, trying to calm herself. 'You mean the call to say they'd found Sanders, to see if Hardy'd been out?'

'Yeah. But I know he hadn't – saw the curtain twitching shortly after I hung up. Like it had been earlier in the night. The guy's not stupid. He knew I was here.'

Eve couldn't begin to take in how dense Ferguson was coming across. When she spoke, it was low and dangerous. 'You brought him to us. Weren't you fired up to prove your point? How could you fall asleep? You gave him time.'

Ferguson scowled. 'I gave him nothing, boss. He never left.'

Eve shot her hand out, grabbed Ferguson by the throat, pinning him against the side window, shock written across his face, probably at her strength. 'And how do you know that? All this time. All the shit you've given me about how I let Sanders down the night Mac-Neill laid into us. She's dead. Do you hear me? She's fucking *dead*.' But what she really couldn't process was how he could've left himself open to more guilt than he already felt after letting Sanders down the first time. His belief that he should've known something was wrong after the length of time they'd been at the call-out.

Ferguson's eyes were wide, his hand grasping at Eve's, trying to release her grip on his throat. 'I'm not fucking proud of myself.' His voice sounded strangled.

Eve watched Ferguson's other hand reach behind him, grappling for the door handle. She was powerless to stop him from opening the door, from falling backwards out on to the muddy street. Eve threw open her own door, all the frustration, all the rage of the last year driving her. She sprang from the car, sprinting round to the pavement, not caring about the ice beneath her feet, wanting to batter Ferguson, needing to make him pay.

But Ferguson was on his feet running around the back of the car – across the road, sliding and slipping towards Hardy's home, slowing as he came closer to the front path, realizing he'd left it too late to run in another direction, Eve inches behind him.

Eve lunged at Ferguson, grabbing hold of his jacket, bringing them both down, landing hard on him. Then they were both rolling across the wet paving slabs of Hardy's front garden. Into the mud and leftover snow of the grass borders. Both of them grunting and kicking, oblivious to anything around them.

Until the flash in the dark.

Not one but two. Three. Four. Stopping them dead, where they lay breathless.

There, standing on the front step, was Hardy. An iPhone in his hand, a smile on his face. The camera clicking away.

Chapter 34

Now

He's in the newsagent's at the bottom of Union Street, the city's main strip, granite-grey buildings stretching to the sky either side. People are coming in and out, moving around him, bumping into him, no clue who he is, of what he's done.

He can't stop looking at the news-stands, his eyes flitting along the row, the whole shelf a montage of the detective. The photos came out perfectly, the rage on her face in sharp focus as she rolled around the garden. The DI making her own headlines. Again.

It worked out better than he'd hoped. They really were useless. Unprofessional. Clueless. So easy for him to notch up the pressure, making sure he was still in charge. But he had to be careful. He didn't want her taken off the case. Definitely not. He wasn't finished, not by a long way. He lifts the paper with the largest photo on its front page, wanting to pick them all up and wallpaper his home with her.

Arthur, the short wiry man behind the counter, smiles. As he's done every morning for as long as he's been coming here. The same smile and the same mundane mutterings about the weather. No matter whether a work day, or the weekend. A creature of habit. He's made sure that he is too, has bought the same thing every day. Boring. Never anything new to draw attention to himself, nothing different about him. Ever.

He smiles back as he hands over his change for the hot sausage roll and newspaper, careful not to touch the two against each other. He doesn't want grease spoiling the picture. He says his goodbyes and pulls open the door, the old bell above ringing as he does.

The cars and buses on Union Street are busy, as always. He walks along to the traffic lights in front of the Tourist Office, waits to cross over towards the Miller & Carter Steakhouse. Aberdeen Police Headquarters a stone's throw away.

The red man changes to green and he steps out into the road, the invisible man, his shoes squelching through slush. He walks fast, with purpose, a smile on his lips as he walks through the crowds, all heads down, walking their own line, no one any the wiser who walks amongst them. How could they, when he lives the lie?

He glances up at the windows of the high-rise police HQ, seeing faces in the odd one, looking out, staring down on him, as small as an ant. An ant amongst hundreds. Not a clue that he's head of the army.

Chapter 35

Saturday, 30 November

'ARE YOU GOING TO let me in?'

Cooper stood on her doorstep. She smoothed her hair, knew she was looking like she'd been run over, the driver reversing for good measure.

She stepped aside, not too happy that Cooper had refused to give up, the doorbell ringing non-stop on the intercom out in her shed. She led him through the cottage, out the door, through the garden and into the shed. She picked up the brush she'd been working with minutes earlier.

'Hastings know you're here?' Eve pulled at the strap of her dungarees, loosening it as she crouched and dipped the brush into varnish.

'Mearns said she'd cover. Nice bruise.'

Eve lifted her hand to her cheekbone, now a deep shade of purple. Cooper looked away and around the shed, his gaze resting on the cork board where Melanie, Lexie and Jenkins stared out at them, each headline found alongside their bodies pinned next to their photograph. No photo of Sanders. Eve didn't need one. She was never free of the women, or her work, even when she was trying to switch off out here.

Cooper lifted the carrier bag he was holding. 'Brought you some breakfast.' The smell of hot and fattening food was wafting from it and, despite herself, Eve's stomach grumbled.

Cooper smiled. 'Sausage roll. Oh, and the morning paper. You made the front page again.'

Eve groaned, placed the brush on the rag by the varnish tin and stood as Cooper passed the newspaper to her. She was sick of headlines.

Cooper shrugged. 'Got myself a butty in here too. You want a cuppa?'

'Yeah.'

He headed into the house. Eve knew he was giving her space to read the paper. It wasn't good. A large picture of her and Ferguson rolling on the ground, the way her face had been caught in the camera's glare making her look like a rabid dog. The article dredging up the old stories about her failures to date, lack of professionalism and how she was proving to be a loose cannon. Great. She put it on the workbench as Cooper came in, two steaming mugs in his hands. She didn't realize she'd been looking at the paper for that long.

Eve sighed. 'Can't believe Hardy has the brass neck to be banging on about bloody police harassment.' It was like MacNeill all over again.

'Yes, you can.' He set the mugs on the workbench, alongside the carrier bag, before helping himself to a softie full of grease. He leaned against the bench.

280

'Christ, what was I thinking?' Eve bent to pick up the brush and placed the lid on the varnish tin.

'You weren't thinking. And no wonder.'

'I bet Hastings doesn't see it like that.' She threw the brush into the sink in the corner.

'He has to be seen to be giving you a bollocking for what happened. But he'll come round. Elliott's working on damage limitation – pacifying the press and hoping to appeal to a sympathetic public regarding what happened and why.'

'At least there's that.' Eve was glad to hear Elliott was still on her side. 'He's good at what he does.' Eve squirted soap on to her hands, turned the tap on and lathered. 'I feel useless. Hastings is going to take me off the case.'

'You don't know that. He just thinks it's best you stay at home until the dust settles.'

'Stay at home?' Eve turned off the tap, rougher than she needed to be, and reached across for a paper towel. 'This madman killed one of my officers. My friend. I don't want to be at home. I want to catch the bastard.'

Cooper nodded his understanding. 'But who do you think that is? Are you still convinced it's Hardy?'

'Aren't you?' She looked straight at him.

'Honestly? Yes. But it's like I said that day at Hardy's, he could just be some weirdo. I agree, it's hard to ignore all the links, and I get why you think it's him. But I can see that you're desperate to make it him.'

Eve narrowed her eyes. 'You think I want to *make* it him?'

'It's been a tough ride for us all. But it's nothing compared to what you must be feeling.' Cooper stopped, searching for the right words. 'What happened to you and Sanders was horrific. The fact people blamed you, or were at least willing to listen to what was being said, Ferguson and Mearns included, must've made it worse.'

Eve stared at him.

'You must've thought you had to prove yourself. But to come back to this? I doubt there's many officers who could.'

'You think I'm making a bad judgement due to stress or some crusade.'

'I think you need to keep more of an open mind.' Eve was surprised at Cooper's backbone. Surprised but not angry. As usual, he was right. He looked worried though, as if he'd overstepped the mark.

'You're right.' She saw Cooper's shoulders relax. 'I need to refocus. Get off Hardy's back. At least until I can prove otherwise. But I'm not going to lie, I still want to punch that smarmy git in the face.'

She watched Cooper put down his bun and reach inside his jacket to pull out a piece of paper. Eve said nothing as he unfolded it and slid it across the work-bench, letting it rest by her bun, still untouched inside the bag.

His tone was soft. 'Maybe this will go towards proving otherwise. Or not. MacLean found it.'

Eve lifted the paper, her hand trembling as she did. 'What do you mean he found it? Where?'

It was a photocopy of yet another original newspaper headline: '*Female Officer Has Long Road Ahead*'. Eve glanced at the cork board, Sanders' face not there, forever in her mind; another space where the headline should've been.

Cooper coughed. 'It was on Sanders' body, tucked inside the pocket of her pyjamas.'

Eve swallowed, her eyes welling. She'd been devastated by the loss of her friend, couldn't handle the headline that would be left behind. She could see the shadow of a bloodstain, clear on the photocopy, and swallowed again. Hard.

Cooper whispered, 'Do you have any idea what he's trying to tell us?'

She shook her head. 'But I can't see how this isn't about what happened. First Jenkins and now this.'

'Do you think it could be MacNeill and his cronies?'

'I don't know what I think any more. Maybe it was wrong to return. I wasn't ready. I'm not the officer I was. But all this?' She looked at the board, to the headline in her hand. 'I can't even think – other than what happened to Sanders and how people held me responsible – what else this could be.'

Eve put the photocopy of the headline on the table, moved to the window. She couldn't look at Cooper. 'I was starting to make things right with her, to move forward. She wanted me to. I don't know if I can handle this being something to do with me again.'

'Do you remember anything about the article?'

Eve turned. 'Jenkins wrote it. A few weeks after what happened. I remember thinking it was a shit headline at the time. But I thought that about everything she wrote, how shit it made me feel. Still, hardly an original headline, was never going to win any awards.'

Cooper was staring at her. 'I'm sorry Mearns gave you such a hard time.'

Eve shrugged, turned to the window. 'Don't worry about it. I know you would've tried to convince her otherwise. Although I was a bit worried that night we went to yours.'

Cooper frowned. 'Why?'

'Bit dangerous sitting next to her at a dinner table with all those sharp objects to hand.'

She could hear the smile in his voice when he replied, familiar with her habit of using humour to diffuse the tension when she found herself in an uncomfortable situation. 'That's the night I think she realized she was wrong. Listening to you talk about visiting Sanders, discussing what happened to her, what she said to you that day.'

'She wasn't to know.'

'Can I ask you something?'

'Shoot.'

'Are you going to tell her you'd been drinking that night? The night MacNeill attacked you both.'

Eve's heart quickened; she felt close to lashing out at Cooper for bringing it up, but she took a deep breath, calming herself. Beneath it all, she knew he meant no ill. Her colleague, her friend, was asking her to be upfront with her team, to get it out there in order to move forward. Something that made sense – honesty, which she'd always prided herself on before.

'Yes.' Her voice was strong, clear.

'Eve, I think Mearns was a little scared. Anxious.'

'Anxious?' She turned around, surprised.

Cooper smiled. 'You think she doesn't worry?' He tutted. 'Harsh. Anyway, I think she had concerns over whether she was safe working with you. Unfounded, of course. I know that. But I think it was more about her trying to be as good as Sanders. And listening to Ferguson.'

Eve could see why. 'I would never have expected her to step into Sanders' shoes. Sanders was Sanders.'

'I think Mearns will be great in time too. She's opening up a little at a time. That night at mine was the first time she'd ever said anything about herself.'

'What?'

'That her mother used to sing to her.'

'Stop press.'

Cooper shrugged. 'It seemed important to her.'

'Yeah. A favourite memory.'

'Funny that, isn't it?'

'What?' She waited, wondering what he was going to say.

'Us remembering all those rhymes, thinking they were soothing songs to help us nod off. But when you look at the words of some of them, what they were supposed to be about, it's the stuff of horror movies.'

'Never thought about it like that. But yeah, "Rock-A-Bye-Baby" and that bloody cradle falling should've been keeping me awake.' She looked to the carpet, thinking about Cooper with his family. 'You've a great thing going, you know. Louise and the kids are brilliant.'

Cooper nodded, a smile playing around his mouth. 'Thanks.'

'You make out you're tortured by all the kiddy stuff, dancing and having to sing the nursery rhymes and all that, but it's obvious . . .' She paused, a thought flickering out of reach.

'What?'

Eve shook her head. 'Sorry. You know, I thought there was something there . . .'

'Something?'

'When we were talking then, about soothing songs and horror films. I . . . I don't know what I thought and then it was gone again.'

Cooper sat quiet. Eve watched him pick up his butty again, happy to take the time to finish it.

Eve was wracking her brain for what had come to her fleetingly and then as quickly disappeared again. She focused on the rhymes, found herself staring at the headlines on the cork board, each one pinned there in order of when the women had been found. She read them one by one. Reading Sanders' headline on the workbench last. She read them again. And again. Knowing she was close to something . . .

Eve lurched forward, springing away from the bench. 'Holy shit.' She was shouting. 'Give me your phone.' Her hand was flapping, urging Cooper to pass it over.

'What?'

'Your phone. Give it to me.'

Cooper reached inside his pocket, looking confused as he did. She snatched it from him, jabbed at the buttons with both thumbs, frantic, her brow furrowed.

'There.' Eve thrust the phone towards Cooper. 'Look. Jesus, it's been staring us in the face.'

dragged his hands down baggy cheeks, bushy eyebrows hanging over hooded lids. 'Fine.' He sighed. 'Do your digging.'

Eve wanted to rush forward and shake her boss's hand, but she didn't move, the look on Hastings' face making it obvious he had more to say.

'Do your digging, Eve, but if you let me down on this, if I find you anywhere near Hardy, it's yourself you'll be burying.'

Hastings stared at her, looked across at Cooper. 'But before you do, get Ferguson in here.'

Eve stood next to Ferguson in front of the boss. Both of them staring straight ahead, no eye contact made since Ferguson had entered the room. Eve's heart thumped, fingers laced together tight in front of her, not trusting herself next to Ferguson if she loosened her grip.

'Sir, what's he doing here?'

'What do you think he's doing here, Hunter?'

'I mean how come he's in the office and I was told to stay at home?'

Hastings sighed, looking like he was in need of a stiff drink. 'Because, Hunter, I called him in to hear what he had to say. Trying to decide whether to suspend his ass for hitting a senior officer.'

'And?' She wanted to know what she was dealing with.

'And whether I should do the same with you for striking an officer beneath you.'

It was only then that Eve glanced to her side, Ferguson's swollen eye giving her cheekbone a run for its money. She was raging. Still as mad as she had been when they'd been rolling about in Hardy's garden, knocking the shit out of each other. But she'd been wrong. Wrong to handle it in the way she had. Temper winning again. Learning nothing after Sanders. And she wanted to learn. Ferguson was a prat, but he was part of the team, one of hers, and it was her job to keep him safe. To protect him, even if he did screw up.

'It was my fault, sir.'

Ferguson's head whipped round.

Hastings leaned back, spindly fingertips joining together in that pyramid in front of his face. 'You think?'

'Yes. It was the emotion of Sanders. The belief that something had been missed with Hardy. The history with me and Ferguson. I lost it, sir.'

Ferguson was staring at her. She hoped to hell he'd keep his gob shut. She watched him turn to Hastings, knew he wasn't going to.

'I fell asleep.'

Eve shook her head, closed her eyes. So this was how he was going to deal with the guilt he'd always felt about Sanders and now the latest balls-up. She forced herself to open her eyes and face Hastings.

Her boss frowned. 'What do you mean, you fell asleep? When?' The words slow, trying to work something out in his head.

Eve heard Ferguson swallow as he rocked on his feet.

'Watching Hardy's place.'

Hastings sat, his features visibly changing as he joined the dots, anger creeping up his neck and spilling on to his face. 'You fell asleep. What the fuck?' He was up on his feet, chair pushed out of the way.

Ferguson stepped back.

'Are you telling me Hardy could've been out?' Hastings' face was beetroot.

'Sir, please . . .' Eve was aware she had a choice. Let Ferguson take the rap or stick up for her colleague. Defend his mistake when he'd never let her forget hers.

She paused only briefly. 'It was a mistake. We make them. Ferguson has to deal with what that might mean. We've both taken a hit out of it. Literally. But what we need to do is catch the sonofabitch.'

'Do we think it's him?'

Eve didn't think her boss had to ask her that. 'Ferguson reckons he saw Hardy at the window both before and after he fell asleep. He thinks he slept for two hours. It would make it tight for Hardy but possible.'

Hastings rubbed at his temple with thumb and forefinger.

'You could report each other. Jesus, I could report you both. Hardy already has.'

Eve stood, waiting for Ferguson to take his chance, wondering if he would try to get her off the job as he'd wanted. Her heart was pounding. It never came. She breathed out.

'Sir, I have no wish to report anything. We need all the manpower we can get. Ferguson is a good officer. I'd like you to allow us to get on with our job.'

Hastings sighed, sat again, picked up a pen, turning it round and round in his hand. The silence was heavy.

'It's all over the papers. You're putting me in a shit situation.'

Eve stood still, Ferguson rigid beside her.

Hastings chucked the pen on to his desk. 'Don't let me down. Get out of my sight.'

Chapter 36

'I SAY IT'S WORTH a look.' The glare of the computer screen gave Mearns' face a ghoulish glow.

Eve, Cooper and Ferguson stood behind, reading over her shoulder. All four of them staring at the Scottish Intelligence Database, where they'd previously got two hits on old cases, Eve surprised they'd found any at all. One had led them to St Andrews, to Helen Black's murder. The other, they'd ignored.

'You think? The reasons for not going any further with it were obvious at the time.' Cooper sounded far from convinced.

'We wrote this one off because the guy was caught, had done his time. Isn't he terminally ill?' Eve was with Cooper. She was aware of Ferguson; neither of them had said a word to each other since they'd left Hastings' office.

She didn't look his way as Mearns spoke. 'Dundee though. Close to St Andrews and here. You never know what it might kick up.' It was obvious Mearns didn't want to let it go. 'Let me put in a call to the station at least.'

'OK. Give them a call. But before you do, I'd like a word.' Eve motioned to Mearns to go into a side office. She looked at Cooper, grateful for his smile of reassurance. He knew what she was about to do. Today was panning out to be one where she was determined to haul her team on side.

'Something wrong, boss?' Mearns looked worried.

'You could say that.'

Mearns looked confused, as if she was ready to fight her corner.

'Don't worry. It's nothing you've done. It's something I've done.'

Mearns didn't hide her surprise.

'What?'

'You didn't have time for me when I came back.'

Mearns looked to the floor, her cheeks reddening.

'And that's OK. To be expected. I hope you've changed your mind.'

'I—'

Eve raised a hand, silencing her. 'This isn't exactly my comfort zone, but I wanted to be upfront with you, to tell you about that night. The night when Sanders was injured. That I had been drinking.'

Mearns didn't look shocked. 'I know. And I'll be honest too – it was the reason I disliked you. I thought you'd shown total disregard for the job. For your colleague's safety.'

Eve deserved what she was hearing.

'But then I listened to you talk that night at Cooper's. About you visiting Sanders. And I knew. Even if I hadn't then, working with you these last few weeks, I know how dedicated you are, a team player. What happened that night, you drinking, was a one-off. A bad call you lived to regret.'

Back in therapy again. 'OK, that's us up to speed.' Eve headed towards the door; Mearns caught her arm.

'Thanks for telling me.'

Eve nodded once and opened the door, glad to be stepping out into the open plan. 'Go ahead and phone Dundee.' Eve couldn't see anything coming of it, but there was no harm in letting Mearns run with it. 'It's something to be looking at in the meantime, something to give the boss – at least until we figure out where the hell we go next.'

Eve caught square on the canteen-wrapped sandwich that Cooper had flung overhead. An egg-mayo bun. Baby bun by the looks of it. 'Wouldn't have to be starving.' Eve's finger gouged the cling film covering the sandwich.

Cooper tutted but with a smile on his lips. 'You could always go yourself.'

'What and take an hour to get to the canteen till, getting ribbed about the front page at the weekend?' Eve tried to keep her voice jovial, pretending it wasn't more about being cornered by every officer in the station wanting to express their sympathies about Sanders. She bit into the sandwich as far as she could, giving in to her hunger for the first time since the takeaway the other night. Before . . . She didn't let her mind go there, ripped another bite out of the bun instead. She was wiping mayo off her lap, her cheeks full, when Mearns walked in.

'Looks a fine barm.'

She looked to Cooper for translation.

'She means the bun.'

'Oh.' Eve might've got used to the Bolton accent, but the words could still stump her.

Cooper grinned. 'And I bet that's not the only buns she's been thinking of.'

Mearns groaned. 'Jesus, Cooper.'

Eve watched Ferguson's gaze following her as she walked to the centre of their desks.

Mearns coughed. 'Here's what we've got.' She clapped her hands together, clearly glad to be changing the subject. 'Managed to speak to one of the officers who attended the scene at the time. Old-timer but a rookie then. Said it nearly made him give up the job before he'd even started.'

Eve put the remains of the sandwich on the table, feeling that her appetite might be about to go out the window. Cooper did the same and came over to join her, both of them letting Mearns take centre stage, their colleague too buoyed to sit by the looks of it.

'Twenty years since it happened. Ronnie Dempster attacked his wife. Knocked her out and when she came to he went for her tongue with a knife. Only stopped when their ten-year-old son, Shaun, woke and came downstairs. Walked right in on them. His birthday.'

'The kid's birthday? Jesus.' Someone else who must've hated their birthday.

'That kind of woke the husband too, because he stopped and phoned for an ambulance.' Mearns carried on, 'Was too late though: wife had gone into shock, massive blood loss, heart gave out on her. When the police arrived, both the husband and the son were covered in blood. The father for obvious reasons. The son because he'd been clinging to his mum.'

Eve couldn't begin to imagine what that would do to a kid. 'What was the story with the father? Breakdown? Drunk? Psycho?'

'His defence went with diminished responsibility – grief.'

'Grief?' Cooper sounded surprised.

'Yeah. They lost their daughter the year before. Freak accident.'

Cooper tutted. 'The poor kid left behind.'

'Yeah, the officer I spoke to said he ended up with his grandparents on the mother's side. They had nothing to do with the father after that.'

'No surprise there.' Eve swung her seat from side to side, thinking. 'Did the officer know where the father's at?'

'Wasn't difficult. Ronnie Dempster never left the family home. Apart from his stint in prison, of course.'

'You're joking?' Cooper screwed up his face.

'Nope. Officer says it's lying empty.'

'How come?' Eve wasn't sure she wanted to hear the answer.

'Seems the guy's on his last legs. He's in a hospice.'

Cooper groaned. 'That's the end of that then.'

Eve could see Mearns didn't agree.

'I still think we should go and speak to him.'

Eve picked up a pen, tapped it against the desk. 'Why?'

'Dunno. I feel we should write it off properly. I mean, OK, it's obvious he's not our man, but don't we want to know why the tongue, why he did what he did, who was connected to him and the case?'

'No disrespect, but I think it would be a waste of time and, even if I didn't, there's no way Hastings'll go for it.' Eve stood, at a loss as to where to go next. The only real leads they had were the days of the week and the headlines. So they'd start there.

'Cooper, Ferguson, I want you to start looking through the *Aberdeen Enquirer* archives. All the headlines to date have come from there, and all from within the last year. Get Elliott on board.'

Ferguson looked like he was losing the will to live already. At least Cooper tried to look keen. 'What are we looking for, boss?'

'Friday's Child. Loving and Giving. Anything that might hint towards that. Community stories of support and generosity, nominations for awards for caring for others. That type of thing. I know it's a long shot and a shit job, but it's all we've got.'

Mearns piped up. 'What about Dundee?' She wasn't giving up. 'It's only an hour away. Like you say, what else have we got? The boys can drum up some theories for us while we're gone.'

Cooper's eyes widened.

Eve came around the front of the desk, stood in front of Mearns. 'We don't even know if this guy will be fit enough to be chatting to us. Besides, even if he is, what's the point?'

Mearns chewed her bottom lip. 'What would you say if I said it's a hunch?'

Chapter 37

Tuesday, 3 December

FOR THE THIRD TIME, Eve found herself on the A90 heading south. This time with Mearns. It was her hunch after all. Eve was glad of the company, which seemed to have thawed considerably.

She flicked the wipers on, the rain chasing them again, light showers on and off since they'd left Aberdeen, interspersed with breaks of brilliant sunshine. Only needed snow and it'd be the typical Scottish four seasons in one day. She hoped the drive would be worth the effort.

'Ronnie? You awake, Ronnie?' The nurse, Annie according to her badge, wore white-soled shoes that squeaked as she made her way around the bed, talking as she went.

Ronnie Dempster looked swamped by the plumped white pillow his head rested on. His eyes were closed, translucent skin seeming to show every vein in his face, wispy grey hair doing nothing to hide the map of blue lines that continued upwards and across his scalp.

Eve and Mearns loitered outside the door to the room. They didn't speak as they waited while the nurse roused her patient to let him know they were here. Eve conscious of her shiner and how unprofessional she looked. The corridor was quiet, scuff marks where trollies had met the wall, posters showing smiling nurses, an open door next to a visitors' water machine.

Annie was raising the bed, helping Ronnie to sit up a little, his groans audible. She held a white plastic cup to his mouth, dabbed it dry when he'd finished sipping, said something meant for his ears only and then motioned for Eve and Mearns to come in, her upper arms wobbling as she did – two seats already positioned for their arrival.

'Not too long, please.' Annie's voice was brisk, no-nonsense, not waiting for an answer before she marched her large frame from the room.

'Help yourself to water. Think I can even stretch to a biscuit if you open the cupboard there.'

Though his eyes remained shut, Ronnie Dempster's voice was unexpectedly strong. And friendly. It was that more than anything that surprised Eve. She glanced at Mearns before answering.

'We're OK, thanks.'

'Say what you came here to say then.'

Direct. Eve had to give him that. Then again, knowing what Ronnie's future held removed any reason for him to waste time. The problem was that Eve wasn't sure what they'd come here to say – she didn't think there was anything to be said. They were here on a whim. Mearns' whim.

301

She leaned forward. 'We wanted to talk to you about what happened twenty years ago.'

Ronnie opened his eyes, turned his head towards them. Eve wasn't expecting his eyes to be clear, deep blue irises, striking against white. Eyes that looked as kind as his voice sounded when he spoke.

'Annie said. She didn't think it was a good idea, but, like I said to her, it's a bit late in the day for me to be worrying about myself.'

'Thanks for seeing us.' There was a softness to Mearns' tone that Eve remembered from when they'd broken the news to the Rosses that their daughter was gone. It seemed Mearns was as thrown by Ronnie as she was.

Eve continued. 'You'll be wondering why we're here about that. I'll be honest and say we're not entirely sure ourselves. Call it a chat. Something we need to explore and remove from our inquiries.'

Ronnie nodded his understanding. 'I've been thinking about it since you called. As you can probably imagine, I've never stopped thinking about it in twenty years.' He moved his head on the pillow, stared at the ceiling. 'I never saw myself making it this far, you know. Wanted to be away long ago but never had the guts for it. Don't need to worry about that now.' He smiled the saddest smile Eve had ever seen. For a moment, she felt sorry for the guy, had to remind herself why they were here, why the room showed no signs of family or friends.

'You sound like you have a lot of regrets, Mr Dempster. Are you able to talk to us about what happened?'

302

'I don't know what there is to say other than what the police files would've said at the time and all the newspapers after that.'

Elliott had got hold of some archive material, and Mearns had given Eve the gist on the drive down. 'It would help to hear it from you. Not the formal interview. Not the media gossip. Your story.'

Ronnie took his hands from beneath the blanket, clasped them upon his chest, thin fingers and wrists looking like they might snap if touched. 'Surely you can't think this is to do with what's going on up in Aberdeen?'

Mearns looked surprised.

'I may be terminally ill, but I can still read and see the telly.'

'Of course.' Eve nodded. 'Yes, it's connected to what's happening. Your case came up on our system and we're ruling out anything that we can.'

'Look at me, officer. Do you think I'm capable of going anywhere?'

'No, Mr Dempster. We don't think you have anything to do with the recent murders. We're here to chat.'

'To chat.' Ronnie frowned, looking as unconvinced as Eve felt. Eve wanted to say something to stop them from looking any more stupid than they already did.

'Mr Dempster.' Eve turned as Mearns spoke, relieved that she had. 'We don't want to cause you any unnecessary pain or distress. As my boss said, this visit is purely the chance for us to talk, nothing else. As you may appreciate, the method that you used,' Mearns paused, 'it's the same that's being used in these murders.'

303

Ronnie's sharp intake of breath was to be expected.

Mearns gave him a moment before continuing. 'We want to know that we've looked into anything and everything that shows some similarity – no matter how tenuous. You're under no obligation to talk though. We respect that.'

Ronnie's eyes focused on the ceiling. 'I've nothing to lose. Call it a final confession if you like.'

Eve leaned back in her chair. 'Thank you, Mr Dempster. In your own time and how you want to tell it. We're here to listen, not judge.'

Ronnie sighed, a deep rasping exhalation. 'Susie was five. The most beautiful wee thing. Inside and out.' He smiled at the memory. 'I know every father says that, but she was. When we lost her, everything changed.

'Of course you try to keep it together. You have to. Your marriage. Your other kid. Yourself.' Ronnie's voice cracked, tears filling his eyes. 'We did that for a year. I think we even managed to fool folk we were managing. But it was a lie. We weren't keeping anything together. Everything was falling apart around us.' A tear slid down the side of Ronnie's face, the pillow sponging it.

'I tried. I tried hard to keep things going. But I felt like we were clinging to each other on a rock that was in danger of being washed away, dragged under. Sometimes I clung to it so hard, trying to save us, that I felt we were fighting each other off.' Ronnie coughed, choking on his tears.

'Can I get you some water?' Mearns was on her feet, helping Ronnie with a tenderness that Eve had to look away from.

'Thank you.' Ronnie lay against the pillow, gathered himself before continuing. 'It was Shaun who found her. Hanging.' Ronnie gulped. 'She'd been playing, tried to hoist herself up on to a wide ledge to hide, lost her footing and became tangled.'

Mearns spoke softly. 'It must've been difficult for your son.'

'It was torture for all of us. I lost my job. Angie stopped looking after herself. Stopped looking after Shaun. He was only nine years old. He doted on Susie.'

'Did he ever talk about it? About what happened?'

'He tried to. I wanted him to. But me and Angie were struggling to deal with the grief as adults. God knows how we expected a child to handle it.'

Mearns gave him a minute and then asked, 'What happened?'

'The honest answer? I don't know.'

'You don't know?'

'How it got to there, I don't.'

'Grief is a powerful thing, Mr Dempster, as is stress.'

Ronnie unclasped his hands, dry skin scratching. 'We'd had a good day. One of the few we'd managed since we lost her. Spent some time together, the three of us. Everything seemed fine – I felt fine when we went to bed. I woke about eleven p.m. A nightmare. I had them often after Susie died.' He lifted a hand to his forehand, rubbed it. 'I was thirsty. Went to the kitchen to get something to drink. I decided to sit at the table, to shake off the dream. Couldn't stop thinking about Susie. About what had happened.'

'What happened then?' Mearns' voice still gentle.

305

'Angie came downstairs. Before, it would've been to check on me, but by then it was to refill her glass.'

'She was drinking?'

'Yes, and had been for some time. Probably since it happened, but she hid it at first.'

'Did she say anything?'

'No. She didn't give me a second look. Headed for the cupboard to get the whisky. Then the fridge to get the water. Not that it was worth it, for all she added to the glass.'

'Strong stuff.'

Mearns glanced at Eve. They were both aware that eventually Ronnie had turned to drink himself. It was the reason he was in here. Liver cancer.

'Yeah. I asked her to sit with me, said I needed the company. It was the look she gave me. Like I was nothing. That she hated me. She didn't even answer – just turned to leave the kitchen.' Ronnie resumed turning his hands. Over and over. 'It's then that I don't know what happened. Something exploded, something that I hadn't even known was in me. Next I knew she was on the floor, the water jug in pieces beside her.'

'You hit her with it?'

Ronnie nodded, tears streaming down the sides of his face. 'I was in shock. Scared. Worried Shaun would come downstairs.'

'What did you do?'

Ronnie gulped, whatever was in his throat seeming to stick as he started sobbing. 'She came to. Started mumbling, but then, when she realized what had happened, started shouting, blood pouring down her face.

Blaming me for what happened to Susie. Belittling me. Pure venom in her voice.' His chest hitched as he breathed in. 'I wanted her to stop. I wanted her to take back what she was saying. I . . . I didn't know that woman. I wanted my Angie. I loved her. Jesus. I still love her . . . I'm sorry. I'm . . .'

Ronnie was falling apart in front of them. Eve spoke. 'Mr Dempster. Ronnie. It's OK. We know what happened next. It's OK.'

Eve wanted out of here. To leave a dying man in peace. A man who had nothing left and probably hadn't had anything for a long time. Eve knew evil. She'd seen it plenty of times in her job and Ronnie Dempster wasn't it. Yes, he'd killed. In the most gruesome way. But it was clear from the court findings and from speaking to him that he wasn't in his right mind that night. That he'd done his time – both in prison and in his life since. She waited for Ronnie to calm himself.

'I'm sorry we made you go there. We'll get Annie to come and see to you and then we'll leave you alone. But I would like to ask one more thing if I could, Mr Dempster.'

Ronnie's face was soaked, blue eyes diluted with grief. 'What?'

'What happened to Shaun?'

Ronnie closed his eyes, his face creasing in pain. 'I lost my son that night. Angie's parents took him in. I never heard from him or them again.'

'Have you ever tried to find him, to get in touch? To explain?'

307

'Explain what? How I took his mother from him? How, after losing Susie, I did that to him? And because of that he lost me too?' Ronnie laughed, a brittle, bitter sound. 'I didn't deserve to see my son. I still don't. He had a chance at a new life, and I hope he grabbed it with both hands. With good people. That he's a good person and he's forgotten I ever was. And that's the only way it should be.'

Eve was glad to be closing the car door and leaving the Dundee Hospice behind.

'That wasn't what I was expecting.'

Mearns adjusted her seatbelt against her shoulder. 'No, me neither. Never thought I could feel sorry for someone who'd tried to cut out a woman's tongue.'

'You're right there.' Eve turned on the radio, low, some background noise while they talked on the journey home. 'Definitely a dead end, yeah?'

'Eh, yeah. Dead as a dodo. Would be interesting to know what happened to the son though.'

'Nosey.' Eve smiled, realizing how comfortable things had become between her and Mearns, glad of it. 'You'd hope that Ronnie's dream for his son did come true. Something good to come out of all that.'

Mearns raised her hand, forefinger and thumb an inch apart. 'You're a little bit curious too?'

'I guess.'

'No harm in me having a casual check on the grand-parents' whereabouts then?'

Eve sighed. 'If you do, then you didn't get clearance from me. I'm in enough shit as it is.'

'No biggy. A wee check. Curious, that's all.'

Eve smiled, noting Mearns' use of the Scottish word, which sounded bizarre in her Bolton accent. She indicated as she joined the dual carriageway, thinking. Her own thoughts, not to be shared. Adrian Hardy still at the forefront of them.

Chapter 38

Then

It's smaller than he remembers. Even standing here on the pavement outside looking in, everything around him feels miniature, different through adult eyes. But there's something else too. Something that he can't figure out.

He's standing by the lamp post, the one that used to shine its light into his bedroom at night, allowing him to read the words on his wall, helping him to see. To see the truth.

Thick snowflakes are coming fast, turning his hair white, resting on his shoulders like a cloak. He's reminded of the night he heard his parents talking in their bedroom. It was snowing that night too. A duvet around him. A different kind of cloak. But always invisible. He remembers this house. More bad memories than good.

There's movement at the downstairs window. The sitting room. He doesn't move, doesn't stop looking. He locks eyes with the man staring out at him. Realizes what's different about the house at the same time he thinks it about the man at the window. Old, haggard, uncared for. A stranger.

Still he stands there, his hands by his sides, freezing, fingertips tingling, burning in the cold; his toes inside his boots the same. He blinks, a snowflake falling off an eyelash on to his cheek. He wonders if he looks real, standing out here, slowly turning white, fading away to nothing.

He breathes out, his only movement, a cloud of white fog escaping his mouth, making him real, showing he's alive.

The man at the window is moving, stepping away out of sight. He sees his shadow moving behind the glass panel of the door, hears the familiar rattle of the chain as the man attempts to unlock the door.

By the time the door opens, he is gone. Invisible. The old man probably left wondering if he was ever there at all.

Chapter 39

Friday, 6 December

EVE AIMED HER EMPTY coffee cup at the bin, threw and missed. She tutted, stood from her desk and went to get it, taking that morning's newspaper with her, determined not to miss with that. A week since she'd scrapped with Ferguson outside Hardy's and the guy was still getting column inches – the same photo of them tumbling about on the ground splashed across the paper again and again – albeit getting a little smaller with each passing day.

How the hell could it be Friday already? Over a week since Sanders had been killed. And all to show for it, a pointless visit to Ronnie Dempster. They'd searched for potential articles and headlines from the *Aberdeen Enquirer* in the vain hope of a link. So many of them a possibility but yet impossible to cover everyone that featured in them. They didn't have the manpower or the justification. Besides, such a move could create chaos. They'd also revisited the Scottish Intelligence Database again, this time concentrating on the nursery rhymes, and explored school teachers, nursery teachers, people that could be connected to the rhyme. All a very long shot but tasks that made them feel they were trying, doing something. It had given them nothing but dead ends – everyone fully aware there could be another murder tonight.

And to think she'd been convinced that cracking the nursery rhyme had been a breakthrough. All it had done was rub their faces in the fact that they knew what was coming but still could do bugger all to stop it from happening.

Friday's Child. Loving and Giving. How could they even know where to start with that? Eve shoved the newspaper in the bin, stomping on it with her foot for good measure. They couldn't.

But she knew where she needed to be tonight.

Eve was struggling to dislodge her foot from the mesh bucket when Mearns walked into the room.

'I know things are quiet but . . .' Mearns raised her eyebrows, motioned towards the bin.

'Funny. I'm taking out some frustration on Hardy's bullshit in the press.'

'How about shaking it off in the staff canteen?'

'You are joking?'

'Relax, we'll all be on the soft stuff.'

'Not what I meant. All? How can anyone be thinking about chilling in the canteen knowing what could happen tonight?'

'We weren't. Hastings is.'

'Eh?' Eve couldn't get her head round that one.

'Yup, bit of a team grouping. He knows no one's going home tonight, everyone waiting for the call that we know is going to be coming.'

'And we hang out in the canteen? No wonder the press are ripping into us.'

Mearns shrugged. 'We've exhausted everything we can. It's all led nowhere. Apart from Shaun Dempster's grandparents. I managed to get a hit on them. The grandmother at least. Grandfather is dead. But she's in a sheltered-housing complex in St Andrews.' Mearns said the last sentence in a hushed tone, aware Eve didn't want anyone to know she was pursuing that line of inquiry. She had managed to uncover a missing-persons report for Shaun Dempster, lodged fourteen years ago, but nothing else.

'Arrange for us to go and see her instead of doing bugger all else but waiting about.'

Mearns nodded. 'I'll get on it. Don't be hard on yourself. What else can we do but wait?'

Eve curled her lip. 'I can think of other things apart from sitting in the canteen. You know, stuff that would feel more useful while we sit and let another woman die.'

Mearns looked like she'd been slapped, a steel edge to her tone when she spoke. 'It's a bite to eat. We've all got to eat.'

'I'll pass, thanks.'

'The boss wants to make it a nod to Sanders too.' Mearns didn't look Eve in the eye.

'I can do that on my own.' Her tone matched Mearns'.

'You're staying here?'

Eve stared at a spot above Mearns' head. 'I need to go out for a while. I'll have my mobile on me.'

Mearns glared at her, like she knew where she was going. 'Eve . . .'

She walked towards Mearns, over to her desk. 'I've got to go.'

Mearns was acting like she might try to stop her, but Eve kept moving, grabbed her jacket off the seat. 'I'll be seeing you in a matter of hours then.'

Mearns stood rigid, stony-faced and silent – her look saying everything.

Eve made it down the stairs and out into the car park without having to answer to anyone. She lowered her head against the biting wind, the clear black sky illuminated by the city-centre lights, and walked straight past her own car. She beeped the doors of one of the service Vauxhalls and got in, hoping not to draw attention to herself when she drove out on to Queen Street. As she made her way from there on to Broad Street, joining the traffic crawling along past Marischal College, she felt anonymous in the HQ pool car. And positive that she'd go unnoticed parked on Hardy's street.

Eve sat in the dark on Seaton Drive wishing she'd worn a thicker coat, knowing better than to switch on the car's engine to try to get some heat. She watched young kids, in need of a good wash, playing in the cul-de-sac long after they should've been called inside. She hoped they wouldn't try to nick off with her wheels. The downpour was bouncing off the bonnet, hitting against the windscreen, cascading down the side windows, obscuring any clear view she might have had of Hardy's home. She didn't care. She was here and that was better than being anywhere else.

She couldn't see Hardy's car, but this area was notoriously bad for snagging a parking place. The car could be parked three streets away. Either way, if Hardy came out, surely she'd see or hear some kind of movement. She was probably kidding herself, but she needed to feel useful, wanted to prove she was right. She couldn't do that sitting in the sodding staff canteen. What the hell were they all thinking?

Or was it her that wasn't thinking straight? Sat here in the blackness, alone, teeth chattering and able to see next to nothing. She should start the car, move away before she got caught. Knowing it would be more than her job was worth if Hastings got wind of what she was doing. Dr Shetty would have a field day.

Eve fingered the keys dangling above her thigh, curled two fingers and a thumb around the one in the ignition, willed herself to turn it and drive. She sighed, let go of the key fob and dropped her cold hand to her lap. Another half an hour wouldn't harm anyone.

It was pissing down. Ernie fought to pull his suit jacket closed but lost the battle to his paunch. The sodden jacket lay heavy on his shoulders, its smell an ancient memory of school blazers and wet walks home. This was why he didn't do work parties. He was too old for this shit – Christmas do or not.

316

Ice-cold rain battered him, tiny needles pricking at his scalp. He shivered hard as water trickled inside his shirt collar, tracing a path down his back. *What a crock of shit.* He'd waved at every orange light in the dark, and not one taxi had stopped for him. Buses had proven to be like his night – not one going his way. He should've worn an overcoat. He should've phoned Sandra, but it wasn't worth the earache.

He looked across Union Street, the city's clogged main artery. More a bridge than a street, propped on huge stone arches spanning the Den Burn Valley. He peered at the taxi rank tucked down a cobbled side street called the Back Wynd. The narrow street boasted pubs on one side and a high granite wall on the other, concealing a graveyard full of crumbling headstones with newly painted park benches dotted between them. Not your average city-centre attraction.

Taxis and death, he thought. Kind of ironic that everyone standing there was waiting on both. Hopefully for them the taxi would come first. The queue snaked further than he could see – splayed white papers full of chip suppers and kebabs spread throughout the slithering mass.

Ernie decided against joining them and carried on towards the Castlegate, where the city's Town House clock shone like a neon moon in the distance and he could see Aberdeen Council's token Christmas tree, a half-decent effort this year. The lights hanging from it swayed in the wintry wind, festive decorations dominating the historic cobbled pedestrianized area, where once upon a time an altogether different type of hanging took place.

The Silver City they called this place. Ernie laughed at the thought. Pile of shite. Depressing grey more like, but, in the right light, and at a push, you could say the granite sparkled. In the oil-boom days, it had been the place to be. Now it was limping along like everywhere else. Many of the shopfronts were vacant after losing out to nearby shopping complexes, others housing discount stores and charity shops. Bah humbug indeed.

Ernie needed to take a leak. Five pints, their taste gone stale, had played havoc with his old-man bladder. He had a vague memory of someone getting fined after pissing in the street. Knowing his luck, there'd be CCTV. But he was bursting. He spotted an alley ahead, the Adelphi, and turned in. The wet cobblestones proved a challenge to his smooth-soled shoes, graffiti either side of him on the walls of the archway that opened out on to the lane. He'd go in far enough to hide.

Ernie stood in front of what looked like a residential building, black bars on every window, overlooking a smaller lane to his right. No chance of anyone seeing him there. He positioned himself by one of the industrial bins lining one side of the narrow lane. Its wide black plastic lid was prised open by overstuffed black bags, more bags piled against the galvanized metal. A couple of seagulls had pulled at them, piercing holes, the rotting innards tumbling on to the ground.

The gulls here were mutant. Big as small dogs, their piercing squawks and frenzied flapping bouncing off the granite brickwork. It was easy to imagine a lead around their neck – wound tight. The mess their shit made around the city, they'd benefit from puppy training too.

He fumbled to release himself and leaned forward to avoid spraying on his shoes. Not that it mattered, not in all this rain. He stared at a bag hanging out of the bin, noticed something else behind it, suspended over the lip of the bin. *It looked like an arm.*

Eve bolted upright, banging her knee on the steering wheel as she did. 'Shit.' She peered through the windscreen, sure it was Hardy walking towards her on the pavement ahead, confirmed when he turned into his path.

'Where have you been?' Eve was only mildly aware she was talking to herself. Her heart was thundering. She wanted to call Hastings, tell him Hardy had been out, get it on record if there was to be another woman found tonight. But she forced herself not to, made herself wait, weighing the repercussions if nothing happened and it was known she'd come here.

She was still wrestling with what to do when she saw Hardy coming out of the garden again. She watched as he lifted his collar against the wind, head down, car keys in hand. Eve craned her neck, trying to get a clear view, letting Hardy slip away into the darkness, but not too far, before she started the engine.

Ernie's heart was hammering. *It was one of those blow-up dolls, dumped after a stagger.* He zipped up and edged towards the bin, his mouth like cotton wool. The seagulls screamed at the interruption but didn't budge.

Definitely an arm, a ring on one of the fingers. Ernie's hands trembled. The limb looked normal. Not discoloured or injured. *Maybe she'd crawled in drunk.* He knew what the chances of that were, but he was struggling to process what he was seeing.

He reached out and lifted the bin lid, holding it open, careful not to touch the flesh. The smell of bleach, of all things, made him want to cover his nose. But, with his free hand, he moved another bag. Sparkly red material. *Her dress.* He nudged the bag further. A leg. Pale. Thin. A shoe missing from the foot. Ernie tried to steady his breathing. His tongue was glued to the roof of his mouth. He looked along the alley. Saw cars through the archway, splashing through the night. Oblivious.

One more bag.

He wiped his hand against his wet trousers, reached over again, his heart feeling like it was going to burst. He pulled the heavy bag towards him. *Her face. Oh God.* Ernie gagged. It was like a deflated football. Misshapen. Multicoloured. The features beaten to a pulp. The blood was still wet. She hadn't been dead long enough for it to dry black and crust over.

Ernie dropped the lid with a clatter, crouched over and spewed – turkey and trimmings splattering all over the cobbled street and his shoes.

Hardy had led Eve to Union Grove, right to Rosie's door. Eve had parked a safe distance away, close enough to see Hardy getting out of his car beneath the streetlights before standing at the main door of the tenement, his finger pressed against the buzzer and going nowhere.

Hardy wasn't giving up though, and five minutes later Rosie appeared at the door, half dressed, hair on end and obviously with a punter indoors. Hardy was mouthing off, arms flapping. It seemed he could lose control after all. And then Eve's phone rang.

Chapter 40

Saturday, 7 December

EVE PULLED UP BEHIND the police van blocking the bus lane and killed the engine. Three o'clock on a Saturday morning. Beneath the Christmas lights, Aberdeen's innards were spilling out across its streets. She climbed out of the car, dodged a mascara-marked drunk wailing into her mobile phone and lifted her hood against the battering rain, thinking about Hardy all the while.

The arched alley entrance was cordoned off with blue-and-white police tape, Ferguson standing guard. She approached him, thinking it was the first time they'd been alone, face to face, since she tried to cover his ass in Hastings' office. 'What's the story?'

Ferguson breathed out – he'd obviously been expecting her to say something else. 'Female murder vic. Found her in a bin.'

An uneasy feeling crept up the back of Eve's neck, crawling under her hair as she recalled the crime-scene photos of Helen Black in St Andrews. 'Who called it in?'

'Guy on a night out.' Ferguson reached into his pocket for his notebook and flipped it open. 'Ernie Fraser. Nipped up the lane for a quick piss. You could say he stepped into shit instead.'

'We got a statement?' Eve was desperate to put a time on this. To see if Hardy's little trip earlier could tie in.

Ferguson nodded. 'Poor sod puked when he found her. Believe it or not, he was worried we'd charge him for relieving himself outside. One of the lads took him home.'

'Any ID on the woman?'

'Yeah, found her bag alongside her. And of course another newspaper clipping. Cooper and Mearns are inside.'

Eve didn't miss the softness in Ferguson's voice when he said Mearns' name.

She looked over Ferguson's shoulder towards the SOC tent ahead. It was off-balance, covering the pavement and part of the cobbled street. The sound of rain drumming on the plastic was deafening in the narrow space, but she could still hear the hum of the generators lighting the spotlights within, throwing shadows against the walls of those suited and booted inside.

'What's MacLean saying?'

'That he'll know more once he gets her to the lab. But looks like blunt-force trauma to the head. Although, by the state of her face, he kept going long after the fatal blow.'

Eve shook her head. 'Doesn't add up. He's not killed out in the open before, and it's sounding like it's the first time he's lost control.' Eve tried to think of anything in Hardy's demeanour when she saw him earlier that could point to this.

'Maybe he's unravelling. About to slip up.'

'I wouldn't bet on it.' Eve played with the idea of saying something to Ferguson about what had happened between the two of them but thought better of it. 'Anyway, thanks.'

She moved past Ferguson, ducked under the barrier tape and looked at the wet cobbles. Eve paused, the dull ache in her right leg taunting her, but she kept walking, her limp more pronounced on the uneven surface.

Within minutes she was kitted out in the regulation white plastic suit, stepping into the tent . . . and walking into what looked like a reconstruction of the St Andrews crime scene. Eve stood stock still, everything around her seeming to slow and stick.

Her eyes scanned the space and then ran over it again, ticking off the similarities against the crime-scene photos she'd committed to memory and the location itself when she'd gone there with DS Jack Allen.

She could smell the overpowering stench of rotting food and God knows what else coming from the industrial bin in the corner. She watched three SOCOs moving about the cramped space, photographing, recording and bagging. All of them dressed in the sterile boiler suits.

The woman had been moved out of the bin and on to a plastic sheet on the ground. MacLean was crouched by her body. She wore a red dress. Festive. Sparkly. Eve remembered that Helen had been found naked. She swallowed as she stared at what she could see of her face, ignoring the piece of paper pinned above her left breast.

She coughed to alert MacLean to her presence, then nodded towards the body. 'Same MO?'

'Yeah, in that the tongue's missing and there's a puncture wound on the upper arm. Hands bound with venetian-blind cord again.' MacLean shook his head. 'But this.' He pointed to her battered head. 'This is a violence we haven't seen from him before.'

Eve was about to say that they had, only it was a year ago and his first kill in St Andrews, but she stopped herself. She didn't want to make that connection until she was absolutely sure, until she'd spoken to DS Jack Allen again. She felt even more sure that Hardy could be in the frame, bringing St Andrews to Aberdeen with his aunt. She stared at the woman lying in front of her, her face as ruined as Helen's had been. 'Any sign of the murder weapon?'

'No, but that's because it's not a weapon that could be left behind. Your guy walked right out of here with it.'

'What do you mean?'

'His feet. Looks like he kicked and stamped her to death. If she wasn't already dead, that is. Poor cow.'

'Jesus.' Eve was scrambling to remember anything about Hardy's footwear.

'Aye, and here's another thing. Unlike the others, she wasn't murdered where we found her. The body's been moved. And dressed again.'

'Moved and dressed again?' A little of the fire left Eve.

'Yup. Lividity isn't consistent with how she was found in the bin. There's wounds to the body that had to be carried out when she was naked. And by the stink, I'd say she's been scrubbed with bleach.'

'How long?' Eve closed her eyes.

'I'd say at first assessment, she's been dead over eight hours.'

In that moment, the fire in Eve was extinguished completely. Was she wrong about Hardy? Then again, she hadn't been watching him for the past eight hours. Eve forced Hardy from her mind – thought about Helen Black, the bleach something that couldn't be ignored. 'How do you know she was naked?'

'The bleach obviously but the marks from his footwear. Bruising beneath her collarbone looks like a footprint, but I'll need my stuff at the lab. Not sure yet whether we'll get anything from that. Oh, and her dress is on back to front – and the zip's broken.'

'Broken by him or already?'

'Looks like it might have been held shut with something when she wore it, but it could've been him and his rage.'

That rage. It mirrored the way in which Helen Black had met her end. She was willing to bet once MacLean got a better look that the footprint would prove to be from Carolina work boots. But she said nothing except, 'Why the hell would he dress her again?'

'You're asking a sane question of someone who appears very much not to be firing on all cylinders,' MacLean said. 'Blind rage, then remorse? Dressed her to move the body? Could mean anything or nothing.'

'Anything else?' Eve asked.

'That's all I've got.'

'OK. Thanks.' Eve spotted Cooper and Mearns over in the corner talking with one of the SOCO team. She was about to go over when Cooper caught her eye, acknowledged her with a nod. He finished talking and strode over to her. 'Is it me or are you getting a severe case of déjà vu?'

'Was about to say the same.'

The SOCOs started to examine the body, Eve and Cooper waited for the obvious to be explored first. Eve held her breath as they unpinned the newspaper cutting and opened it.

'*Charity Worker Hailed a Modern-Day Saint*'. Eve wanted to scream in frustration; instead, she looked over at Cooper as she spoke.

Cooper sighed. 'I reckon it's time we got to HQ, grabbed a crap coffee and gave Jack Allen a call.'

Eve nodded, started for the tent door where Mearns had arrived. 'I'll call Jack, but I'll leave you to drink the crap coffee. Mearns, we'll fill you in on the way.'

'OK. One thing you'll want to know before you do though.' Mearns caught Eve's elbow.

'What?'

'Your little camping trip at Hardy's tonight was a waste of time.'

Eve reddened, not surprised Mearns had read her easily. 'The time frame still means he could've been here.'

Mearns shook her head "Fraid not.'

Eve felt like her heart had hit her protective soles. 'How come?'

'Found out from one of the guys that Hardy was picked up early yesterday. Complaint for harassment from Rosie. He only got out three hours ago and looks like he went home and then straight out to find her. Seems him and Rosie had a little set-to about some punter. Got nasty. She's in A&E and he's back in a holding cell.'

The tent wall was swimming in Eve's vision. She'd been there. While Rosie was still safe. She'd been wrong that Hardy was their man for the murders. If the tent that they stood inside hadn't been plastic, Eve would've punched it.

DS Jack Allen didn't take kindly to being woken at 4.30 a.m. – not until he realized who was calling and what she had to tell him. Eve listened to Jack lighting his second fag in the ten minutes they'd been on the phone, a full run-down already given of what had been found on Adelphi Lane.

'It has to be the same guy.' Jack coughed for the ump-teenth time.

'That's what I'm thinking. Cobbled lane. The bin. Where the body was. Beaten black and blue. The use of feet instead of a weapon. But most of all the bleach.'

DS Allen inhaled sharply. 'Yup. But does it fit your guy?'

Eve had told him about the nursery-rhyme theory but definitely not about Hardy, thank God. 'Yeah, not the violence though, but we found ID beside her. Sarah Crawley. Turns out she was a children's charity worker. Got a bit in the press a couple of weeks ago about all the work she'd been doing.'

Jack spluttered as he inhaled. 'Friday's Child. Loving and Giving.'

'Yeah. Sick guy. I can't see what the link is. Why that rhyme. Who we need to be looking for. How we start to confirm a connection to St Andrews a year ago.'

'Could be a million things. Is there anything different between the scene of Helen's murder and Sarah's?'

'Helen was naked, wasn't she?'

'Yeah. Never did find her clothing.'

'Sarah was dressed. But according to our pathologist he'd attacked her naked and then dressed her afterwards. I can't get my head around him dressing her again.'

'Was MacLean sure?'

'Yeah, markings on the body pointed towards it, plus the zip-up dress was on back to front.'

DS Allen started to say something but then began wheezing and coughing hard. Eve had to hold the phone away from her ear. 'Jack? You OK?'

It took a while for him to answer. 'Sorry, yeah. You caught me there with the dress.'

'What do you mean?'

'Helen was wearing a dress that zipped up too, but nothing unusual in that.'

Eve was on alert nonetheless. 'Anything else about the dress?'

'Erm, yeah. We interviewed her flatmate after the murder and it stuck in my head that the dress we were looking for was a zip-up because she gave us a story about having to help Helen get dressed before they went to the pub. About them having a laugh about it after a few wines while getting ready.'

'What, was she too drunk to dress herself?'

'No, the flatmate said she had to use her initiative to fasten the thing. Said the zip was broken.'

Every hair on Eve's arms rose. 'Say that again, Jack.'

'What? The zip was broken?'

Eve closed her eyes, not wanting to ask what she was about to. 'Jack, what colour was the dress?'

'Red. Sounded totally out of character for Helen, but the flatmate said she wanted to dress fancy for a change and she'd lent it to her. Real party dress. A sparkly number.'

Eve took a deep breath. 'Jack? I think we've got our link.'

'How?'

'Sarah was wearing Helen's dress.'

Chapter 41

'ARE YOU COMFORTABLE, RONNIE?'

He nodded once at his nurse's question without looking away from the telly in the corner of his room. Usually they'd chat at this point in the evening. Meaningless chit-chat that broke up his day. She'd move around his bed, checking charts and equipment, tidying what little there was to tidy, getting ready to clock off from her shift, and he'd think of any old drivel to keep her there. To have company. But he didn't want her to stay tonight.

Annie stepped into his eye line. He craned his head to the left of her. She looked at him, surprise on her face, then turned to look up at the telly, shuffling sideways as she did, eager to keep her patient happy.

'Terrible business that.' Annie shook her head, a plastic cup stuffed with used tissues in one bloated hand, an empty water jug in the other.

Ronnie's eyes flickered from the telly to the water jug, his mind seeing broken glass on a cold linoleum floor.

He closed his eyes, inhaled long and slow through his nose and made sure his eyes were focused on the TV when he opened them again.

Annie sighed. 'Poor woman. That's five in as many weeks.'

Ronnie dug his nails into his palms beneath the bed sheets.

'I mean, imagine dumping her in a bin. Left lying there like a piece of rubbish. God only knows how her parents must feel.' Annie tutted, stood looking at the telly.

Ronnie stared at her back, thought about how proud her parents must be that she spent her working days caring for others. He thought of Susie, didn't have to imagine how a parent felt to lose a child. To lose two children. But he knew his daughter would've grown to be an adult whom he could've been proud of. His eyes wandered to the jug again.

Broken glass. Shattered dreams.

He clenched his teeth, nails drawing blood from the thin, ageing, useless flesh of his hands. He didn't want to think about that night. Had never allowed himself to, no matter what he'd told the coppers.

But he had permitted himself to think about Susie. Had never stopped thinking about her over the years. About how alive she had been. About how she was found. Reliving every second that he'd stared at her small lifeless body hanging there. Her delicate, inno-cent, beautiful face turned ugly, her tongue hanging limp. How he'd watched his wife fall apart, had felt his son slipping ever further away from him. Loss. Ripping the seams of their life apart. Stitch by stitch until there was nothing left but rags.

Thinking about Susie was what he'd had to do. The only way he'd been able to find comfort. The reason that justified that night. The one thing that made what he'd done right.

'How many are there going to be, Ronnie? Before these numpties get their fingers out of their backsides and catch him. How many, eh?'

Ronnie swallowed, guilt a bitter pill. 'Annie, I want to go to sleep.'

Annie put the cup and jug on the chair by the door, jumping to attention when her patient spoke. 'Of course, of course. Been a long day.' She fussed at his bed sheets, plumped his pillow. 'Do you want the telly left on?'

He shook his head. She lifted the remote from his bedside cabinet, pointed it at the telly, humming a tuneless song as she did, binned bodies forgotten. 'There's your buzzer, pet. I'll be seeing you in the morning.'

Ronnie watched her leave the room, then stared at the ceiling, beyond the roof tiles and into the past. He was still staring when the lights went off in the ward, one by one. It was only then that he let the tears run free. In the safety of darkness. And only then that he let himself think about that night.

How many more indeed?

Chapter 42

NANCY MORRISON RESEMBLED A GNOME. At least Eve thought so. Shaun Dempster's grandmother smoothed the loose grey strands of her hair towards the bun they'd fallen from, chubby gnarled fingers trembling as she did. Nerves, perhaps, but most probably age.

'When did you last see Shaun?' Eve's voice seemed too loud in the low-ceilinged room. Everything about the sheltered-housing cottage felt like it had been built in miniature. She wanted to get to why they were here, the small talk starting to grate.

The old woman stood from her armchair, offered the plate of warm scones again to her and Mearns that she'd not long put on the coffee table. 'Please, help yourselves.'

Eve declined, wondering if the woman was ever going to answer a question.

'He was sixteen the last time we saw him.' Nancy's voice was raspy, her round face and ruddy cheeks quivering as she spoke.

'When you filed the missing-persons report?'

'Sorry?' Nancy cupped her ear, shouted the word, the hearing aid tucked amongst her wiry hair failing in its job. It was the reason they'd had to travel to her when they realized a phone call wasn't going to work. Eve repeated the question.

'Yes.' Nancy pushed at the round-rimmed glasses perched on the end of her nose. 'We reported Shaun missing three days after he left.'

'Why did you wait so long?' Mearns was doing her best to balance a broken scone on a napkin as she shouted.

'Shaun had gone off before but never for that long.'

'Where would he go? To friends?' Eve glanced at Mearns as she asked, wondering what the elderly woman might do if she let a crumb fall – the sitting room was pristine, floral cotton protectors on the arms either end of the beige sofa.

'I'm not sure Shaun had many friends at home. We thought about moving.' Nancy looked to the floor. 'But it's true you can't run from your problems.'

'Memories of your daughter? Of your granddaughter?' Eve kept asking the questions while Mearns did her best to eat the crumbling home bake.

Nancy shook her head. 'I never wanted to run from memories of Angie or forget Susie. I just didn't want to be near where that bastard had been and was again after prison.'

Mearns coughed, struggling to swallow what was in her mouth. Nancy didn't falter. 'I didn't care even when he was in prison or not. He was still there, everywhere we went. Then he had the brass neck to return to that house after they released him. Not even a life sentence, though he took my daughter's. Got off with murder, literally, because of some cock-and-bull story of grief. What do you call it now? Post-traumatic stress?'

Mearns nodded and finally crumpled the napkin, careful to place it on the coffee table without anything falling to the carpet. 'And you never saw him?'

Nancy shook her head. 'No. I heard he was reclusive. It was tough for us. With Shaun.'

'You must've wanted to protect him.' Mearns softened her tone but maintained the volume.

Nancy looked to the floor. 'It's all I wanted to do.'

Mearns nodded, understanding. 'Losing his sister and then what happened with his parents might've made him confused. Angry. Distant. He was only ten, wasn't he?'

Nancy worked her wrinkled lips against each other, crops of wiry grey hair on her top lip and chin visible from where Eve sat. 'Yes. I . . . we tried to reach him.'

'Did you ever get help?'

'We tried. It wasn't good, keeping all that inside. What he must've seen.' Nancy sighed. 'We worried we weren't enough, that we were doing something wrong. Even with help it didn't work.'

Mearns leaned forward, took hold of the old woman's hand. 'I'm sure you did the best you could.'

Nancy patted Mearns' hand with her free one, reversing roles. 'Thank you, dear, but I sometimes wonder if, having a father like Shaun did, if there's anything we could've done.'

336

Eve wasn't shocked by Nancy's words, could see why there was no understanding of Ronnie's state of mind. He had taken her daughter. She wanted to take the opportunity to introduce the subject.

'Shaun's father said he doted on his sister Susie.'

Nancy froze. 'You've been to see him?'

Mearns nodded. 'Yes. I told you that on the phone. It was the reason we looked for you.'

Nancy glowered. 'My hearing's not the same as it was, neither's the mind. But you would've heard me if I'd caught that little snippet.'

'I can imagine it must be hard.'

'I hear he's dying.'

Her voice was devoid of emotion.

'He's in a hospice, yes.'

'Good. I hope it's slow and painful.' Nancy clasped her hands under her bosom, seemingly satisfied.

Eve changed tack. 'What was Shaun's relationship like with his parents? With Susie?'

'Happy. Or at least I always thought it was. Mind you, I used to think that Ronnie was a good man.' Nancy laughed, not a merry sound. 'Susie was great for Shaun, took him out of his shell when she was born. She did that to people. Such a contented baby. Loving. Was growing into a fantastic wee girl.'

'Sounds like they had a good relationship,' said Eve, trying to prise more from her.

Nancy nodded. 'She idolized her big brother. Would play whatever he wanted to play. Do whatever he wanted to do. It was his idea to play hide-and-seek that day . . . Can you imagine?'

'Her death must've been difficult for him.'

'He found her. Hanging there.' A crack in her voice.

Eve closed her eyes, imagining what that must've done to a ten-year-old kid.

'There were days when I wondered if things might've been different if it had been Shaun.' Nancy's words sliced into the silence.

Eve's mouth opened involuntarily. She heard Mearns' sharp intake of breath by her side.

Nancy's eyes were brimming. 'Terrible, isn't it? But I wonder if the family would've been torn apart like it was if it had been him instead. If my daughter would still be alive.'

The room stilled but for Nancy's heavy breathing.

'I don't mean what I said to sound bad. Susie was the apple of my daughter's eye. The girl she'd always wanted. I used to wonder if Ronnie was jealous, the way he'd watch them together. You'd expect that from the sibling, wouldn't you? Not the father. Losing Susie . . . my daughter never recovered.'

Nancy's hands were shaking, the shame she felt in her admission clear to see.

'It certainly didn't bring back the wife Ronnie might've felt that he'd lost. I'm not saying she loved her son any less, I just always wondered if things would've been different. After what Ronnie did to our Angie, I wondered if maybe Shaun went through more than I knew in those four walls. If our inability to help him was about more than losing his sister.'

Eve didn't want to get on to the subject of Ronnie but couldn't help herself. 'When we went to visit Shaun's father, he was full of remorse. Spoke about how everything fell apart after Susie's death. It seemed grief and stress, mental illness, played a large part in what Ronnie did.'

'He would sell that story, wouldn't he?'

There was no point in discussing it any further. 'Was there ever any news on Shaun after his disappearance?' There hadn't been anything in the media – Elliott had done an extensive search.

'His wallet was found washed up on the beach three months later. Everything still in it. Always had it in his back pocket.'

Mearns flinched, neither of them expecting to hear what Nancy was telling them.

'Do you think he was capable of taking his own life?' Eve watched tears drop from Nancy's eyes as she nodded.

'I knew as soon as they found it. Some woman walking her dog. Never questioned he was dead. We even held a service for him. Wanted to remember him, to let him rest with respect. Even though I knew he was gone, I tried to kid myself for a while that it might've been an accident. Thought maybe even someone else did it. But I think he wanted to be free of it all, you know?'

Mearns nodded. 'Maybe he thought he'd be with Susie again.' She looked around the room, at the photo frames dotted here and there. Pictures of an older gent whom Eve took to be Nancy's husband. None of her daughter. Not one of her grandkids. 'You must miss him.'

Nancy closed her eyes. 'Every day. Six weeks after his wallet was found, my husband dropped dead. Massive heart attack. I blame the stress of it all. You can see why I hate Ronnie Dempster. What that man took from me.'

Ronnie. The hopes and dreams he'd had for his son. Not knowing about his disappearance. None the wiser about the wallet or that a service had been held in his son's memory. A man imprisoned and then inebriated throughout his freedom. She wouldn't be the one to deliver the news to him. There was no need.

Mearns passed Nancy a tissue from her pocket. 'You have memories, Mrs Morrison. Good ones from before. He can't take that.'

Nancy dabbed at her eyes. 'Memories can be as painful. They were such beautiful children.' She straightened, seemed to brighten a little. 'Would you like to see a photo? I have some in my loft. I can have Charlie, our caretaker, find them. He put the stuff up there. Was too painful to look at them every day. He'll know where to look for the photo albums. I could ask him.'

Eve felt for the woman, didn't want to refuse her offer, even though she knew there was nothing left for them to find here.

'We'd love to see a photo, Nancy. If I give you our address, could you send us one?'

Chapter 43

Wednesday, 11 December

HASTINGS RAPPED ON THE desk at the front of the packed incident room. Chairs scraped, backsides hitting seats as fast as possible. Eve leaned against the wall, bracing herself for the fallout.

'Quiet, please. Quiet.' Hastings' voice was gruff, his sickly face glistening with sweat, patches visible on his shirt beneath his arms as he raised them to hush the room. 'Thank you.'

Eve looked around at the officers who had been working non-stop over the last five weeks. Her team. All of them desperate for a lead. To feel they were doing their job, to believe they might glimpse justice for the women murdered. They'd tried hard and she wanted more than anything to shield them from her boss's imminent rant.

Hastings picked up that morning's newspaper, flapped it in the air. 'We are being damned in the press, doubted by our public.'

Here we go.

'But this is not about failure. I don't think we can speak about that with the efforts that have been made by this team.' Hastings glanced around the room.

Eve straightened, stepped away from the wall.

'I have to commend you all in the hours that you've put in, the countless lines of inquiry that you've followed, the things that you've had to deal with.' Her boss turned to the whiteboard behind him, five A4-sized, coloured crime-scene photos a reminder of what they'd had to endure. Ferguson sitting up front, panting at his boss's feet.

'This case has not been without its setbacks and difficulties.' Hastings glared at Ferguson as he spoke, stopping the officer's adoration in its tracks, and then looked over at Eve. 'But like any case, we've looked for the facts, for the answers. Ryan Phillips, Michael Forbes, Johnny MacNeill, Adrian Hardy. All viable suspects. But all dead ends.'

Eve felt each name like a punch to her stomach, didn't need to be reminded that it had all led nowhere.

Hastings rumbled on. 'Old cases have been revisited, tenuous links explored. But nothing.' Hastings threw down the paper, Eve waiting for him to finally lay into them.

'However, we've had sound leads too. Working out why these women are losing their lives on the days and in the ways that they are.'

Eve dropped her gaze to the floor as her boss turned in her direction, feeling like an idiot for blushing as all eyes focused on her, thrown by her boss's uncharacteristic positivity.

'But it hasn't been enough. It didn't stop Sarah Crawley losing her life. A woman thrown away like a piece of rubbish.'

It was good while it lasted.

'Most would say we deserve to be getting battered. Perhaps they're right. But I know we've felt every one of those murders, whether the press have reflected that or not.' Eve looked over to Elliott, saw him flinch.

Hastings continued. 'Yes, they lost Jenkins. But we lost one of our own too.'

Murmurs round the room, everyone pulling back their shoulders at Hastings' motivational speech. At the mention of Sanders. Even Eve felt her shoulders straightening. She wondered where her boss had got the new approach from, could imagine that he'd been practising in front of the hallway mirror that morning. She had to admit it was a tad cringy – real American sports locker-room stuff, but it kind of suited him, might even lose him his Grinch moniker. That thought could've made Eve smile if it wasn't for what he was talking about. Eve tried to refocus on what her boss was saying.

'Time to prove them wrong, folks. To find that link we've been looking for. If we're correct the murders are linked to this nursery rhyme, then we have two women left. Two women we can still save.' Hastings let his words sink in. Eve thought the officers were in danger of rising in rapturous applause. 'As I said, this is not about failure. We can still salvage something. But we need to revisit everything, to think about what hasn't been looked at. Our killer is not going to come walking through that door.'

With that, the incident-room door opened, all heads turning towards it, out-of-place laughter rippling through the room as the acne-faced mail guy stood there frozen, not used to being anything but invisible. He edged the pile of mail on to the already overloaded desk by the door and scurried out again.

Hastings looked deflated that he'd lost his audience and was searching for the right words to buoy the team again when he spoke. 'If there is a positive to come out of this, the concerns we had about one of our suspects have been proven right.'

Eve stared at her boss, willing it to be Hardy. For her to know that her gut instinct wasn't completely off radar.

'Adrian Hardy has been charged with GBH as a result of his attack on Rosie Donald. She's in intensive care but should pull through.' The room broke into chatter before Hastings regained control. 'All right. All right. It's time to regroup and refocus. We can find this guy. We need to believe that. Go get me something, people.'

Hastings swept towards the door, Eve not missing the nod in her direction as he left the room. She wanted to enjoy the moment as Elliott reached over to clap her arm, to feel reassured that she still had what it took to do the job, but it was a bittersweet consolation when she thought of Rosie lying in that hospital bed.

Chapter 44

Now

He smiles at the man sitting in the doorway in the Back Wynd off Union Street. Passes a newspaper to him – a fiver too.

The man's eyes widen. 'Cheers, mate.' Throaty. A roll-up, dirty from the hands that made it, waving in his mittened hand as he salutes him. And so he should. Little does he know that he's looking at the front-page news. At least he's trying to share it with him. After all, everyone deserves to know.

He salutes back at him, hiding his disgust at the chip-pan hair, the grime on his hands and the smell that wafts up from the stained sleeping bag. It's nice to be nice. That's what the normal folks do.

He strides on to and down Union Street. Inhaling the exhaust fumes, believing they are fuelling him. He's on a set course, moving for no one. Not flinching when he's elbowed and sworn at. He moves among them, no closer to being caught. Invincible.

He stops, looks across the road at the Adelphi Lane; still a police presence there. No fear of them and their incompetence.

The papers haven't made enough of their failures. The Hardy witch hunt not so scandalous now he has been arrested for something concrete. Such a shame. He could've had so much more fun with that.

He misses Jenkins. She made it fun. Her replacement at the Aberdeen Enquirer *a jobsworth out for recognition as a serious reporter, not one for scandal or hearsay. Another woman in a man's world but one who is no use to him. Someone had to tell the new bitch that she worked on the local rag, and always would if she didn't at least try.*

Not to worry. Two more women and the whole story would be told. The new reporter would break the rules then, especially when she found out whom he'd picked for his ending.

Chapter 45

Saturday, 14 December

IT WAS THE TOILET brush clutched in Shelley Anderson's hands, bound by venetian-blind cord, that made a mockery of the mess her body was found in. Nothing clean about it, apart from the cut that had taken the young mother's tongue.

Frustration and guilt swept over Eve in waves. She'd failed Shelley. She'd failed them all. But how could she have saved her? Seemingly random selections, two close to Eve, the others never known to her. Maybe all part of the plan to stay one step ahead of the game.

There was a cloying smell of drying blood, a whiff of urine and faeces beneath it. From where she stood outside the cubicle door looking in at her she couldn't be sure if the underlying smell was coming from Shelley or the toilet. Shelley's work uniform of blue tabard and trousers was drenched in blood, the walls around her sprayed bright red, mimicking some grotesque graffiti. But somehow her murderer had found a clean space to pin the expected headline, neatly folded as always.

Shelley was seated on the lid, facing Eve, propped against the wall. Mouth open, tongue gone.

Eve stared at her, seeing Shelley's three-year-old son instead. An innocent boy whose mummy wouldn't be coming home tonight or ever again. She swallowed and stepped back, the space so tight she banged against the wash-hand basin behind her. She turned and pulled the door open, breathing deep as she stepped out into the small open-plan office that was teeming with bodies, none of whom worked here.

'Shelley's mother's been notified.' Cooper's voice was soft, the bodies around him silent apart from the muffled rustle of their white suits as they moved about the premises, the overhead strip lights harsh against the winter skies outside the windows.

'Is there someone with her?' Eve couldn't bring herself to mention the boy.

'Family liaison should be with her. The boy's in bed, has been since half an hour after Shelley dropped him with his grandmother.'

Kai. A name making the kid all the more real, impossible to ignore. His mother forever to be known as the sixth victim. 'Saturday's Child Works Hard for a Living.'

Cooper nodded. 'Worked a supermarket job in the mornings Monday to Friday while Kai was at nursery, and then her mother came to watch him five nights a week while she cleaned here after hours and once a month on a Saturday morning when she did the carpet clean, etc.'

Eve was willing to bet the article that went with whatever the headline was would be some kind of feature on the struggles of single parenting. 'Only her that cleaned here?'

Mearns glanced around the office. 'Small place. Had keys to let herself in and out. Worked seven to nine p.m. weekdays and seven to ten a.m. on the Saturdays. Mother called it in at eleven thirty a.m. when she failed to come home and she couldn't reach her on her mobile.'

'How did he know she'd be here? That she'd be on her own?'

'Like the rest of them. Watched her in advance or knew her somehow. Didn't have to worry about CCTV. Too small a business to be shelling out for that kind of thing.'

MacLean came into view over Cooper's shoulder. Anything he had to say would be nothing new, the pathologist only confirming that when he spoke. 'Little point in even saying it.'

Eve tutted. Forensics would be the same. 'It's hardly a comfort, but if this guy is working the way we think he is, then there's one more. And hopefully we'll be able to get to her first. We have to get to her first. Then at least it'll be over.'

MacLean raised his eyebrows. 'You think?'

Eve shrugged. 'I have to. It's the only thing keeping me going.'

Chapter 46

Sunday, 15 December

'MORNING, SUNSHINE.'

Ronnie gritted his teeth at the sound of Annie's sing-song voice, kept his eyes shut as she rattled the blinds.

'Beautiful day.'

As if he gave a shit. He listened to her shuffle about the room as she performed the usual morning routine, knowing he'd have to open his eyes soon to watch her poke and prod at him before scoring her chart for the first of many times that day.

He heard her lift the TV remote from the adjustable bed-table that had been pushed to the side the night before, same as usual. The sound of other voices from far-off places filled the room, and he was glad they were at least drowning out hers. Until he realized what they were saying, his eyes opening as he listened, his brain knowing it was coming before he could even make sense of the words; wishing in that moment, more than anything, that he could trade what he was seeing and hearing for being poked and prodded.

Six thirty a.m. Eve had been in bed three hours, not one of them spent sleeping since finding Shelley Anderson the day before. She listened to her phone vibrating on the bedside table, watched the light from the screen bouncing off the ceiling in the dark hole that was her bedroom. At this time in the morning, it could be nothing good.

'Hunter.'

'Good morning, ma'am.'

It was the barrel-shaped call handler who had quashed her hopes four weeks ago when he'd burst into the incident room with the news that their one and only suspect at the time, Ryan Phillips, had been found dead in his car. Eve wondered what happy news he would be delivering today.

'I have an urgent call.'

Eve slumped against her pillow. 'Surely someone at the station can take it?'

'Says it's for you.'

'Doesn't—'

'Guy's name's Ronnie Dempster.'

Eve sat up. 'Put him through.' The line crackled. 'Hello?'

'I saw the news.' Ronnie's voice was a whisper, the kindness in it replaced by what sounded like grief and a raw desperation.

'Did you know Shelley?'

351

'No.'

Eve let the silence stretch, waiting to hear what Ronnie was struggling to say. She heard him swallowing, pictured him lying there, his head resting on the oversized pillow plumped by Annie. Eve gripped the mobile phone tighter, wanting to take a deep breath of her own when she heard Ronnie's, knowing he was about to talk.

'I didn't know Shelley, but I know who killed her.'

Chapter 47

'DO YOU BELIEVE HIM?' Hastings sat on the edge of his desk, arms crossed. Eve sat in between Cooper and Mearns, while Ferguson loitered around behind them. All five bleary-eyed but in the office within an hour of Ronnie's call.

'He believes what he's telling me.' Eve didn't know what to think. 'Says his son came to see him a year ago. Or rather he saw his son.'

They'd been through this part once already, were going over it again, trying to make sense of it.

'Standing on the street.' Mearns sounded excited that maybe her hunch about Ronnie had been right after all. 'Outside his house.'

'Yes. Says he knew it was Shaun as soon as he saw him. Was like looking at himself when he was the same age.'

'And he stood there, on the street corner, staring at the house.' Ferguson this time, sounding less than convinced.

353

'That's what he said. It was snowing. Heavy. Said Shaun was standing on the pavement, not moving, snow gathering around him. Ronnie was in shock, couldn't move from the window at first, was too scared he'd leave. Or that he wasn't real.'

'And that's the problem.' Mearns sighed, having to admit facts. 'Ronnie was at the height of his drinking at that point. What's to say he wasn't blotto, hallucinating?'

Eve nodded. 'Exactly what I thought, especially when he said Shaun was gone by the time he managed to get his feet to move and went to the door, wanting to ask him in.'

'What changed your mind?'

This was as far in the story as Eve had got before they'd started asking questions.

'When Ronnie told me that he woke the next morning to the news of Helen Black's murder.'

Eve was expecting the silence, but it was still deafening when it came.

It was Hastings that broke it. 'And he automatically thought it was Shaun?'

'Not straight away, no. Says it niggled at him that the two incidents happened close together.'

'Niggled?' The sarcasm in Ferguson's voice was clear. 'That's all it did?'

Eve sighed. 'I'm only repeating what Ronnie said. He wondered if it was some kind of message from Shaun. About what he'd done. To his mother. To them all.'

'Bit of a long shot, isn't it?' Cooper seemed unwilling to buy into it. 'Father kills mother, and son turns into a killer too? And why Helen?'

'Maybe, but we all know it can happen. Look at Johnny MacNeill and his son. Both hard men, both wife beaters, both drug dealers, both rapists.' She swallowed. 'But what makes it probable is that Helen went to school with Shaun's sister. She and Susie were best friends. Ronnie told me about an article that appeared in the local press afterwards: kids and teachers paying their respects, and Helen was right up there.'

'Shit.' Cooper was connecting the dots.

'Tell me about it. But you're still right that it's a long shot, and eventually that's what Ronnie thought. Blamed his thinking on the drink and guilt. Told himself he hadn't seen Shaun. Got lost in the bottom of a bottle again.'

'And then what?' Hastings uncrossed his arms, more open to what Eve was saying. He rested his hands either side of him on the desk.

'And then Melanie Ross. By then Ronnie was sober and dying. In the hospice. Didn't think anything of the murder at first, but by the time Sanders was killed Ronnie knew it was Shaun.'

Mearns frowned. 'How?'

'Ronnie had worked out the rhyme before we did. Before he knew about the tongues. When we went to visit him and told him why we were there, he knew for sure.'

'Why didn't he say anything?'

'It's his son. You heard him that day. You saw him. He wanted to believe that Shaun had gone on to a make a better life for himself.'

'But he knew.' Mearns sounded like it was all making perfect sense.

'Maybe he was still clinging to that hope, even then. The guy had lived a life of guilt after what he did to his wife – his kids' mother. Maybe he couldn't bear the thought he was responsible for what had happened to his son too. That his actions caused all these women to die?'

'Didn't you tell him about our visit to Nancy?' Mearns obviously didn't want to leave anything unexplored. 'That Shaun's grandmother had told us about his disappearance and that she believed he was dead?'

'Yes, but there was never any concrete evidence.'

Mearns couldn't argue with that. 'You believe what Ronnie's saying?'

'Yes. I do. But only because I asked him the one question that you haven't yet.'

Mearns' eyes widened. 'What?'

'How he knew about the rhyme.'

She shrugged. 'Thought maybe he'd been as clever as you – you worked it out one murder later.'

Eve shook her head, wishing that were true. 'Shaun's sister, Susie, had "Monday's Child" hanging above her bed when they were growing up. Embroidery. Cute gift from their grandmother. At least it was until his sister died. Ronnie says Shaun became obsessed with the rhyme after that. Wouldn't sleep without reciting it over and over.'

Hastings looked confused. 'Why?'

'Funny how a kid's mind can work. Things they can obsess over to make sense of chaos. But you're talking about a kid who found his sister dead. A child whose mother had all but given up on him in her grief. A father that was unravelling as fast.' Eve let all that sink in before continuing.

'Ronnie said Shaun was being bullied at school too, for being different, for being fat, for his connection to his sister and, whether the rumour was true, for playing a role in her death. You name it. But Ronnie and his wife didn't know about it at the time. Too wrapped up in their own stuff. And then Shaun watched his mother being murdered.'

'Still doesn't make sense of the rhyme. Why's he killing these women?' Mearns wasn't sounding as sure.

'Shaun found out he was born on a Wednesday. Full of woe. Maybe he believed whatever the bullies were saying. Felt that he deserved to be ignored by his parents. That he wasn't the child they'd hoped for.'

'Oh, come on. Bit of a sob story.' Hastings stood away from the desk.

Eve shrugged. 'I've known people to kill for a lot less than what Shaun went through. We all have.'

No one argued with her. She thought, not for the first time, about where she might've ended up herself, had it not been for joining the police.

'Ronnie says it didn't help that the mother had always made it clear that Susie had been the favourite, that she went to pieces the way she did after losing her. Ronnie tried to be there for Shaun, thought he was coping. Susie was born on a Sunday. Bonnie and Blithe and Good and Gay.'

'Beautiful, carefree, good and happy.' Mearns translating it for them, starting to buy in to what Eve was saying.

'Everything Shaun loved about Susie too. Everything he'd always felt he wasn't.'

Mearns nodded. 'Why the killings?'

'I think it's fair to say we're dealing with a guy who is seriously mentally ill. Whatever the reason is, it makes sense to him. The same as any crime, any murder is justified in the eyes of the wrongdoer. Only he can tell us that.'

Cooper leaned forward. 'I don't know. All seems a bit far-fetched to me.'

'Maybe, but think about it. Not about the tongues and the rhyme. About how these women are being tied up. What they're being tied with.'

'Venetian-blind cord.' The cynical note in Hastings' voice was gone.

Eve looked at them one by one. 'Susie Dempster, Shaun's sister, was found hanging with venetian-blind cord wrapped around her throat.'

Chapter 48

Then

He's found her, but she's not playing any more.

Warm wetness trickles down the inside of his leg, soaking his sock, pooling around his feet, a dark stain spreading out across the carpet. He doesn't move. Stands there. Staring.

Her tongue is sticking out. But not like all the times she's teased him, wanting him to chase her.

No. Not anything like that.

Her head's tilted to the side, like she's listening. Listening out for him. Wondering if he's going to find her. If he'll seek her out.

She's staring at him, her big blue eyes bug-like, jutting out, like her tongue. Not normal. He takes a step towards her, imagines her jumping towards him, giggling in that tinkly way that she does, telling him it's all some silly joke. But she doesn't.

She's getting closer. He's not aware of his feet moving, cold trouser material clinging to his leg. He stops when he sees the cord. Pulled tight against her tiny, smooth neck. Holding her there. Upright. Her skinny small body half-hidden, milk white against the brightly patterned curtain, pale beneath the lurid purple of her face.

He sees the garden through the slats of the blinds. Blinds new to the window. Modern. His mother's idea. Rain batters against the glass, blurring the wet lawn where normally they would have been playing, hiding amongst the rose bushes, ducking behind the hedging. He wishes more than ever they'd been out there today. His eyes flicker as a bird flies past the window. Movement as normal out there. Not frozen. Changed for ever, like in here.

He's right in front of her, can smell the Vosene shampoo in her long straight hair. He lifts his arm, stretches out his hand, stops mid-air.

He wants to touch her. To touch it.

Repulsed by the swollen tongue, too big for the small plump lips it hangs from, but unable to stop looking at it, to get rid of the need to feel it. He wants to stuff it back in. To make things the way they were. To make her the way she was. But he knows it's too late for that.

He drops his hand to his side, her bloated face blurring in front of him. Nothing to do with the rain this time. He feels tight. Rigid. Like he's being squeezed by some giant fist and will surely burst. Wanting to explode. To be nothing, which is what he is and will be without her.

And then he hears it. Shrill and raw. Outside of him but inside too. He's screaming. Sobbing. One hand grabbing her chubby cheek, the other pushing at her too-long tongue – pushing it, forcing it, trying to put it where it should be.

She can't leave him. He won't let her.

He's panting, hears footsteps in the distance, rushing towards him. Someone else screaming. His mother. He turns to her, heart lurching in his chest, his hand still clutching flesh, pulling his little sister ever tighter against the cord.

What he sees when he looks at his mother makes him let go, gives him something else to grapple with. Something that confuses him – terrifies him. Clear and confirmed only when she speaks. Barely a whisper, her voice someone else's.

'Oh God. What have you done?'

Chapter 49

Sunday, 22 December

EVE DABBED A FINGER on the underside of the dresser to check that the last coat of varnish had dried and was no longer tacky. Satisfied, she prepared to sand again. She lifted the face mask from beneath her chin, paused and found herself staring at the cork board. Who was she trying to kid? There was no escaping. The women staring out at her from the wall wouldn't let her and the truth was, she didn't want to. Another week had passed. No developments to speak about, apart from Dr Shetty being convinced Eve was getting stronger every day. What a joke.

Sunday. D-day.

When no news had come, Hastings ordered her to go home at the end of another long day – to get some rest, something to eat. She'd gone along with it, had told Cooper and Mearns to do the same – nothing they could do sitting in the office – knowing herself that neither of them would have a stomach for food or a mind for sleep.

She'd come out here as soon as she got home, but she knew she could've brought a sleeping bag to the office, the amount she'd been here lately. Not that it had got them anywhere. Not when they were looking for a ghost. They'd checked on every Shaun Dempster they'd managed to find, knowing it wouldn't be the one they were looking for but doing it anyway. No trace since the missing-persons report had been filed. Fourteen years ago. When Shaun was sixteen years old – six years after his father murdered his mother. For all they knew, Shaun was dead too, as his grandmother believed. But Eve had to believe that teenage boy was responsible for what was happening – that he was living off radar – or they had nothing.

She looked at each woman in turn. Melanie, Lexie, Jenkins, Sanders, Sarah and Shelley. A blank space next to Shelley. Space for the planned seventh victim and one that Eve felt helpless to save. No idea where Shaun was. No clue as to who he would target next. She thought about Ronnie, about all the hopes and dreams he'd had for his son, about his failings and his guilt. How hard it must've been phoning Eve to turn in his son. Ronnie had called from his hospital bed every day since, desperate to know if there was any progress.

It was strange, but part of Eve wanted to be able to tell him they'd found his son, that he was responsible after all. But another part of her wanted Ronnie's dream to come true, for all this to be a terrible mistake. To give him some peace at the end of a shit life. Eve kept staring at the photographs, frustrated. Not a clue where to start

363

trying to find that peace for Ronnie. Too late even if she did. No matter how many hours she'd put in. Sunday. Another woman tonight. The last line of the rhyme. Would it stop then? How could they even try to save whoever was in the killer's sights when they didn't know where he was?

She lifted her mask again, adjusted the strap of her dungarees, went to fetch the sandpaper and stood looking at the dresser. Being here was wrong. This was all a crock of shit. She threw the sandpaper to the floor, yanked off her face mask and walked to the door. There was no way she was staying home.

Mearns slipped off her shoes, wriggling crushed toes in sheer stocking soles before padding the short distance across the heated wooden floor from her front door to the kitchen. She opened the fridge, pulled a bottle of white out and closed the door with her foot as she reached to the cupboard above the black marble worktop for a wine glass. She laid them on the kitchen worktop, opened the drawer, hesitated on lifting the bottle opener, wondering whether a drink was a good idea, knowing what day it was, aware she could get a call in the early hours. She'd wanted to stay at the office, but, between Hastings and Eve, she'd eventually given up arguing. She looked at the wine glass. One wouldn't hurt, to help her relax. She opened the bottle and poured.

Mearns turned to the sink, a breakfast bar behind it separating the kitchen from the living room. Across the spacious open plan was a floor to ceiling arched double-window looking out over the city. She loved the layout, could see her reflection in the glass from where she stood in the lit kitchen, the space between there and the window still in darkness.

Mearns jumped as she felt her mobile phone vibrate in her pocket. She walked towards the window, fingers curled round the wine glass, walking around the coffee table in the centre of the room, her other hand fishing her phone from her pocket. It was him. It would be. She sighed. Unsure what to do. Thinking he might be what she needed to take her mind off things, ignoring the doubts that she was using him for nothing more than that.

She typed a reply with one thumb saying she was home, pocketed the phone again and then pressed her forehead and nose against the freezing window, her breath clouding the glass, snow falling outside once again. She felt small against the large frame, looking out to the deserted roads and buildings below. It looked like a scene from a Christmas card. All white and glittering in the streetlights that bounced off the snow in the dark. Christmas. Days away. The thought of that, of today's date, stirred something in her memory, something she couldn't grasp. She could see the odd set of lights twinkling here and there behind windows, the outline of Christmas trees. Her flat felt bare in comparison. Maybe she should have made an effort, but in her job you didn't get the chance to feel festive.

She looked out to the small balcony outside her window, if you could call it that: enough space to stand outside, wrought-iron railings surrounding it. She could count the number of times she'd been out on that balcony since she moved in – feeling unsafe any time she had, avoiding leaning against the railings as she had no idea how long they had been there or when they'd last been maintained.

There was a thin line of snow balanced on the railing, a white carpet on the balcony floor. She had a sudden urge to touch it, to stand out in the cold air, to feel free and part of something else for a moment. To forget about the stuffy office, the ongoing case, the bodies, the blood. To be surrounded by white. By nothing.

She lifted the brass handle of the window, shunting it with the heel of her hand as it stuck, wine sloshing in the glass in her other hand. Mearns pulled the heavy window in towards her, hinges creaking as she did. A blast of cold air stung her cheeks, making her feel alive. She stepped out on to the balcony, icy cold seeping through her stockings, snow turning to slush between her toes. She gasped, feeling a little stupid. The outside car park was below, more parking hidden beneath the building. Headlights bounced off the cars as another turned into the gap between the high red-brick wall. It was him. She smiled, despite herself, as he parked – even waved to catch his attention as he got out of the car. He looked up, waved, probably thinking she'd lost it standing out there.

Mearns stepped backwards into the flat, closed the window and went to get a second wine glass from the cupboard. She didn't care that her feet were cold and wet, or about the puddles of water she was leaving behind her, dotted along the floor, as she walked. All she cared about was that he was on his way and she'd decided he was what she needed.

Chapter 50

THE OFFICE WAS DEAD, overhead strip lights buzzing in the silence. Eve sat at one of the incident-room desks working through the mounds of paperwork she was always being told was essential but that she found to be essentially pointless. Still, the monotony went halfway towards numbing her brain to anything else. She picked up her vending-machine coffee, grimacing at the bitter taste as she swallowed, nothing else in her stomach. She heard a noise from far off down the corridor – the creak of a door opening, the echo of it closing. She waited, staring at the door, and relaxed as she saw Cooper appear.

'About as hungry and as able to sleep as me?' Eve sighed as Cooper nodded, taking the desk by the door.

'Needing a hand with anything, boss?'

Eve pointed towards the pile of envelopes she was working through. 'You could help me out with the mail backlog.'

Cooper picked up a batch of envelopes and headed over to his desk, both of them knowing that while they muddled along with the mundane, another woman could be dying at the hands of Shaun Dempster.

Mearns stood at the open door to her flat, a glass in each hand, her heart quickening as she heard the double door in the corridor squeak open before swishing shut again. She smiled as he came into view, let herself be gripped in his embrace, wine in the raised glasses in her hands above his shoulders slopping over the sides and on to the hallway carpet.

'What's in the bag?' she smiled, teasing him as she walked backwards into the flat, pulling him with her, one hand free of a glass.

He stared deep into her eyes – that look that made her want to keep on meeting him. 'I was hoping I wouldn't be leaving until morning.'

'Presumptuous, but I like it.' Her voice was throaty, surprising her like it always did in his company. She stepped around him, closed and locked the door, wanting this to feel real, for her world tonight to be about living. To forget all about death and their search for a ghost.

Eve and Cooper worked in silence, both their minds on the same thing. The need to be doing something but no way of knowing how to start or where to be tonight. That knowledge physically hurting, knotting their stomachs and spreading throughout them, the strain heavy, limbs rigid, everything clenched and no way of release.

Eve banged yet another sheet of paper down on one of the growing piles in front of her and lifted the next envelope. The scrawl on the front of the recycled brown paper was almost illegible, Eve taking a minute or two to make out that it was addressed to both herself and Mearns. Something pricked her memory. She turned the envelope over in her hands and ran her thumb beneath the gummy overlap, the contents spilling out on to the desk. Eve frowned as she picked up the sheet of notepaper, the same thin scrawl scratched across, a paperclip fixing something to it. She peered at the note, struggling to read it too.

'Photograph as promised. Such beautiful kids, Nancy Morrison.'

Eve's mouth went dry. She was unsure why, questioning her blood pumping, rushing through her veins, the knot in her stomach tightening ever more as she lifted the paper to expose the photograph beneath. Something felt wrong. It was a family photograph. What she took to be a mother, father, daughter and son. Her eyes skimmed across the faded faces, feeling the pulse throbbing in her neck, honing in on the son, her breath catching as it did. Eve's heart hammered, making her feel sick. 'Jesus Christ.'

She was aware of Cooper's head snapping up from his desk, saying something to her, could feel herself pushing back her chair, stumbling over to his desk, never lifting her stare from the small boy's blurred and faded face on the old photograph in front of him – the realization of who it was as sharp and as clear as if it had been taken that day.

Mearns pulled away from the kiss, sighing as she did. 'Shit, sorry.' She walked over to the sofa to where her mobile phone lay ringing, the sitting room still in darkness, seeing the reflection in the glass of the domineering arch window, of where he still stood in the lit kitchen. 'Mearns.'

'The photo.' Eve sounded panicked, wired.

'What?' Mearns didn't know what she was talking about.

'Nancy Morrison. She sent us the photo.'

Mearns' heart skipped, remembering the old woman's promise, wondering what Eve was about to say. She jumped as she felt a hand on her shoulder, too caught in the call to have noticed him walking towards her in the reflection of the window. She raised her hand, made herself smile to soften the abrupt request for him to give her a minute. He stepped back, turned towards the kitchen.

'And? What? What is it?' She could feel Eve's urgency over the phone.

'We know who Shaun Dempster is.'

'What?' Mearns was trying to make sense of what was being said.

'We *were* looking for a ghost. Shaun Dempster's dead. At least that's what he wanted everyone to think.'

'You're not making any sen—'

'He changed his name.'

Mearns was frowning, looking out at the blackness, hearing wine being poured into glasses behind her. 'What?'

'We know him.' Eve sounded gutted.

Mearns swallowed, her voice a whisper, trying to deal with this new information. 'Who?'

'It's Elliott. It's Elliott Jones.'

Mearns took the glass being offered to her, returning his smile, hoping he couldn't see her hand shaking. Elliott cupped the side of her face, leaned in and kissed her cheek before walking away again.

'Mearns?'

Her legs felt like those of a newly born foal. She gripped the phone tighter against her ear, having to hold on to something, anything. She had to think, go over what she'd said to Eve so far. 'That's a shame. Sounded like it could've been a good lead. Don't beat yourself up about it.'

'What? . . . Mearns?'

'OK. Good night.'

'Where are you?'

'Don't let the dragons bite.' She forced a laugh, watched Elliott walking over to her. She tensed as he looped an arm around her waist from behind, nuzzling his mouth into the side of her neck. Mearns closed her eyes, everything inside her wanting to pull away. She held her breath, trying hard not to run, hoping he hadn't sensed anything in her words to Eve or in her body language.

She opened her eyes as he raised his other arm, bracing herself for him cupping her face as he always did. Her lips trembled as she tried to smile when he spoke.

'You're so beautiful.'

Her skin crawled, tears springing to her eyes for who she thought the man in front of her had been, now knowing who and what he was. 'Thank you.' Her voice cracked, her head churning with how she was going to break free of him.

'Such a shame we couldn't have had some fun, one last time.'

His words were clearing in her head, the realization of what he said coming at the same time she saw what was in his hand. Too late. She gasped, jumping as she felt the jab of the needle plunge into her neck.

The phone dropped from her hand, clattering to the floor. The last thing Mearns saw was black.

Eve was limping for the door, aware more than ever that she was paying for all the morning and evenings she'd missed her exercises in recent weeks. Cooper almost banged into her as they reached the door at the same time, asking what the hell was happening.

'He's there. Elliott's with Mearns.' Eve watched Cooper race ahead. 'Bring the car round. I'll call for back-up.' Cooper was already crashing through the door to the stairwell, not waiting for any lift, unlike her, cursing her leg as she stabbed at the elevator button and fished in her pocket for her phone.

Cooper was already at the kerb, engine running, window down, shouting to Eve as she exited the station doors into the car park. 'Elliott's who she's been seeing?'

Eve moved around the car as fast her leg would allow, nodding as she opened the door, got in and started jabbing at her phone. 'Suddenly Ferguson's not such a bad option.'

'You thought she was seeing Ferguson? Did she say Elliott was there?'

Eve lifted her hand to silence Cooper as her call was answered at the other end. 'Ferguson, I need you at

Mearns' flat at the Bastille. No time to explain, but Cooper and I are en route. Get there as soon as you can.'

Eve remembered Cooper's question as she pocketed her phone. 'No, she didn't say Elliott was there, but what she said was enough.' Eve buckled her seatbelt as Cooper put his foot to the floor.

'Eh? What did she say?'

'Don't let the dragons bite.'

Cooper looked towards Eve as he sped out of the car park on to Broad Street, heading up Gallowgate towards George Street, Mearns' flat minutes away. 'You've lost me.'

'That night we were at yours and I gave her a lift home. She told me that the bank of mum and dad paid for her flat at the Bastille.'

'They do know what she does for a living?'

'Yeah, go figure. But she made a crack about being a princess in a tower – you know, a regular Rapunzel. I said something about not needing to be saved, about how she'd probably be able to slay a few dragons on her own. When she got out of the car, I said goodnight and "Don't let the dragons bite".'

'She's telling you he's there, that she needs to be saved.'

The car was flying across the junction at George Street on to St Andrew Street, Cooper taking the right turn on to Charlotte Street on what felt like two wheels, Mearns' flat one street away on Maberly. Eve leaned forward, staring out of the windscreen at the dark deserted roads, willing the car to go faster. 'I hope we get there in time.'

Chapter 51

MEARNS OPENED HER EYES and saw white. What had happened? Elliott. *Dempster.* Christ, how long had she been out? She tried to lift her head, but it wouldn't do what she was telling it to. She was sitting, hard against something, her chin slumped on her chest. Her breathing was heavy, like a bull snorting, forcing air from flared nostrils. There was no other sound. She couldn't calm herself enough to breathe any other way.

Her tongue felt thick and heavy. When she tried to force the tip of it through her lips, she felt nothing. She couldn't see her lips, only the blurred tip of her nose. It felt like there was a knife slicing in and out of her skull. She tried to lift her hand to press it against her head, but her arm didn't move. Was she tied? She couldn't feel her arms, but she could feel the panic that was knotting inside of her. Imagining her wrists bound in venetian-blind cord.

Elliott, where was he? Not Elliott. Shaun Dempster.

She blinked, unbelievably grateful for the small movement, and tried to focus on what she could see. White. Her work blouse, its collar hidden beneath her chin, long sleeves pulled back out of view. Her chest was heaving beneath, but she had no sensation of burning in her lungs. Her eyeballs felt strained, like overused muscles, but movement was becoming easier to them. She was blinking faster and was able to squeeze her eyelids shut against the pain in her head.

She looked to either side of her and saw she was on the floor. Wooden flooring. The sitting room. She knew where she was. Propped against the breakfast bar, facing the window. She thought of Melanie, found in the same position but against the bathroom wall. Dempster's first victim. Mearns knew in that moment he intended her to be his last.

She had to move.

Mearns looked up as far as she could, still unable to lift her chin from her chest. The orange light from the kitchen behind her was enough to see her legs stretching out in front of her, flat against the floor, her fitted work trousers, a perfect crease down their middle, still on. She could see her reflection in the window, looking like some drunk slouched in a doorway. Her feet, nothing tying them together, lay still when she tried to wiggle her stocking-covered toes.

Where was he?

Tears filled her eyes, further blurring her vision. Her heart was racing, her head dizzy. She tried to calm herself. Think. The phone call. What she'd said. Eve must've known what she was trying to tell her, would be on her way. She had to stay alive until then.

Eve was bouncing in the passenger seat as the car sped over the cobbled surface of Charlotte Street. She saw a group of teenagers on the corner ahead, smoking, craning their heads towards them, looking at the car going far too fast on a side street. Cooper slammed on the brakes as they neared the junction on to Maberly, the street where Mearns lived, the wheels' rubber screeching as he did, prompting whoops and shouts from the smokers.

Neither she nor Cooper turned their way, concentrating instead on what they could already see of the edge of the high granite-brick wall that surrounded the Bastille, Mearns' building, and getting ready to turn left. Eve saw the barrier and the red ROAD CLOSED sign at the last second and shouted at Cooper, prompting her colleague to pull on the wheel before slamming the car into reverse, dumping it at the kerbside by the congregated drunks outside the pub. The group cheering them on as Cooper jumped from the car and Eve followed, watching Cooper as he disappeared around the corner.

Mearns heard the bathroom door open in the hallway, then footsteps. Coming into the kitchen. Coming towards her. Passing by her. Stopping in front of her.

Her stomach lurched. She fought to look up. She managed a small movement but could only see shoes. His shoes. Boots, the thick leather tongues of them sticking out from beneath the hem of his jeans, the word 'Carolina' imprinted on them. An image of Helen Black's battered body flashed into Mearns' mind. Carolina. The C imprinted on her bruised flesh. Stamped on to her face. Why had she never noticed those boots? Had he changed into them? Mearns fought to move, mumbled instead of the scream she was trying to release. This was not how things were supposed to end for her.

Dempster crouched in front of her, low enough for her to see his face. Her heart knocked harder against her chest. He looked different. His features tight, distorted. No trace of the man who had seduced her. Was it the drugs he'd pumped into her or was Shaun Dempster finally revealing himself?

'You look like she might've done.'

Even his voice sounded different. Mearns held eye contact, unable to speak but desperate to keep him talking.

'I loved her. Too much maybe. She did that to people.'

Mearns took a deep breath, bracing herself as he moved, exhaling only when he came out of his crouching position and sat on the floor in front of her, legs bent, arms closed around his knees. Relaxed.

'They used to make fun of me. At school. I wasn't like them. Never was. But she understood me. They didn't get that though, thought it was something sick in my love for her. But it wasn't. It was pure. Good. Honest. Everything they thought, said and did to me was a lie.'

Dempster stared at the floor, and Mearns wondered if he'd done this with all the women. Spewing forth his story as if anything would make sense of what he was doing. She didn't care; she wanted him to keep talking.

'When I found her that day, it was like I'd died. That it was me hanging there. Her tongue was huge. Unnatural. Purple, swollen and sticking out at me, goading me to touch it. Still talking to me. Like she was sending me a message.'

Mearns was strangely glad she could hardly move her face, knowing she would've been unable to hide her look of horror.

'My mother walked in that day. The day I found my little sister. And I felt like I was dying all over again when she looked at me. I knew in her eyes that she blamed me. For Susie. Even before she asked what I'd done. My own mother. Thinking I'd be capable of that.' He shook his head, eyes still staring at the floor.

'Of course she tried to take it back. Afterwards, when Dad forced her to apologize for what she'd said. He tried to tell me she hadn't meant it too. But I knew that she had. That, like the boys at school, she'd always thought I was different. Not right.'

Mearns wondered if that was true or if it was Dempster's warped memory of something that never was. Her heart jumped as he locked eyes with her.

'You're wondering why. Why all this. It was the rhyme you see. Above Susie's bed. "Monday's Child". Gran made it and Mum hung it above her bed. It never meant anything to me, not until after Susie.'

Mearns stared.

'She used to lie there at nights reciting that poem to me, telling me she didn't believe that I was a Wednesday's

Child, full of woe. Trying to help me. But she was a true Sunday's child, and I realized after she died that if she could lie – if even my Susie could lie – then anyone was capable of deceit. After she left, I used to read that poem until my eyes couldn't stay open any more. Every night. Punishing myself, telling myself I was the odd one out, that everyone else was better than me. Normal. But slowly I could see why that poem was there. What it was she was trying to tell me. Hearing Susie's voice as I read it. Like she was talking to me from her grave. Sending me a message. Like her tongue.'

Mearns closed her eyes, not wanting to look at him any more. Realizing how ill he was. Struggling with trying to figure out how he'd been able to hold it together as Elliott.

'Don't you see? She was telling me it was lies. All of it. All of them. The bullies, the gossiping neighbours, Mum. Dad. I knew then that I had to be the one to show the truth. To be the man she knew I could be.'

Mearns opened her eyes, trying to give the impression of understanding in her stare, keeping him there, looking at her face as she tried to move her fingers, her toes, anything.

'But I needed to take my time. To grow stronger. Be ready. After Mum died, when I went to live with my grandparents I did what was expected of me, but I was planning, always planning, until the day I was able to disappear.'

Mearns tried to wiggle her fingers behind her but felt nothing. She forced herself to concentrate on what he was saying to her, aware of the total lack of emotion in

380

his voice as he brushed away the death of his mother and what he'd done to his grandparents. Blind to the fact that his own disappearance was just as big a kind of lie as the ones he claimed to hate.

'I thought it was time a year ago. In St Andrews. I went home. Saw him. Dad. I wanted to talk to him. Wanted to thank him for giving me the chance that he had. Letting me know in his own way that I was meant to go and do what I had to do.'

Did he think his father had killed his mother as a favour to him? Mearns was always amazed at how diseased the human brain could be. Did he honestly see it as a sign that he was supposed to go off and live this other life? To undertake this mission?

'I thought I was ready then. With Helen Black.'

Mearns had known as soon as she saw his boots this evening. No. Before that, when Eve had voiced her suspicions after the visit to St Andrews – that Helen had been the killer's practice run. She wanted to know why and it looked like he was intent on telling her.

'Helen was a liar. One of Susie's friends at school. Or at least she pretended to be. There was a local newspaper article in the days after Susie's death; the reporter had talked to the teachers and pupils who had known her. Helen took the headline, going on about how she'd lost her best friend. Upset when she died and then two weeks later playing in the same bit of the playground as she always had. With another little girl. She'd completely forgotten Susie. I wanted to kill her then. That's when I first realized that headlines lie.'

Mearns was staring at him. His voice was changing, becoming rougher, more menacing. She realized that his act of leaving a headline at each murder scene probably stemmed from that early memory.

'She seemed the perfect fit, years later. To be the first in the rhyme, but I gave her an overdose before I could kill her the way I'd intended to. I couldn't control it when I saw her lying there.'

Exactly as Eve had said.

'I wanted each woman to know why she was being killed. To think about their lie in the last moments of life. To watch their tongue being taken. To think of it as a final confession. Removing the lie – their sin – if you like.'

Mearns was reminded of the words spoken by Ronnie, Dempster's father, when they'd visited him at the hospice and asked for his version of events when he murdered his wife. 'Call it a final confession if you like.' Had Dempster overhead Ronnie saying that to his mother as he watched his father take her life? Had he been unbalanced even before that or was that night what pushed him over the edge?

'I accepted I wasn't ready. Went into hiding. But I took Helen's dress – didn't want her death to be a total waste.'

Mearns thought about Sarah Crawley, found wearing Helen's dress. He wanted them to know.

'By then I was living as Elliott, had been for a long time. Enrolled at Napier University. Journalism. Alongside Jenkins, would you believe?'

Dempster smiled, widened his eyes as if they were having a friendly little chat. As if anything about this was normal.

'She was a cut-throat bitch with ambition even then. But I never lost that friendship. It proved useful to me when I moved to Aberdeen. She helped me see what I needed to do. Not only work for the press but to do it for the police. The biggest liars out there.'

Mearns thought about how Elliott had fought Eve's corner when Jenkins had tried to destroy her in the press after what happened to Sanders. She wondered if he had been feeding Jenkins information about that and everything since.

'It didn't take me long to find the worst offender. Eve. Lying that she didn't chase Johnny MacNeill's son off the road. I knew her history. How close what she saw that night was to what happened to her own mother. I knew that she had lied. It was me that set up the disturbance call later – the one that sent them to MacNeill and his boys. I managed to get Eve to the pub beforehand – didn't even have to try hard to get her to have a drink with me. She believed, still does, that a half bottle of red wine affected her. No idea what I dropped into her glass. I led her to that trap. The pictures of us at the pub were a nice touch too. One of MacNeill's men was only too happy to play cameraman. Liars have to pay. MacNeill and I had that belief in common, at least. And she continued to lie about how drunk she was that night, about her past and why everything had affected her. She needed to pay. And MacNeill paid me handsomely for my part in that. It was a shame about Sanders, but she lied too. To cover up for Eve being drunk that night.'

Mearns couldn't believe how easily Dempster was able to justify himself.

'I wanted to give Eve long enough to think about her lie. Knew I had to wait, that she needed to be the officer who would work on my case. After all, only a liar would see the truth of what I was doing.'

Mearns was surprised to hear herself moan as she thought about the fact that Melanie was murdered only three days after the management decision that Eve was allowed back on the job.

Dempster stared at her. 'I can hear your frustration at not being able to talk. And it would be nice to chat. Don't worry. The drugs will wear off before too long. I didn't give you too much. Anyway, I'm sure you're wondering why the women. How I picked them.' A note of pride coming into his voice. 'Readily available in the job I do. Important to keep an eye on the local news. To know what's going on around you.'

Mearns didn't know what he meant, but she knew he was about to explain.

'I first found Melanie through a piece I read about a local modelling competition she entered. All those grand dreams of making it in London as a model. She was beautiful. I was captivated by her photo. I could see she had the same energy that Susie had. Ryan was with her the third time I tracked her down, leaving the chemist's where she worked. The times before I'd just observed her while she worked. Her mannerisms, interactions, the way she held herself.'

'That night with Ryan, I could see from their body language that they were close. It reminded me of us. Me and Susie. I was jealous of what they had. I wanted to be near them. To live through them, believe that's what Susie and I would've been like if we'd grown to adulthood together. I watched them many times. It didn't take long to realize that there was more going on between them. What they had was impure. Nothing like me and Susie, but what the boys at school always accused us of. I knew then that Susie was right all along. Everyone had their secrets and their lies. That it was up to me to expose them. To show them the only way I knew how – through the rhyme. I knew Melanie would be perfect for my "Fair of Face", and Ryan was the perfect person to frame and take the heat off me for a while.'

Mearns felt sick that he'd picked these women at random through pieces he'd read in the local paper. Making the headline fit the rhyme and then following their lives until he found something that he saw as a lie against that headline, a reason to kill.

'The thing is I never had to watch them for long. Like I said, everyone lies. Unspoken truths. If you listen, the world is silent with them. Look at Lexie. There was a bit about her and her stage-show success before she moved here. About her hoping to emulate that here while her husband worked. Start lessons for under-privileged kids. My "Full of Grace".

'She was selling herself as this graceful dancer, her body a temple. And all the time she was shoving buckets of coke up her nose, poisoning that body.'

Dempster smiled. 'Just after Lexie came the perfect opportunity to point the finger at someone else.'

Mearns wanted to scream, moaning instead, louder this time.

Dempster didn't seem to notice, too lost in his memories. 'That day in the office. Pure chance that I was sitting there when Eve started on about hunting down vets. Hardy came winging into my mind and made sense on so many levels. But I couldn't be the one to bring him to you. So I tipped off Ferguson, told him to say it was all his idea, that I'd keep quiet. He didn't suspect a thing when I told him he deserved a break and should shine. I knew his blustery arrogance wouldn't let him refuse.'

Mearns felt sick to learn how they had all been played.

'Then we had Jenkins. A so-called friend. I never had friends and never wanted them. Susie was all I needed. Jenkins was on to me. She made the connection to Mac-Neill with the drugs, suspected he may have supplied Lexie, or at least that his cronies had. Say what you like about her, but you've got to admit she was bloody sharp at her job. She met with one of them, offered a good payout if he spoke. Anonymous. He would've been able to tell her I knew MacNeill a lot better than she realized. She started digging into my past. But I didn't have one, at least not as Elliott Jones. She had to go. It served two purposes. The dealer shut up.'

Mearns was reeling. Jesus, Jenkins was just trying to do her job. To tell the truth, as seemed so important to Dempster. And he'd killed her for it. How must've Jenkins felt the night she became the third victim?

'Of course, I didn't need Jenkins' tongue. Wednesday's Child. It's who I am.'

Mearns couldn't start to see the sanity in that answer. Didn't try to.

'Still, I was surprised at how hurt she looked at the end. Like she believed we were friends. Or maybe she was just shocked that someone had got one up on her. Nothing compared to Sanders' expression though.'

Mearns closed her eyes. Glad Eve wasn't here to listen. She looked towards the window. Where was she?

Eve was limping uphill, breathless, cursing her useless leg. Cooper was nowhere to be seen as Eve followed the edge of the red-brick wall, skimming her hand along it, using it for leverage against her pathetic speed.

She struggled into the car park, the lit foyer empty, only the lift, an artificial plant and the stairwell off to the right-hand side visible. Cooper was still standing at the door pulling at the oversized handle of the heavy double glass as if surely it had to eventually open. It clattered, but nothing. Eve started buzzing every button on the wall by the door as Cooper continued yanking on the door – not stopping to buzz more than a second at each. Avoiding the penthouse, so as not to alert Dempster to the fact they were coming. 'Come on, someone has to answer.'

Mearns was able to wiggle her fingers, careful not to move anything that Dempster might see. She listened to him still talking.

'I liked Sanders. She was a good woman. But she lied for Eve. A lie that cost her the life she'd known. I knew her death would shatter Eve.'

Mearns wanted to shout at him, wondered if she might be able to try and talk at least. To tell him that it was *his* lies, about who he was, that it was him going behind Eve's back that had put Sanders in that wheelchair, but, even if she could, she knew that him talking incessantly was the only reason she was still alive.

'And then there was Sarah. The children's charity worker. Miss "I'm saving the children one by one". She put on a great act. Yet away from the limelight, the glory, I found out she was dipping into the fundraising pot any chance she got.'

Mearns was shocked at that. There'd been nothing to suggest it in the investigation they'd carried out after her death. She didn't ask how he found out.

'So you see, she deserved what I did to her after all.'

Mearns felt nothing but disgust.

'Who next? Ah, yes. Shelley. I can't deny she did work hard for a living. I read about her in an article exploring the pressure of being a single parent on the breadline. But not working as hard as she'd have her poor mother think.' He shook his head. 'I went to pay a wee visit to her work. To see if she really was telling the truth. Quick glance through the window and I could see work was the last thing on her mind. Yet she made that old woman look after her son all hours so that she could roll around the office with one of the partners that worked there any chance she got.' He tutted. 'How can you care for your little boy when your lie keeps you away from him?

And not even for something that will benefit him. The work – yes, that's commendable. But sex?'

Three-year-old Kai. Motherless because Shelley might have tried to have a little snatched time for herself. A lie, maybe, but one to be killed over? No. Never.

They were nearing the end of the rhyme. She was beginning to doubt that Eve had understood her underlying message on the phone. Please God, let him keep talking.

'You'll be wondering what this has all been for. Maybe it'll bring Susie back to me.' He laughed, a sharp, harsh sound that was nothing like the gentle laugh she'd often heard from Elliott's mouth. 'Come back from the dead. But I guess that would make me crazy.'

As crazy as they come, you psycho. 'Tough time.' Mearns struggled to form the words, slurring, her voice alien to her.

Dempster raised his eyebrows. 'I see the drugs are wearing off. You think I had a tough time?'

Mearns concentrated on answering in as few words as possible. 'Bullied. Susie. Father killed mother.' She felt exhausted, unsure Dempster would even understand what she was trying to say.

He stood still. 'As if anyone could ever understand what I've been through. Losing Susie destroyed me.' He looked at her, and Mearns was shocked to see a smile slowly growing across his face. 'But my father killing my mother? That was the biggest lie of all.'

Chapter 52

Then

It's dark at the kitchen table. My nose twitches at the smell of cinnamon. Mulled wine that was made earlier. I hate cinnamon.

It's quiet. There's snow on the lamp posts and I wonder if there'll be enough to build a snowman in the morning. That's what Susie would've been wondering too.

My deep sigh is loud in the dark room as I turn towards the glass door. Mum and Dad sprayed white foam into the corners of the glass, and through the spaces above the fake snow I see the tree in the corner. It's old, the decorations Susie made at school still hanging from it. Mum and Dad couldn't throw them out. I lean against the cold wooden chair and close my eyes.

The moan disturbs me.

She's moving. Mum. The back of her white nightdress looking rust-coloured in the shadows as she drags herself across the linoleum. If only she'd stayed in bed.

I take another bite of my biscuit and watch her matted hair as she crawls across the floor. Like a slug leaving a trail in the dark. I can hear the glass crunching beneath her. I stand, careful not to scrape the chair legs against the linoleum. I don't want Dad to wake up. I walk over, crouch and move the glass handle away from her side. It's the only thing that didn't break when I smashed the water jug against her head. I bend over, tuck her wet hair behind her ear like she's done to me many bedtimes after a bath. I whisper, 'It's all your fault.'

I roll her on to her back. It's hard, but I manage, weight on my side. I need her to see me, to see that I'm my own man. Not dependent on her. That Susie was right. I'm not Wednesday's Child. Not full of woe. I'm happy. Especially with what I'm about to do.

Her breath comes in short rasps and her eyes are wide, pleading, trying to understand what happened, what is about to happen. I jab my finger towards the ceiling and put it to my lips, smiling. I signal for her not to wake him.

I get up and go to the kitchen drawers. In the top one, I see the pink plastic spoon next to blue, the only ones Mum and Dad kept: a reminder of our baby years. In the next drawer, I curl my fingers around the worn wooden handle of the breadknife. It will do. She has to pay, and today is the perfect day. My birthday. I see the kitchen tongs and smile as I lift them from the drawer too and move towards her, the knife blade shining.

'Please, I love you,' she says.

She's a liar. I kneel, drop the blade and tongs by my side and clamp my hand over her mouth. I stare into her eyes. She's struggling to keep them open, blood pouring from her head wound. I listen, still not believing that I haven't heard movement from upstairs. Nothing.

I sit on top of her and open her mouth, my dirty nails digging into her tongue's strong, slippery flesh. Pulling at it, I lift the tongs and hold her tongue fast. With my other hand, I lift the knife and cut.

Her eyes fly open. Her hands claw at mine but slip in the fresh blood that I know is filling her throat, killing her. Choking her with her lies.

I feel her kick her legs against the floor, impressed at what little strength she has left, she's using it to jerk her groin upwards in the vain hope of throwing me off.

The knife's edge is blunt. I press harder and drag it back and forth, faster, with one hand, the other hand squeezing the tongs together. She stops fighting, the shock numbing her. Her wet eyes never leave mine, but I don't stop.

I hear the creak of the floorboards overhead, soft footsteps making their way down the stairs. It's the cry that makes me look towards the door, deep into Dad's terrified eyes.

For that, I am sorry.

Chapter 53

MEARNS COULDN'T BREATHE. The enormity of what Dempster had told her. He looked exhausted. She was now able to rotate her wrists in the shackles behind her.

'She bought the blinds. The ones that killed Susie. She dragged my dad down with her grief and her hate. But he was too good a man to leave her. It was all her fault. And yet she blamed me. She had to die. Dad covered for me that night. Let me go free.'

The sacrifice Ronnie had made for his ten-year-old son. *Ten*. Dempster had killed his mother on his birthday. That was what Mearns couldn't remember earlier. About today – it was Dempster's birthday.

Why had Ronnie let him go free, taken the blame? For the guilt he felt over not being there to save Susie, to save his wife? Or because he truly believed that there was good in his son, that the horror of what he had done was an illness that he could somehow recover from, given the chance? A better life. But all he'd done was to allow Dempster to go on and kill again.

Mearns flinched as Dempster lifted his hand, feeling her body awakening, praying he hadn't noticed, her hands working behind her, trying to break free of the cord. He cupped her face as he had done often, catching the tears streaming down her face.

'Why me? Sunday's Child?' Her voice was stronger now, less slurred.

'You're how I imagined she might have been as an adult. Brave, dedicated, conscientious, kind. You came into a situation others wouldn't have, you've worked tirelessly to be accepted and make your mark on the team and you've been kind to others, even Ferguson. Perhaps not Eve, but I'm with you there. Don't get me wrong, you're not perfect – not like my sister. Never as happy as she had been, but enough for my needs.'

For his needs? For her to fit the rhyme? That's all her life would come to? 'What needs?'

Dempster looked thrown for a second, confused, before regaining control of himself. 'It's my birthday today, on the same day of the week Susie was born. Don't you think that has to mean something?' He looked as excited as a schoolboy. 'Maybe it will bring her back to me.' Dempster laughed, a crazy tinkling sound. 'Or maybe I'll be joining her if Eve gets to me before I get to her. Either way, me and Susie? We'll be together again. I've always believed that.'

In that moment and in that face, Mearns saw madness. True madness, for the first time. She looked at Dempster, a man far removed from who she thought he was. How could she have not known?

She was crying, feeling snot bubbling at her nose, wondering if it really was there. The feeling. Or if it was just her imagination. She wasn't supposed to die here. 'What was my lie?'

His gaze pierced through her. 'Me.'

The answer hit Mearns hard in the stomach. The fact she'd kept her relationship with him a secret from everyone. She watched him lower his hand and pull a bag from behind him – the bag they'd joked about, laughing about him taking it for granted that he'd be staying over. He rummaged in it, pulled his hand out, a scalpel in it, and what looked like pliers.

Pliers. Mearns remembered what Dempster had told her about his mother.

She moved against the restraints, loosened but not enough. Kicking her legs out in her mind, them barely moving in reality. Fighting to live. Wanting to live. Thinking about Eve as Dempster leaned towards her, smiling.

Eve and Cooper took the stairs, the lift still out of action. Cooper went two at a time, Eve not far behind him. Clenching her teeth against the pain, willing her limb to move faster, knowing she would pay for the adrenaline spurt later. She cursed the fact Mearns was on the top floor. Each and every step felt like she was dragging a burning limb. Just when she thought she could take no more – would have to leave Cooper to go ahead alone – they reached the top. Eve's arm stretched out, breaking the crash of the double door as Cooper broke through it into a small hallway, a lift door and the door to what must be Mearns' flat in front of them.

She prayed the door would be unlocked. She watched Cooper take hold of the handle, push. It didn't budge. She was beside Cooper, batting his hand from the handle, wanting to take control. She looked at Cooper, both of them knowing they had no time to worry about the noise they would make alerting Dempster to the fact they were there. Eve had to let Cooper do what he was about to do, her leg too sore to cope. She stepped aside as Cooper took three steps back from the door, until he was hard against the opposite wall, and charged, his left shoulder turned inward to take the hit.

Nothing.

He staggered from the door, ready to try again. Eve hoped they wouldn't have to try too many times before the door gave way.

Dempster was dragging Mearns to her feet. The noise from the door deafening, echoing around them in the flat. She was here. Eve. She was here.

Mearns could move a little more but didn't, keeping herself relaxed, like a deadweight, making it harder for Dempster to move her. He started to pull her over towards the window, leaning her against the side that didn't open while he went to lift the handle on the side that did. Her heart was racing. What was he doing? She told herself he was trying to get as far away from the door as he could, nothing else. He pulled back the window, cold air rushing into the room, the curtains billowing either side of the glass.

He crouched beside her, out of breath, struggling to lift her, trying to pull her out on to the narrow balcony.

Mearns wondered if she'd be able to stand, keeping herself heavy in the meantime, hearing the wood start to splinter on the front door as the constant thuds pounded against it.

Dempster moved away, over to where the bag and its contents lay across the floor. He picked up the scalpel, came towards her. She jumped against the glass as the front door finally gave way, the crack sounding like it had taken part of the wall with it.

Eve froze in the doorway, Cooper by her side. Mearns was on the floor by the window, Dempster's forearm wrapped around her neck, the scalpel blade at her throat.

'Stay there,' Dempster shouted, a tremor in his voice.

Eve didn't move, scoping out her next move. 'There's nowhere to go, Dempster. Back-up's on its way.'

Dempster looked surprised that Eve knew who he was. She hoped she was right about the back-up as she watched the grip on Mearns' throat tightening. Dempster was shaking his head. 'I don't need to go anywhere. I have everything I need right here. It's the end – Jo is the final show.'

Eve kept eye contact with Dempster, risked taking a step into the room, stopping as she looked to the point of the blade pressing into Mearns' throat, a bright-red dot of blood appearing against the white of her skin. Eve looked into Mearns' eyes, her terror clear.

'Why?' Eve asked the question, not knowing whether to try to get Dempster talking or not.

Dempster smiled. 'Why? Isn't that for you to figure out, Detective?'

'Do you think this is what Susie would've wanted? What your father would've wanted? He wanted you to make a new life for yourself. A good one.'

'Nice try. Don't forget I know how you work. I spend every day of my life feeding a story to the press, manipulating them. This is all for Susie. Mearns knows that. As did all the other women. My father will too.'

'Tell me. I thought you were my friend.'

Dempster looked surprised by the raw emotion in Eve's voice. 'You don't need to know. But you will. First I need to finish what I started.'

Dempster raised his hand, clutching at Mearns' cheeks, pressing against them until she couldn't hold her mouth shut any more. She was white, her eyes wide. He was going for her tongue.

And then Eve saw Cooper moving, running towards Dempster, who let go of Mearns and was springing to his feet in preparation for Cooper's onslaught. Eve shouted at Cooper to stop, brushing his clothing as she tried to hold him. She watched as Cooper's feet slipped on a patch of water on the floor and he fell backwards, cracking his head against the corner of the coffee table, thudding against the wooden floor. Blood spread out across the floor. Eve saw everything in slow motion, forcing her feet to move, wanting to run to Cooper, needing to get to Mearns.

Eve devoured the space between them, dodging the patches of water leading to the window, her limp forgotten. She lunged for Dempster, her hands grasping either arm, the momentum pushing them both over the windowsill and on to the balcony.

Eve tried to hold him fast against the wrought-iron barrier, Dempster's eyes wild, rage fuelling his strength as he pushed against Eve, pulling her round so that she was against the railings. The scalpel was still in his hand as he attempted to slash at Eve's arms, hands, anywhere it could make contact with flesh through fabric. Eve held his arms tight, not wanting to let Dempster have any real force behind the blade.

She saw movement behind him. Mearns was trying to pull herself up, using the glass of the window as leverage. Her legs were shaking, her feet unsteady. The strain of trying to move was clear on her face but she was up. She was standing. Eve watched Mearns swaying like a drunk as she took a step on to the balcony. Eve wanted to shout at her to stand clear but didn't want to alert Dempster to the fact she was there. Mearns' hands broke free of the cord at her wrists and her fingers gripped at Dempster from behind. Dempster's hands let go of Eve to fight Mearns off as she tried to pull him backwards, her strength still not fully restored. Eve ducked, moving out from against the balcony, and stepped around Dempster and Mearns, attempting to help Mearns pull Dempster into the room.

There was a scream, the sound piercing. Eve wondered where it was coming from, realized it was Dempster, the rage changing his features, giving him a strength that Eve could feel him unleashing, even as she tried to pull with Mearns.

And then Mearns was moving towards Dempster, being dragged on to the balcony, screaming as she went. Dempster was bent backwards over the balcony, trying to take Mearns with him. The rotten iron rails groaned under the strain, starting to move in their foundations.

Eve could see what was happening and lunged towards Mearns, flinging her on to the ground by her side in order to deal with Dempster, who was coming towards her. Before she could think, Eve lifted her bad leg, balancing on her good one, before kicking Dempster square in the stomach, winding him, sending him backwards, full force, against the railings. Dempster was crouched, clutching at his stomach. Dazed.

A noise behind her made Eve turn. Ferguson was striding towards her, stumbling as he passed Cooper, who lay on the floor, his mouth hanging open in shock at what he was seeing out on the balcony.

She turned to Dempster, who was still stunned, slumped against the railing, only seconds having passed. He didn't hear what Eve could: bolts starting to spring, one by one, from the wall. The balcony being ripped free. By the time Dempster realized what was happening, it was too late. Eve reached for Mearns and grabbed her, feeling Ferguson behind her, pulling them into the room, clear of the balcony as they watched Dempster flailing, suspended in mid-air before falling backwards, screaming through a rush of snow-filled air as he fell, hurtling, towards the ground. A last shout for Susie as he hit the concrete.

Chapter 54

BEADS OF RAINWATER GLISTENED upon the waxy black material stretching across the broad shoulders of the man in front of Eve at Aberdeen Crematorium's West Chapel. She stared at the perfectly formed transparent drops as they trembled but stayed put, as the man shifted from one foot to another, limbs restless after standing for the entire funeral service.

Sanders' funeral. Five weeks since her death. Eve heard the delay was down to key family members from overseas travelling and attending around the festive period.

Whatever the reason, well-wishers had arrived in droves – familiar faces, eager to crowd the chapel. Eve hadn't got any further than the entrance foyer. Outside. Where she felt she should be, regardless of Cooper and Mearns trying to convince her otherwise, and where she effectively had been since the day MacNeill had dealt the blow to Sanders' back.

She looked to the floor, concrete flagstones blurring in her vision, hands clasped tight in front of her, hearing the final song being played, picturing the blue-velvet curtains as they were drawn around the coffin. The final goodbye.

She pictured Sanders, everything she had been, before saying her own silent goodbye and turning to walk to her car. She wanted to disappear before she was seen, like the outsider she was. To keep on hiding like she had been since Dempster. Off work in the guise of a festive break. Shut off from the world, only the thoughts that she was to blame again keeping her company.

'Eve?'

She stopped outside the chapel, turned, already knowing who was behind her. Mearns looked different. Still dressed in black as always, but softer, a little make-up, loose hair. Longer and blonder than Eve had thought. Eve hadn't seen her since that day with Dempster. The same day that DC Ferguson had taken Eve's official statement, later letting her read Mearns'.

Eve had been congratulated on a job well done. Except it hadn't been – not with Sanders gone and so many others dead.

'Some turnout.' Mearns looked uncomfortable, as if unsure what else to say.

Mearns' account of her time alone in that flat with Dempster had been harrowing reading for Eve, exposing the mind of a madman she'd thought of as a friend, a mind more damaged than Eve could ever have imagined, than any of them could have – a miracle that Elliott had functioned as he did. They'd found all five

402

tongues in the bag he'd brought to the flat – only Jenkins' missing, and Mearns', of course.

Eve looked at her, unable to hide the relief in her eyes, grateful that Mearns was still here, even though Sanders wasn't. 'Yeah. She was a great woman.' Eve saw the congregation starting to spill out from the chapel and wanted to go.

Mearns stepped forward, stuttered as she spoke. 'I . . . I'm sure Cooper would like to see you.'

Eve glanced at the crowds and, as if planned, Cooper was there, one of the first out, Hastings and Ferguson right behind him. Eve acknowledged Hastings' nod with her own before he walked off in the direction of his car. Eve's mouth went dry as Cooper and Ferguson headed in her direction.

'Hey, you.' The emotion clear in Cooper's voice.

She felt bad for ignoring his calls, ashamed she'd hidden all the times he'd come to her door. But she hadn't been ready to deal with the real world. Still wasn't.

'Hey, Cooper.'

He looked like he wanted to give her a hug but was aware she wouldn't thank him for it. She looked at Ferguson, standing there with his hands in his pockets, and braced herself for the attitude. Instead, he looked to the gravel at his feet.

The atmosphere between them was heavy, far too dangerous for Eve. She stepped forward, clapped Cooper on the shoulder. 'The bold hero.' She watched her friend's face redden.

Cooper smiled. 'Yeah. I'm never going to live that one down, am I? Out cold on the floor.'

'Nope.' She was glad to see a smile on Mearns' face. Even Ferguson raised a smile.

She turned, the four of them walking towards the car park in silence. Eve stopped as she reached her car and looked at Mearns, her heart thumping. 'How are you?'

Mearns cleared her throat. 'Fine. Struggling.'

Eve wanted to offer comfort. She opted for words, easier than physical contact. 'Hey, don't beat yourself up. None of us knew.'

Cooper stepped forward. 'Eve, you should take the same advice.'

They all knew that Cooper was talking about Sanders as well as Dempster. The four of them stood in silence for a moment, black suits and skirts bustling past them, returning to cars and life.

'I should've known.' Mearns' voice was hoarse. 'I got the closest to him.'

'No. No, you didn't. You got the closest to Elliott. They weren't the same person.'

Mearns was shaking her head. 'All those women. Dead. How can I be a copper and not know something like that?'

Eve laid her hand on Mearns' upper arm, the other two members of her team watching. 'Hey, if it's any consolation, I thought you were seeing Ferguson.' Eve watched Mearns' small smile appear at the feigned look of disgust on her face; Ferguson groaned.

Eve dropped her hand, changed the subject. 'I spoke to Ronnie. Thought it was only fair that he heard from me what happened. Even when I told him that we knew about Shaun being the one who killed his mother, he stayed silent.'

'Protecting his son. Loyal to the end.' Mearns breathed heavy.

Cooper spoke up. 'Keeping the lie alive, I think Dempster would've said.'

'Will anything happen to him?' The soft spot for Ronnie was still evident in Mearns' voice.

Eve shook her head. 'I think he'll give in to it. Let himself go, hoping to be with his family.'

'And you?'

Eve frowned, not sure what Mearns meant.

'I mean, how are you? After Sanders, after stopping Dempster? No one but Hastings has heard from you, and he's told us bugger all. Are you coming back?'

Eve looked towards her car. 'Haven't had time to think about it. All I can think about is Sanders. How I couldn't save her. Again.' Eve's voice cracked.

'But you saved me.'

'You can hold your own, Mearns.'

Mearns tried again. 'You know you saved me, Eve. If you hadn't got there when you did . . .'

Eve couldn't look at her.

Mearns sighed. 'Anyway, I'm not sure that you're right.'

Eve didn't like where this was going. Ferguson and Cooper's expressions matched her own. 'Why?'

'Maybe I'm not cut out for this. I was blind to Dempster.'

'Mearns—'

'I know what you're going to say, but I don't know whether I can trust my judgement after this.'

'Christ. Your judgement? I thought Elliott was my friend. I shared so many things with him. I thought he was trying to help me all this time. After what happened to Sanders that night at MacNeill's, I returned to work six months later not knowing who I was, plenty of people waiting for me to muck up again.'

'Yeah, and I was one of them.' Mearns looked to the ground.

'Me too.'

Eve hadn't thought Ferguson was capable of surprising her. She fought to keep her mouth from hanging open.

'Look, I'm not great at all this apology shit, but I was wrong.'

Mearns stared at him. 'Jesus, Ferguson, you could've given us some warning. I would've got my phone out, started filming for posterity.' She smiled.

Ferguson's face reddened. Cooper was kicking at the ground, obviously feeling like a spare part.

Eve felt the lump in her throat, wondering what the hell was wrong with her. 'Yeah, you were one of them. But you weren't wrong. I did muck up. Ryan, Hardy, MacNeill. I was hell-bent on all of them when Dempster was right there in front of me. A friend. Playing me.'

Ferguson shook his head. 'We all thought the same. Anyone else would've thought so too. We were being led all the way along. Jesus, I took the shit he fed me about the Hardy connection and pretended I'd found it.

I didn't see what he was doing – too intent on taking the glory.'

'But—'

Ferguson shook his head again. 'No, let me say this. That bastard even had a hand in what happened to Sanders at MacNeill's. I doubted you. He spiked your drink, Eve.'

Eve said nothing.

'Jesus, I was a shit to you. And look what I did the night I should've been watching Hardy. It's irrelevant whether it turned out to be him or not. And the thing is, I hated myself for not getting to MacNeill's quicker that night. Minutes too late to stop Sanders being injured. You being injured.'

The lump in Eve's throat was growing. She swallowed, coughed. 'You did everything you could that night at MacNeill's and you pulled me and Mearns to safety on that balcony. Yeah, outside Hardy's was a mistake, and I should've dealt with that better.'

'But you still covered my ass in front of Hastings the next day, after what a prick I'd been.'

Eve shrugged. 'We're all capable of being a prick.'

'You excel at it, Ferguson.' Mearns made them all smile. No mean feat.

Eve stared off into the distance, towards a black funeral car pulling away from the curb. She watched it crawl in their direction, motioning for the other three to step aside and let it pass. It passed silently, wheels slicing thorough air, the passenger unmistakeable.

Archie. Sanders' husband.

His head was lowered, his frame looking a decade older. Shrunken. At the last moment, and as if sensing Eve, Archie raised red-rimmed eyes, their glare as strong as ever. Eve stepped back. It was a look that didn't need any words.

She watched the car go. There was no forgiveness in those eyes; the pretence had been for Sanders. Yet she'd had no expectation of forgiveness from either of them.

It was whether in time she'd be able to forgive herself. But as she looked at Cooper, Ferguson and Mearns – her colleagues, the closest thing she had to friends – and thought of what they'd said, she dared to believe that she might.

Acknowledgements

WHEN I FIRST SAT down to write this, I was so excited and grateful that I was in danger of thanking everyone and their dog. So, this is the pared back version (believe it or not!), but I hope those dogs know they are loved.

Firstly, I would like to thank my wonderful agent, Oli Munson, at AM Heath for taking a chance on me and my book. You've made this process such a joy and always been on hand to guide me, no matter how dense my questions – and, my God, some of them have been questionable! I couldn't ask for a nicer, more down-to-earth champion fighting my corner than you.

Thanks to my fabulous editor, Tash Barsby, at Transworld for the phone call that made my dream come true. I can't thank you enough for all your help and support to date in realizing that dream. You rock.

Of course, I can't thank Oli or Tash without thanking the fantastic team of people behind them. Florence, Alexandra and Vickie at AM Heath, and Ailsa, Katie, Beci and Josh at Transworld. I'm in awe of all you've done for me and continue to do.

Now to go back in time. Thank you to the members of *Writing Magazine*'s online Talkback Forum for the monthly flash-fiction One Word Challenge, and the seed of an idea that eventually led to *Hold Your Tongue*.

To Julian Gough and Susie Maguire for your input, guidance and support at that early short-story course at magical Moniack Mhor – and for seeing something there that made me want to keep going.

To the Professional Writing Academy, especially to organizer extraordinaire of the Introduction to Crime Writing course, Susannah Marriott, and my wonderful tutor, Tom Bromley. Tom also provided first-class guidance and professional insight during two online Faber courses – Write Your Novel and Work in Progress – which helped me to shape early drafts of *Hold Your Tongue*.

Thanks also to Sarah Hilary and Doug Johnstone for their invaluable critiques of early versions.

Thank you to my fellow students who joined me throughout, allowing me to read their work and very kindly providing thoughtful and constructive feedback on mine. Special thanks to Katherine Slee for being there through it all, and for still being there now. I've never met you in the real world (yet!), but you are my friend.

And, speaking of friends, I am lucky to have the best ones. Love and hugs to my bestie and childhood chum, Nicola, and to the 'Cheers Bitches' crew – Dalgarno, Jobbers, Pam and Fiona. You guys have always had my back – throughout the good and the bad. There is no way to thank you enough for being my buddies and for making life that bit sweeter.

I also have to thank the school mums who are in my life every day and are as excited about this book as I am. You brighten my mornings and I love you all.

Then there's the love for my kids, Holly and Ellis. Thanks to them for showing me that siblings really can fight 24/7. Seriously though, I couldn't love you two mini-monkeys any more than I do. I hope that Mummy's book being out in the world shows you that anything is possible.

To my wider family, thanks for making my childhood as happy as it was and for supporting me into adulthood. But thanks especially to my bro, Chris (who has promised me he'll read this even though he doesn't do books), my sister-in-law Carrie, and my adorable nephews, Aiden and Aaron. You are the best.

And, of course, I can't sign off without bigging up everyone on Twitter for sharing the book and writing love; you have made me feel so welcome. A million thank yous to all those fabulous online bloggers who champion books day in and day out.

And finally, to you. The reader. Thank you for giving this book a go. I owe you one.